Ten Journeys

By ten top authors

The celebratory fifth in the acclaimed Short Story Reinvented Series

Legend Press

Independent Book Publisher

Legend Press Ltd, 2 London Wall Buildings,
London EC2M 5UU
info@legend-paperbooks.co.uk
www.legendpress.co.uk
www.twitter.com/legend_press

Contents © Cassandra Parkin, Dave Foxall, Guy Mankowski, Alistair Meldrum, Paul Burman, Ari O'Connell, Josie Henley-Einion, Brendan Telford, Anne Devereux, A.J. Kirby 2010

The right of the above authors to be identified as the authors of this work has be asserted by them in accordance with the Copyright, Designs and Patent Act 1988.

British Library Cataloguing in Publication Data available.
ISBN 978-1-9065581-9-2

All characters, other than those clearly in the public domain, and place names, other than those well-established such as towns and cities, are fictitious and any resemblance is purely coincidental.

Edited by Lauren Parsons-Wolff

Set in Times
Printed by J F Print Ltd., Sparkford, Somerset.

Cover designed by Gudrun Jobst
www.yotedesign.com

All rights reserved. No part of this publication may be reproduced, stored in or introduced into a retrieval system, or transmitted, in any form, or by any means electronic, mechanical, photocopying, recording or otherwise, without the prior permission of the publisher. Any person who commits any unauthorised act in relation to this publication may be liable to criminal prosecution and civil claims for damages.

Legend Press
Independent Book Publisher

Contents

Interview #17   7
by Cassandra Parkin

I'm afraid to fly...   33
by Dave Foxall

The Willows   55
by Guy Mankowski

The New Head of Deaths   85
by Alistair Meldrum

At the Rawlings' Place   115
by Paul Burman

Ukini Nageni   141
by Ari O'Connell

Dear   179
by Josie Henley-Einion

Angel Wings   203
by Brendan Telford

What If You Slept   235
by Anne Devereux

Curious Case of Jenni Wen   275
by A.J. Kirby

The Short Story Reinvented series

Legend Press' unique short-fiction series, The Short Story Reinvented, is designed for today's busy, but discerning, reader. Short fiction is a perfect answer in a world where everyone wants things to be easily accessible, sleek and tailored to fit their needs.

High-quality, thought-provoking short fiction can perfectly fill what before may have been an enforced gap of 'dead-time' in a daily routine. Dipping into short fiction is not as daunting as delving into a thick novel on a commute or during a lunch break, when you know that you might soon be interrupted mid-chapter; yet the subject matter in this popular series is weighty and meaningful, providing something new to think about and feel inspired about for the rest of the day, week, month and year.

Legend Press receives hundreds of submissions for the collections, from all over the UK as well as from all around the world. The successful entries for each book are chosen so that all stories combine and contrast compellingly to make the most varied, yet at the same time the most cohesive, collection possible.

A Note from Legend Press

Not only this short story series but Legend Press itself, at the very beginning of its journey, began with a visit to a local shop one bright afternoon in London. There occurred the thought of how interesting it would be to have a glimpse into the minds of each person rushing, or strolling by, no doubt packed with their dramas, concerns, hopes and opinions – probably more fantastical than any fiction.

The collection became a flag-bearer of the importance of the short story and its relevance and enjoyment for a society now seemingly pressed to rush more than ever, bombarded with images, adverts and promotions; and harried away from the never-dying power of storytelling.

Five years on, its relevance and fit for the modern reader is as strong as ever. And the diversity, power, depth of the collection seems to have grown and grown.

We want to say thank you to everyone who has worked on the series – special mention to Gudrun, who has produced all of the covers, apart from that first one. Most importantly, thanks to all of the authors that have submitted and those that have been included – whether those such as E.C. Seaman, who have become regulars in the series, to those that have provided one memorable and brilliant story.

Since starting the series, there have undoubtedly been strides – for instance, large competitions – to boost the short story. These have been welcomed, although there is still a way to go before collections are on those front-of-shop bookshelves, deservedly basking on bright afternoons.

We really hope you enjoy this celebratory fifth collection, and in your own way add your voice in support of the power of the short story.

Tom Chalmers
Managing Director, Legend Press

1

Interview #17

Cassandra Parkin

Oh, right, now you're gonna try and *buy* me off, huh. Well, I ain't for sale, and neither's my life story... what did you bring? *Glenfiddich Ten-Year-Old Single Malt*, are you shittin' me? You bought a bottle of well-aged Scotch whisky to a down-and-out bum living on Skid Row? Ah, knock that off, would ya? I ain't dying, you loser, I'm *laughing*. You finally managed to do something entertaining. And civilised. I hope you brought glasses. You can't drink *this* stuff outta the bottle... You *did* bring glasses. Huh. Well, OK. I'll make a deal with you. I ain't gonna tell you *my* story. My life journey's my business, and that ain't for sale. But I'll tell you a fable of the streets, a true morality tale for our times; a story every wet-behind-the-ears starry-eyed idiot oughta hear, at least once. This is the story of a man who managed to get himself a ticket for a ride on the Money Train. This story is about a man called Jack.

Jack English was a farmer-boy, grew up in the bible-belt of Idaho. Classic smallholding, the kind there ain't really room for no more in this fine and copasetic country of ours. Father was killed in one a them bizarre industrial accidents farmers are strangely prone to. You know the ones I mean. Jack's daddy went through a potato washer. Came out in lumps, apparently.

So anyway. Daddy went through the wringer; the farm went to the wall.

Jack, he was a college boy, great with numbers but a hopeless farmer, didn't have his daddy's magic touch with the soil. I guess these things sometimes skip a generation. Saw disaster crawling over the hill towards him, black and inevitable. Did everything he could to hold it off, but he didn't have it where it counts. Farming ain't bean-counting. You can't grow the crops or get the hens to lay, you ain't never gonna make it work.

Had to sell the land off, piece by piece. First the arable – Jack was always more of a people person, and a cow's closer to human than a cucumber. Then the pasture, along with those pretty-eyed ladies Jack was so attached to. Cows can be quite attractive, you know, in a big-tits-long-eyelashes kind of a way. Day the sale went through, Jack watched as his Jersey girls, his daddy's pride and joy, went wandering down to the milking shed as usual, only the farm hands hitching 'em up to the milking machine weren't working for him no more. The great cycle of grass, lactation, machinery and cow-shit kept right on turning without missing a beat. But he wasn't part of it. He'd never been part of it; he was just some damned idiot who couldn't hang onto what he'd inherited. He watched those ladies lining up, listened to them lowing in pleasure – hey, you don't think it feels good to get milked, you ask any nursing mom. He rustled the banker's draft in his pocket, and he bit his lip until it bled. Then he drove into town, found a bar, and got drunk. Pass that bottle, will ya? I notice you ain't drinkin' yours. Don't worry on my account, I ain't gonna freak out at the sight of someone else drinking my booze. It may or may not surprise you to know that I ain't actually an alcoholic. I mean sure, I've been drunk every time you've been down here, and the first time you found me I was so completely pissy-eyed I could hardly speak, but that ain't because I *got* to be. Alcohol ain't never been my poison; I just really, really, *really* like to drink. Well, take a look around; living here, who wouldn't? I'm what you might call a *contextual drinker*. Down here, I'll drink every drop I can get my hands on. But take me outta this particular context you happen to find me in, put me somewhere clean and decent, and I can leave the booze alone with the best of 'em.

Although I admit my liver probably don't know the difference.

There's all kinds a drunk, you know. Down here we mostly like to indulge in the *drinking to forget* drunk; although the *drinking to stop the voices* drunk's kinda popular too, with a certain discerning clientele. But in the world above the gutter, there's *thousands* of ways to get acquainted with the bottom of the bottle. There's the fun drunk, where the gang's altogether and the food's just grand, and everybody's so fuckin' witty you can't even believe it. There's the summer-afternoon drunk – ah, that was one a my favourites, back in the day. Sitting in the shade with a couple a six-packs, watching the sky and the grass and the water, waking up just as the sun slips behind the hill. There's the *meaningful* drunk, when halfway down the bottle, damn if that ain't the secret of the universe, who fuckin' knew that was it all this time? Only you can't quite get the cap off the pen, so you have to let it go, and when you wake up the next morning all you can remember is how righteously good it felt to know how the world fits together. The sloppy drunk – sprawled all over your girl, begging her to marry you, so god-damn horny you want to do it right there on the bar-stool; only the booze takes all the starch out of you, and she has to carry you up the stairs and put you to bed in the spare room. The mean drunk, where you catch a glimpse of your reflection and try starting a fight with yourself. Right now, you and me are having an *educational* drunk – that's where one of you sits in respectful swinish silence and gobbles up the pearls of wisdom cast before you. So many kinds, so many kinds... I gotta take a leak. That's better. Where were we? Oh, yeah, kinds a drunk. Well, Jackie boy, he went on an *epic* drunk, genuinely Homeric in scale. He drank and he drank, and he ranted and raved, and waved his arms around, and stumbled around the room. He was a cabaret, a floorshow, an entertainment all in himself, better'n anything you'd see this year in Stratford, little old England. People actually stayed there to watch him. He did this whole speech on the inequities in the modern capital marketplace that meant that just when you most needed help with your cash-flow, all the checks and balances the money-men had in place would automatically kick in and prevent you from getting it, and how the perverse incentives of Wall Street would bring the whole system crashing down around our ears one day... Kinda prophetic, huh? Well, when you're looking in the rear-view mirror, everyone's a friggin' genius.

Then he got started on the cows. Took out his wallet, started showing everyone a picture of this one damn cow he'd hung onto. "This is Genevieve." Slurring his words, barely able to stand up. Everyone nodding respectfully. "All I got left... that and an acre of land to graze her on... "

Other end of the bar, there's a guy on a different kinda drunk. The steady, mean-eyed, drinking-just-to-get-drunk kind. He's working his way down a bottle of vodka, shot after shot after shot, not speaking. Jack catches sight of him. Their eyes meet in the mirror.

"Wh'r you?" slurs Jack, sliding onto the barstool. The man shrugged.

"I," he said carefully, "am a financial wizard. I'm a giant of Wall Street. I have made and lost more money for myself and my employers than you could *dream* of... And I would trade the whole damned lot for a life I could be proud of."

"I'm drinking," said the man, every word enunciated with the care of the truly shit-faced, "because I have just been to the memorial service of a man who used to work for me. He wasn't a *friend*, mind you. He was a salesman; they never have any friends. Just golf buddies and drinking partners. He was killed by the system."

"Whatcha talkin' 'bout?" mumbled Jack.

"The system," repeated the man calmly. "The system you were railing against just now. It chewed him up and spat him out."

"Y're all a shower of bastards," said Jack indistinctly. "You and y'r damned rules and y'r freakin' cash flow projections."

"Indeed we are. A shower of heartless bastards, all of us dressed in expensive suits and red suspenders and Rolex watches, and not one god-damned soul between the lot of us. I'll trade you." Jack looked blank. "I'll trade you," said the man, looking straight at Jack. "I'll trade you that house, and that acre of land, and that pretty-eyed cow of yours."

"What do I get in return?"

"I will give you a reco... a recomm... " the man sighed. "I will give you a *recommendation* to my manager, who'll be frantic since receiving notice of my resignation and desperate for a replacement. I will call in the morning and give my personal assurance that you are a fine young man, deserving of a chance to prove yourself. Oh, and the keys to my apartment."

"Yeah, but I don't wanna be like you," growled Jack. "Money men took my farm, the farm my Daddy spent his life building up, won't do that to anyone else, there should be a better way."

"Perhaps. But, as you so correctly observe, *we* are all a bunch of robbers. Who's going to change the world if the good guys won't come and work for us?"

"What makes you think I'll even be any good?" Jack asked, baffled.

"I have no fucking idea," said the man calmly. "And I couldn't care less. But I want out, and you want in. The rent's paid for a month. After that, you're on your own. Do we have a deal?"

Jack squinted across the top of his glass. "Why're you doing this?"

The man looked into his vodka for a minute, and shuddered. "Because," he said, "the system *eats* people. It eats us from the head down, chews us up and discards the empty husks. It is a carnivore, with a predator's instincts, and I do not intend to be its next victim. And since you're so angry and determined to get us all, let's see what the system makes of you."

"I'll show 'em all, you know," said Jack, swaying. "I'll be decent. Ethical. Not like the bastards who took *me* down. And if they won't let me... I'll fight the system from the inside. I'll take 'em down. I won't be a corporate whore."

"Yes you will," smiled the man. "Yes, you will. Here." He put a bunch of keys on the bar, then a business card. On it was a name, and a corporate logo. *Red Giant Investments Ltd*. Jack's ticket to board the Money Train.

"'Kay," mumbled Jack, and shook the outstretched hand. Then he slid off his stool and passed out.

Was I the Red Giant financial wizard? Ah, just give over, wouldja? Ain't no point trying to work out where I come in this story, cos I ain't in it anywhere. The men in this story, they're all dead now. Chewed up by the system.

Jack's mother, ah, she was mad. Selling off your birthright, completely insane, chasing dreams, not the man your father was, you know how it goes. And how do I figure that one out? On account of *your* wastin' those hard-earned college dollars, trailing up and down the country collecting stories off people like me, that's how. Don't try and tell me your folks are thrilled by the path you've taken. Anyway, Jackie boy, he shouted her down for once in his life. He was like a man possessed; he'd been given a strange, singular chance, and damn, he was going to take it. He packed up his car, his mother and his underwear, and set off to take a bite outta the Big Apple.

New York crashed into Jack like a series of divine revelations. It shook the heart outta him, left him gasping and lost. First revelation was the architecture; ornate fingers of glass and concrete that pierced the clouds. Visited St Patrick's to ask for God's blessing on his new life, felt uneasy, couldn't work out what was wrong. Finally figured out it was the scale. God's house is supposed to be the biggest place in town, but Wall Street residents bow their heads down at somebody else's altar. When he realised *that*, he had a moment of panic. He actually went back over to Grand Central and looked at the departures board. Looked again at that bit of card in his hand, that ticket for the Money Train. No contest. The Money Train won. Always does. Jack turned right around and headed back into town.

The second revelation was the apartment. Only four rooms – two bedrooms, living room with kitchenette in the corner, miniscule bachelor-pad bathroom – but in New York, it's all in the address. His was Ninetieth and Park. His mother looked at the view, and for a blessed minute, she stopped complaining.

The third revelation was the office. He snuck into the building like a thief, convinced he was going to be found out. A woman met him in reception, a certain age as they say, but damn, she looked good.

"I'm Cornelia," she told him. "You must be Jack."

"Yes," he said, thinking *damn, even the secretaries here are hot, all those years I wasted in Idaho...*

"You've got one month's trial," she said. "You'll report direct to me until we re-staff, picking up where Bradley's team left off. And I warn you, we're up against it. Nick's dead, Ruby's on sick leave, and Brad's idea of a useful contribution is to throw it all up to live in Idaho and send you down here instead." She looked him up and down. He felt oddly naked, oddly exposed. "So I hope you're everything he said you were."

"What did he say I was?" asked Jack, busily adjusting his ideas.

"He said you were a bankrupt farmer-boy with a grudge against the system," she said absently. Jack nearly swallowed his tongue. "But he always knew how to spot talent, that man. Well, I guess no-one lasts forever. Come with me."

Took him into a high glass palace up in the clouds. He had a desk, a phone, a computer, a window, a pile of paperwork, a compensation package he didn't even begin to understand, a desk neighbour by the name of Jerry. Sat down, made some small talk, him and Jerry getting on famously, and then this... *vision.*

Blonde hair in a chignon, beautiful blue eyes behind thick-rimmed glasses, lovely body encased in a grey suit, pretty black heels. Only the heels gave her away at first. Other than those, she was pure Wall Street, a suit with a head on top. But those heels told a different story. Her smile was the other clue, warm and sweet, unexpected.

Jerry caught him looking, grinned.

"That's Aisling Carroll. You know McLain Carroll, right? Red Giant's founding father? She's his daughter, interning for a year. She's doing an MBA at Harvard. Way too good for us."

The daughter of the Red Giant, thought Jack. *She's beautiful*. Then, across the office, he saw this huge slab of meat with a shock of red hair, inexpertly crammed into a pinstriped suit by some poor, terrified tailor. The slab glared at Jack, like it wanted to kill him.

"That's why we don't mess with her," said Jerry.

"That's her daddy?"

"Booya." Jerry lowered his voice. "So, d'you reckon the story's true?"

"What story?"

Jerry looked at him incredulously.

"Where'd you say you were from?"

"Idaho."

"They have negotiable currency yet down there in Idaho?" Jack lobbed a pencil over the partition; got it right in the middle of Jerry's forehead, perfect bulls-eye. "*Ow*... well, the story goes like this. Mr Carroll got his start at one of the other big places – Lehmann's, I think – then he went out on his own, founded Red Giant from nothing. Grew overnight, just about. Man's got the magic touch. Somebody at one of the big firms wasn't happy. One more at the feed-trough means that much less for everyone else, right? So, he decided to try and take Red Giant down. He got a couple of other Masters of the Universe lined up, and they made a plan. Horned in on his deals and priced him out of the market. Tried to cut off his lines of credit, that kind of thing. Mr Carroll got word of it. Next thing that happens... "

Dramatic pause; Jack's eyes like saucers. Jerry glanced over his shoulder, whispered so softly Jack had to strain to hear him.

"The guy who started it all off? They found him in the Hudson River."

"Doing what?"

Jerry laughed.

"Floating, you dimwit."

"Floating? What -?"

"Face-down. And that isn't even the worst part. The worst part is that all his teeth had been pulled." Jack swallowed. Jerry shrugged. "Red Giant never looked back."

Jack stared at McLain Carroll, his new Lord and Master. McLain Carroll gave him a look like Jack was next in line for a one-man river-cruise. Jack looked away and bit his lip.

"Shit. He hates me already."

Jerry looked Jack straight in the eye.

"Maybe," he said. "But he'll leave you alone as long as you bring in the money."

Jack flicked rapidly through the files, gradually realised he was supposed to be doing a deal with a couple of maverick inventors for the rights to a voice-recognition system for MP3 players. He stared at the pages of figures. And something clicked. *I can do this*, he thought. *I can actually freakin' do this.*

Like I said; the men in this story, they're all dead now.

Course they got to know each other, Jack and Aisling. She was beautiful, and outta reach, more than enough to attract him. As for Jack, he had that farmer-boy physique, the build that comes effortlessly when you work on the land. In that polluted corporate ocean, filled with hungry young sharks fighting to stay in shape, he stood out like a tall ear of corn; strong, golden, and totally outta place. Plus, as it turned out, they both had this fantastic idea that they were going to be *good*. Shared dream; bringing ethics to Wall Street. How could they resist each other?

First, the high-octane business discussions, the junior staff all working crazy hours, Aisling and Jack fitting in nicely. Meeting by the coffee machine, nothing planned just more often than not. Come break-time they'd both be there. Next, that wilful blindness. You both act like it's all still spontaneous, but still, a lull in the working day and God *damn*, there you both are by the coffee, what are the odds? All the rest of the coffee crowd getting wise to it, making a point of staying out of the way; Jerry giving way last of all, a bit jealous, a bit reluctant to concede defeat. Then at last, the first time you slip over into the edge into personal...

"Why are you here?" she asked him one hot October night. Just the two of them left in the building. "You seem far too... nice."

So he told her the story he hadn't even told Jerry, the farm in Idaho, the shame, the guilt of losing his birthright.

"I want to do better than they did by me," he said earnestly. "I want to make the money-men play fair."

She looked at him like she'd just seen him properly for the first time.

"So why do you do it? He asked her. "Why work so hard? With your dad running the place and all?"

She blushed like a rose. He felt his heart squeeze with it.

"That's why I have to work so hard. Everyone else has to fight for the chances I've got. I've got to... " she sighed and pushed her glasses up her nose. "I've got to earn it."

You can fall in love with the smallest damned things. Jack fell for the way she looked when she pushed those glasses up her nose. Just that, and he was a goner. He kissed her, soft, innocent. She let him, for just a second, then pushed him away.

"No," she said, her face little girl serious. "I don't do office relationships."

But he could hear her breathing faster; he knew that, with time, with patience, she'd be his.

Could have been happy, too, if they'd met on any other street than that one. But as it was, the Money Train was already waiting at the station, the porter beckoning them aboard.

You ain't married. No, I ain't asking a question, I'm telling you.

Fact. You ain't married. How do I know? Cuz you're down here at one in the morning drinking with a homeless guy, that's how. So *you* won't know what it's like to build a life together. Jack and Aisling. A pigeon pair of starry-eyed dreamers. She wouldn't even date him till she went back to Harvard, and when they did get started they took it slowly. Both afraid of damaging this precious, fragile thing that was slowly growing between them. They finally fell into bed together one golden Spring afternoon when Jack got his first promotion. Ah, they came fast to him then. Wall Street's good to its golden boys.

Still, they kept it quiet for the longest time, hiding where no-one from Wall Street ever looked. Took the boat to see the Statue of Liberty, holding hands like teenagers. Went to the top of the Chrysler, took in a view even better than the one from Red Giant's offices. Rode the subway to Coney Island, Jack winning and winning on the shooting galleries.

The monster in the closet was Mr Red Giant, who still didn't know Jack was slipping around with his daughter. Coupla nights Jack actually woke up in a cold sweat, dreaming of deep water filling his lungs. But by that time, the little ole farmer boy from Idaho was an established asset to Red Giant. A lead producer, bringing home the bacon time after time, and they rewarded him accordingly. First an office, then a corner office. All the time that compensation package creeping upwards and upwards. Then came a suite with its own bathroom attached. Can't have the reigning monarchs pissing in the same urinals as the aspiring heirs, one of those hungry little suckers might just reach over and chop his dick right off. You think I'm joking, dontcha? Easy to see *you* ain't never ridden the Money Train.

Ah, the Money Train; God help us all, the Money Train. First you hear the scream of the whistle, so loud it hurts your ears. Then there's this – unearthly *thing* – twice the height of a man, and maybe a hundred feet long, thundering down the rails towards you, grabbing the air out from your lungs, sucking you into its path so you have to hold onto something. It rolls into the platform, you think, *Man, that's the scariest thing I ever saw.* You look at the wheels, the steam, the sweating men shovelling coal. Looks like one of Lucifer's Angels, sent forth from the gates of Hell to claim you.

And then, the door opens, and there's a man waving you on, and damn if that ain't a ticket in your hand.

You pat the red velvet seats as you sit down. *Just a few stops*, you think to yourself, *then I'll get off.* You can't quite believe it when the wheels start turning. And to start with, man, what a rush. You take your turn shovelling coal; brutal, backbreaking work, so hard you can hardly take it, but it's worth it, because you know what's coming up next. And then you take your break in the restaurant car, and you just can't believe you made it. They invited you in, you're sat right here on the Money Train with the crisp linen napkins and the bottles of champagne. *Just a few stops. Just a few stops and then, I swear, I'll get off.*

Then, the scary thing. You get used to it. That speed, that noise, it starts to seem *natural*. You get used to the heat, the swaying motion, the world going by in a blur. You remember how it feels to be one of those folks at the level crossing, forced to stop while the Money Train goes by, and you like the feeling. The whole world stops for you! People bring you stuff on silver platters, the prices are insane, but hell, who cares, right? You're on the Money Train! Who gives a shit about the mark-up?

And before you know it, the Money Train's got you good. Ain't no way you're getting off, not until the Money Train has taken everything you had when you got on. Not until the man in the uniform comes by and says, *Hey buddy, this is your stop*. You want to stay on longer, but it ain't never been your ride, someone else was working the strings the whole time, figuring out when to shove you back out into the cold. The whole infernal contraption screeches to a halt, and the porter flings open the door and tosses you out. And then you're standing on the platform in a cloud of smoke, watching the train roll out again, and you're poorer and older and dirtier. Stood someplace you never intended on going, and you can finally see again how fucking insane the whole thing is. But the Money Train don't care. It just rolls on and on, out of the station, taking the next poor suckers on to the end of their personal line.

So where did it all go wrong for Jack and Aisling? They started out with such high hopes, such magnificent fuckin' ideals. But there ain't nobody alive can reform the Money Train; it gets to everyone in the end. And then one night, Jack met Charlie. After that, it was only a matter of time. Doomsday clock at the station counting down, numbers flicking over one by one, counting the hours and minutes and seconds till the crash.

Jack and Jerry in a bar in Harlem. Two City slickers out on the razzle, celebrating their first truly obscene bonus. Jerry introduced them, maybe just being friendly, maybe trying to drive the thin end of that wedge between Jack and Aisling, who knew? Nobody made him say yes. "Hey, Jack, say hello to Charlie," said Jerry, slumped on his stool, and there was no denying the buzz between them, the instant connection. Five minutes later, they were locked in a cubicle in the men's room, Jack lost and screaming in ecstasy.

"Oh, my God, Jesus fucking Christ, that's so fucking beautiful."

And when he came down from the peak, the sound of someone in the next cubicle banging on the wall, "Hey, buddy, you wanna keep the noise down in there?" Jack laughed and banged back, "whatsa matter, pal, you never been in love?"

Jack and Charlie lost in each other. He didn't care who heard them together, didn't care about anything. He'd never felt anything like it. She set him on fire, every part of his body buzzed, tingled, sang. He felt like he could conquer the world.

He staggered back into the bar, swimmy-eyed and grinning like a madman.

"Pretty good fun, huh?"

"Pretty good fun," said Jack, in a daze.

Next morning, he couldn't stand to look at himself in the mirror. Had to go to work without a shave, screaming horrors sat on his shoulder, gibbering in his ear. What had he been *thinking*? He was a nice boy, a good boy, raised right and clean and decent, knew better than to behave like that. Charlie was poison, she was toxic, the deadest of cul-de-sacs. He was meeting Aisling for lunch, their favourite restaurant. Couldn't make himself walk over there, felt like he didn't deserve to be near her. Felt like he wanted to die. Felt like he wanted to see Charlie again, need burned into his brain, pushed the thought away.

He called Aisling, put her off till the evening. Took a company limo down Fifth Avenue to Tiffany's, marched in and laid his sliver of necromantic plastic on the counter. "I want to spend as much money as I possibly can," he declared firmly, and naturally they obliged. He wasn't the first one, not even the first that day. The clerks at Tiffany's all know when Bonus Time rolls around on Wall Street.

Proposed that night over a criminally expensive meal; she cried as soon as she saw that little turquoise box. She was a nice girl, but she had the same weakness girls have everywhere – the rainbow flash from a diamond blinds them.

She should have seen that night it was already too late for them. Spending enough on one meal to keep a poor family afloat for a year; beguiled by a rock mined in conditions so obscene they'd neither of 'em have lasted a day there. They'd set out with good intentions, but the system already had its claws in them.

But there ain't nothing so blind as a woman with a ring on her finger. Nothing apart from the man who thinks he's just bought her off with it.

Fast-forward a little. Mr Red Giant's first instinct was to take Jackie boy somewhere nice and quiet-like and get going with the pliers, but they finally came to an arrangement. One thing Jack had learned by now, just about anything's for sale for the right price. Ole Red laid out Jack's targets for the next quarter, an impossible number that made Jack swallow hard. Then he doubled them. Then he grinned, and tripled them. If Jack made his numbers – Red would consent to the wedding.

Nearly killed Jack, but he did it. The look on Red's face when Jack brought him the paperwork. Enough to turn milk sour through an iron door.

Wedding of the century, naturally. Tulle and ribbons; live music and dead guests. Jerry was Best Man; from the look on Red's face, Jack was the Worst Man He'd Ever Laid Eyes On, but Jack was too happy to care.

"I guess I was wrong about New York," said his mother, sniffing.

"The day you step out of line's the day I kill you," growled Red, glaring.

"I'd buy a gun and keep it handy," said Jerry, only half-joking.

"Do you take this woman... ?" said the priest, on auto-pilot.

"Yes," said Jack, to all of them. He'd raided the palace and carried off the princess. Red could rant and storm, but Aisling would be in Jack's bed that night. And in the bathroom, while Aisling danced with her daddy, Jack the little laddie was biting his lip and trying to keep quiet as Charlie took him up and up into that high, soaring emptiness only she knew how to help him reach.

Afterwards he leant his forehead on the mirror, staring at his reflection. Flushed cheeks, bright eyes, powered by his pounding heart.

"Never again," he told himself.

Never again.

The Money Train just kept rolling for Jack and Aisling, deal after deal after killer, impossible deal. After Jack closed on the voice-rec deal, there was the Freedive project – supposed to go to Prickly Tree, but the boss-man topped himself and Jack managed to buy the rights while the company floundered. You ever Freedived, College Boy? Nah, I thought not. Strictly for the super-rich, probably only a few thousand people in the whole world can afford it. Little nosepiece that pulls the air right outta the water, damnedest thing you ever saw in your life. After that, some domestic-appliance work – dull but profitable. The money just kept pouring in. Seems we Americans just can't get enough of our cute little toasters and our adorable little waffle-makers.

What, the Freediving thing? Nah, I ain't tried it either. Maybe I ain't even *heard* of it. Maybe I'm just making it up to mess with ya. This is a story, remember, not even my own; just something I heard in a bar one day. You ain't never getting my tale outta me, College Boy. All I got for you is Jack's train-ride, and it ain't got the happiest of endings.

For a while, you can fool yourself you've got the whole thing under control. Jack had it all, or so he thought. He had Aisling; he had the stratospheric career, the swank Manhattan penthouse, the gracious New England country home, the simple beach-house on the Cape; the staff, the cars, the use of the personal jet. So what if in that crazy, sleepless run-up to their wedding day, he'd had to make the odd deal that didn't quite live up to the standards he'd set himself, right? It had all been for love. And if over time, he was gradually letting things slip a little, cutting corners, squeezing percentages, investing in companies who weren't as squeaky clean as he'd like... well, he was still doing a thousand times better than that black-hearted reprobate lurking at the end of the corridor, clawing dollars and cents into his personal hoard. Told himself Aisling had it all too. The homes, the lifestyle, what he had begun to think of as *a nice little career of her own*.

She wasn't as willing to sell out as he was, you see. Still shooting for the coffee-machine vision. She gave investment advice to charities, ethical portfolio, reduced fees, great returns too. They loved her, swore she was a saint who'd change the world one day. Jack's take on it? The first time he made a deal he knew Aisling wouldn't – the first time he screwed over some poor sucker with a good idea and no capitalisation – he smiled tolerantly and thought, *Ah, but it's only because of me that she can be so ethical.* Yeah, he actually let that traitor thought slip past his defences, that *he* was the one making the sacrifices.

Truth was, he fucking loved it. The power. The terror. The money.

And, naturally, some of that money went on Charlie.

It began as an occasional thing, just the odd stolen night in the bar. He told himself it was nothing to do with Aisling, nothing that would ever touch her. The lies men tell themselves. The next day he'd wake up alone in his cherrywood sleigh bed in the clouds of Manhattan, sweating and cold with the shame of it, and craving her company again.

Just the odd stolen night at first. Maybe once a month, maybe less, usually when he and Jerry were really tying one on. A clever girl, Charlie; always knew how to find him. She was an expensive habit, but he could afford her. Hell, he could afford anything.

Just once a month started creeping up to two or three times a month, but he could handle that, right? He always picked nights when Aisling wasn't around, didn't want her to see him when he crawled home barely able to speak. Nonetheless, she knew, the way women always know when their man's playing away. She took on a junior – bright young thing she poached from her Daddy – made fewer road-trips and came home early. Jack tried to act pleased. Truth was he wanted Charlie so bad he could hardly think straight.

Where to meet her? What was the smallest risk? He could meet her in a bar somewhere, but then going home to Aisling afterwards... could smuggle her up to his office, but the risk of Red catching them... or go to a hotel... yeah, that could work...

He engineered a fake trip away, meticulous planning, conscious all the time that ole Red was watching, waiting, with murder on his mind. Would you believe Jackie boy hadn't never booked a hotel room his whole life? First he was too poor, then he was too rich. But he found a nice place in mid-town where the concierge understood. Cash payment, and no questions about visitors who didn't check in at the front desk.

Spent the night in Charlie's arms, didn't sleep a wink. Dragged himself into the office the next morning looking like a walking corpse.

"You all right, boss?" his secretary asked him.

"Fine," he muttered. Staggered into the bathroom and threw up.

The lies men tell themselves.

After that, there was no chance he could keep it under control. Charlie was on his mind the whole time, every minute, every second. He met her in airports, in hotels and bars, every business trip he took Charlie was along for the ride. He craved her constantly. Couldn't never get enough. Aisling had been talking about a baby, but naturally there was no fuckin' chance of *that* happening. Charlie took all his energy. Blamed it on pressure of work. "Tell me about it, maybe I can help?"

"Get off my back, damn it, what the hell would you know about it with your fucking charity work and your..." – then hated himself for the look on her face. A hurt little girl, no defences to hide behind.

Thing was, he really *was* feeling the pressure. Work was harder now, the money not so easy to find, holes starting to appear in the numbers. His particular trip on the Money Train was reaching its end. It was nearly time for the porter to open the door and toss him out. The deals were tougher to make, or maybe they just seemed tougher, maybe he was just losing his touch. By now he was doing the one thing he'd sworn he'd never do – smuggling Charlie up to his plushy office, getting it on with her right down the corridor from Red. Looking at his hands shaking afterwards as he tried to pour the coffee and thinking, *Shit, this really has to stop, she's going to kill me*. Of course she wasn't a cheap mistress to keep either; she was the best of the best his Charlie girl, the cream of the fucking crop. Had to take short cuts to keep it all going, dancing around the edges of the law. Then he had to stop dancing and start walking, all the way over that line and down, down, down into the murky world of *corporate malfeasance*. Screwing over the people he was investing in. Juggling money. Hiding losses on one deal with profits from another, moving the hole around, hoping he'd find a way to fill it before someone caught on. Sometimes he came home sweating with fear at the thought of the secrets he was hiding. The things he'd done, the stuff he'd stolen, the damage he was doing, the lives he was destroying.

But he was on the Money Train, and he didn't know how to get off. Just knew he was heading for an almighty crash. Jack was smart enough to see it coming, but there wasn't nothing he could do. If you'll forgive me an abrupt change in my metaphorical direction – even the world's lousiest farmer knows that eventually, your chickens come home to roost.

You got any more in that bottle?

Hmmm. Ain't nothing like the burn of a quality Scotch whisky.

No, I am not avoiding the fucking subject. Stop tryin' to analyse me, you friggin' know-it-all sanctimonious prick, or you're gonna see my ugly side. You know *nothing* about me College Boy, and you never will. That's the one fearful beauty of this godforsaken shit-hole. Nobody knows who you really are.

The last day of Jack's life started no better and no worse than many others. He and Aisling were barely speaking by now, barely even *meeting*, just lying in that big wide cherrywood sleigh-bed, back to back. Both lying awake, Jack counting losses and wondering how much longer he could hide it from Ole Red, and Aisling... ah, ain't a man anywhere knows what a woman thinks about at a time like that, and I'm no fuckin' different. Sometimes Jack heard her crying. He just couldn't see how to make it stop.

So it was a shock to hear Aisling's voice out there in his assistant's office.

"I don't care what he's doing in there, Beatrice, I'm his wife. I need to see him. Right now." And Beatrice doing her best to stall her, "Mrs English, ma'am, I do know who you are, of course I do, I just really don't think that – "

Trapped in his office with Charlie, his wife at the door. Like a moment in a nightmare. No way out. The door opened.

Close your mouth, boy. Lotta flies down here.

Jack had Charlie all spread out on the desk, just the way he liked her. He was crouched over her, eyes half-closed, face flushed, futile attempt to hide her.

His wife, his beautiful angel wife, staring straight at him. In her hand, a bundle of papers spelled D-O-O-M in the reddest of inks. She'd come in there to save him from Ole Red's wrath, convinced her Daddy had it wrong. But for all his faults, Red was never wrong about the money, and Aisling was finally staring at the truth. End of the Money Train. End of the line.

"God help me," whispered Jack.

Aisling looked at him. At his face. At his hands. At the six rows of white powder Jack had chopped out in front of him. Finally understood.

"Cocaine," she said softly. "All this time I thought – I thought you were with – and it was – " Her face was white. "Oh, Jack,

Jack – " Trying to hold it together. "And these papers – these deals... " Tears pouring down her cheeks.

"It's not what it looks like," said Jack, ridiculous, because how the hell else could the situation be construed? He'd ruined himself, destroyed his marriage, damned near bankrupted Red Giant. He was a junkie, a thief, an embezzler and an all-round bastard. Everything he'd sworn he'd never be.

"Yes, it is," she said. "It's exactly what it looks like, Jack." She held out the papers, her hands were shaking. "And *this* is what it looks like too. These things you've done. This missing money."

"No," he whispered softly.

"Yes," she said. "Nobody can think straight when they've got an addiction to feed. Oh, Jack -"

She wiped tears off her chin with the back of her hand, and pushed her glasses up her nose. "I thought it was a mistake," she said. "I thought, *My Jack, there's no way he'd do something like this – he might fall in love with someone else, but not lying – not stealing – this is a mistake* – but there is no mistake, is there, Jack? Jerry was right. It's all true."

"Jerry?" The name was like a slap in the face. Even when your insides are black and numb with the bad things you've done, you can still feel the pain of betrayal. "That little bastard, I'll – "

"My dad made him check, he was getting suspicious. Jerry was trying to save you, Jack. He called me before he sent it, so I could warn you."

"You came here to *warn* me?" Her goodness in his heart like a bright knife. "You thought I was cheating on you, and you still came here to warn me?"

"I thought there was still a chance to save us," she whispered. "But there's no point, is there? There's nothing to save. You're not the man I thought you were. We were going to change the world, remember? And now you're worse than any of them."

Jack stared at her, groping for the words. Couldn't find them.

Then he heard this almighty roar. Heard Beatrice scream. Then McLain Carroll, the Red Giant himself, exploded into the room.

"You...You fucking little thief. Thought you could put it all right, did you? Thought you could put the money back before anyone noticed?" Jack saw his hands twitch. "I've been waiting for this moment since your wedding day, you asshole. I told you then I'd kill you if you ever stepped outta line – I've been fucking *praying* for the chance to do this – "

"No!" screamed Aisling.

Red was quick, but Jack was quicker, and coked out of his head into the bargain. He reached into his desk drawer. Pulled out the gun Jerry told him to buy.

For a moment, the universe stopped. Jack remembered his wedding day; the way Aisling looked when he lifted up the veil, the first time he ever kissed her, that night by the coffee machine; the way his shirt stuck to his back when he first walked in off the street into the air-conditioned office, the way the sun looked coming up over the hill at the back of his daddy's farm in Idaho spilling over the horizon like corn syrup.

Then he pulled the trigger, and shot McLain Carroll right through his old black heart.

Jack and Aisling looked at each other over the body of her father.

"I'm sorry," he told her. "You're right. I'm not the man we both thought I was. Every word you've said to me is true."

She stared at him wordlessly, her father's blood pooling around her feet. Too much happening in too little time. A crash always seems to happen in slow motion.

"I'm not as strong as you," he whispered. "I never was. It was all too much for me. I'm so sorry, Aisling. For what it's worth, there never was another woman, I always loved you." He held the gun to his head.

"Don't – " she said, on reflex.

"I think you should go now," he said. "I need to pay the bill. This is the end of the line for me."

She would have stayed, to be with her daddy if nothing else, but Beatrice grabbed her by the arm and dragged her away. Dragged her to the elevator, fast as they could go. But not far enough to get away from the sound of that second gunshot.

Bottom of the bottle, pal, end of the line. The Money Train stopped, threw all the Red Giant employees out at the station. Jack had done what he'd always said he'd do, after a fashion; he'd brought down one of the giants of Wall Street from the inside. Company went to the wall. Aisling buried her father. Jerry died in a car-crash.

What the heck you talking about, *What happened to Jack?* You got all the jigsaw pieces, pal; you can't put together a suicidal coke-head who just shot his father-in-law and a gunshot in a deserted office?

Sheesh, once you get an idea in your head... look, even if there was a way for him to get outta that office, d'you think I'd tell you if I was Jack? Think I'd admit to being that sorry excuse for a man? Think I'd confess on tape to embezzlement and murder? I told you, College Boy, I ain't in this story anywhere. The Money Train crashed, and took Jack and everyone else down with it; I just crawled out from the wreckage. I'm just a travelling pilgrim hiding out in this City of Angels, doing penance for all my sins, 'til I can finally hitch a ride outta here in an empty railroad car.

2
I'm afraid to fly...
Dave foxall

Author

Dave Foxall was born in the Black Country. He started commuting at the age of 11 and so came to appreciate the escapist value of a good read. Eager to see the world he swapped his small town roots for the bright lights of Coventry (45 minutes down the road) and the seductive glamour of studying law. 19 years later – the law career having been abandoned along the way – he finally managed to live the dream of being a wealthy writer. The 'wealthy' bit still requires a little work. Contrary to what his story, *I'm afraid to fly...* may lead you to believe, Dave is actually very happily married.

1 tsp cumin seeds
tsp ground cinnamon
3 tsp ground coriander
1 onion
6oz diced turkey
1 small butternut squash
1 small sweet potato
2 fresh bird eye chillies
1 tin plum tomatoes
1 tin red kidney beans
1 small glass red wine
2 tsp dried mixed herbs
brown sugar
6 squares dark cooking chocolate
juice of half a lime
salt and pepper

... and the old woman in the window seat next to me, she's a stranger but I already know that she's going to keep on annoying me for this entire long-haul trip. Now she wants her boiled sweets that she's left in her carry-on; which is, of course, in the locker. *Would you mind? I do really need them; my ears, you know.* Yes, but that's descent; we won't be landing for 10 hours. Oh God! 10 hours. Never mind the old baggage, I've got to spend the next 10 hours on a plane. Still, desperate times require desperate travel arrangements.

My fear of flying cows me into retrieving her barley sugars

for her. Now quickly, before she can ask me where I'm going or tell me where she's from or show me pictures of grandchildren I put the earphones in. Send her a solitude signal. I'm listening to music; don't bother me and don't, under any circumstances, ask me what I'm listening to. I really wouldn't know what to tell her. I consider closing my eyes and pretending to be asleep just to make sure that my terror is undisturbed.

Take-off. I hate take-off. It's a beginning that feels like an ending. All that fussing about. Bags in the overhead lockers. Flight attendants fluttering here and there. Pay attention while we tell you the procedure in the event of imminent disaster. Basically, you're to put your affairs in order so that should we fall from the skies then at least our corpses and belongings will be neatly identifiable. We blithely overcome the law of gravity with no thought for consequences. The casual miracle of flight and the ignorance of casual death. All brushed aside and made deceptively commonplace by a moron in a nylon neckerchief asking me to make sure my seat is in the upright position.

Sorry, I'll get a grip; it's just that I don't like flying. Don't worry, I'm not an idiot. I know (better than most, in fact) the crash statistics and how 'safe' flying is these days. But a plane is the one place in which I can't access my rationality. I check in my logic with my hold luggage. I look outwardly normal, of course I do. And I know – statistically – that I'm not alone. On a plane this big, there'll be dozens like me, wearing an outward coat of calm over their churning inner panic.

We're moving. This is it. The proverbial point of no return. The earphone ruse seems to be working. I'm not really listening to music, of course. The earphone lead is just tucked into my inside jacket pocket, allowing the assumption that there is an ipod or suchlike in there. In fact, I can't listen to music in flight. The paranoia that I might fail to hear a wing start to shear off or an engine stutter and die is too great. So my right ear contains a silent earpiece; my left, which my fellow passenger can't see, is empty and alert to the out-of-the-ordinary sounds of possible disaster.

But no-one can survive 10 hours of this sort of brain-simmering fear, so we phobic flyers each have our own distraction. Some can do the music thing. Some read. Some crossword or sudoku. The young guy across the aisle has a soft porn magazine; filling his airtime with tits'n'bums (although how he's going make a single top-shelf periodical last for a 10 hour flight is something I don't want to think about.) Bet the woman next to him is pleased. As for me, I cook. I don't fly often – as little as possible, as should be obvious by now – but I've found that when I can't avoid it, when flight is absolutely essential, like today, then cooking works for me.

Before you think me deranged, I don't mean I get out the pots and pans and a gas ring and start frying onions in economy class. I mean that I pick a meal and imagine cooking it. From choosing the fresh ingredients, chopping and preparation and then each stage of the actual cooking until the finished dish is ready for imaginary eating. Granted, it takes a lot of focus and willpower to do this and not cut corners. But that's not a problem, I have plenty of both. If it takes three minutes to soften chopped onion over a medium heat in reality then that's how long I take to imagine it. It's almost a meditation.

So, today's in-flight meal is: Winter Chilli. As follows...

First, heat the powdered spices in a dry, non-stick pan over a high heat. You'll know when they're hot enough because the powder will crack like earth in a drought and the room will be filled with a rich, almost curry-ish smell.

I've always been a keen (but strictly amateur) cook. I like to try new things, experiment. And I have a well-equipped kitchen in which to do just that: Le Creuset pans, Sabatier knives, KitchenAid mixer, a proper butcher's block; you get the idea.

This recipe is a sort of cross between a tex-mex chilli con carne and a Mexican mole. A true mole has over a hundred ingredients and takes up to a couple of days to cook (which, I suppose would be perfect for a flight to Australia) so I just sort of mole-d a chilli recipe and ended up with something unexpectedly good. It's become a special dish for me. Something I cook for milestones: celebrations, commiserations and reconciliations. Fixing those 'special moments' in the memory more firmly. I cooked it the first time my ex came to dinner.

It was early on in our relationship and it was winter. I liked her alot but wasn't sure how she felt about me. As it turned out, I realise now that right up to the end she kept her secrets. It was too cold to meet in town and she had agreed to come over to my place and be cooked for. This felt hopeful. Two previous occasions had shown that we were physically very attracted to each other but we hadn't yet had sex.

I spent the day tidying and cleaning so that my mid-terrace might appear as inviting as possible. I wanted her to think that it might also be worth seeing in daylight. Put bluntly, I was hoping for breakfast as well as dinner.

My ex arrived, appropriately late and over warm winter beer we continued the courtship dance of exchanging information, opinion and belief. That evening we told each other everything and everything we told each other was in perfect accord. Obviously subsequent events proved that to be wrong, but the point is that at the time, that's how it felt.

We both loved all of Miles Davis' music, but felt that John Coltrane had lost the plot in his later career. Both without siblings and so we knew how to share. Dogs were better than cats; eating and drinking were pleasures too good to lose for the sake of a flat stomach; and terrorism was a theoretical worry that the West had theoretically brought upon itself through centuries of poor foreign policy. Two liberals falling in love. Everything felt nicely inevitable.

Add some oil and the chopped chillies and onion. Reduce the heat a little so as to soften but not burn, otherwise the result might be bitter or unpleasant.

By the time the beer was gone, we were sitting close and the food was ready. We moved to the dining room and started on a spicy and heavy Shiraz while she paid me compliments on the food which went beyond simple social politeness.

I don't actually remember words from that evening. Neither am I going to do a Proust's madeleine and evoke the entire experience from the smell of a cumin seed. But what has stayed with me is the feeling of excitement, optimism and perfection that nothing could spoil. That evening was everything that I had hoped it would be.

From then on, my winter chilli became a sort of half-joking code for an evening that would end in sex. If one said to the other, "Do you fancy chilli tonight?" the other knew exactly what the menu was offering. It's nice when a relationship begins to develop that interpersonal shorthand that only the two of you share, isn't it? But the excitement, optimism and perfection? Well those are things that never last.

Raise the temperature, add the diced turkey (or your preferred alternative) and seal the meat in the hot oil and spice mixture.

Well, here we are at 33,000 feet, safely ascended and now cruising without incident. The seatbelt signs are off and the drinks trolley is almost here. About time, I had a few brandies at the terminal bar before boarding but they're beginning to wear off. Grandma in the seat next door has actually taken out some knitting of all things. Maybe she's scared of flying too and knitting is her back-up plan if annoying fellow passengers fails. I wonder how she got the needles through security? That would almost be worth asking but I really don't want a conversation. I imagine she has a peevish voice. Anyway, a quick drink for the chef and then on with our dish of the day.

Add the diced squash and the (similarly diced but also previously parboiled) sweet potato. Stir well and allow the heat to singe the edges a little.

One particularly memorable occasion when chilli led to sex was after an awful row that we had. My ex had moved in a few weeks earlier. Everything was continuing to be wonderful and it seemed only natural for her to move out from her parents' home and into mine.

We had a lot of fun playing house, buying a few key items together – a picture, an oil burner, a lamp – so as to make the place more 'ours'. And, I suppose, there was always some to-be-expected storming going on as we discovered new, cohabit-y things about each other. Seeing each other day-to-day, 24/7 for the first time. Really seeing the details of domestic hygiene values, kitchen storage preferences and finding out how the other has been spending their free time. That is, the time that was free of the other. The time that is no longer free now that all time is shared time.

Don't get me wrong, it was an adjustment that I wanted to make, but it was an adjustment nevertheless. You don't realise how little room you've got in your life until you try to fit another person into it. Maybe you don't agree. Maybe this is just my experience. Maybe one of us doesn't know what he's talking about. Anyway, I really was enjoying it, living with the ex; there was just some occasional friction.

The trouble was, we thought that all that was left to discover about each other was where on the tube we squeezed the toothpaste. Turned out that there was something a little bigger still hidden away. And it came out in those first few weeks of domestic bliss.

To this day, I can't imagine how we got to the point of moving in together – by modern standards, basically a certificate-less marital commitment – without finding out that we disagreed completely on the subject of children. Perhaps we assumed that, being so in tune regarding everything else, this would be the same. Or perhaps in some immeasurable way, we both knew that we would disagree and so put off raising it for as long as possible; forestalling the awful day. Either way, once the disagreement occurred, it would take the best chilli in the world to resolve our difference.

To sum up: I wanted kids; she didn't.

The subject came up one evening out of nowhere over a glass of wine; a cheap Chilean merlot, as I recall. (Incidentally, so strong is the association with domestic disagreement that I've avoided Chilean wines ever since.) The ex's basic position rested on her logic; namely that children completely changed (read: ruined) everything. Childbirth was a prolonged and painful process, and raising them was an expensive lifetime sentence commuted only by death. I was just being driven by some blind biological imperative over which I, as a civilised and intelligent being, should be able to exercise more control. It was her body and damned if she was going to have it deformed and damaged for anybody, even me.

All good, sound, rational arguments I had to concede. I agreed with every point she made and yet I still was adamant that I wanted children, that she should want them too and that she should have them with me. Have I mentioned yet that another thing we shared was stubbornness?

We stuck to our guns, elaborated on our arguments and increased our vehemence. All night long.

Debate? Argument? Row? Who knows but it was proverbial

thirsty work, and before we realised just how drunkenly engaged we both were with the other's recalcitrance, the best part of a three-litre winebox was gone.

By now we'd moved on from digging our trenches, finished taking potshots at each other and were now engaged in a mutual bombardment of emphatic insults. Not good. Luckily, in a sense, the sheer volume of alcohol meant we reached oblivion before armageddon. That night I slept on the sofa in my own house. This struck me vaguely as unfair but I was drunk enough for my inner gentleman to emerge; on this point, at least.

Chop the tomatoes finely and drain the beans. Add both to the pan and stir well. Reduce the heat so that the mixture simmers gently for about 5 minutes.

The next morning, looking at each other across the breakfast table, sharing the paracetamol, we were at least subdued enough to feel the mutual shame and talk a bit more rationally. We might even have listened to each other; we were both too weakened not to.

I don't think we ever resolved the issue properly. Certainly not to the extent that either of us changed their fundamental views. Behaviour, yes; views, no. And that evening, I made a batch of peace-making winter chilli and we shared a bottle of the hair of the dog (South African pinotage this time) and the making up was almost worth the argument of the night before.

Time for another drink as the trolley dollies (and I do mean that in a most non-gender specific and disrespectful fashion) serve some real food. Of course, when I say 'real', I mean not imaginary. In terms of sustenance, I'm not sure that the rubber chicken, bashed potatoes and boiled-to-death green beans have as much to offer as the chilli. And this is just the first of two on-board culinary treats.

Grandma's asleep. I decide not to wake her for lunch. She might be hungry later but better that than we actually talk to each other. Besides, I'm doing her alimentary canal a favour. Small acts of kindness with thanks neither expected nor sought; that's what life is all about.

So far, so not too bad. There's been no turbulence; no crying brats (my own I wanted, other people's are to be avoided like the plague they are) and the co-pilot's just announced that we're ahead of schedule. Only the crushing claustrophobia and the ever-present fear of plummeting with which to deal. A good flight. So far.

The chilli's really coming on quite nicely. The secret at this stage is not to let it simmer too long without adding the next ingredients. If the mixture reduces down too much, gets too dry and viscous, then you end up having to add quantities of water just to keep the consistency right. And all water will do is dilute the richness you were after in the first place.

Before things go too far, add the red wine and mixed herbs. Stir well. Continue simmering.

"Why don't you want to marry me?"

We'd been living together for two years now. The subject of children hadn't been discussed again but I think we both knew that it hadn't gone away. So, unconsciously waiting for that particular shoe to drop as I was, the ex really caught me by surprise with the marriage question.

It had been a lovely day; a sort of Hollywood movie. The sort of day the young, loved-up couple enjoy just before one of them is diagnosed with cancer or runs over their favourite cat or something.

Breakfast in bed, sex, a walk into town, pub lunch, cinema in the afternoon and chilli for dinner; why did she want to go and spoil it? Busy looking the other way, I'd walked right out into the traffic and been blindsided while washing up.

Unlike the question of children, we had actually talked about marriage properly (and soberly) and I'd thought that we were in complete agreement. Marriage was fine for those who want it, but in the modern civilised world it was hardly necessary as a means to demonstrating commitment. There was no real social pressure any more. It was even faintly hypocritical to get married if you didn't have a religion; which neither of us did. As I said earlier, two liberals in love. Or so I thought.

Well, she was right, I didn't want to marry her. But I also thought she didn't want to marry me. Had she changed her mind? Had she been lying all along? Or if not lying, perhaps just going along with me, humouring me, hoping that sooner or later I'd see my error and drop to one knee? Ridiculous. Or was it?

I hadn't responded quickly enough to forestall the obvious follow-up question:

"Don't you love me?"

Christ! Not even *"Don't you love me <u>anymore</u>?"* This was serious, the past was suddenly, momentarily irrelevant. The only thing that mattered was did I love her now; did I want to marry her now. The danger was clear. Having spent two-plus years fitting her in, there was going to be a big hole if she left now.

I blurted and stammered out reassurances and protestations of devotion. Of course I loved her. (Good.) Of course I wanted to spend the rest of my life with her. (Even better.) I hadn't suggested marriage because I thought that she didn't believe in it. (Only partly true, but the right thing to say under the circumstances.) She knew that I wanted children with her, surely that showed how committed I was? (Watch it, thin ice.) In fact, if she'd agree to have my children, I'd marry her tomorrow. (Damn!)

It was the Chilean merlot all over again: I was trying to blackmail her into carrying my child. In fact, it was worse than that because I wanted children, plural. I didn't care what happened to her; she was just a breeding pod to me. I wouldn't love her after she'd been pregnant and given birth which means I obviously didn't love her now because of what I was asking; it was scientifically proven that men had affairs after their wives became mothers. Why didn't I just go and have an affair now and be done with it? Tune in next week, folks, for more of the same; this programme could run and run. I had to do something.

Now sprinkle in a heaped teaspoon of brown sugar. Stir well. Continue simmering.

The ceremony was in the spring. It rained.

Grandma's starting to stir; her knitting has just fallen off her lap. I wonder what she's making? A little Aran straitjacket for some unlucky grandchild, no doubt. Said child will be forced at gunpoint by grim-faced parents to say, Thank you, Grandma, and any complaints about the scratchiness of the wool will be firmly shushed. I nip down the aisle to the toilet before she wakes up properly and realises she's missed her cordon bleu lunch.

Contrary to what you might think, I find the extremely confined space of airplane toilets rather comforting. My fears about flying aren't sensible and neither are my contingency plans. I don't pay attention to the arm-waving presentation on emergency procedures before take-off. I already know my procedure. Should any plane on which I'm a passenger start nosediving towards the ground, I will grab as many seat cushions as I can and then lock myself into the toilet. Wedged into such a confined space with enough foam padding and I stand a better chance of survival than if I just assume the 'crash position'.

On a rational level, I know that this is no more than an urban myth and that death is certain. But that doesn't stop me believing. Faith is unreasoning and born of fear and desperation. Put that on a t-shirt and sell it to Catholics.

By the time I return, Grandma has been provided with a foil coffin in which her late chicken lies in state. She glares accusingly at me as I sit down. I ignore her. She's hardly likely to want a nice, friendly chat now. Job done.

Even the most experienced cook can't afford to look away at the wrong moment. After a year and a half, we were still married, there was no sign of any children and it wasn't me who had the affair.

I don't know anything about him. I don't know who he was. I don't know how they met. I don't want to know how he made her feel. I don't want to hear how lonely she might have felt until he came along. I didn't want her to tell me it was all my fault. That's why I didn't ask any of the usual questions that are asked in TV soap operas, cinematic relationship dramas and chick-lit novels. I had all those questions, naturally. I just didn't ask them. I did tell you I had focus and willpower.

All I know for sure is that I came home early one day (what a cliché) and there was a scuffling and fumbling and dashing about upstairs accompanied by much hoarse and desperate whispering. When I went to investigate, I found the ex only partially dressed, my bed unmade and some man looking undecided: hide in the wardrobe or jump out the window (cliché heaped upon cliché.)

I decided to improvise rather than play the outraged cuckold and/or denounce them both from my moral high ground. I went downstairs again and started preparing the dinner, chopping onion, butternut squash and sweet potato and measuring out the spices.

The house is small and the foot of the stairs is next to the kitchen door. I kept the door shut and my back to it to give them a chance to sort themselves out. After twenty minutes, the door opened and she came into the kitchen and started to talk. Or tried to. I cut her off. I'm not interested, I told her, in excuses and explanations, in whys and wherefores, in lies and recriminations. I don't want to know who. I don't want to know when, or how often. I don't want to know what he's got that I haven't. I don't even want to know if it's going to stop. All I need to know is whether you are staying.

That did it. No dancing around the issue. No playing by the accepted rules of extramarital fallout. Just straight to the bottom line, everything else is mere detail. Are you staying or going? The answer to that decides which set of details then needs working through. I still had my back to the door, and to her, but I could feel her shock. Good, I thought, I've had one; have one back. Now, what's it to be? I could tell from the tension in the air that she didn't think I was playing fair. She had a dozen explanations, all carefully worked out in those post-coital reveries when the adulterer asks themselves, what if I get caught? So I deprived her of her speeches and self-justifications and reduced her available responses to just *yes* or *no*. She said, yes. So we had dinner. And I opened a bottle of good Spanish cava because I felt as if I'd won something.

At this stage it is worth testing a piece each of the butternut squash and sweet potato to check they are cooked properly. There should be no resistance to the bite.

That night, whether because of the chilli or the situation, we certainly had sex. I wouldn't say we made love exactly – although, to be honest, I've never been too clear on the difference – but the sex definitely had more energy than it had had for a while. With the rear-view mirror of hindsight, signs, events and contributory factors are often much clearer: months of sexual drought, her new clothes, her increased happiness with life in general. Clichés are clichés for a reason: they're so often true.

The morning after, things felt clearer and more settled. She was staying. With me. That was all the distance I thought I needed from the interloper. Warning: items viewed in this mirror may be closer than they appear. Within a month, a home test said she was pregnant. The doctor confirmed it.

Things are simmering nicely so I take a break and look around the cabin while they serve meal number two. Grandma's awake but making a point of ignoring me by facing the window as she puts away her knitting. Suits me fine. Little Jack Porno across the way seems to have got bored of staring at nude girls and sharing the view with the woman sitting next to him. She still looks like she'd wants to kill him, though. I hope for his sake that the plastic cutlery is blunt. I'm not sure why she doesn't change seat, there're plenty of empty ones. Pride probably: why should she move, he's the one doing something offensive and socially unacceptable. True, but that only works in a fair and just world, this is not that world. It's always surprising to me the energy people put into pretending that it is.

Ah well, the illusions and delusions of others. To return to my own pretences, the mental cookery is keeping me nicely occupied and distracted. But I suppose it's not just the chilli that I'm stirring up.

I made winter chilli a lot during her pregnancy. It was something she craved. Some women want banana pizza, some peanut butter and Marmite on toast, the ex wanted my winter chilli. I think it brought us closer together. Sometimes the craving was so great that I had to make up batches especially for her.

Of course, one of the many side effects or signs of pregnancy is that the taste of familiar foods can change. She loved the chilli but would sometimes complain that it tasted 'different'. Nothing she could put her finger on, just not quite usual. That's the thing about using fresh ingredients, there'll always be variations in the flavour; and in a dish, which combines so many different flavours, the end result will always vary from batch to batch. That's what I told her.

On the whole, it wasn't too hard a first pregnancy. She said the morning sickness was manageable and the food cravings weren't too strange (like I say, I was happy to make her as much chilli as she wanted) and although she felt exhausted all the time, I was only too happy for her to rely on me for whatever she might need. Yes, it all went well until a routine checkup at the two to three month mark.

From what the doctor said, the baby had died. He couldn't tell how or why. And what we thought were signs of the pregnancy proceeding (less nausea, less fatigue, etc.) were actually signs that the pregnancy was over. Given how little enthusiasm she'd shown for motherhood in the past, you might be surprised to learn how distraught the ex was upon receiving this news. Mind you, the dilation and curettage procedure that followed is apparently quite unpleasant and would, I suppose, upset anybody.

And so my role changed subtly from that of carer for mother and growing baby to carer for bereaved parent-to-be. At first, she refused to believe that it had happened; she wanted so badly to believe that she was still pregnant. I genuinely believe that the irony was lost on her. But the d&c made that sort of denial difficult to maintain and she rapidly progressed to feeling depressed.

Most days she didn't want to even get out of bed and it was all I could do to get her up and out for a walk in a nearby park. Mixed up with all the grief and sense of loss and the mourning was her belief that she'd let everyone down by losing the baby.

On more than one occasion, she said that I should feel let down by her. After all, I was the one who'd wanted children; she was having the baby for me. To make me a father.

She thought that I should let my feelings show; express them, mourn with her. But, do you know, I could never quite bring myself to one hundred percent believe that it had been my child. There was always a nagging doubt, a slight statistical possibility. I suppose there are tests to decide one way or the other, but if it had been his child then she would have had to leave me. My preference is to be certain about things and as long as doubt remains, well, that doubt prevents me from feeling too much one way or the other.

Finely chop the chocolate and stir into the chilli with the lime juice. Bend low over the pan and let the smell remind you of chocolate limes, the green boiled sweets from childhood with the chocolate centres. Simmer some more.

So I held her hand through it all. I comforted and I soothed. And after a year or so, things began to return to something approaching normality. There was always a slight shadow, naturally, but the events of the past year or two were behind us. I really don't think she would have got through that difficult time without me and I'm sure that in her own way she was grateful. We were moving on. Together.

Time to get up and move again. Crashing isn't the only scary thing about flying. Deep vein thrombosis is an equal albeit less dramatic danger. I get up and go for a walk up and down the aisle. After all this trouble, the last thing I want is to arrive at my destination and die of a blood clot. That said, I like to think that in my last moments I might appreciate the ironic symmetry of it all – given the events that have led me to be here.

Back in my seat, I lift my legs in turn and point my toes. Feels good. Economy class seats seem to be built for midgets. I rotate my shoulders and then lift and stretch each arm. Grandma grunts, annoyed. I'm not encroaching on her space, but by now I could shower her with compliments on the artistry of her jumper and she'd want nothing more than to shove a knitting needle up my nose. Ah well, there are risks to every course of action.

The ex never asked me to make winter chilli again and I only cooked it with her one more time. Life continued but we never talked about children again. Whenever I tried to raise the subject she refused to talk about it; it was 'too soon'. When would 'soon enough' be? I didn't know and she wasn't giving any clues. Surely the most sensible thing to do would be to try again as soon as she was physically fit? Sort of getting back on the horse after you've been thrown off. Or getting a new puppy after your dog has died; it's not a replacement – of course it isn't – but you love it and it helps you deal with the gap left by the old dog. Obviously, I was careful about expressing this reasoning to the ex. She was quite sensitive about anything to do with pregnancy and children and I didn't want her to misinterpret my point.

The chilli should be a dark reddish-brown colour by now and have a thick, rich consistency. Taste and add a little salt and pepper if necessary.

Funnily enough, although I never actually mentioned the dog and puppy analogy to her, we did get a dog. It was her idea, she found some tatty mongrel that needed a home and gave it one. She also gave it a name: William. No consultation with me on any of this, but I was just pleased that she was showing signs of interest in life again.

At first, I worried that William might be some sort of baby substitute and would delay our second attempt at parenthood, but I told myself that it was early days and besides, any sort of connection was a good thing; for now. Then I wondered if perhaps William was meant to be my baby substitute. If she was hoping that in focussing our affection on a dog I might forget about wanting children. It seemed unlikely that she could be so subtle but from then on I kept my distance from William. Our relations were polite and friendly, but not too warm, just in case my position was misconstrued.

A possibility that worried me more lay in the choice of William's name. It wasn't a name we'd considered for the baby but I knew it would be in our book of baby names. William means 'protector' or 'protection'. The ex maintained that it was simply that his scruffiness reminded her of Just William from the Richmal Crompton stories she'd read as a child, but I remained concerned that she unconsciously felt the need to be protected from something or someone. I have to admit to a touch of jealousy towards William on this point. After all, I was the husband; surely I should be the protector. What need could there be for a william as long as I was there?

The seatbelt sign has just come on, accompanied by that irritating chime. Grandma and I buckle up. I try not to let it strike too much terror into me. It's probably just my imagination, but the stewardess has just rushed past and she looked worried about something. Two of the cabin crew are huddled in the kitchen area, whispering. I tell myself that it's only the possibility of a little turbulence and return to the chilli. It's almost finished.

She died in the autumn. In her sleep. It would be alot more pleasant to say that faithful William woke me, with his pining and whining for his mistress who'd passed away during the night. But actually, it was the smell that roused me.

Our society is very coy about death. Preferring to ignore it whenever possible and when it can't ignore it, romanticise it. We're sold a nice, reassuring image of dying in one's sleep, peaceful, easy, with dignity. The physical realities are glossed over, including the fact that once the brain dies it ceases all those automatic little functions that we take for granted. Like bowel control. She didn't appear to have much dignity, lying in a pool of her own urine and excrement. To be fair, she also didn't appear to care very much.

William was nowhere to be seen and I was in bed with my dead, messy wife. I got up and had a shower. While I was in the bathroom, I thought about how my life had changed overnight while I slept. Our time together was over. I was alone again, no chance of children. William was irrelevant, he wasn't my dog and he had failed to protect her. I could already feel that her-shaped gap opening up. All the time and effort expended in making room for her and now she was gone. The unfairness of the situation was not lost on me. The practical issues began to become apparent: the call to a doctor, the death certificate, possibly an inquest, embalming, a funeral service, then cremation or burial. I imagined the fake sympathy of the other mourners as they mourned themselves. The platitudes: "At least it was peaceful." ... "She'll always be with you." ...

The more I thought about it, the less right it seemed. She should stay with me. She could stay with me. I didn't have to let her go. Nobody knew yet and I was still in control. She would always be with me. If I acted quickly.

Serve with plain corn nachos, rice, tortillas, soured cream, jalapeño chillies and freshly made guacamole and salsa. Best enjoyed with either a robust Cabernet Sauvignon or one of the darker Mexican beers, such as Negra Modelo or Dos Equis Amber.

Funeral rites and customs vary greatly between cultures. Look widely enough and you'll find a precedent for anything. Someone else has always set the example. Ritual ingestion is one way of respectfully honouring the loved one, making them a part of you and your life both symbolically and literally. And cannibalism is a word with such ugly and inappropriate connotations.

To spare the details, let's just say that by the end of the day the rites, so to speak, were done. William took a keen interest in everything and I saw no reason why he shouldn't share the honours as her faithful, if incapable, protector.

So that was the last time I cooked the winter chilli. And if it was a special dish before, it really had significance now. I may eat it again one day, but it will have to be a very special occasion and, to tell the truth, I think I may have had a bit too much that last time. A surfeit. I can't quite get the taste out of my mouth.

Looking at the time, we should be starting our descent soon; coming in for that blessed landing. Grandma's asleep again and will probably only wake up when her ears hurt enough for a barley sugar. The sad pervert across the aisle has got his porn out again (much to his neighbour's disgust) and the cabin crew look relaxed. Perhaps it was all in my imagination.

The one thing about my journey for which I am truly grateful is that it's a one-way trip. There's no reason to go back. And besides, to wish to return always implies some sort of regret. Don't you think?

Serves two.

3

The Willows

Guy Mankowski

Author

Guy Mankowski was raised on the Isle of Wight before being taught by monks at Ampleforth College, York. After graduating with a Masters from Newcastle University and a Psychology degree from Durham, Guy formed 'a Dickensian pop band' called Alba Nova, releasing an EP. Guy now works as a psychologist in Newcastle. Guy's writing also featured in Legend Press' 2009 short story collection *8 Rooms*. Guy's story *The Willows* is about an elderly man's recollection of a summer in which he first experienced love, jealousy and the transience of life.

As I am drawn back to that summer, my mind is enveloped within a sleepy, silky web of memories, interwoven like waves breaking crisp on a shore. I sleepwalk through these memories, some so vivid and clear set to the backdrop of a rolling sea, the sound of innocence. Every sadness and melancholy still return to me when I set foot on the sand and hear that watery procession that chants and chants, seducing me into a slumber.

The Willows is there as it used to be, paled slightly with the crime of time. It still resonates with a glacial beauty that is ominous and cool. Its aged palm trees, tired and golden green still sway, wrapped in the cold autumn wind. When I was thirteen the white pillars and slate porch that looked out onto the blue mass seemed menacing to me. Now they are all a part of that web, shrouded in beautiful sorrow and ghosts.

Some barrier, written in ink or printed, tells me now that I can't walk into that garden and skirt around the pond or look out at the sea from the comfort of that green canopy of leaves. It's unattainable, lost, irretrievable in the silver, but still clear and shimmering like shards of glass in my mind.

The ghosts come alive in the seaweed, driftwood and stones; the pale, hard sensations under my feet. I had never met Aunt Bella before my parents sent me to The Willows, only heard her name tossed into the tumult of a conversation. But when my mother, concerned with how thin I'd become and convinced that a summer by the sea would revive me, said that she was eccentric but wonderful, I knew I'd love her.

I'll have to tell you about her, as soon as I've whirled with my memories a little longer, as soon as they've settled down. Those mere words 'the summer holidays' still bring a certain chill to me, like a heady gulp of wine on a still evening. They send shivers first, phantoms second. It's the soft ride of the words, ripe and warm. It's the beauty of those spectres that chime around the trees, the clefts, the sandy gorges, that wrap their shroud around the bodies, that hang over the paint-flecked boats clinking in the wind under the aroma of sea air, forming a crystalline 'o' in the wind which breathes its voice around me, sighing and drawing endlessly, like the sea.

I'd spent the first part of my life naked and blonde in warm rock pools fishing for cockles and sculpting sandcastles, which to me were as strong as the imaginative figures that swept around them in limitless adventures. But when dusk fell and I was taken inside I never realised that the lapping of the sea eroded those castles and their characters into a gold wet sludge, before heaving it slowly into its body, to be washed up further along the shore.

That summer represented two months away from my parents and the faceless cruelty of boarding school, which crushed my spirit and tucked it away in desks and pencil cases, endless corridors, cold mirrors, and continual silences. Besides the sea, which was the backdrop and my first love of the summer, there was another who was just as eternal and crazily poised. Aunt Bella was my mother for July and August. Bella lived by the sea all year round, and swam only in the sea even in the dead cold of winter, where she suspended herself frail and trembling in the waves.

I remember the first time I watched her step into the ocean, the waves washing mercilessly against her body, slim and downy in a chequered swimsuit that damply clung to her. The sky yawned over her and she looked brave and lost. Submitting herself, she rose in paroxysm of bliss, the corners of her mad old mouth tugged into a sheepish smile as if she was almost ashamed of the pleasure the water gave her. She was as much a child of the sea as any driftwood or rope.

The Willows was filled with canvases of her impulsive paintings of the water; smashed and scattered with paints, portraying movements and rhythms that showed she had been watching it for years. In the summer her paintings were lively with webs of gold and white, and in the winter they were still with silver and green.

When I skirted The Willows for the first time, its emptiness vaulted me. My room looked over the sea and the expanse of pale sand, and I remember the faces that passed in front of it, busy with their own thoughts. Somehow the sea brought a fresh honesty into everyone who passed it; glazed bodies broke free just as the air broke out of its winter shroud. To that sea I owe my first flirtation, because silhouetted against it girls in pale dresses passed, slim and calm, with infinite mysteries. All I knew was that women, like Aunt Bella, could be eternally comforting and yet also silently, mercilessly cold. In the first lights of summer I fell in love with every apparition that slid past my window, delicately rounded and full of exotic dreams. Every single one broke my heart. Each imaginary affair moved as a series of intense, glistening emotions with a veiled promise never to betray, and every one did, every one slid across the horizon and disappeared. Their minds were as desperate and frightened as my own. It seemed they all had secrets that could make me recklessly happy; but that could only happen when I knew myself, and I did not then.

Even in early summer, with bright sky and transparent water, the sea was too cool to slip right into. I had to become intimate with it, bring my heat down to its level and then ease myself in. I learnt to swim, plunge, twist and float underwater and I saw through the sandy fug to weeds suspended under the surface. I would touch the ground, and kick up sand storms, which I dared myself to swim through, and I rise to a blast of white sky, which stretched over my head.

The water broke like blossoms and dripped from me as I shivered in its grip. I gambolled recklessly in the water, washing away the dirt of school, the stale dormitories, the frozen sinks – they all dissolved in the beautiful August sea as I plunged and plunged and plunged.

When the winter came, I would lie in bed and listen to music, which took me back to the graceful sweep of that ocean. But I couldn't capture its essence, except from when I was immersed in its arms, its waves breaking over me in a turquoise shimmer.

How do I describe this to someone who has never stood on a beach in a summers evening, with the sea painting itself endlessly in its own colours? What am I hoping to achieve as I immerse myself in my memories so deeply, to try and recapture that essence? Perhaps I am hoping to gain something I lost, or hoping to achieve the greatest of indulgences – to shed all responsibility to the future. But inevitably I must accept that I have to let go.

When the train first slid into the station I looked for Bella, trying to seek out a mad vision perhaps muttering to herself under a mess of hair, but no-one stood out. Unlike other relatives who'd be keen to find me on arrival, Aunt Bella couldn't be seen. I often entertained the thought that she could appear on will. There were a few occasions during the summer when I desperately tried to find her in her favourite haunts (that word seems so relevant now) and she couldn't be found at all, not sitting by the pond pushing pages, nor under the shade of the willow tree. She appeared when she wanted to appear, she seemed to have assumed the rhythm of life and in her mad dexterity was able to influence it, to appear and disappear at will.

I searched for her through the smudged grey window of the train, distracted by the noise and the heat, but she wasn't amongst the men in suits, the tourists smiling to themselves and the slim girls in blue. I was wild-eyed, and frantic and then she arrived without a greeting. Startled, I was clutching the bunch of flowers my mother had given me and I held them out to her. Bella seemed unable to smile, except faintly when she was by the sea and even in that first meeting she was very distant.

I never knew her in the way most people know others, through a shared secret or a similar pursuit; our bond came about through a mutual understanding, which I thank the sea for. At no point did she try to talk to me about school, and her efforts to make me study in the holidays came purely out of guilt; she would have hated to see anyone work in the summer.

My mother had instructed me that Godfrey, her husband who had recently passed away, was not to be mentioned. She'd told me they had been 'two peas in a pod' and that when he died, she wouldn't be far behind.

But this world still had her for a few moments yet. Bella had accepted his death with the quiet, helpless inevitability of one who knows the cruelty of the world only too well.

She asked me if my parents were well and how my brother was, and said how she'd been looking forward to meeting me. She never seemed unhappy, but I felt infectious moments of bliss rise through her occasionally, when the sun blasted white onto our lithe bodies, making her complexion shine. She never looked wrinkled to me, only ruddy and strong, despite her frailty.

I wonder whether or not I sent secret messages out to the sea when I arrived, and whether or not it responded to me in some sensuous way. I'd been brought up for the first years of my life by it, so I had grown to know its rhythms, and I felt in some strange way that it welcomed me when I arrived at The Willows, as it beat down on the shore. The Willows soon seemed more like home than home did, and I realised as I walked through it that even though I didn't know where everything was, it would soon come to represent an oasis to me. I had my room, and unlike my room at home it was full of the spicy airs of the sea. I longed to slip into the soft and warm water, and I knew that when I did all responsibility would be shed from me.

I slipped out alone and laughed. Out loud; it shivered in the wind. I was free – I knew no-one. It was a beautiful feeling. Summer was clear around me, full of mysteries. I had the promise of romance, the sea and a mad apparition to live with, and I loved it all.

Bella later said, in her more affectionate moments, that I was beautiful like only a child who'd lived his first year by the sea could be. She said she doubted my eyes would be as blue if they hadn't reflected the waves for my first year. She was full of these mad ideas. And she promised that I would also spend my dying years by the sea, and in that respect she was right.

I felt recklessly happy as I stripped off my travelling clothes and slipped into the water that lopped around me, its cool lip rising with a thin line of bubbles over my slim knees and up the twist of my body. As I looked down on myself my body was pale and white in the water. I hoped it would soon ripen in the sun. I dived under, felt the water splay through my hair, and I rose invigorated. I kicked around in pleasure and when I was too tired to swim any more I walked back to the shore and let the sea dry on my body as I shivered and dripped on the sand. I got to know the boats, the faces and the sounds of that corner of the beach so well.

As I sat with her on the third night, she poured us wine and stared at the sky outside our window.

"Did your dear mother tell you that you would be having company?" she asked.

I shivered all over. I knew it would have to end.

"One of my closest friends has a daughter – who I admit I've not seen in a long time. He wants her to spend a little time away from home, as apparently she's become withdrawn. And what better place than here!"

She said the words with a quick wave of her hands.

"She's coming tomorrow, and if her father's anything to go by she will be a gentle, sweet thing. Her mother died two years ago and she hasn't been nearly the same since. She was a dear woman, but we know how the world takes its toll."

She took a nervous sip of wine, and shook slightly.

"Her name's Olivia. Dear me, I shall feel like quite the mother figure what with you both here. I shall have to steel myself." She quivered again, and then looked back at me firmly. "Here is the only place to be in the summer. When your mother sees you next, you will be different boy, you mark my words. I can see the grey around your eyes starting to fade already. I shall watch you blossom." She paused, and then murmured to herself affectionately, perhaps imagining it.

Olivia arrived the next evening. She came in tattered city clothes with eyes that I saw myself in. Standing at the station wrapped in smoke she was bewitching. She greeted me with an awkward smile, and then averted her gaze. But what flashes she gave me of it told me I could hide nothing from her.

She touched Aunt Bella shoulders gently when she greeted her, and I felt the glare of her gaze on the side of my face when she realized I was watching. Aunt Bella made quick inquiries about her father and then, perhaps afraid of uncovering some shadow, left us alone together. It was exactly what I'd wanted, but I was afraid I'd say something inappropriate.

She had a strange, gentle allure, and though I wasn't yet close to her I promised myself that I must be soon. She wasn't quite the fragile flower I'd expected and the apparition that appeared so thin and fragile was in fact furiously intelligent and bright. Her eyes were china blue and searching, and they gave you the feeling of being naked under their gaze. I often felt that no-one could lie to those eyes, and if they tried they would search among the knots and crevices of your mind and triumphantly seize on the truth. Life to her seemed intense and fleeting, she was almost ashamed at the brevity of it, and she treated it with a passing ecstasy and despair, all dispatched with the same weary reverence. So far she sounds just like a fireball, but she wasn't; she was beautiful and dark, and I was desperate to know the her she was trying to hide.

Another moment haunted me when she first came to The Willows, and that was the strange twist of a smile she gave when she first saw the shimmering sea. The intimacy the three of us felt just seeing it made us seem complicit in something. How could something that distant still remain so intimate? It was as if we were part of a secret tribe, and we knew our secrets but they were so powerful and intangible that we could never share them with anyone, not even each other. All at once I wanted to pour it all out to Olivia; shamelessly, recklessly. I wanted to tell her I that felt close to her although I knew nothing about her. I wanted to tell her about the emptiness I felt at school, about the release of the sea when I sank in it, about all of the ecstasy and confusion I saw ahead of us – but social timing made me refrain. She seemed to know, and when it was difficult, as at first it was to think of something to say, her gaze rested on me and I was at once exposed and settled.

She played the guitar, singing in a gentle whisper that I was drawn into. It was as intimate as a late night confession between strangers. When she sang she lightly carried the melody of the song but hid the words, which I imagined she felt were too personal to reveal. I watched those slim, long fingers flicker delicately over the strings of the guitar, and as I write now it seems impossible to convey the ecstasy I felt when she plucked those chords and coaxed my soul.

"Teach me," I said. "Teach me all of them."

She smiled slightly, as if seeing that she'd met someone who cared, someone whose soul was made from the same odd, awkward stuff. We'd be soul mates; I'd tell her all my visions and I'd want nothing back. For a moment I thought there were strange runes carved into her guitar, which gave her the ability to touch the nerves of life and dance on its fingers.

I went for walks with her, long searching walks where we trespassed around the curve of the beach and scrambled up the sandy mound, looking out at the sea. I held her arm and helped her along and she looked at me inquisitively. We sat out of breath at the summit, and looked at the beach and the sea below us along the horizon. Ships passed quietly out on the water, children pushed out dinghies and put on bright lifejackets. The smoke, the soft glow of barbecues wafted around, even laughter and the clink of wine glasses. I breathed in, smelt life.

"Don't you *love* it?" she whispered, her eyes alive. She looked at me and said louder, "isn't it so beautiful?" The slim girl beside me was everything anyone had promised. The same soft posture as the other girls, with brighter eyes, more mysteries, more promises.

"I'll take you out in the boat," I said. "Can you row?"

"No, but I'd love to learn. Can we fish as well? I can't fish, but how hard could it be?"

"Not hard at all," I replied. "You can see right through the water early in the morning. When no-one else is up we'll take the boat down to the shore. OK?" She smiled her agreement.

"If you teach me to play the guitar, I'll teach you to row" I said, keen to further our intimacy into the realms of somewhere reckless.

"You've got the best end of the deal there," she said, carefully putting her shoes back on. "There's nothing like learning to play the songs you coax yourself through with." She seemed to say it more to herself than me, and as she began the climb down to the sand she looked suddenly distant.

London had packed its bags, made its way south and now had begun to flood our beach. The creamy waves of sand were washed away by the trudge of sandaled feet, and the clear ocean was peppered with speedboats, dinghies and half-naked swimmers. But I didn't resent any of it, I loved it all. I loved the milky smells and the peace after the bodies deserted the sand for home, and the surrounding solitude of the falling dusk.

I soon realised that it wouldn't last forever, that the machine would soon want me back, turning me from a wild-eyed child into a custom made adult with fitting degrees.

I realised something else; that the bewitching girl who I longed to know beside me had everyone's eyes. Moving with grace through the beach she cut an air of serenity amongst the ecstatic havoc of the tourists.

The sea stirred me awake in the morning, and a sleepy morning sun lit the room. I looked out of the window to see Bella gazing out at the sea, the waves finishing their crawl in a confusion of foam at her feet. She was looking out at the still ocean, and the beach was silent and empty. She was a solitary silhouette in the morning sun.

Pulling the covers around me I moved onto my knees and watched her slim, bronze feet shuffle into the waves as they broke in circles around her. Did she quiver slightly as she breasted the water, her head held high like a swan as she swam out to the horizon? I sat there and watched her for a while, as her shoulders and head arced around in circles on the brink of the waves. She stood on a sandbank in the distance; she got tired and held onto the stern of a boat and finally, chin still high, with a look of ridiculous dignity, she paddled back to the shore. Her clothes were waiting for her on a rock and she patted herself dry. The air was still bright. I stepped out and across the landing, and seeing the door slightly ajar I tiptoed to Olivia's room; this was the perfect morning for a row.

The blankets were swaddled around her and she was still, swathed in sleep, her blonde curls scattered over the pillow. I whispered her name, and she stirred. She lifted her head sleepily, and croaked, "What is it?"

"This is the perfect morning. Look out the window." She groaned. A second later a slender wrist yanked back the curtains and sunlight spilled onto us in a hot, slanting ray. She sat up, her hair falling around her strangely uncreased face. She pouted cheerily. "You're not going to take no for an answer, are you? Let me get dressed."

We ran out of the porch and onto the grass, down to the bottom of the garden and opened the gate. She'd left her hair an awry, beautiful mess. Sleep hung over the houses; it felt like we'd made a break for our liberty. I found Eeyore under a blue tarpaulin and turned it over. We limped with it down to the water's edge and pushed it quietly into the water.

It was still and silent at sea as she lay back, looking at the sun with her eyes half-shut as the boat rocked and splashed on the water. I remember seeing fish dart in strange movements, like secret arrows backwards and forwards under the web of the glowing, undisturbed waves. She let her hands trail in the sea, and she picked up shooting stars – clumps of seaweed attached to stones. She taught me how to whirl them around my head like a lassoo and let them fly, and they would dive like spinning, falling missiles into the sea. I was near her while she span them around her head, I could smell the softness and warmth of her body. These were the most beautiful of moments out there in perfect isolation while the village slept.

Bella probably saw us while she sat on the porch with iced tea as we frolicked in Eeyore, the small powder blue rowing boat, secluded from the world. We rowed up to the moored dinghies and peered inside at the possessions; lifejackets, penknives and flares. There were beautiful names for the boats like Juno, Serena and Barnacle, painted in intricate letters on their sides. The sun caught the edges of the varnish and lit them up in shallow flames. Their hulls splashed on the water, which sloshed around them.

On the way back I taught her how to row. She sat beside me and took an oar in each hand, and as I looked at her I saw that her eyelashes were dark blue, almost violet. Her oars bashed the water, we got nowhere. She laughed and dipped her hands back in the cool sea, and screamed with pleasure when she saw a silver fish, pulling her hair back from her face, peering into her own swimming reflection on top of the transparent water. I was madly in love with the girl at the other end of the boat in a cotton skirt who constantly smiled. Now I wish I'd rowed slower and preserved those moments more carefully.

On the way back she craned her head over the edge and tried to catch a crab as we neared the land. The water spread around the boat like doves. She toppled into the sea and I caught the hilarious look on her face as she realised she was falling. She fell onto her knees, with a charming look of complete helplessness on her face. She screamed, pretending to be angry when I laughed at her. The water dripped from her hair as I wrapped a towel around her, and she clung to me. I took in her smell. As she looked up I felt a glowing sense of content as she shivered under my arm while I rubbed her hair dry. She looked up at me and said, "The crab got away."

A half-smile crept over her face, and I leaned in. I heard her lips part, we moved closer and then her fragrance enveloped me as we kissed. I tasted the salt on her moist lips, and her fingers snaked through my hair as she pulled me nearer. I felt a sharp, passionate intake of breath against my body. I was wrapped in her, for a second I was suspended in the glow, splayed with reckless desire, but my awkwardness stopped me. It lasted a few beautiful seconds. It wasn't my first kiss, but the first time one had affected me. I felt the huge silence of the morning, the lapping of the sea, the wet smile that spread over her mouth. She held her head to one side, still dripping. We kissed again, and the taste stayed on my lips when she drew back and laughed. "I'm all wet!" She turned quickly and pushed me into the water.

That afternoon, we decided to leave the beach for the first time and walk to the nearby town. Olivia took off her shoes and we walked the dusty track that led up the hill. Neither of us knew exactly where we were heading, so we followed the scent of suncream left by people who'd abandoned the midday heat to find shade in a café. There were no signs on this side of the coast, so all we had to follow was that elusive scent, and the bowed heads of those who knew better.

We walked past the youths smoking their cigarettes wearily in the heat. None of them seemed in any hurry; each seemed to pause as they inhaled, swilling the smoke around their chests. Their smoke only travelled one way, drifting towards the slate roofs of the town. On the way in Olivia talked without pause. I wish I could remember more of what she said; all I can recall is that her words seemed to roll from her tongue as if uncoiling from the very part of her she'd kept secret. I remember her telling me how her mother used to play the violin in the evenings, and of the time she ran away from home, returning before anyone had even noticed.

I remember looking at her as she spoke. Years later I was told that at university people would be drawn over by the sound of her voice as she talked in the corner of some bar. Her voice had a curious mix of something I have never heard before or since; it was at once assured, flirtatious and rapt. I was able to imagine even then the magnetic effect it would one day have on people, an allure made more potent by the sense that her voice had been restrained for so long. That afternoon I told myself not to interrupt that flow, thinking I may never hear it again. We chirruped like children up the long hill to the houses; both of us seemingly chasing the tail of some feeling that seemed difficult to define.

In the village we found a café to sit outside, somewhere we could watch the people around us. I noticed boys were looking at her and then smiling to their friends, though they ignored her when they passed by. I knew what that meant only too well.

At her bidding I reluctantly went inside to find a menu and when I returned I found one of the boys leaning over our table, talking to her. She was smiling up at him in exactly the same way she smiled at me, with the same air of familiarity. As I angrily neared the door, I heard her laugh and the boy smiled at his own cleverness. I dropped the menu in front of everyone and then snatched it up again and walked outside. Her laughter was subsiding. "Did you get it?" she asked, her eyes wide with innocence. I passed it to her wordlessly. "This is Joshua," she said, waving a careless hand, as careless as the vision that had just crushed me. I didn't look at him; I knew I would hate him. "Hi" he said. "Hello" I answered, throwing the word out to no-one.

Olivia seemed to register the pause between us before interrupting it lightly. "He lives near us, in the bay. What did you say your house was called?" I noticed his watch looked very expensive and his hair was layered and blonde; he had a sun-beaten public school charm that I loathed, perhaps because it always seemed to have some effect. She gave him that inimitable smile again as he said 'Providence'.

"Oh I know," she replied. "Along by the café?"

I missed the rest of their conversation. I looked determinedly down at the menu, and tried to block them out. The words on it had become ugly symbols that I could no longer comprehend. I despised the creature standing opposite me, and wished there was something I could do to make him leave, but instead I slowly learnt to smile at him. He said he'd seen us rowing together in the morning, and though I resented knowing that someone had spied upon our blissful seclusion I managed to keep smiling. The world forces us to pretend respect to those we disdain and often causes us to relieve this anxiety on the ones we love. I hoped Olivia would not have to feel the delusional swing of my jealousy.

"He's teaching me to row." she said gaily, cocking her head towards me. "Though I'm completely incompetent." I saw the next line coming.

"I can row," he said. "In fact, last year I won two cups at the regatta, one for racing speed boats, and one for rowing."

"You have a speed boat?" Olivia asked.

"Oh yes," he said, effusively. "It's the Boston Whaler. I've seen you row past it quite a few times in the morning. I think I saw you looking at it."

The last sentence was aimed more at me than her. It seemed he had already signed me up for some sort of materialistic competition with him, which only showed how wrong his assumptions of me were. I wondered how many times he'd watched us in the morning, spying on our tranquillity and planning its wreckage.

"You must show me!" Olivia said.

"I'll take you out on it," he assured. He prodded me. "You as well."

I feigned a grin, perhaps even giving him a thumbs up – the sort of gesture I would never normally undertake, which only demonstrated how far from myself I felt at that moment.

We glared at each other. In that moment we'd both communicated to the other our objective; Olivia was the battleground.

"By the way, I'm having a party at my house," he declared, before I had even thought of an evasive response. "This Wednesday night. I'd love it if you could come. Both of you."

"We'd love to. Wouldn't we?" She looked at me, which made me smile. She took this as an affirmation. "What time?"

"You can come early if you like, everyone else is arriving at seven but if you come before I can show you the grounds." He looked over my shoulder as a tall, blonde woman passed by. He didn't wait for our response, instead rising to his feet and waving over his shoulder as he walked away. I think I even managed another smile.

"How sweet." she murmured. "That will be a lovely way to spend an evening. Have you ordered?"

Aunt Bella was, of course, delighted to hear of the invitation and insisted that I wore a clean shirt for the occasion. Olivia worried for quite a while about which dress she should wear. When she asked me my opinion I was tempted to choose the uglier one in the hope that it might make her look less attractive to Joshua. But as she posed in it, it became obvious that it wouldn't make any difference.

I wondered why love was this selfish. After all, could I really I make her any happier than he could? Was my chief concern her contentment or did I secretly want her to help me solve myself? You probably think I'm shamefully self-centred but until then, those days had been completely untainted, by anyone. I'd refused to admit to myself that she'd even looked at other boys, though of course I am sure now that she had. At that age I was a limp little puppet, and my new mistress was the smiling controller of my strings, who stood amongst the mesh of all these emotions, toying with them with little understanding of the marks she left on me.

In effect I've described Joshua's introduction with the exaggerated slant of a historian who tells the story of his own nations defeat. Olivia was only ever polite and friendly, I'm sure she didn't even know how to flirt with anyone then. The kiss she'd given me the morning before had hardly been any sort of promise; it had been the natural consequence of a boy and a girl of a certain age spending an unnatural amount of time together.

I didn't have Joshua's confidence or self-gratifying charm. I'd spent my life so far easing myself gently into the company of others or in the safe harbours of my own imagination. On the rare occasions I'd wanted to get closer to someone I'd approached them with a mixture of shyness and curious sincerity. Later this developed into a careful wariness, but back then I was too young for such caution. Polished, artificial Joshua with his clear skin and perfect blonde hair would never have need for such careful approaches. I moved into the events that followed next like a fly fluttering blindly into a web, and allowed her to proceed similarly. I had not yet learnt that some undesirable occurrences were inevitable, perhaps even eventually useful.

Aunt Bella moved in her own mad, semiconscious circles over the days that followed and became quite excited by it all. Somehow Joshua spoke to Olivia again before the party and asked about her 'brother'. I don't think she corrected him.

She decided to wear her blue dress for the party, the exact one I'd rather she had just worn for me. I can't pretend every moment of that summer was happy, because the days preceding the party, where I fretted and sulked resentfully, simply weren't.

That evening she wore her hair up; her blonde curls framing her face. There was even a touch of lipstick, if I remember rightly. As I watched her prepare herself in her room, speculating aloud whether she should darken her eyes, she wasn't the girl who had sat on my bed with her fingers curling over a guitar. It was a new, pouting, preening Olivia who was becoming a woman.

I looked in the mirror. My skin had mellowed with the sun, and my hair had brightened. I was no Joshua and I never would be, that much was certain. Bella called me down and we began the long trek along the beach, which had never looked so desolate.

Olivia didn't guess my feelings; no-one ever would. It was a lonely thought. Further along the coast we could see a house lit up, and within it I could see writhing shapes in the window. As we neared, a hypnotic dance beat shattered the serenity of the coast. If that makes it sound as though I resented the music then I must make it clear that I didn't; I loved it. Despite my concerns the euphoria of the song in the distance cascaded through me. I felt the huge sense of possibility you can only have before a party at a very young age. The sense that something monumental may happen, that perhaps I could shed my skin, burn out and find a new body by the end of the party, be an improved model, perhaps with Joshua's looks. There would be girls at the party, hundreds of the exotic creatures. I couldn't help but feel excited at the thought of what might happen. Olivia whispered that she was scared, as we walked up the steps.

Faces glowed everywhere, radiant and beautiful, set alight by each other, or so it seemed. Friends danced and hugged and the girls swirled around me in skirts and jeans; boys licked their lips, girls pursed their shiny mouths. Fragrances hung in their slipstream, delectable and soft. There was a lingering, sexual buzz between the bodies as they fluttered amongst each other, and a sweet aroma, one of raw, polished flesh.

Joshua greeted us with a nonchalant wave of his hand and offered us wine. I noticed he had an expensive scarf draped around his neck. I accepted the wine and swallowed it in one go. Olivia stood beside me as I did, holding the glass nervously by the stem as perhaps her mother had taught her to long ago.

The gulp of wine made me feel dizzy and I leant against a wall to steady myself. When I turned to laugh with her about how giddy I felt she was talking to Joshua. She nodded; he took her slender wrists and led her onto the makeshift dance floor, which seemed so lawless to me. I found myself merging into it, girls twirling and dancing around each other, encouraged by the confidence in their revealed bodies. Time passed as the music blurred – the bass was so loud that it quivered in my chest. I kept looking over at them, her mouth open as she laughed and I saw him lean in. It was unbearable.

I ran upstairs asking someone for the toilet, past couples kissing frantically. I stepped over their bodies and found a balcony full of evening sun, where people were flirting clumsily. The relentless gasping of the sea and the promise of a crisp sunrise where flames would spread like smoke and smear the sky in orange clouds, cleansed the ocean air. I looked out at the sea, glad to inhale the clean air, the music from the house a muffled beat below. I was right in the centre of summer and that infectious, floral feeling was still coursing through my veins.

A drunken couple burst onto the balcony and looked for a corner. The girl had torn her dress; her smile suggested she was amused and frustrated. I made my excuses and ran back downstairs.

Olivia was dancing in a circle of boys, and I watched her smile amongst her coterie and realised there was only one thing I could do. The music was growing louder and as the evening progressed it seemed to lull me into some sort of trance. I'd never really danced before and didn't really know how to. I took some more wine, and drew on a cigarette someone offered me. I tried to take in the hot fumes, but they just seemed angry and bitter so I left it smouldering beside me.

A boy started to chat to me while a blonde-haired girl slept on his lap. Laughing at something he'd said I turned and saw Olivia embracing Joshua, leaning back as the weight of his body pressed her over a chair. After the initial shock I reminded myself of the only remedy. I forced myself to stop watching them and tried to dance again, after finishing another glass.

In the haze a girl stepped forward and said something to me about the music, something I only partially understood. She had blonde hair streaked by the sun and a small, kind face. We danced and her body was soft and flushed and I hoped badly that Olivia could see. She was exactly the sort of girl I'd seen passing The Willows in the days before Olivia had arrived. I even tried to imagine it was her, but she wasn't as slender, she had dark rings under her eyes, and she was more assured, clear-minded. Full of irrational guilt I excused myself and tried to squeeze my way back onto the balcony.

I had been there for quite a while, watching the ships in the distance when I heard something behind me. Olivia was stood at the top of the stairs, her eyes a blur.

"Where have you been?" she screamed, throwing her arms around my neck. I could feel her drunkenness as she held me, and I caught a glimpse of her eyes, ugly black circles, which used to be so delicate and violet.

"I'm so stupid." she said, trying not to cry as she smudged her eyes with her palm. I looked at her for a moment and realized that all of this had been inevitable from the moment Joshua had first spoken to her. Now she'd been discarded and was unable to ease her way through the confusion. I led her home along the shore, neither of us saying a word. Seagulls passed like lights.

Outside The Willows I cleared her eyes with my sleeve and made her laugh a little through the black and tears. She held my face and said "Thank you. You're so sweet." Despite myself, part of me hated her as I took her hand and led her inside.

The next morning I went rowing on my own and was glad for the comfort of the morning air. As always I had blown something out of proportion, taken a suggestion and turned it into a promise. I knew that looking back all of it would be a haze; that I was too young to take love seriously. I let the oars fall into the hull of the boat and allowed myself to drift, looking up at the blue sky.

I trailed my hands in the water. It was a peaceful and clear morning. Looking over to Joshua's house I could see the wreckage of the party, and I even saw a few lost souls wander past, their heads down, deep in their own thoughts. I took off my top and exposed my back to the morning sun, which lit up the waters silver ripples. I submerged my hand until it felt warm underwater and after tying the boat to a nearby buoy I dived into the sea. It was so deep I couldn't even see the floor but I kicked as hard as I could under, into the watery fog. I saw the green weeds swaying, the slope of dull gold, and then I kicked upwards and let my air go in one crazy gulp.

I laughed out loud and slapped the water, felt it spin in cool spirals around my body. I clambered back into the boat, dripping and shivering and sat there for a few minutes, looking around me at the ships in the bay, clinking softly on the morning tide. Then I patted myself dry, slipped on my shirt and went home.

Bella was teaching Olivia to paint. I'd often looked reverently at the colour-streaked canvases that filled The Willows, and had wondered what state of mind she'd had to have been in to paint them. Bella was looking quietly pleased. Olivia was smiling at her, the two of them standing in front of an easel. Bella shakily drew a line along the middle of the canvas and said, "Now, imagine that is a horizon. They all need a horizon." Then she saw me and slipped off her glasses. "Good morning dear boy," she said. "You weren't in your bed so I assumed you had gone for a row." Olivia looked at me and smiled.

"And a swim." I said.

"And how is the water?" Bella asked, selecting a new brush and mixing her blues and reds together. "Delightfully embracing as always?" She squinted, before leaning back into the canvas and swiping an arc of blue across the page. "The water in August here is unlike the water anywhere else in the world. I can only compare it to the mountain pools in the highlands." She withdrew her brush from the page, a far away look filling her eyes as she gazed down at the floor. "I do remember Godfrey always returning from a dip in the highlands with an invigorated look that would colour his cheeks for weeks." Olivia and I looked at each other. This was a special moment; she had mentioned Godfrey.

"Ah yes," she said, blinking and returning her glasses to her nose. "Your breakfast is waiting. I can't remember which cereal you prefer, so I put them all out for you just help yourself. I'm just teaching my dear girl about *colour*."

It transpired that morning that Olivia had a natural ability with paint. She painted with an accuracy different from Bella's abstract sea-pieces but with a precision that nonetheless delighted her. Bella called her 'My Little Rembrandt' and Olivia laughed, looking very different from how she had last night. A few times our eyes met and she smiled nervously, before the moment was broken by Bella pointing out something in her painting, or asking again whether we were yet to eat.

That night Olivia called me into her room. Steadying my thoughts, I told myself that she hadn't promised me anything and that my feelings were merely the summer talking. In the corner of her room she looked alone, she asked me to hug her and I curled my hand around her body and held her tightly against me.

"I just want to say sorry for last night," she whispered. "I was a tease to you, I made you go to a party you didn't want to go to and I was such a flirt. He tried to touch me."

She suddenly looked very sad, as if something she had hoped for had shattered before her, and her eyes welled up. I held her tighter and heard her breathe against my chest. She seemed to be pausing before saying something important. "Thank you," she whispered. "I deserved it, I led him on. I wanted to be desirable, that's what it was. But I told him I didn't want it like that, and he left me, and kissed another girl. And I know you were worried about me, and you could see what was happening but I didn't even talk to you about it. I realised as we came home that it wasn't him I wanted."

Glancing up, she looked so fragile, like glass shot through with a spiders' web of shards, ready to break at a single touch. "Can you forgive me?"

I cleaned her up. She fell into silence. I moved over to the window, at the sea falling onto the beach, the waves heaping onto themselves. "Do you think I'm far too sensitive, to let a little thing like that hurt me?" she asked, and I heard her turn on the bed.

"Not at all."

"I am sorry," she said.

"There's no need to be." I paused before I said it. "I would never do that to you." I whispered."I know," she said, before looking up and smiling at me.

That night the still breeze that had floated over the water knotted into itself and twisted into an awkward, powerful strength, building into a storm that span around the shore. I had felt it gather through the beach as the night closed in, collecting in pockets of strength that tore the green palm leaves from the trees, sucking them into the landfill of the sky. Twisting branches of driftwood were wrenched across the shore, to be caught between the rocks and the sea like soldiers in barbed wire, struggling to free themselves from claws as the clear sea cascaded over them. I lay wrapped in my blankets and heard its frenzy; it howled and whirled outside, I heard the casualties fly across the beach, heard the crash of the sea and saw the occasional glance of the inky black sky, bruised and hollering over the shore, turning this paradise into a huge swollen scar. The sand opened like pale wounds under the dark sky, the scars blossomed.

The next morning all was still, it was eerie and menacing. A bloated grey covered the sky like a cool smear and I saw the leaves and palms and branches scattered around, the wreckage of the beach. I saw fish, hurled up by the sea and thrown onto their bellies, surrounded by dry sand.

I walked down the steps to where Eeyore had been covered by a tarpaulin to find the tarpaulin in tatters; part of it wrapped around the tree, clinging to it limply, another part flapping like a trapped bird between iron railings. Eeyore was exposed like tender flesh, and stones and rocks had been sent by the claws of the wind and had covered its hull in bruises. The delicate hull that had floated over the morning ocean.

Its paint had been scratched off in long scars, it was scattered with holes and part of the palm tree had dislodged and smashed along its spine, tearing my beautiful boat in half. It lay dead on the sea wall, its blue and brown body scattered amongst the trees, the stones and the sand, in thousands of broken pieces.

I picked up a small piece of the hull from the collapsed wreckage and tucked it into my pocket. I still have it now and it reminds me of when we used to tug it down to the shore to let it bob on the waves. It seems impossible to accept Eeyore won't ever float again. Today that small piece of wood has dried; it's lonely and pale and makes me want to cry.

Olivia and I swam in the sea together. The heat was starting to thin a little, the sea was starting to cool, and we danced in the carnival of waves.

She forgot it all and laughed and skipped and twisted in the water, her lithe, golden body diving and rising and her thin arms around my neck, trying to push me underwater. We laughed and fought and I dragged her down with me and then let her go, and she held me under. I shot up to the sky, at least it felt that way, and we laughed and swam until we couldn't anymore.

She dragged me onto the sand and kissed me, deeper, for longer and the taste hung on my lips. Even now the sharp taste of seawater reminds me of Olivia's kisses; she showered me with them.

We sat in a warm rock pool in our costumes, our tummies rising, falling and dripping, as it was quiet around us. Her pale flesh had warmed with the sun, and her hair had lightened into a near-white glow.

I could feel ghosts surround us as the air drew in. We sensed a movement in the air, the sound of a shroud being pulled over August as its bright freedom was clothed. We both felt the melancholy; the urgency of our time together and we agreed that we would never forget these trysts. Sitting in the rock pool with the setting sun on one cheek she told me about her mother, and that the shame of the other night had been partly due to her wondering what she would have thought of her. She told me she spoke to her some nights, she felt her around her, that she was always close. She told me her father didn't understand, that he wouldn't talk of her, and her brother and sister were too young, that it had been left with her. But every night she said she sat in the dark and waited for her to come back, every morning she hoped it had all been one long, drawn out nightmare that the morning would clean away.

There was an impenetrable sadness in her pretty face that I couldn't heal. But I held her, and promised myself I would never give in and do more, that although she wouldn't recover I would help her, talk to her and never expect anything in return. She said I was the only one she trusted, and the only one she ever had.

I knew this bliss couldn't last. Already the deckchairs that used to pepper the shore in stripes of blue and white were thinning, and every day the beach emptied earlier.

One evening I smelt one sad barbecue and went out to see it. A silver foil tray had been left on the wall with the charred remains of meat, and sitting on her own was an oriental girl in pale jeans. I watched her for a while and she looked around herself, at the sea. I imagined it reflecting in her eyes. I wondered what secrets she had. Then she got up and walked away, and I never saw her again.

Less pale girls came past as the last day approached. I walked sombrely along the beach and told myself to be prepared for whatever happened this year; that the sea, which had felt like a brother, wouldn't be there for me, that Olivia wouldn't be with me and that it was back to the corridors, the routines, the faceless humiliation. I tried not to be bitter. Nothing that happy could have lasted any longer. I kissed Olivia goodbye, and we promised to write. She said she didn't want to think of it without me and I felt pulled apart by the cruel dignity of the world, the way it makes us cower and hide and deal with it all. I kissed her and tried to drink in enough of her smell to last me, and I hoped one day that smell would be mine.

Bella looked sad, and she kissed me, trembling on my cheek and said, "Dear boy, I wish you never had to go. You are golden and revived. I shall miss you." She was frail.

I was going away, and leaving behind me The Willows, the

beach, Olivia and summer. I gathered my possessions and stood on the wall, and shut my eyes, for those nights when I would try and bring myself back. I left before Olivia. I waved to them from the window of the taxi and I had never felt so tired. She was so beautiful and lost, in that silver web, and everything told me to run back and stay with her. I tried not to think of her on her own, walking along the beach and remembering it all, as the sea beat down on the shore.

Twelve weeks later I was in a lesson at school when the secretary came into the classroom and told me that my mother needed to speak to me urgently. I took the phone in her office and my mother told me in a flat voice that Bella had died in her sleep, alone.

The funeral took place on a bright, cold day in November. I had since seen Olivia for weekends and she had been so bright and alive. But when I saw her at the funeral her face was ravaged, even though she had only known Bella for two months like me. I wondered if I'd ever recover; I wasn't used to loss, though I suppose no-one ever is.

Perhaps it was because, like me, Olivia knew that summer would never be recovered; there would always be an empty place at the table. She knew that The Willows wouldn't be the same without her, her air and her madness and that it was all lost.

We spoke about her occasionally, but our relationship moved on, and strengthened, but sometimes we looked at each other and the happiness of that summer and the sadness of it all came back into her eyes. We were careful how we talked of it, so that we didn't tear open a wound that had started to heal. My tears were a comfort; they were not like the vaulting emptiness I had felt while I held the phone and listened to my mother's voice through a wire far away.

We were allowed to go back to The Willows one last time, and we wandered in the garden, and sat in the shade, and heard the sea. The windows were still full of blue, loaded with memories. I imagined she was behind me. The house had her clothes, her comfort, even her scent. It hadn't faded even a little, and I wanted to absorb enough of it so that summers from then wouldn't be painful to me or to either of us. When we walked out of it we knew we wouldn't ever come back. But we were together, that wouldn't change, there was happiness to think of in that.

But I could always remember it. It always swam into my mind in flashes and sensations, and always would, forever. I'm sure her smell faded from the house, and from the walls. Through the winter I sat in my bed and heard the breath of the other boys in the dormitory, and imagined it was waves, but it was no use. I couldn't bring it back. I lay in darkness and shut my eyes. I had to leave it behind, disentangle the web from my fingers and discard it. I used to turn over and try to go to sleep, but the memory of the sea through the trees left an imprint on my mind that wouldn't fade away.

4
The New Head of Deaths

Alistair Meldrum

Author

Alistair Meldrum was born in Edinburgh, and brought up and schooled in East Lothian. Alistair studied Psychology at university, but now works as a computer programmer for a pensions company in Edinburgh, a job forgettable enough to allow him time to write in the evenings. He lives in the Borders with his wife and three children. His story *The New Head of Deaths* is a story about the modern detachment many people have from the inevitability of death, and why that is a loss to us.

As I reverse into my new parking space, I catch a look at myself in the mirror. The clothes that make me look like a corpse; white shirt, charcoal grey suit, and black tie against a pallid face, elongated by the baldness which has long since stopped surprising me in the mirror.

Daniel is looking in front of him, at nothing in particular, as he often has in the past few days, though he maybe did before then too. Has he always done that? I don't know – it's the sort of thing I should.

"You OK?" I ask, redundantly.

He looks to me, in the same way as he looked in front of him before, and nods.

"I'm really sorry that I have to do this. Are you sure it's OK?" But this question is redundant too. I'm here now, and I don't have a lot of choice.

However, Daniel doesn't say so, he lets me off the hook and just shrugs. "I'll be fine, I'll just play this," he says, and takes that damned handheld gaming thing out his bag. It smugly sits in his hand, taunting me and reminding me of the clumsiness with which I gave it him. "This might take your mind off things," I'd said at the time. Indeed.

I pause for a moment, which I suppose is to make it seem like I'm still considering whether or not to go upstairs, though it's not conscious. Then I unclip the seatbelt – "OK, I'll try not to be long. Sorry," and I slip out of the car.

The garage, and the rest of the building is just how it was fifteen years ago when I first stepped in here. Concrete walls, faded white paint marking out the space numbers, the floor painted a now discoloured light blue, and all of the colours just weaken into grey.

I buzz in, and make my way upstairs.

"Hello, Mr Cross," the security guard says as I get to reception, "pleased to meet you. Mr Hughes will be down shortly." The subordination of it was not false, the man was just being cheery, and it seemed to fit with the marble desk, marble floors, large bay windows, and oval blue carpet – all an attempt to project a confident, extravagant image.

Steve came through the glass doors from the main building and grinned at me.

"Martin, hi!" he said warmly and shook my hand. I'd been looking forward to working with him again, but I wasn't feeling as comfortable as I'd pictured. Mind you, what a different job interview it would have been had his familiar face, clearly in my corner, not been there, highlighting my strengths, smoothing over any weaknesses. It's very safe to say, I wouldn't have this job were it not for my old friend. "Come on this way," and he led back through the familiar glass doors, behind which there was a corridor leading to a large oak door.

It's amazing how it comes flooding back. This image of indulgence portrayed on the ground floor is immediately thrown out of the window as soon as you pass through the oak door and head up to the office. Extravagance makes way for the austerity of the coalface. The stairs are steel open risers, the walls, more whitewashed breeze-blocks like in the garage.

Steve holds the door open and walks up beside me, though with his six-foot-five frame, I struggle to keep up. "Full suit and tie then!" he mocks. "As I said, we're mostly business casual here, but I suppose it's appropriate, all the grey and black." he says with a well-meaning smile. Does that mean he knows? Would that make it easy? Or is he talking about the first day? I'll be ambiguous.

"It's only proper." I said.

"Well," he said airily, "I know you've joined the death team but you don't have to take it that seriously!" And he laughs again so I know I'm going to have to make him feel awkward. We reach the top of the stairs; ready to go into the office so I pause, to spare him a little.

"Ah. Look, Steve, I'm not just wearing this because of the job. Louise died last week."

As expected, his face falls.

"Don't worry about it, you weren't to know. I wasn't sure, by your comment, if you did."

"Shit, sorry Martin. I had no idea. What a twat's thing to say."

I laugh a little to ease him up. "Show me someone who hasn't said something like that though. I'm forever doing that – 'you're dressed up, got a job interview?' – and they always answer, 'no, a funeral'. You'd think I'd learn."

He raised his eyes, apologetic and grateful at once. "Yes, I know what you mean. How are you? You OK?"

"Yeah, but I feel like a total muppet about this – I can't stay. Daniel's in the car downstairs, and I have to take him to the funeral."

He waves his hand, and goes to open the door. "Don't be silly, of course you'll have to."

I stay still, just to make my point a bit more. I can't believe I didn't give more warning about this. First day on the job. How I thought I'd get out of the funeral is beyond me now. It took three days to even occur to me that I'd need to be there for Daniel, and that was only when I was slapped in the face with it.

"It's just she died late on Wednesday and I didn't find out until Thursday evening. I should have let you know on Friday, but I don't know, it slipped my mind." Slipped my mind that I needed to comfort my son.

Steve continued to shake his head, and dismiss, which of

course he would. He's not very well going to tell me I can't go.

"Still, it's appropriate. First day as Head of Deaths, and I have to go to a funeral," I try and say brightly. Steve's eyebrows flicker, a little unconvinced, then he recovers and smiles.

"Hey, look, thanks for coming in and telling me anyway," he says. "I really shouldn't ask this, but it's just I'm off for the rest of the week – I couldn't just give you the five-minute tour could I? Introduce you to the team? Some of them have come in early, especially to impress, so you ought to show your face – if you can manage it, I mean?"

He says this kindly, and means it that way. He's a good-natured man, like many tall men seem to be, gentle, and with a face which generally expresses calmness, benevolence. Of course I'll do what he asks.

We enter the open plan floor where I should be starting my new working life, were it not for the unforeseen delay. "I'll not keep you long," Steve says as we walk through on the dark green carpets, an attempted touch at luxury.

We walk half-way through the room, and there is an office, of sorts, a partitioned space, which he enters. I assume this is his office. Steve is head of customer services, and as such, my new boss.

I sit down opposite him.

"Must be odd being back is it? How long has it been, ten years?"

"Eleven since I left. It's hardly changed on the face of it; it's like being back at school. How long have you been here now?"

Steve laughed, and idly looked around as though surveying – he started on the same day as me, so I know full well. "Seventeen years!" he says, shaking his head. "Some things are different – some, well, just aren't. Anyway, I don't want to keep you, I'll just give a quick overview. I don't expect you to pick up too much this week, first week in the job and all that. Just get to know people. I'll introduce you to Julian in a minute, he's been dealing with the allocation of work while we recruited – well, you. So you can rely on him for the next week or so."

I nodded. It was a strange sort of office now I looked at it afresh. I'd worked in plenty other open-plan offices before since being here, and this is unusual. Usually they have the odd office in the corner for department heads. To have, effectively, a little bullring, partitioned by pin-boards and cabinets for the head of customer services, was odd. Then he explains.

"I shouldn't be this side of the desk though," he says laughing, a little insincerely, as though he'd set the whole thing up as a slightly under-whelming surprise. "This is your area, my office is upstairs. So this is it, what they call round here, the 'Inner Circle of Death'".

The death jokes will take a bit of getting used to. My own effort had seemed decidedly crass, given that I was talking about a real funeral. Steve's had been more general, I suppose.

"The main thing I want to stress, and the main thing that's changed is the culture, the feeling of this place," he starts, his voice altering into a presentation-style tone. "We take great pride in our death benefits product, and the support we give. It's central to our brand, crucial to the customer offering. We offer a high-end support proposition to the widows and widowers, including a quick release of a portion of death benefits, assistance in funeral planning, and a service to gather and centralise all benefits from other financial products the deceased might have…" I suppose you get used to this, in the industry. Steve talked about the deceased, as neutrally as a pharmacist probably talks about condoms.

"…and so it's a tough job for the guys there on the phone. That's where you come in, as the Death Benefit Servicing team manager. Balancing the work they do so it doesn't get them down, keeping them focussed and positive, it's absolutely crucial. On the whole, we need to ensure our customers see us as – " and at this, he held his hands apart, palms open and facing each other, as though holding up a large sign–"sympathetic and compassionate. Simple as that. But to do that, we have to keep our staff happy, and keep them understanding. For that, you, above everyone, need to be that too–sympathetic and compassionate."

My son is downstairs in the car, playing a handheld gamer, which I bought him to console him (no pun intended) for the death of his mother, while I sit upstairs at my new job. He waits, on his own in a dreary garage, playing – what game is he playing? I don't even know – until I'm ready to take him to his mother's funeral. Sympathetic and Compassionate. I may be in the wrong job.

Eventually, having been through a ten-minute meet-and-greet with my new team, I get back down to the garage. It had been as uncomfortable as expected; one person referring to their team as the 'death squad', and one other guy making the same mistake as Steve before cringing about what an idiot he'd made in front of his new boss. Then at Steve's behest, I'd given a short speech about 'me', paraphrasing from memory a similar speech I got from my last boss when he joined – "I'm a work-hard-play-hard kind of manager" – that sort of utter nonsense, since I'm a get-by-and-go-home sort of boss really, but that wouldn't have been what Steve was after.

Daniel looks pretty impassive, as they say on the news. People don't really say impassive. They say more dramatic things; he looks drained, or dazed, or defeated by the world. But he doesn't look these either; he looks blank, he's quiet, like he's tired. He probably is tired.

As I climb into the car I ask him again if he's OK, and I get a nod and a shrug all at once and it's clear he'll be a teenager soon. Losing his mother before he's at high school, no wonder he looks like that.

We pull out of the garage, and out onto the city streets,

which are now recovering from the rush hour traffic and starting to bustle with shoppers and tourists, as well as the businesspeople.

He's so quiet though.

"You OK, Daniel?" I've asked him that already. I ask him that too much. Leave him alone. "Do you want to talk about it?"

I must be reaching the age where you have children and you wish you could chat to them like adults, or at least like they do with their friends.

But Daniel switches off the handheld, and says "no thanks, Dad, I'm fine," and nothing else, as he looks out the window and I'm left wondering how to move it on from there.

Of course he's not fine. He's practically an orphan for all the use I am. Hardly knows me, hardly sees me.

If he would just ask something about his mum, we could speak about her, speak about things. It would be healthy for him. Speak, Daniel, speak.

He looks out the window at a couple of late teen girls, walking along shrieking, who should possibly be at school.

I can imagine it, his head turning, and looking ahead slightly hazily asking how me and his Mum met. He's never asked me that. I wonder if he ever asked Louise.

If he did, I wonder if she told him the truth. Not the story any boy wants to hear about his parents, even if his opinion of them is as low as Daniel's must be of us. Or me at least.

How would I answer it? Tell him the truth? Your mother and I met at a concert, I could say. Or maybe, to make it sound more salubrious, I would say 'we met when we were out at a show', like we were from the '30s.

I couldn't think how to get it across how it really was. A night in the Barrowlands, watching Julian Cope. Sweaty, like it always is, the place just reminds me of beer-stained clothing and sweat. Even the ceiling perspirates, dripping condensation on those below. I saw her at the bar about half way through, her t-shirt cut down from the collar to be loose, and showing a small amount of chest. Twenty-three and mostly there to size girls up when not watching the band, she caught me at it. She scowled, frowned, and I shrugged a who-can-blame-me shrug. I saw her again toward the end, and to talk to her, exchanged a lame 'great gig – yeah, great' type of conversation with her.

Then I saw her up Sauchiehall Street soon after when we'd both had a lot more to drink, and despite the lecherous start, an hour later we were back at her flat, drunk and stupid.

Not that I'd be saying that to Daniel. It seems wrong even to think about it now she's gone. One-night stands were rare at that age for me, (not like they were ever common) I couldn't believe my luck. I didn't even have to try very hard.

Poor Louise. I can't help but picture her. One minute, in the gym. She must have just had pain, and collapsed. Could she have known? I can't imagine, and I shouldn't imagine. What were her thoughts as she crashed off whatever machine she was on? What would you think – "I'm going to die?!" Probably not.

No, I'd tell Daniel we met at a concert, then started going out. Though that's not true either. After we slept together I didn't see her again for six weeks, and when I did, it was awkward smiles all round. A short conversation, trying to establish if the other felt guilty, or worse, hurt. It was probably the lack of guilt, the lack of attachment, or interest either of us had in the other, which did the trick. Of course, it should have been a sign of things to come, but it meant that instead of the atmosphere being icy and weird when we kept bumping into each other, on the train, at the supermarket, we'd exchange a smile and a hello, and move on.

She was pretty though, back then. She put on a bit of weight in the past while, but she had smiling eyes, and what you'd call a wholesome figure. Full-chested and at twenty-three, a tapered waist.

I shouldn't think of her this way. It's been a while since I've thought about Louise, how sexy I found her there. But today's not the day is it? Or maybe it is, I'm hardly thinking ill of the dead.

Then at Nick Cave, back at the Barras, it stopped being a one-night stand. We fell into bed again, then again and again, and two months later, she was pregnant.

We're getting out of the city now. Daniel watches out the front window with the same stare. We pause at a traffic light, with a supermarket on the right. "Do you want anything to eat?"

He looks over at me and looks me plainly in the eye, looking like I broke his train of thought. "No, thanks" he says with a soft smile.

So there's no excuse to stop, but I have to, I need the toilet. Ten minutes after I leave the fucking office. "Couldn't you have gone before we left?" I'd have asked James and Sally, my two younger kids, if they were here. Hypocrite.

"Sorry, Daniel, I just need to nip to the loo."

The toilets are empty, and I'm grateful. I stand at the urinal. I wait. Nothing. Try not to think about it. Think about something else. Nothing. Nothing. Someone may come in. Nothing. Goddammit, I need the toilet.

I go into a cubicle just in case anyone comes and I have to give in. Eventually, something comes. A weak stream. A pause. Another weak stream. A pause, then another weak stream, followed by nothing. I have to get this pissing problem seen to.

I give up. I have to do something about this. I know I still need a bit, but I also know I could stand here for twenty minutes and not feel like I was finished.

I wash my hands and go back out to the car. There's nothing like going to a funeral to make you resolve to sort out your own health problems. Nothing like starting a new job in the death benefits department of a life insurance company; nothing like realising your relationship with your practically estranged son is in tatters; nothing like the sudden death of your ex-girlfriend.

It could be me next. It could be Daniel here again, with no family dropping him next time.

Stop it. Not worth thinking this way. Just sort it out.

But sort it out this time, Martin. Don't bottle it, talk to your wife, you twat. I've tried – countless times, I've tried to talk with Kathy about it. I prepare myself for talking with her, but whenever I sit down to open my mouth, it's always seemed like nothing. A bit of stage fright. Just too distracted by other problems to properly concentrate on urinating.

I've pictured myself telling her, getting the support I want to visit the doctor about it. Getting the chat about it to put it into perspective – it may well be nothing. I'm probably making too much of a meal of it. I would tell her, and she would nod and listen and say, "don't worry, just go to the GP, it's probably nothing." And I could tell her I know it's probably nothing, but it's the biggest reason I wanted to come home, get a job back up here. To be closer to my parents, to Daniel, as well as with her and the kids. That it makes me think about the fact I'll not be here forever. That it might not be nothing.

No, I've never had that chat. But nothing like all this to make me resolve, again, to do so. Maybe I'll just go straight to the doctor about it, not bother Kathy. But it's serious, I have to do something. I can't leave Daniel alone.

I get back to the car, and Daniel's sitting still, looking in front of him again, not annoyed or impatient.

He does seem a good lad. What must he be thinking? "What's this old man turned up here for?" Maybe. Probably. Couldn't blame him.

Oh, pull your head out your arse Martin, why would he be thinking about you? He only sees you two, three weeks a year. He's thinking about his mum, or Newton, or his brothers. Or more likely himself. More likely since he's my son, anyway.

He's probably weighing it all up. What's it all mean for him?

The lights are green and we move off.

Or maybe he's thinking, what does a boy do without a mother as he enters teenaged life? Or, a miserable thought, he might be asking what sort of genes he has.

Christ I hope not. It makes my little scenario all the harder to think about.

But that's why I'm here, that's why I took this death job – to help him out, to see him more. That's why I'm able to take him to his mother's funeral, instead of hiding four hundred miles away and giving him useless, empty consolation over the phone. Poor little bugger, left without a mother. The least I could do is offer him a half-baked father. Even *he* knows that I wouldn't have gone to the funeral if he hadn't actually asked. What the hell was I thinking? In what sort of world would it be OK to miss the funeral?

I can't think like this, it's not good for him. He'll be able to tell.

"Are you..." I start, but I can't ask him if he's OK again. "Are you nervous or anything? About the funeral, I mean?" That's not right. "Not nervous," I add, as he looks confused at me, "but anxious?"

He frowns momentarily, then resorts to his Gallic shrug.

"Good," I nod, a little too vigorously. What is the matter with me? I can't even talk to my own son. Come on. "I think I probably am," I glance over at him, one eye on the road, which, as we approach the outside of town, is getting less busy. "I've never actually been to a funeral."

"You're joking?" he says, and for a moment, he looks normal, relaxed, comfortable in my presence, and I get a surge of pride in myself for dragging it out of him at last.

"No. Thirty-six years old, and I've never been to a funeral. Have you?"

He nods his head. "I went to one two years ago, when Mr Burns, my old music teacher, died." He sadly looks down to his feet as he says this, though I doubt it's for Mr Burns.

What sort of a question was that anyway? Sympathetic and compassionate? Er, no.

Twelve years old, and he's been to more funerals than me. This one, though, this is the big one. Not for the first time in his life – though not as often as I probably should have – I wish I could take it on for him. If I'd been around more, maybe I could have. Cowardly twat.

I wonder if I could take it though. How would I feel if my mother died? Fucking awful, that's how. And that unfortunate, sad little soul beside me has that to bear.

"No, I haven't ever been to one. It's probably something to be pleased about, getting to my age without being to one." I soliloquy. I may as well, Daniel probably won't ask me. "My grandparents all died before I was born, except your Nan's dad, but he died when I was two. I suppose I may have been at that one, but I don't think that counts."

He smiles and looks at me, wide-eyed and earnest like he does, looking from one eye to the other, and I hold his look as long as I can before I look at the road again.

"You're still young though," he says, and looks back down at his feet.

Young? I am, in the grand scale of things. Although when I was his age, I thought everyone out of school was old. I thought you had kids when you were twenty-five if you wanted to wait a while and live a bit first.

When I was twenty-five with a child at home, I thought differently, of course.

But that sort of remark sets him apart, I think. Most boys wouldn't be that grounded. It's his Mum, I take no credit.

When I was at school, maybe Daniel's age, come to think of it, I had a friend, Mike, who moved away. I found out, about nine months after he left, that he'd died of leukaemia. It was terrible, I knew, and I was sorry that he'd died, but I didn't grieve. He'd been a bit of a friend, but not much, just someone I mucked about with at lunch and went round to his house a couple of times. Simple truth was I didn't really know him that well at school, and much less by the time he died.

Yes, I know nothing of death, and that's modern life. Real reference to death is frowned upon, any sight of the sick and needy shuttered away, chances of your own demise abstracted in statistical terms. The news will talk about other people's tragedies, but with so much 'reality' on the television, I'm pretty sure I'm not the only one who's desensitised.

You only get real feelings like this in hospitals. Three times in my life have I been reminded at close quarters about the fact that we're just animals sharing the same fate as all other animals. All three times it wasn't even me who was facing the fate – it was the child-bearing women I was with. Louise first, and worst, with the blood pouring out of her after Daniel was removed, and Daniel, blue, taken to the back of the room to breathe. Everyday occurrences for the people in the hospital, but for me, the boldest reminder I could have that both of those humans might not make it through the next hour. The other two times were with Sally and James, when it was Kathy, screaming and panting, and me, realising it could all go wrong any moment.

Then what? You leave the hospital and forget all about it – it's just normal after all. Forget that for a moment, you knew what actually mattered.

That's typical of how it's been for me. People have died that I've known, sure, but not until long after I've known them. Or it'll be someone I was in a meeting with twice, or something like that. Knew them? No. Heard of them maybe – or I once knew them, at best.

Louise, that's a different sort of matter. I'm not grieving, not really. I didn't know her either, not for a long time. I shared only cursory conversations to arrange which weeks I'd take Daniel. I haven't had a conversation more than three minutes long with her for, I don't know, maybe five years.

So I'm not grieving. I hardly knew her even when we were together. We'd split up eighteen months after the Nick Cave concert, and I was the heartless arsehole who'd left a woman with a child of not even a year.

But, all that aside, it's strange, thinking of her as dead. You can't argue with the connection, however misguided and accidentally, that a child can have. She is Daniel's mother, my son's mother. Otherwise she'd just be my ex, and I'd maybe hear like Mike – "Oh, Louise has died? That's scary, so young".

I've had friend's brothers who've died. Parents of friends. My parent's neighbours. My ex-girlfriend's friend from school died – when was that, when I was twenty-one, twenty-two maybe? I didn't know them, but she was really upset, and it had been sudden. It, like when so many of these people pass, made me wonder how it would be if it were me. How would it feel to be me with a heart attack, or leukaemia, or post-operative issues gone badly wrong? How would it feel to be me with the dying parent or friend? I have thought about it, for a while, and moved on. Louise, she gets the prize, she's the person I've known best so far who's died.

"Dad," Daniel says out of nowhere, and it takes me by surprise – I'd given up on his speaking. "Why did you leave Mum and me?"

Careful what you wish for, I should have thought. Here he's opened up, and it's not the question I'd have asked for. The 'and me' resonates particularly. It's a question I've dreaded being asked anyway, for years, but today of all days. I really wouldn't have picked today. How can I look anything other than selfish? And why should I anyway?

"What did your Mum say?" is the best I can come up with.

Daniel fiddles with the straps of his rucksacks, and looks out at the window, in no hurry to answer. That is just like his Mum too. She's a dreamer – was a dreamer. It drove me nuts the year

I lived with her. I'd ask her a question, and she'd look at her feet, pick up a magazine and flick a couple of pages without looking at them, or twiddle her hair around her fingers, then, if I'd waited that long, answer. For a while, I found it endearing, but then pretty quickly I'd get to the stage where I'd ask the question again, and then leave the room, annoyed.

Now Daniel is doing it, and I can live with it. That is one fairly clear distinction, a good reason that it didn't work out. Mostly, she irritated me, and I didn't love her enough to not hate it. With Daniel, I have no such problems. But I can't tell him that on the day of her funeral.

Eventually he looked back at me, and responded, "she said that you just didn't go. Actually," and he looked a little sheepish, "she said that there was nothing wrong with custard, and nothing wrong with chips, but they didn't taste great on the same plate."

I laugh out loud. Louise was a lovely person, and that proves it. No bitterness, nothing betrayed to Daniel, just a simplistic explanation of the truth – we just didn't go together well. For the first time, I feel a genuine sadness that she's gone. The first time, four days after she died. Four days! What sort of a prick am I?

"That's a funny way to put it, but she's right. Your Mum was a lovely woman, but we just didn't get on. There must be people at your school, who you just don't really click with?"

Daniel takes a moment, then squints his nose a little. Apparently not.

"People who, even though they seem OK, just aren't your friends? It's a bit like that, but stronger."

He doesn't look convinced, but I just try smiling and stick to my guns. It's hard to explain. But I just didn't love her. And she just didn't love me back, it wasn't all my fault.

"I'll be honest Daniel, I still feel like a terrible father for leaving you when you were so small. I would not have judged anyone kindly, if I'd heard of them doing that." Daniel, as so often, betrays nothing. His mouth remains neither in a smile, nor frown, his eyebrows steady, no flicker across his face. It's too much to expect that he might chirp up in my defence. But I have to try. "But I wasn't leaving *you*, I was leaving your Mum. We weren't getting on, and your mother didn't want me to stay any more than I wanted to."

I stop at this, as I'm suddenly reminded that I shouldn't be saying any of this. I'm not saying it for him, nor for her. I'm just saying it to get it off my chest. I've time, I hope, to explain all this to him. Today is not the day.

Sympathetic and compassionate. I have a lot to work at.

"She was a nice girl, I don't want to make anything else out like that. You know that anyway, but..." Lord, I'm struggling here. This is what Louise did too, just sit there and not say anything to save me as I dig my holes. Why should he say anything? "But it wasn't just me. We were both unhappy. It was a sort of favour for both of us." What a thing to say. Take it back.

"Yes, that's what Mum said," he mumbles. And he shows he's not his mother – he's himself. Five words, and he's put me at ease. More than that, I could just about weep.

Lord knows, Louise may have irritated me many times, but isn't this a surge of gratitude to her? She didn't have to defend me to Daniel.

I feel almost free of a burden. With only five words.

I've looked back over it, looking at my mistakes, hundreds of times. It would be easy to say that the mistake was not splitting with her early on, when we knew it wasn't working. But that would have meant no Daniel, and I can't bring myself to think that. Staying together wouldn't have made things better. Louise was quick to notice we were making each other miserable, both of us. She was right too. I had to leave. So what did I do? Messed around for a couple of years drinking, and not managing to sleep around, probably best given the situation I'd found myself in. Then I moved down south for a job. That was definitely a mistake; though I think I'd convinced myself they'd be better off without me back then. Maybe I didn't need much convincing. Worst was not arranging for more visits from him – once a year. He must have hated those trips. He looked more uncomfortable when I met Kathy, and worse still when the kids came along.

But early on? No, I don't think so, there's not much I could have changed with Louise, which wouldn't have led to misery of one sort or another.

Leaving your wife and nine-month-old child. It's an arsehole's thing to do. It really is I've come to terms with that. Daniel may too, with age. I bloody hope so.

But now, all that matters to me is that Louise told him otherwise, so maybe I still have a chance with the boy after all. Selfish prick, I only mourn when it suits me.

Here's the crematorium. I pull in and drive down a long tree-lined lane, well-cut grass on either side, and see the car park at the end. I've never been here before.

We are here with perfect timing, actually, just short of ten minutes before it starts. I'm sweating a little at my collar, and can feel my pulse beating, just gently, in my wrist against my sleeve. As we pull up, the faces of people I know, barely, and always dread seeing, come into view. First is Louise's mother and father, short, unhealthy-looking people at the best of times, now absolutely grey with grief. I can see Newton, Louise's widower, holding the youngest of her three children, Thomas (I think). What is he, eighteen months old?

Newton is a reasonable man, someone I feel I could have actually been friends with in other circumstances. Never an angry word from him, the slightest hint of jealousy or grudging, he was always a pleasant, grounded man. So I see him and feel terrible, imagining myself in his situation. He's with his brother, a guy I've seen but never spoken to. I never really have to. My meetings with Louise have been very short since I moved down south, especially since I met Kathy.

There are various friends of Louise's around, and a number of people I don't know – they may be there for Louise's funeral, or maybe someone else's, I wouldn't know. All of which re-affirms my initial instinct: I shouldn't have come.

Nonsense, of course I should. It just takes me too long each time to remember. In the first case, three days. Not until the Saturday, when Daniel came over for the weekend – Newton, on the doorstep, asked, just checking (he thought), that I knew where I was going on Monday. Daniel, there beside Newton would have seen the whites of my eyes as it sunk in. Sure, I'd be able to find it fine; I struggled my way into saying. Newton, open as ever to visual clues, insisted I was welcome at the funeral. Could I imagine doing that? Saying to any of Kathy's ex-boyfriends, please, come along to her funeral?

Not until then did I realise that perhaps, at the wake of one parent, Daniel may like the support of the other. By which time, of course, it was too late to let my new work know.

I park the car, and unclip my seatbelt, keen to get going, but Daniel pauses.

I nearly ask him if he's OK, but he's probably just thinking, and I give him some moments to prepare himself.

Newton has spotted us now, and nods at me in acknowledgment. He looks tired and drawn too. How much time does someone take off after the sudden death of their wife? He's a GP, so you'd think he'd have to be in the right frame of mind. How do you get in the right frame of mind?

Daniel shifts in his seat and turns to me. "Dad, I want to come and live with you." His earnest eyes search for traces on my face, and I wonder what he finds.

What I hope he sees – joy; relief; love.

What he might see, if I can't hide it – fear; doubt; guilt.

He'll definitely see surprise. You can't account for a surprise like that. I can hardly believe he's asked me. It is all I've been hoping for this past few years, and yet...

"Well, that'd be..." I have to try and be sensible about this. "What about Newton? And your brothers?"

I don't want to hurt his feelings, and thankfully he doesn't interpret my tactless question like that.

"Newton is nice," he shrugs his near teenage shrug again. "But he's not my actual family, is he?"

I should be delighted, and I *am* on a certain level. But it's balanced, against a fear that he doesn't really mean it. Emotions of the day, getting on top of him. I can't blame him. His eyes, still dry four days on, I can't expect a rational conversation with him here.

"Listen, I would absolutely love that Daniel. Really I would. But we have to go now, so we'll talk about it later. OK?" It doesn't sound like my voice, doesn't sound natural, but Daniel nods and opens his door.

There is a stiff breeze, and I wish I'd brought a coat. Newton makes his way over, and says something to Daniel I don't catch.

I shake his hand. "Hi." I say, and then shake my head. I can't think of a thing to say. "I..."

"Hi Martin," Newton says with a soft, sympathetic smile, and Thomas struggles in his arms, trying to get down to Daniel.

There's a loud voice from behind, and I don't notice it's directed at me until half way through the sentence.

"... a bloody nerve coming here. After what you did to her. After what you did to HIM!"

Louise's mother, her grey face turned to an angry red. I haven't seen her for a couple of years, maybe four or five, and she's aged very suddenly. She's put on weight around her jowls, and her waist, and her hair has greyed, her eyes have four times more wrinkles.

"Why did you come? Eh? WHY?" And her anger is turning

to tears now, but not faded totally.

"Martha, please. I asked Martin because..." Newton starts, a gentle, calm voice, not the voice I think I'd be using on such a day. I would be stropping like a teenager.

Martha actually beats Newton's chest as he starts to say this, and it's a struggle not to be utterly swept over by this sort of open anguish. "I don't want him here, Newton. He ruined her life, ruined it."

I don't even want to defend myself on this. I am doubtlessly among the last people she would want at her daughter's funeral. But I start, "Martha, I'm here for Daniel, to try and..."

"For Daniel?! Now?!" she shrieks, and tears are streaming now, her eyes, showing sorrow more than anger. Looking towards me, but somehow not at me. She shakes her head as though to add something but instead just moans, before Daniel steps in.

"It's all right, Dad," he puts one hand on his grandmother's arm and the other round her back. "I'll be fine. Maybe you should just wait here."

Martha is no longer looking at me, her hand covering her face, making heaving, grieving groans. Newton looks on pleadingly, and I know I'm not going in. What surprises me is that I'm quite disappointed about it.

I nod, and am actually shaking as I get back in the car.

I'm a little embarrassed, but nobody is looking at me. They are chatting amongst themselves, meekly smiling at each other, trying to make the best of the situation.

At once, I'm reminded again that Louise is gone. Her brain has stopped operating, her heart stopped beating. Her body lies in that building, an empty carcass. I will never speak to her again. Clearly that's the point of a funeral, to bring some finality to it. To slap us in the face with it: she's gone.

I know these thoughts I'm having are clichés. They're nothing different than those that have passed through the minds of a billion humans before me. I've heard people saying these things before, too. I've even thought them in an abstract way before, but I've never actually put a real person I know to those clichés. And I'm shaking now at the bluntness of that undeniable truth, death, grief, finality. I close my eyes and wait for it to pass.

Everybody is moving in to the crematorium, and I'm out here alone.

I have to phone Kathy. Nominally, it's to talk about Daniel and what he said. Realistically, it's to take my mind off death, and back to life.

I pull out my phone and speed-dial the number, but I have to stop and think about this. How am I going to word this? What will she say?

She said again last night she didn't think Daniel liked her. I can't tell, really. Maybe he doesn't. Maybe, he's just being quiet.

Actually, he's definitely being quiet. But maybe there's no motive behind that. He's quiet with me too.

What will she say? She'll say that he doesn't like her. She'll say there isn't space. And there isn't much, I'll have to put James and Sally in together for a few months until we can convert the loft. She'll ask why there is room for Daniel, but I don't think there's room for another baby.

How can we have another baby just now? But then, how would she know about that particular worry, if I don't tell her?

We could have another baby. I'd be happy to, if it makes Kathy happy. We could possibly afford it, now that we've moved up here. We'd need a bigger house, but we could struggle by until then.

So, what's my plan? Phone her up and say, Daniel is coming to live with us, so you can have another baby? A little crude.

The phone is ringing.

"Hello?"

"Hi, it's just me."

"Hi. How are you? Aren't you at the funeral?"

"I'm at the crematorium. Long story, but I didn't go in."

Kathy sighs quietly. She knows I didn't want to go, and she'll be making that assumption. That I got out of it. I can't blame her for that, can I?

"I didn't want to, I tried to go in. Martha, Louise's Mum, she... well, she didn't want me to."

"Right. Poor woman."

"Yes, I can't even imagine." I say this on autopilot, blathering out the words, which fit the conversation. In fact, I'm imagining what she's going through, me standing here at the funeral of one of my children. But I don't want to, so I speak instead. "Daniel is still very quiet. I hope he's OK."

"Mmm," she says, a little distantly.

"How are James and Sal?"

"A bit wild, this morning. James has had about three meltdowns. How was work?"

"They were fine, didn't mind me leaving, like we thought."

"Good." She's being very terse, waiting for me to get to a point.

"Look, Daniel asked this morning if he could come and live with us. I know it'll be a bit tight, but I don't know, I would really like to talk with Newton about it. Not today, obviously."

"Oh right," she says, quite breezily. "That's good, actually. It'd be good for you. And really good for James and Sally."

"Are you sure you wouldn't mind? I know you and him haven't got on so well recently..." I trail off. I'm starting to sound like a soap opera, the way I talk.

"Of course I don't mind. It'll be hard, I suppose. You know, because he isn't actually mine. But he's yours. And the poor little boy's just lost his mother."

What did I think she'd say? Get lost you can't have your son?

"I know. But still. I wanted to talk with you about it before it went anywhere."

"We'll speak to Newton next week some time, when everything is settled a little," she says. "We could maybe just put James and Sally in together for a bit, they'd like that."

And as she talks practically for a while, I stop listening, and start thinking about how I don't deserve the family I've got.

They're definitely Louise's friends. Out they come, pale, streaked eyes, thoughtful. I get out of the car, and wait for Daniel. Eventually, he comes out, holding hands with his little half-brother, Richard, who is six, and will only understand enough to know he's sad. Daniel, who probably doesn't understand an awful lot more, looks like he's been crying, and I think for the first time in my life, I'm glad to see he has. He's talking to Richard, smiling at him. Richard, like Daniel and Louise's other son Thomas, have the look of their mother. I have always found it odd to see two children I don't know at all, looking so similar to my own boy.

Newton follows shortly after them, and Louise's parents, the last out of the crematorium. Have they done a line-up? They do them at weddings; surely they don't do them at funerals too. I've no idea. Hopefully I'll not find out soon.

Newton comes towards me, with his two children, and Daniel.

"Martin, hi," he says, "how are you?"

"I'm OK, Newton. How are you?" I cringe slightly that I even asked.

"Honestly, I'm glad that's over. It's weighed on me a bit over the past few days."

I nod, the burden he's had to carry as his two young children stand around him, lost, is unthinkable to me.

"If there's anything I can do, I hope you can ask me. I'm really sorry for what's happened. And I'm really sorry for before..."

"Please, don't worry about Martha. I should have prepared

her for you coming. She's taken it particularly hard, I'm sure she'll feel terrible."

"Well, she shouldn't. I totally understand."

"Listen, I'd really appreciate it if you came along to a wee get-together we're having at the house – Martha is fine with it. I'd like it if you could come. Not just," he says with a wry, if tired smile, "because I need you to give Daniel a lift."

I laugh a little too hard, nervously. "I'll pop in for a while. Thank you."

I'm never comfortable drawing up in front of this house, but today is worse than ever. Usually it's to avoid an awkward conversation, steer clear of the hints Louise would make about my not doing enough with Daniel. Today, well, it's different, clearly.

Only a two-minute drive from the crematorium, and Daniel had given nothing away. If he had been an adult, I might have asked if it was a nice service, but Daniel is twelve. Apart from the actual occasion, I expect his first impression would have been that it was a bit boring.

I let Daniel lead the way into what is, still, his house. He bumbles up the front path, a weedless bed on either side to the front door, shining black, with sparkling gold numbering. Newton's work, I knew, and I wouldn't be surprised to hear he'd done it since Wednesday. A bit of solitude, a meditation. The door looked clean enough.

Daniel opened the door, and there's a bustle inside. Most of the guests are forcing themselves not to be too gloomy.

"I've just got to use the toilet," I tell Daniel, withholding the 'again' which rang in my head. As I go, I hear two women, neither of whom I recognise: "God yeah, I remember that. It was so funny," one says, failing to hide a sad smile. "She must have been mortified," says the other, managing little better.

The toilet is a poky room, like most downstairs loos are. The décor is sparse, white and light blue, with a few small maritime models on the shelves over the piping, little carved boats and lighthouses. I stand, and nothing comes again. Come on, come on, come on. A small amount comes.

There, just above the sink to my left, there is a familiar picture, baby Daniel in his mother's arms. You can't see much of Louise, if it weren't for the signs of a nightdress, you wouldn't know if it were here or me. I have the same picture at home. I remember that day, clearly, and all the details of it, but emotions are so easily dropped from my memories. I don't always remember, for example, the force of fear, and love, that I suddenly do feel again, now. It brings a small, unexpected jolt to my chest, forcing me to breathe in sharply, and for a moment, I feel like crying.

Hold it together.

I see myself in the mirror again, greying, wrinkling, jowl spreading slowly. Standing in this tiny room, holding a malfunctioning cock. Louise is dead. And I am not a well man. I zip up, wash my hands and leave.

As I come out, Newton's over there by the kitchen shaking his head serenely, as one of Louise's friends weeps.

Suddenly I get an urge. I could tell Newton. He's medical, he would be able to tell me if I was foolish. A father, he could understand my fears with Daniel, could tell me if any of my worry is well founded.

Sympathetic and compassionate, though, I will say nothing.

Louise's mother is across in the conservatory. She sees me, and nods sadly and I nod back. I hadn't realised I'd been concerned about a scene until I feel the relief wash through me.

The woman with Newton starts to leave him alone, and he comes over to me. Daniel, at the same moment, comes in the room with a full rucksack.

Oh, Christ, no. Surely that's not what I think it is.

"Hi, Daniel," Newton says. He looks confused, so he's

definitely not privy to the conversation Daniel and I had a little over half an hour ago, "you not unpacked yet?"

Daniel looks over his shoulder as though he'd forgotten the rucksack was there. "Oh, that. It's just my stuff, Dad says I can come live with him."

Oh fuck.

"Daniel, I..." I open my mouth, but I don't actually know what I'm going to say. Newton looks confused and a little hurt, so I change my audience. "Look, we haven't decided anything yet, we just had a short chat – he asked, and I...."

Now it's Daniel who looks hurt, like he's going to crumple right there. No, shit, no. I can't have that.

"Daniel, listen," and he turns his face away. Don't cry, please don't cry. I bend down and hold both his shoulders and look at him. "Daniel, I do want you to come stay with me. I really would love that, more than anything else. Kathy too. But we have to talk it through with Newton first. I didn't necessarily mean today." God, that sounds like a cop-out.

Daniel, a little wounded, looks from me to Newton and back again, as though it's only just dawned on him that this is bad timing. So he is my son after all.

"OK," he mumbles at the floor.

Newton nods a measured nod, "it's a tough day today Daniel. Tell you what though, we'll get together next week and talk through what to do, OK?" he says, securing his place on the list of the world's most reasonable men.

I catch Newton's eye, and he doesn't look hurt any more, nor angry. He looks rather blank all in all.

Daniel now looks unsure, he doesn't believe me. I know it, and I know why. I'll give it another go. "Daniel," I start, but that's about the fifth time we've used his name directly this minute, and it's starting to sound silly, "I moved up here to be closer to you. It would be brilliant if we could work something out about moving. But you, Newton and me need time to get over today – it's been a tough morning." He looks like he'll cry, but this time it's more like grief. "You can come stay with me tonight though, I don't mind. You just choose. I can bring you back tomorrow if that's what you want, or you can stay here." I glance at Newton to check, and he doesn't seem to mind.

Daniel looks at him, and then looks across to the corner of the room. Thomas, his two-year-old brother comes toddling over and holds on to his leg. Daniel puts his rucksack down. "I think I'd better stay here, actually," he says, as Thomas grins up at him and attaches himself round his leg. Thomas hoists himself up on to his shoe, so he's fully hanging off Daniel. "Come on Thomas, I'm hungry," he says brightly, for the child's benefit, and swings his leg, Thomas clinging to his leg like a limpet, and makes his way to the buffet.

I turn to Newton, a dim, proud smile on his face. "Look, I'm sorry, I shouldn't have come. That wasn't as it... I'm so bloody clumsy."

He shakes his head. "Not at all. Daniel needs you about." Then he shakes my hand firmly, and says, with conviction I think I could never manage – "if he decides he wants to move back, then he can, you know, I understand. If he doesn't, he's welcome obviously; I love having him around, as do the boys. But you're welcome too, whenever you, or Daniel, need".

It's all too much for me this. I'm too emotional – I should have been in that funeral and let it flow out. Instead, I turn my head away to stifle the hint of arriving tears, and look over at Daniel. Sympathetic and compassionate, his mother's son.

5

At the Rawlings' Place

Paul Burman

Author

Paul Burman was born in Northamptonshire, England, but currently lives in Victoria, Australia. Paul Burman's debut novel *The Snowing and Greening of Thomas Passmore* was published by Paperbooks in 2008. Paul has worked in a wine-bottling factory, a deep freeze, a plumbing warehouse, as a maize 'castrator' in the south of France... and once had a newspaper round until a neighbour's dog bit him. Having decided to never become a teacher, he became a teacher and has been learning how to teach English and Literature ever since. Paul has been compulsively reading and writing fiction from the age of six, following a childhood indiscretion in which he was caught inadvertently telling the truth. Making up stories has remained a happy obsession ever since.

There used to be a house there, but not anymore. They knocked it down years ago. Piled all the timbers together and burned the lot. Brought in a bulldozer to clear the rubble. I'd like to have seen that. There's something healing about flames. I could've done with being there and watching it burn.

It's been an empty block ever since, isolated here on the edge of town; trying to drift away but attached by a raw and bloody thread all the same. And although I say it's empty, it isn't empty of course. Apart from all those nettles and brambles scrambling through the dead orchard at the side, there are those dark walls of cypress and the wild memories that still fly back to nest there, even now.

After Mrs Rawlings died and the place fell into disrepair, we spent whole evenings, entire weekends, scaling the buttresses and crawling along the ramparts of those trees. Claimed them as our own did Kaz, Tad and me. For a short while, they became our territory, our castles, our sanctuary. At eleven and twelve years old, what better way to explore the world than to clamber up and twist our way through the branches? To conquer each new crow's-nest, learning the rough gnarls and accommodating smoothness, the inaccessible prickliness and welcoming embrace of each one?

Sometimes, we'd spend days swinging around, hanging upside down by our legs, teasing the feral cats that haunted the wilderness below, playing Hide-and-seek and Feet-can't-touch-the-ground among the darkness and shadows and the sweet scent of sticky resin. Sometimes, we'd forget about the trees for cold, rainy weeks at a time, but then we'd return and they'd still be there, waiting for us like the oldest and most understanding of friends.

It's still a huge block, but not quite as large as I remember. The world looks bigger when you're a child, I guess, even if it seems more conquerable too. All the same, though it's got far more land than you'd ever get your hands on in the city, where developers would dump several units on it quick as a flash, no-one'll buy it. Not this block. Not here. Not for a generation or two at least. People grow big memories when they live in small towns. And there are some things that refuse to be forgotten, no matter how hard you try, no matter how far away you live.

That spring, I was only three weeks shy of my thirteenth birthday and more excited than I could ever admit to at the idea of becoming a teenager. It seems a silly thing now, but everyone – Mum and Dad, my brothers and sisters, Gran and Pop, my aunties and uncles – made the biggest noise about becoming a teen, so that, even though I got into the habit of pretending I couldn't give a stuff, really I felt possessed by the sense of being on the brink of something new. Something different, momentous, and special.

Only friends like Kaz and Tad didn't harp on about it, but probably because they were being put through the same fuss by their families. That spring, I felt as if I was about to leave the plainness of childish things behind and discover the thrilling, steeper contours of a more exciting world. In my head, I associated it with being taken seriously, having more freedom; with warm, sunny, adventurous days, after the cold grey of winter.

Until around this time, old Mrs Rawlings' house and its gardens had remained as much an occasional feature of Kaz's and my childhood landscape as the Milk Bar where we bought our lollies, the tiny Primary School we'd not long finished attending and the few wide streets of this small town of ours, stuck squat in the vast emptiness of the Western Plains. What a place to grow up in. There was nothing outside the town, beyond the town, other than this sweep of enormous paddocks stretching wide and flat in every direction, towards whichever horizon you'd care to stare at. An environment which, even now, depends on the diminishing peaks from that distant range of power pylons, stretching from one infinity to another, to break the insane monotony of its flat immensity and lend it some other form of definition.

Later – during the summer which followed that spring – there were days when the sky too, in mirroring the plains beneath it, seemed impossibly broad and impossibly high. It became too easy to imagine such a sky drifting further and further away from such a land, simply because there was nothing on this earth that could anchor one to the other. Nothing.

There were times when Kaz and I would look at those horizons and fantasise about the places that lay beyond, further than we could see. We'd dream and tell each other stories about how one day we'd move there, even if our imaginations relied on TV programmes and films to shape them.

She might've told me that one day she'd live in a big house by the sea, with a small, private beach. I'd have probably described to her the mountain lodge I'd one day own and how it would be surrounded by drifts of winter snow and how we could go skiing anytime we wanted. We'd live in a forest or on a mountain or by the sea, in a place where the seasons played in keener harmony with the landscape, and in which exotic pleasures, like skiing or reef-snorkelling, would become commonplace. Sometimes Kaz would fit into my picture and sometimes I'd fit into hers, but usually it didn't matter because we'd known one another forever and, after all, we were just kids.

Up until that spring, Kaz had always been a part of my life. Our mums had been good friends and I guess we must've learnt to crawl together. I imagine us being parked in our prams side-by-side as they drank coffee and nattered, as Mum used to call it.

When we weren't squabbling with our brothers or sisters, Kaz and I played together in one another's garden or house or garage. She had a Wendy house and I had a wig-wam. She had a swing and I had a sandpit. She had dolls and I had model soldiers.

When we were four or five, we made a tent in the middle of her lawn. We threw a picnic blanket and a tablecloth across the swing rails, clipped in place with clothes pegs, and set up house there. We had shoeboxes for cupboards, her tea set with real water in the teapot, and a box of Smarties to share and lick and turn into lipstick or teabags. It must've been a fine, summery day because I still remember the bright chequered light as she sat cross-legged opposite me and I remember the lush smell of freshly cut grass. However, what I chiefly remember is how we decided, in those moments of sitting in front of one another, that we'd marry each other one day, when we were old enough. Definitely. It was the easiest decision in the world.

"You'll be my husband," she said.

"And you'll be my wife."

She'd have giggled at that, but then said: "Promise?"

"I promise."

"But not until we're old enough."

"Not until we're eleven or sixteen and we're allowed to. And then we'll travel around the world together."

It seemed the most natural thing to agree upon, and it wasn't something we, or our parents, forgot about for a couple of years at least. In fact, it probably only drifted into one of those jumbled corners of childhood memory because it was supplanted by something more significant, like the memory of that time we played doctors and nurses, or the time she borrowed my penknife and cut open her hand and had to have stitches.

We explored and mapped out our childhood together. Our

discoveries were, for the most part, joint-discoveries. And Mrs Rawlings' place existed on the perimeter of that world. For many years, it was this property that defined how far we were allowed to wander in one direction, whether we were on our bikes or taking her Aunty Nan's dog for a walk or struggling with roller blades along the grass and gravel. It formed an outer edge of the township, after which the vacuum of the Western Plains might suck us out into the nothingness of space.

I'm not sure what I expected. It's still a large, rectangular block at the dusty intersection of two rarely used roads, with that shelter-belt of untended cypress running the three sides of the property, carving a large corner from Home Paddock. There used to be a picket fence across the front when Mrs Rawlings was alive, with the privet hedge behind, but she kept it neatly trimmed and lower than the fence. Once she was gone, that soon got out of hand; became wild and thick and tall.

There used to be a driveway just there, leading to a garage, and behind that was a shed, I think. There was a quaint cottage garden out front, here, with brick paths dividing it into sections, and the house was an old, weatherboard place with a wide, return verandah and gable windows in the roof. It wasn't so very different to many houses in the township, I guess, except for the upstairs windows and its old-fashioned garden, which made it seem like a fairytale cottage to Kaz and me. Mainly, it was Mrs Rawlings herself who made it special to us.

These days, I can vaguely remember what she looked like, although I believe I'd forgotten that spring. She'd died a couple of years back, when I would've been about ten, and two years is a vast eternity of its own for a child, whereas twenty-five years becomes nothing for an adult. Time, like distance, is not a constant, whatever they teach you at school.

She was short and slight, with a thin perm of hair that was white rather than grey, and I've the impression of her as a generous and kindly person. Although I have a memory of Mr

Rawlings too – a man bent double, who leaned heavily on a thick and polished walking stick, with a round face and ruddy cheeks that looked like polished apples – I could've only been five or six when he died, long before we'd have ventured that far by ourselves, so maybe I'm manufacturing that memory from next-to-nothing or maybe I saw a photo of him once.

I've tried to remember anything I can about Mr and Mrs Rawlings and about how this little town was during our childhood. Anything and everything, from the clattering ring of the doorbell whenever we shoved and pushed our way into the Milk Bar, to the names of all our favourite and not-so-favourite lollies; from the names and nicknames of our neighbours and the occasional drifts of gossip that'd hang like mist across the roof tops for a day or two, to the taste of summer dust storms roaring across the paddocks or the acrid stink of burning-off in the stillness of autumn. And maybe, through doing this, it's one way of trying to reclaim some small part of what we lost back then, however late, however insignificant.

On the first couple of occasions that Kaz and I found ourselves out by the Rawlings' place, Mrs Rawlings smiled and greeted us from the other side of her fence and seemed to know who we were. She held onto the fence with one hand as she asked how our parents were and about our brothers and sisters and so on. Then she'd reach into her apron pocket, pull out a small, crumpled, white paper bag and offer us a lolly each.

After that, we often headed in her direction, on our bikes or walking Kaz's Aunty Nan's dog, and if Mrs Rawlings was in her garden, pruning her roses, dead-heading hydrangeas or simply wandering after one of her two cats, she'd stop at the sight of us, hobble over to the fence and offer us a mint humbug or lemon sherbet or sometimes a toffee.

"Here, have a mint humbug," she'd say. And we'd dig our grubby fingers into the bag and pull out a treat. "Give me your wrappers, so you don't go dropping them." Then she might tell us about the games she used to play when she was our age, the schoolteachers she suffered and the antics she got up to; perhaps by way of forming a connection between her childhood and ours. Or between the girl she could remember being and the person she now was.

Sometimes I regret not spending longer talking with her or asking about her cats, which were clearly dear to her. I regret never offering to cut her lawn or chop wood or trim her hedge or doing anything extra that might've shown a fonder degree of respect for her. At the same time, I know this is the adult in me looking back and that, at ten years old, I might not have had the strength to split firewood let alone manage an antiquated lawn-mower.

What I really regret, I suppose, is that I didn't fully realise how good that time of my life was and didn't grasp onto it more firmly. I regret those things I might've known or could've known or should've known, but didn't.

Was there an occasion when we noticed that she never appeared in her garden anymore? That she didn't wave us over and offer us her lollies? Did we worry whether she was unwell or had a fall or whether she'd been carted off to a poorly run nursing home? I doubt it. I can't imagine we'd ever have noticed or considered such things. Mind, it's also possible that we only learnt about her death some months later and that there'd been a long period when we hadn't even adventured out to that corner of town, so wouldn't have noticed anyway. Like gardens, memories can become overgrown; like houses, they can fall into disrepair.

She's probably buried in the town cemetery. A weathered headstone among the crop of weathered headstones. If there's time – now I'm finally here – I'll wander down to the cemetery and look her up. Mr Rawlings too. They'll be snuggled together, side-by-side, I imagine. I hope. Maybe I'll learn their first names and when they were born; maybe I'll learn the dates of their passing. As if in reinventing my memory of them and reclaiming that part of my past, I can displace all that came after.

Undoubtedly, there was a season when we honoured the boundary of her abandoned, overgrown garden because we associated it with her kindness. After a while, though, we'd have forgotten all about the person she was, enchanted instead by the exotic wilderness her absence had created and the opportunities for exploring it that grew there. Children, for the most part, know instinctively to live in the present rather than dwelling on the past.

Whether there were problems with the will or she died intestate, I don't know. Perhaps the place was put up for sale but, with the hard economic climate, no-one in the district could afford to buy it, as they couldn't now even if they wanted to. Except, naturally enough, none of that stuff concerned us and the property sat there falling into disrepair. The garden becoming more and more gloriously entangled with itself.

Of course, when Tad moved into town and we biked round the streets together, ending up at the Rawlings' place, all he'd have seen was the adventure of an overgrown garden, surrounding an abandoned house. Our boring little town suddenly grew interesting, and Kaz and I discovered some pride in our connection with the cottage. More so for the timber boards and sheets of plywood that had been nailed across the windows, giving it a mysterious, haunted appearance – shut tight like a coffin.

Tad's family moved into town several months before that last spring of childhood. His dad was the new bank manager and had some clout in the district, but all that concerned Kaz and me was the new kid we could hang around with, who came from somewhere exotically outside of our town and beyond the Western Plains. I vaguely remember him having a younger brother or sister, but don't ask me what their names were or what they looked like. Sometimes, I think, even Tad's image would've vanished years ago if it wasn't for the two school photos I've got from that time. There's so much I don't remember and too much I do.

It was Tad who created a leading role for the old Rawlings' place in our collection of childhood myths and legends by describing it all too clearly in a story he wrote for school and which was so good the teacher read it to the class: *The House on the Hill*. Although the entire district is pancake-flat, anyone who lived here would've recognised Tad's description of the abandoned house, even though he chose to tenant it with an evil witch instead of a fairy godmother.

After we'd stopped ribbing him about the praise Miss Jacobs heaped on him and how much she must love him, Kaz said, "But seriously, it *was* good, Tad. I didn't know you could write like that."

Tad kicked the dirt at his feet and grinned. "It should be good. It's the third time I've used that story. Just changed the description a bit to fit in with that old place."

"The third time? You mean, like at the other schools you've been to?"

"Yep. Too right. I can't help it if the teachers all use the same worksheet or have the same dull imagination, but it's the third time they've given me *The House on the Hill* as a title so I keep handing up the same story. There was another title that old Jacobs used, which always crops up: *The Best Days* or something like that."

"*The Best Day of My Life*," said Kaz. "Yeah, that's what I wrote on. I wrote about my sister leaving home and not having to share my bedroom anymore."

"Well, there you go. No kidding, if you moved schools as often as I have, you could keep submitting the same work. Just change a few details, that's all. Too easy."

"Really?"

"Really. While you suckers were doing homework, I was watching TV."

"Neat idea," Kaz said. "I might hold onto mine now instead of chucking it out. It might come in handy."

"I reckon mine's good for another two schools yet – if we move again, that is. But I'll amp it up next time. Have more blood and gore."

And we'd have encouraged him in that. As friends should.

"A ghost with a chainsaw."

"Acid pits, blood fountains, cannibals, vampires."

"I've already got the ghost with the chainsaw," he declared. "She didn't read that bit."

"Save something for the year after," Kaz said. By then, she'd developed what Mum called a dry sense of humour.

The acid pits and chainsaw murderers were as familiar to us as the images of ghosts in white blankets and the universal Bogey Man. We fed our imaginations with them, were always hunting for new, thrilling delicacies. Sometimes they were just plain silly and sometimes we succeeded in secretly scaring ourselves, but for the most part they were as clichéd as that stock image of the house on a hill: a derelict, three-storey mansion, brooding over a graveyard garden, timbers creaking and moaning in an incessant wind, silhouetted against a howling half-moon or illuminated against a backdrop of gnarled trees by fork lightning and screams.

And it didn't matter that there wasn't a pimple of land in town, let alone half a hill, because at least the Rawlings' place had boarded windows, a wickedly wild garden and the densest crop of shadows growing from the broad limbs of those old cypress trees.

"*The House on the Zit* would suit it better," Kaz said later, when we were leaning on our bikes, outside the Milk Bar. We rolled about laughing, made zit jokes for half an hour, learnt a new irreverence for the town we called home. She used to say lots of things like that, did Kaz. We laughed a lot together, the three of us.

Not long after Tad arrived in town was when we built our den – over there, across in that corner. We 'borrowed' a wooden palette from the yard at the back of Western Agricultural Engineering and we carried it all the way here. Hauled it up into that tree – that furthest one, that tall one, I think it was – and lashed it across a couple of branches; then we nailed old fence pickets across it for a platform. Probably thought of ourselves as a gang at the time, the way kids will, revelling in creating a sense of belonging at last, even though there were no rivals to make it really fun: no-one to challenge our territorial rights to this spot or to battle against.

Together, we'd see how far we could get round the property without touching the ground, from one horizontal branch to the next, tree to tree, clambering along the bare and rotting fence rails, getting marooned on hardwood posts. Or we'd set dares for one another. Or sit and out-tell each other's tallest stories. And once, when my older brother came canoodling round this way with his girlfriend, we kept silent and spied on them a few minutes, but then gave ourselves away by squawking and pretending we were crows.

Tad had a catapult, and we'd take it in turns to scare the feral cats that roamed the block or dozed in the shadows of the building. We'd probably get done for animal cruelty these days, but back then it was just a laugh.

The funniest time was when this big, black and white tom was snoozing next to the old, water tank. A fortnight before, from our hideout forty metres away, Tad had put a stone through one of the rust spots on the tank and we hadn't known whether to laugh or cry when two thousand litres of water started pissing into the garden. We almost fell off our perch with holding our sides, but kept quiet for the rest of the day, half-expecting to get in trouble from some busybody. Not that anyone else ever seemed to go near the place.

On this particular occasion, it was my turn to have the catapult and I'd collected a pocket-full of small pebbles for ammunition. My attention had been taken up in the opposite direction, shooting at the cowpats in the paddock behind us, aiming to hit a steaming, fresh one. Until Tad nudged me and pointed in the direction of the old house, the water tank, the sleeping cat.

"No," Kaz said. "Leave the poor thing alone." But even though she liked cats far more than I did, I could tell she wasn't serious about stopping me.

In case I needed encouragement, Tad said, "It's a *cat*-apult, not a *pat*-apult. What's the point of having it if you don't *pult* cats? You might as well give it back to me. Here, let me have a go."

I shook my head, loaded a stone the size of a lemon sherbet and pulled back on the rubber. Closed one eye and aimed at the cat; then shifted my aim about a metre higher to the middle of the metal tank. Stretched the rubber further. Thwang – boom! The cat nearly shat itself. Jumped from the ground so fast, I swear it was running on the spot before it took off at a million miles an hour.

Kaz nicknamed that old black and white tom Greased Lightning.

"Fastest cat in the history of fast cats," Tad acknowledged.

"Probably left scorch marks across the block."

"And a long streak of cat pooh."

It was from the crow's-nest we'd made at the top of our tree that we could see beyond the roofline of two streets of houses to where the main Broughton Road skirts close to the edge of town. Which is how we caught a glimpse, that spring, of the two TV vans heading back to the city – outside broadcast vans, with their channel logo plastered across them. The story had been on the radio and in the local rag a few days by then, about the girl who'd run away from home after an argument with her mum and step-dad, but who the police were now concerned for. But that evening it was on the six o'clock news of both TV channels. She came from Hinchley, thirty kilometres away, where we went to Secondary School, and we thought we were dead special, we did, as if we were famous by association.

And it was from this same look-out, at around the same time – maybe even the same day – that we caught sight of the buses transporting rail passengers following the derailment just ten kilometres down the road. From our vantage point, the highway seemed busier than we'd ever imagined, as if everyone in the Western Plains had somewhere to be other than where they'd just come from.

It suggested a need for busyness that I'd recently begun to feel, if not to fully understand. With my thirteenth birthday only three weeks away, I too felt impatient to be somewhere else, impatient for bigger challenges. So when Tad suggested we spend the first Sunday of our fortnight school holiday riding our bikes to where the train had derailed, to see the tangled mess and to watch the engine being lifted back onto the tracks, his idea answered that need.

We must've covered a good few kilometres that day in search of the derailment, but all we found was an open gateway where a nest of heavy-duty tyre tracks snaked across the bitumen in one direction and bit a rutted trail across the paddock in the other. The paddock tracks disappeared into the dry distance, crossing a terrain too rough for our bikes and further than we could be bothered walking.

As the three of us stood there, talking down our disappointment at the absence of drama, but still staring hopefully at the horizon, we began planning an adventure that might surpass this one. It was, after all, what the holidays were for. And this is more or less how we hatched our plan to not only meet at our den that evening, but to finally find a way of getting into the old house.

"I can't believe you've never done it before," Tad said, and he might as well have accused Kaz and me of cowardice or dullness. One would've been as bad as the other.

"Well, neither have you, Captain Courageous," Kaz said, and pushed him so that he almost fell over his bike.

"I haven't lived here all my life," he countered.

"It hasn't always been empty," I said.

"And it never really seemed interesting or creepy before," Kaz admitted. "Not until that story you wrote."

Tad would've grinned and recognised that with the compliment came the opportunity to add yet another layer. "That's because it wasn't completely made up, you know," he told us, beginning to wheel his bike forward. "There was some truth in it. The old dear who lived there really was a witch. My Dad heard the real truth about her. And I wouldn't be surprised if she haunted the place. Witches' spirits never rest, you know; they can't."

"Mrs Rawlings?" Kaz and I said together, following him and laughing.

"She was no witch," I told him. "She was married to Mr Rawlings. Witches don't get married. Everyone knows that."

"That's why she killed him," Tad said straightaway. "That's something else my Dad was told. The police told him. They couldn't arrest her because they didn't have any proof, but they reckon she poisoned him or put a spell on him or something."

We laughed at that too, and then Kaz said, "Don't be daft."

"No-one knows how he really died," he told us. "Do you?"

We had to agree that we didn't.

"And those toffees she used to offer us... maybe she was trying to poison us."

"Of course she was," Tad said. "That's the oldest trick in the witch book."

Over the course of that afternoon, as we rode back to town and then hung about on the Memorial Park swings, our story about the Rawlings' place and old Mrs Rawlings grew until she no longer resembled the dear old lady who'd let us pick apples in autumn. She was transplanted by another character: The Cat Witch. Someone to inhabit the wilder reaches of our imagination.

"In the daytime she takes the shape of a cat, but at night she's an old woman again and can be seen creeping through the house, prowling through the garden. My brother heard her crying once."

Kaz stroked her chin. "Actually, now you mention it, a couple of blokes did see her once, not long before you moved here, Tad."

"The ghost?"

"Well, *a* ghost. A real ghost. Yep. Not a story-ghost."

"What happened to them?" The question was obligatory.

Kaz would've measured her moment, looked about her, hushed her voice. "One of them was found lying next to his chainsaw. It was half in him and his guts were hanging out. A coil of intestines steaming in the morning air. He had claw marks on his face and the petrol tank was full... of his blood."

"Juicy," Tad drooled. "What about the other bloke?"

"He went mad," I said. "You remember, Kaz, don't you, about the Malleroo guy and the chooks?" And my appeal would've had a ring to it because this part was a well-known story around town. "He was the one who worked on the Malleroo property. You know, the one who clubbed the chooks to death with a cricket bat one night, then shot himself. Stark naked, he was. Mr Bailey found him in the chook run – well, most of him. Chunks of brain were snagged in the chicken wire. It's a well-known fact."

It didn't matter who said what. Not really. The stories grew from us, found strength in the details we might add.

"Gruesome," Tad said, and I could see him storing all this for his next version of *The House on the Hill*.

"Worse than gruesome," Kaz said, turning to me. "Especially for you. You shouldn't have shot at that cat the other week. Poor old Greased Lightning."

"I didn't aim at the cat. I aimed at the water tank. Missed the cat by a mile."

"But scared it shitless all the same," Tad laughed.

"Scared it into the middle of next week," Kaz said. "What if it ran in front of a truck because of what you did? It'll come back to haunt you. And if Greased Lightning doesn't, the Cat Woman will."

"Ooooh," groaned Tad, clawing close to my face with outstretched fingers. "Meooow."

"The Cat Woman's gonna get you."

"Not a chance," I said.

"Well, we'll have to see about that tonight, won't we? If you're not too chicken, that is. See if she wants your blood."

"I wouldn't mention chickens, if I were you," Kaz said.

I wasn't scared. In fact, I was the first to turn up. I dumped my bike in the ditch and then skirted the trees on the paddock-side, before hauling myself up onto the first branch and then into our den.

I have, at times, incorrectly remembered the sequence of events, which followed. Deliberately so, I suspect. Memories, I've discovered, can be broken apart and cast in a new mould to suit what we think we believe or want to believe or need to believe. What begins as a self-preserving lie takes the shape of an established truth. For years, I half-convinced myself that we scarpered at the first sight of torchlight – grabbed our bikes and fled – without ever looking back or hearing a sound, but that's not true. I don't think there was any torchlight because I can now accept that it wasn't dark. To be able to lie to yourself like this isn't as absurd or as difficult as it sounds.

For a while, I used to dream that we were actually in the house, downstairs, when we suddenly discovered we weren't alone. In my dream, I could always feel someone breathing down the nape of my neck, although I haven't had that dream in a while now.

What actually happened was that we pretended we were commandoes, sneaking for cover, as we dropped silently from our den and crawled through part of the old orchard, before inching our way towards the water tank near the back door. We were all whispers and belly-crawls and hand signals, and we were happy to take our time and make an even bigger game of it because we were mustering our bravado, trying to decide if we were really going to do this thing or not. Was it 'Breaking & Entering' or 'Trespass', or both? What would Mum and Dad say if I got caught? How long would they ground me for? Would it spoil my birthday?

But it was then, just as we were making elaborate signals about which window we'd crawl to – which boards looked the easiest to prise off – that all hell broke loose inside.

Even now, I'm not sure about the order because it was a tangle of noises, impressions, all mixed up, coming too fast, too unexpectedly.

Footsteps on floorboards, running; pounding down the house. One pair? Two pairs?

Rumble and clatter, smashing and banging – a chair or cupboard knocked into, knocked over. A crash. Loud.

Footsteps on floorboards, running.

Breaking glass. A fight? A fall?

We're frozen in waiting. Staring at a blank door.

A shout, a yell – several shouts – surprised, alarmed, angry. A man's voice, swearing and cursing – no words, no word, no names, no name.

Groaning and crying. The same voice; I'm sure. I'm sure. A tone and pitch I can't forget – not ever – that voice.

And pain and hurt and anger and fury. One pained and furious shouting.

The Cat Woman got him. Whoever *him* was.

And then...

A ghostly wailing. A single cry.

No signal needed, we stood and ran. We dashed across the garden, through nettles, round brambles, across and over to the trees and between fence wires into the paddock – run, run, run, scramble, scramble, scramble – along the ditch to where our bikes were jumbled together.

We stopped, we breathed, we held the stitch in our sides. We looked back, we waited.

We waited.

And Tad laughed first.

"Jesus, Mary and Joseph," he said, and laughed some more as he crossed himself. His eyes were bright and his face was glowing. "Holy shit, someone lives there!"

"No, they don't," panted Kaz. "No-one lives there. Unless a tramp or a dero or someone's moved in."

We crouched in the safety of distance – forty metres or so – and watched some more. Finding our breath, our laughter tinged with hysteria, but quiet laughs that wouldn't carry.

"Definitely a dero," Kaz said.

"Whoever it was must've fallen over, hurt himself. Or had a fight with another dero. A drunken fight."

"Or fell through the ceiling."

"Perhaps the Cat Woman got him."

"He sounded well-pissed off, whatever."

We were dragging our bikes upright, ready to make a move towards home, when Kaz grabbed the cloth of our T-shirts, Tad's and mine, and nodded back in the direction of the house.

What we saw was the back door being shoved open and the figure of a man staggering out. He was clutching a black and yellow sports bag, and he struggled to force the door shut again behind him; had to kick it twice to close it. It was obvious he'd been hurt, because of the way he hung his head and held one arm, and he seemed dazed or frightened – it was hard to tell which.

"He's been sleeping rough," Kaz whispered. "He's just a dero. A tramp."

"The Cat Woman *almost* got him," Tad said.

But we'd stopped laughing. Like all well-nourished creations, our ghost story had outgrown us at that point.

A moment later, we heard a car start close by and listened to it tear off down the Old Hinchley Road.

"Funny he's got a car," Kaz observed; "a dero-on-wheels." But a piece of timber fell away from one of the windows just then, dropping onto the verandah, and we practically cacked our pants.

I'd never cycled home as fast as I did then. I reckon we three broke the land speed record that night. Faster than Greased Lightning.

Night is one world, day is another. We slip through from one to the other like passengers on a train, and the way we see ourselves changes as the landscape beyond our reflection in the window changes. As an adult, attempting to articulate the roots and routes of my endless travelling – my too many goalless journeys – this is how I sometimes see my life.

By the time we met up next morning, each of us had rationalised the previous evening's events and we were ready to laugh at one another's foolishness in seeing ghosts and demons behind the harmless antics of a dero, or whatever he was. Probably some traveller looking for a place more comfortable than the back of his car to kip down overnight, or a prospective buyer wanting a quick look-over; fell through the stairs and broke a bone or two, perhaps. We should've helped him, not run and hidden like little kids. Our curiosity had found its courage again, and we were eager to see what the place looked like inside. Maybe we'd discover how he'd hurt himself. It was midmorning and no ghost worth its salt would be stirring.

We tugged at the back door and then we all three shouted together: "HELLO, IS THERE ANYBODY HOME?"

It wasn't so bad once we were inside.

The first room was bare, except for the laundry trough and several shelves. It smelt damp and the entire corner of one wall was blackened with mildew. Beyond this was the kitchen; with its lime green fitted-cupboards and the kitchen sink still in place, although there was a gap where an oven had stood and a mess of glass on the floor where a windowpane had smashed.

The hallway was littered with newspapers and we had to step over an old-fashioned hall stand that had been thrown over, and I began to wonder why we'd never ventured this far before. What babies we'd been. Nonetheless, we stayed together as we moved from room to room, while trying to appear bravely, independently adventurous.

When Tad opened the bathroom door, we were met by the stink of shit and piss, and Kaz quickly slammed it again.

"Shit," Tad said and held his nose.

"Hmm," said Kaz, "you think so?"

The rooms downstairs were empty, and even the carpets had been pulled up. Only the carpet grips remained, nailed round the edge of the floor. Then we moved to the stairs, where we might've hesitated a moment.

"There's no-one here," Tad said, assuring Kaz and me, and himself too, and he shouted up the stairs: "IS THERE?"

"Keep to the side of the stairs," Kaz whispered. "They might be rotten. Maybe that's how the guy hurt himself."

All the same, the stairs looked and felt solid enough and our wooden movements, step by step, resounded through the hollowness of the house. It was then I thought of Mrs Rawlings climbing these stairs with a softer tread and what a waste it was to have such a home standing empty, year after year.

There were two rooms upstairs, and in the first were scraps of furniture – two chairs, a bookshelf, a disgusting mattress, half a carpet and strips of crumbling underlay – and a built-in cupboard. I tried to imagine being a dero and sleeping on such a mattress, but it was beyond me. The other room was bare. Cleaner, but bare.

Kaz returned to the first room, and I followed, while Tad lingered on the small landing.

I don't know why she hesitated in front of the cupboard – I never asked her – but she did and, because she did, it was me who pulled open the door.

I didn't recognise it as a person at first, only saw it as part of the rubbish of shiny black bin bags and loops of old carpet that had been dumped hurriedly on top, but I turned at Tad's footsteps, then felt Kaz gasp and stiffen.

None of us screamed, not like they do in films. We might've done, all three of us, but I didn't hear. I froze. Every pore of my skin froze. Then the axis of my world shifted: turned upside down, inside out. Struggled not to buckle at the knees. A black hole sucking me down.

All this for mere seconds, perhaps.

"Oh," Tad groaned, deep and long, and rushed to a corner and threw up, while Kaz and I remained frozen against time and all new sensibility. I wanted it to be an optical illusion, a trick of light, and tried to see how it might be something else, but the more I saw – not a matter of looking or looking away – the more I understood what I was seeing.

Her eyes were open and staring right at me, through me. Picking each bone bare. In seeing nothing, they saw everything.

It was the missing girl, the one in all the photos. Recognisably a once-person to that extent. She had brown eyes, but her skin was such a cold, pale colour that I remember it as grey, and her lips were blue. But what I saw most –

and can never un-see – was the look of surprise and sadness on her face.

It took three years for the police to catch the filth that did that to Alison Honiton.

More than our childhood games ended that morning. Our friendship fell apart because there was something too terrible propped up in the middle of it. It was only a small town, but there were enough reasons – excuses – to avoid calling at each other's house, to steer clear of one another if we were down the street and, anyway, I think I missed a fair whack of school that term. I spent a lot of time at home, sleeping, reading comics, watching TV and 'staring into thin air', as my mother too frequently declared.

Being part of the end of someone's life like that – hearing the ugly commotion of her death – and wondering if we could've prevented it is enough of a ghost for anyone to carry around with them, through childhood into adulthood. It's enough of a coming of age.

It wasn't long afterwards that Mum told me that Kaz had been given a scholarship to a boarding school a couple of hundred kilometres away. As if I needed to know. As if it ought to make a difference. And then, that Tad's family had abruptly moved to another town, interstate, where his dad would be the new branch manager.

Except for those bleak days when we were brought together at the trial, I never saw Tad or Kaz again.

Things must've been bad at home. I must've made them bad with the sourness that clung to me, from which I couldn't let go. Else Mum and Dad wouldn't have packed me off to live with my eldest sister in the city. And I don't mind admitting that I had ulterior motives, several years later, in encouraging my dad to sell up and move four hundred kilometres closer to my sister and me soon after Mum died. Anything to avoid coming back to this place, from which I've never properly taken my leave.

Until today.

Although I now know that the ghosts which haunt us don't belong to a place as such, but live within us, maybe it would've been good, after all, to have been here and to see the fire when they burnt the old place down. To watch it burn. If we fail to bury our ghosts where they belong, then we end up dragging them with us through life.

I don't often think about Tad these days, but sometimes I imagine Kaz with a couple of young children and a husband who adores her, with an uncluttered house and a neat city garden. Picnics under the swing.

Other times, I imagine her travelling, always travelling and moving on, unable to settle, unwilling to commit, wary of getting too close to anyone, wary of trusting anything to ever remain the same.

Sometimes, I imagine her life has qualities I'd like mine to have; other times, I imagine her life is what I fear mine has become. And sometimes, like now, I wonder whether either of them, Kaz or Tad, have ever returned to this place – to the Rawlings' place – and stood where I'm standing now, in order to finally lay their ghosts and begin again. Or at least to try.

6

Ukini Nageni

Ari O'Connell

Author

Ari O'Connell spent much of her mid 20s travelling, including a stint in the neon wilderness of Osaka, Japan. Her story, *Ukini Nageni*, explores Japan's nocturnal world of hostessing, where appearances are deceptive and people are not always as they seem. Ari has worked as a journalist and in Communications and PR. She is currently completing a PhD and her first novel, a black comedy about renegade corporate soldiers, cubicle hell, anxiety and death. She lives in Perth, Western Australia with her family and her Labrador Coco, who has food and entitlement issues.

There's been talk that someone spotted Trick and Katherine Daniels in Cardboard Town by the Dotombori River. The rumour's spread through the gaijin community like a mangy dog on heat. I head for my shift at Amber and even the customers know about it.

The Mama-san pokes my belly and tells me I need to lose weight. Then she hooks me up at my usual table with Lucy, the goth girl from Canada. I call her Satellite because she's always in orbit checking out what's going on. When Trick introduced us a few months ago she said, "welcome to the family, darling," and gave me a sake shot and a gap-toothed smile. I grinned hello but all I could see was her corpse-like beauty. The blue-white skin with purple veins tracking so close to the surface I wondered if I should be frightened for her.

Lucy calls everyone honey, sweetie or darling, even if she hates them. We don't have much in common but we work the same table every night, so we've got eachother's backs. There's safety in numbers when you don't belong. She's younger than me but an old hand at Amber and she's protected me from Mama's maneuverings more than once. Lucy's the club's most valuable asset – partly because of her fractured charm but mostly because she understands the deal. Over here she's known as the 'number one hostess'. It means she earns a lot of money.

Lucy has dark cropped hair, wears blood-red lipstick and diamond studs in her nose and tongue. Mama pairs us at tables because the contrast between her slender neck and deathly appeal, and my blonde curls and beach skin make for "very foreign beauty", whatever that is. I think she means it's good for business.

Being a bargirl in Japan wasn't something I planned. It grew up around a goodbye I couldn't speak; the way flesh encircles an embedded splinter of glass. You feel it but it's hidden.

I was 23 when they rang and said, "Evie, it's Hopey." And I knew he was dead. Everybody loved him, but Hopey died smeared in vomit and alone. "A hotshot," they told me, shaking their heads. "Stupid kid. The junk was too pure."

At the funeral they played REM's Everybody Hurts and I stared at Hopey's coffin and wondered if it was suicide. I realized we'd never sit in rocking chairs on the verandah when we were 60, or strap on backpacks and sturdy shoes and follow the sun.

"Do you children know what you do to your mothers?" my Mum asked me, when she sat me down after the funeral for one of her talks.

"Don't start Mum," I warned. She looked at me, red-eyed and hopeless, and tried to reach across the void. She said Australia was still the lucky country, especially for generations born after the Great Depression and Vietnam. This may be true, but a loss is a loss however you find it. Our tragedies are small scale and domestic: divorced parents, a casualised workforce, loved ones decimated by drugs or fast cars. We have no noble truths.

Mum was holding me with her eyes, willing me to speak and all I could offer was that my happy, lazy country had left me ill-equipped to deal with grief. She talked about seeing the good in things and believing, but my temple throbbed and the white-noise came up between me and the rest of the world. Then she gave me a quick, stiff hug and made me promise to have faith in my luck.

I tried, but when the grey makes waves within you, luck is a four-letter word and faith doesn't mean much. When people here ask me, I tell them Australia is mostly desert, with cities clinging to the coast gasping for breath. It's all sand and sea and salt, with a never-ending blue-dome sky.

My hometown is full of light and heat and room to breathe but I couldn't find room for my grief. So I packed my life up tight. I moved fast, so it couldn't keep up.

Japan offered easy money and it kept me moving. It was something to do. Amber was a drag sometimes, but the boozy camaraderie and the chatter made my days slide more easily into night. Sometimes people questioned what I was doing there. I said I was saving to buy a camera to travel and take photographs; that I might map a course and follow the sun. If they asked me what I wanted to shoot, I'd tell them whatever catches my eye.

Everything changed when Katherine Daniels disappeared.

HOSTITUTE! screamed the headline on the front page of the Yomiuri Shimbun above a grainy photo of a plump, fair-haired girl holding a can of Kirin and laughing into the lens.

There are fears for the safety of 22-year-old Briton Katherine Daniels who has been living in Osaka for the past six months but has not been seen since 11.30pm Friday 22 July.

Ms Daniels, who entered the country on a tourist visa, had been working at the Sakura Club in Shinsaibashi's entertainment district the night she disappeared. Ms Daniels went on dohan, an off-premises date with a customer, before bringing him to the club as her guest for the evening, and working her regular shift.

Ms Daniels' disappearance raises uncomfortable questions about the participation of foreign women in Japan's mizu shobai, or water trade; a loose network of bars, clubs, nightclubs and restaurants, often bankrolled and controlled by the yakuza.

Police are concerned Ms Daniels may have been pressured into prostitution, drug running, or assaulted by a client.

Noriko Shimizu, the Sakura Club's Mama-san, dismisses such claims as ludicrous.

Katherine's father, James Daniels, arrived in Osaka yesterday to meet with police. In a brief written statement he said: "The Daniels family is very concerned for Katherine's safety, however we are convinced she is alive. We have found media reports linking Katherine with prostitution and/or drugs particularly distressing and ask that the media and the public respect our feelings on this matter and refrain from what amounts to character assassination."

Later, I saw James Daniels on TV at a press conference full of Japanese and foreign journalists. Sweat patches spread across his shirt as he appealed for information, bug eyed and desperate. There was no trace of Katherine, at least not then.

As we wait for the customers to arrive, Lucy shifts nervously in her seat and asks me if I've heard that Trick's back in town. I nod and she pours me a shot of sake and we raise our glasses in a triumphant salute to the night ahead. "Kampai! Ganbatte ne!" The sharp sting of the liquor relieves me and the world loses its edge.

The first couple of hours at Amber are always slow. The customers trickle in around 9.30 or 10.00pm but we have to punch in at 8.00pm, just in case. If we're late, even five minutes, Mama docks our pay. This sucks, but being late for anything in Japan is one of the Seven Deadly Sins so after the first few times you get organized. If it's something unavoidable, Taka-san, the perma-tanned barman, might take pity and sneak the amount Mama's docked back to you via the till. This means you owe him a favour though because Taka-san won't do something for nothing.

Amber's pretty standard as far as hostess clubs go. It's in a small, narrow room on the twentieth floor of a skyscraper near one of Osaka's busiest subway stations, Umeda. On the wall outside, neon letters flash 'The Amber Club' and inside there's a bar stacked with the customers' bottles of whisky and sake, each identified with a neat name tag. Wooden tables with chairs are scattered around the room and three soft-leather booths are tucked against a wall. A small raised stage for karaoke and dance performances is opposite the bar and the place is decorated with mirrors, disco balls and an ugly fake chandelier.

The club's main attraction is its 'global girls' who serve drinks and light cigarettes while making small talk about nothing much. We're from all over; Brazil, Thailand, Canada, Holland. But the Japanese call us gaijin, which means foreigner or outside one. This makes us sound unified, as if our difference earns us a place, but I know we're just flotsam and jetsam drifting along. Gaijin. Ukini Nageni.

"Trick'll be back poking around sooner or later, Evie honey," says Lucy, pushing a greasy tempura prawn around her plate with her chopsticks. Lucy can eat just about anything and stay slim while the rest of us get fat and puffy on the booze, the starchy food and sleeping all day. It can be a problem: the customers prefer thin.

I shrug my shoulders. "So, who cares? As long as Mama's happy with us, Trick stays off our backs, right?"

I wink at Lucy and pick up a couple of the traditional wooden coasters on the table and slip them under the cushions for later. I figure if I collect two a night I can put together some complete sets over the next few weeks and offload them at the Saturday Flea Market in Shinsaibashi. I do that a lot. Collect souvenirs from around the place.

Back home, Hopey and I'd go to swapmeets every month, and even though he's not around anymore I still have the habit of trawling. I don't really know why. It can be hard work selling stuff on a sweaty day or a winter's morning but you can earn some money. You'd be surprised by what people buy if they think it's a bargain.

Lucy doesn't say anything about the coasters. Just throws back another shot and exhales. "I've got a bad feeling. I think things might get nasty," she tells me and picks nervously at a scabby sore on her arm.

"Jeez, don't do that, Satellite!" I snap. "It'll get infected. What are you so worried about anyway? Trick's just a gaijin making bucks like the rest of us. He's an idiot but he's not Charles Manson."

Lucy flushes and lights a cigarette, pale pianist's fingers shaking slightly, nails bitten down to the quick. I sigh under my breath and signal Taka-san for a couple of beers.

When I first started at Amber, Lucy seemed old-movie sophisticated, like Lauren Bacall, but she's been wound up and jumpy lately with greyish half-moons under her eyes. I'd heard she used to be a speed demon but that she'd cleaned up a few months ago. Maybe she's back riding the pony. Or maybe she owes Trick money. A lot of people owe money over here. You can earn a lot but you can spend it too.

When Taka-san brings us our beers, I mention we're missing two coasters and it'll look sloppy when the customers come in. He looks suspicious but I smile and tell him that he's looking very tanned and he grins, makes a quick trip to the bar and then slaps two of the carved wooden squares down in the middle of the table.

"I betcha all the customers' bottles that he goes to a tanning salon," I whisper to Lucy. She nods and smiles but her eyes are on the door.

"You want something else to eat?" I ask, figuring that some more food might settle her nerves.

Lucy shakes her head then leans across the table and pushes

a folded piece of paper into my hands.

"Check this out but don't show anyone," she hisses.

I open the paper in my lap and feel a familiar clench behind my right eye. There's a manga cartoon of a half-naked girl, breasts spilling out of her tiny singlet, skirt riding up over her splayed thighs and an ugly slash across her throat, blood spattered across her neck. Two people, their faces in shadow, stand over her. Written in neat romaji at the bottom of the page, are the words: Lucy desu!

I grimace, fold the paper and push it back across the table.

"Is this a sick joke? Where did you get it?"

"It's no joke, Evie. It's the seventh one this week. Four in my letterbox, two pushed under my door and one taped to the seat of my bike. All the same kind of thing."

I take a gulp of my beer. The throbbing behind my eye threatens to unfurl into a migraine so vicious the world will become glaring white noise. I pop five painkillers, drain my beer and then signal Taka-san for some whisky shots.

"Sickos. Don't take any notice of it. It's probably schoolboys who're reading too much manga and their imaginations are running wild. Or maybe it's a customer with a crush. Don't let it rattle you."

"Yeah, I know. It's weird though and freaking me out a bit."

"It could be a love letter from Hiroshi-san," I tease, trying to lighten the mood. "Maybe you're missing some cultural nuances here."

Hiroshi-san is a blue-suited executive from Sumitomo bank. People say he does business with the Yakuza, but you can't believe everything you hear. He's one of Lucy's regular customers and he's besotted with her gappy beauty, everyone knows that. He comes to Amber most Friday nights and books her for dohan at least twice a month.

Going on dohan with customers before bringing them to the club is part of the gig and bumps up your commission, but the dates are usually a drag. Lucy makes sure Hiroshi-san takes her to top-end restaurants for fugu, or shopping for clothes or jewellery, and says all those dohan are worth her while.

Hiroshi-san has got a wife and two young kids at home but that's just how it is here. Maybe that's how it is everywhere. I don't know.

"Hiroshi-san might be a loser salaryman but he isn't a chikan," says Lucy, snatching the note from me and tucking it into her sleeve.

"I know, I'm only joking. But seriously, it could be a customer. Maybe you should tell Mama. Or, if you get any more you could take them to the police, I guess. It's practically stalking. Have you kept all the others?"

Lucy grimaces. "You're kidding right? Even if it is a customer, Mama isn't going to do anything to interfere with her profits and do you really think the police are going to help a hostess, let alone a foreign one? I'm here on a tourist visa, I'm not even legal. Besides, they sell this kind of stuff everywhere and no-one bats an eye."

"True, Satellite, true. It could be worse. Someone could be stalking your laundry bag and stealing your knickers to sell in vending machines."

It's not funny but we laugh because it's true. Neither of us mentions Katherine Daniels.

"Promise not to tell anyone?" she asks. "I don't want any problems right now."

I don't see how telling anyone is going to cause trouble but I don't ask Lucy why and she doesn't elaborate. That's just how it is here. People only tell you what they want you to know. They roll their lives up tight.

"I promise," I say and raise my whisky shot in a salute. "Hostesses' honour."

Lucy clinks her glass against mine then pulls two cigarettes from her delicate silver case and gives me one. We sit in silence as the club unfolds around us. I draw the smoke deep into the core of me then tilt my head back and exhale a long grey streak into the air. It floats above us for a few seconds then dissipates. By the early hours of the morning Amber will be so choked with smoke and sweat and exhaustion that it will seem as though we're perching on the edge of a dream.

Lucy gnaws distractedly on a fingernail. "What's happening with you, sweetie? Saved enough for your trip yet?"

I've told Lucy the same story I run by everyone else: there's a camera I want to buy and a trip I'm dying to take. It's easier than trying to explain Hopey.

Hopey called me most days and he'd always say, "Hey Evie, it's the man on the moon," and I'd always ask "Who?" and he'd sing REM's Man on the Moon. Then we'd laugh non-stop for about three minutes. I don't know why. We used to laugh a lot about stupid things.

Hopey was really into music and he played guitar in a covers band. They had a few gigs around town. He didn't have any formal training but he could hear melodies in his head, so he'd just close his eyes and feel out the notes. He could really play. Sometimes he'd write his own songs. Just sit there and pick them out on the guitar, eyes drifting, cracked smile splitting his face. I told him the band should play his originals as well as the covers. He'd grin and say, "maybe one day."

Hopey liked to sing too, but he had a terrible voice. I guess he wanted to be a rock star but had to settle for being the guitar player. I always told him Keith was cooler than Mick anyway. He liked it when I said that. Hopey really dug the Stones but the band he loved most was REM. Everybody Hurts was his favourite song.

Dragging myself back to the present, I stub out my cigarette and pull a new one from my pack. I give Lucy a tired smile.

"I think I'll only have to do a couple more months here and I'll have enough money. I thought I'd go and hang out on a beach in Thailand for a while then maybe I'll head to Alaska to photograph the Northern Lights. I've always wanted to see them. I was going to go with a friend once but we ran out of time."

Lucy smiles at me but her eyes are opaque. "I'll miss you when you go," she says softly and I feel a sharp sting of surprise. Lucy and I look out for each other but it's not the same as the friends you grow up with. It's intense I guess, because it can get pretty lonely over here but it doesn't last. Everyone's always moving on.

"We'll stay in touch. You can come and visit me if you like. That'd be pretty cool."

"Maybe," she says stubbing out her cigarette and signalling Taka-san for a clean ashtray. "You've done well, Evie. Most hostesses don't save enough to do anything useful."

"Yeah well, this isn't a career move. I'll be well and truly ready for something new in a month or two. I'm ready to go now but I need to earn a bit more cash."

"Damn, I wish I could do that," Lucy says and starts drumming her foot against the floor and picking at her scab again.

I press down hard on my right temple with my thumb. My eyes are gritty and I feel tired and dirty, like we're at the end of the night, not the beginning.

"You should focus on selling more of the jewellery you make and work out a plan to ditch this gig, Satellite. I reckon you can only do this kind of job for so long before you start to lose it."

"Yeah, maybe I will but I've got more important things to worry about at the moment," says Lucy, and I guess she has.

I didn't tell her but I'd be pretty spooked if someone was sending me those pictures. Especially now that Katherine Daniels has disappeared.

Maybe it's an Amber regular or some stupid schoolboy. It could be a screwed-up gaijin's idea of a joke or a warning; lots don't approve of hostessing. Maybe Trick's on another power trip and he thinks the pictures will put Lucy in her place, whatever that is. As far as I know, they had something once, but the gaijin community is always at love or war and you never know what's really going on. Someone steals money or food, or takes off for Paris owing rent, or leaves all their gear in someone's one-room apartment for five years instead of five days like they promised.

People come and go and even if you don't know them you do, because your fellow English teacher, barman or hostess has lived, worked or slept with them and they'll tell you all about it as if it's World News Tonight. It's like having Christmas Lunch with your extended dysfunctional family. Permanently.

When I arrived in Osaka I moved into Banana House, a crumbling two-storey accommodation for foreigners in the working class suburb of Taisho. Taisho was cement-filled and charmless but it had cheap rent.

Everything in Banana House was old and covered with the detritus of the travellers who'd gone before: torn books, bags of clothes, battered pots and piles of stained futons on the bedroom floors. The scabby kitchen bench always had dried rice and toast crumbs all over it, so the place was humming with flying roaches dive-bombing your ramen. It was off-putting at first but you got used to it after a while.

Officially five housemates paid rent but there were all these Saturday night lovers who stayed 'til Wednesday and most nights the place shuddered with a cacophony of moans. Half the time you never saw who owned the moans. They arrived at 3.00am and disappeared like ghosts. They were faceless but they left their dirty coffee mugs in the sink.

The longest-serving resident was Sandra, an Environmental Science graduate from San Francisco. When we first met, Sandra told me there were no jobs in America so she taught Conversational McEnglish at one of the big chain schools, UIES.

"You'll all regret in the future when the polar ice caps have melted and it's too late," she said, and pulled at her curls so they rose in a dark halo around her head. Sandra was pretty in-your-face but she walked the talk, which is more than most people do. She carried lacquered chopsticks everywhere, so she didn't have to use disposable wooden ones, and when she bought something she deposited the wrapping – plastic, cardboard boxes, bags and string – back on the counter, and put the product in her hemp shopping bag.

This annoyed most shop assistants, who liked to wrap everything individually, and often three times, even basic purchases. They didn't say anything though because there were two types of gaijin, pretty ones to photograph, touch or practise English with, and weird ones to avoid. Sandra was in the weird category and people kept their distance, mostly.

Sandra could be hard work sometimes but she had some useful connections and she hooked me up with Trick. "He's a loser-gaijin, but he's been here forever and he knows the business," she said, leaning out of her bedroom window sneaking a joint. We weren't supposed to smoke in the house because it was a fire hazard. It was on the list of House Rules, stuck on the message board by the door:

1. REMOVE your shoes before walking on the tatami!
2. NO loud music after 9.00pm!
3. NO drugs, NO drunks!
4. SMOKE OUTSIDE or suffer the consequences!
5. NO people staying over!
6. WRITE DOWN phone messages. No, you WON'T remember them!
7. DON'T steal bikes, umbrellas or FOOD! IT'S BAD KARMA!!
8. DO I LOOK LIKE YOUR MUMMY?? CLEAN THE BATHROOM AND THE TOILET!!!!

The rule sheet was typed up and laminated and it looked pretty official but no-one took any notice of it, except Matt from Minnesota who taught Business English and hiked every weekend.

Sandra finished her joint and pulled herself back inside the window, grabbing Carol King's Tapestry CD from her stack of music against the wall.

"I hostessed for a few months when I first got here. It's completely demeaning. Why don't you just teach? I can get you a gig at UIES if you like."

I gritted my teeth and forced my lips into smile. Ex-hostesses were like reformed smokers, always wanting you to learn from their mistakes. I just wanted to be left alone.

"Thanks for the offer but I need to earn some money quickly. I want to keep moving. Japan's just a pit stop for me and teachers' salaries are rubbish in comparison to the bucks I can earn hostessing, no offence. I'll probably pick up some private classes on the side though. I've heard they pay pretty well."

Sandra glared at me and tugged at her hair. "Why are you in such a hurry anyway? The world will wait won't it?" She flicked on the CD and grinned. "My absolute favourite singer."

I thought about telling Sandra about Hopey and me. How we'd been friends since we were ten and that REM and a freshly-dug grave were never part of the plan. How his melodies and cracked smile got lost in the needle, the spoon and the flame. That the world didn't wait for everyone but you never knew who was staying or going until it was too late. How the grey made waves within me and the white-noise came down between me and everything else. That moving helped.

I took a sharp inward breath and grinned. "Carol King's a classic. I'm not in that much of a hurry. I'm just trying to stick to a travel plan, keep things ticking along."

"Plan, sham," Sandra said dismissively. "Well it's your funeral. At least I've done my duty by telling you it sucks. Try

The Amber Club, the money's good and Trick'll get you the best rate. Not because he's looking out for you, although he'll tell you he is, but because he'll get himself the best deal in the process. But watch your back. Trick's real slippery. He's got connections with the local Bosozoku Boys, who are mostly all talk but they can turn. Some people say he's in with the Yakuza but I don't know for sure. He'd probably like people to think that. Hell, he probably started the rumours. Whoever heard of a guy called Trick anyway?"

Trick was an odd name, it seemed undignified.

"Well, we're all on show here in a way," I offered. "You even have to perform in your McEnglish classes. You said so. Maybe it's a stage name like Harry Houdini or David Copperfield."

Sandra snorted and rolled her eyes. "Whatever. Here, have a spliff." And she rolled me a new one.

"Thanks," I said and shoved it in my pocket for later.

"I'm going to the store, do you want anything?"

I needed everything but I figured I'd just nick food for a while so I said I was OK and watched her try to jam her hair under a cap.

"You've got wicked hair," I offered.

"I have to hide it whenever I can because people pull it here. I'm on the train and people just yank my hair then giggle behind their hands. Can you believe it?"

I could, because I wanted to pull her ringlets and watch them spring back but I just shook my head and watched as she strode out the door.

Sandra hooked me up with Trick who told me three gaijin had up and left for a spiritual retreat in India. I guess he was scouting for new blood and couldn't afford to be too choosey.

We arranged to meet at 2.30 outside Mr Donut in central Shinsaibashi. I had a quick shower then headed into the humid bustle of the street towards Taisho station. I walked down the main drag, past the takeaway noodle bars that sold ramen for 700 yen, the video shop that only stocked porn and the local Lawsons where gaijin picked up dinner on their way home from teaching or hostessing or 1000 yen/hour bar work. The clammy air pushed down on me and my legs were wet with sweat.

I'd missed the push and throb of rush hour but the train was still crowded and I had to stand, gripping the plastic strap above my head. The other passengers avoided my eyes and pressed their bodies and faces away from me towards a safer space. Lots of gaijin got offended by how some locals treated you as if you were a cross between a maniac and a monkey but I didn't mind the extra legroom it gave me and it was better than being mauled by a chikan.

Like most gaijin, Trick was easy to spot. He was tall with pale freckled skin and blonde dreadlocks, and wore a flared suit and coloured sneakers. He stood outside Mr Donut squinting into the sun.

Trick took both my hands in his and squeezed them so tight I gasped. "Evie-chan, welcome to the wild ride that is Japan," he said in a low American drawl as his eyes skated across my chest and back up to my face. His skin felt like aged leather, cracked and soft.

He led me to a small table by the floor-to-ceiling windows that overlooked the hurried mess of the street. Outside, Irani illegals sold counterfeit phone cards, dissolving into the crowds as soon as they spotted a policeman doing the rounds. Expensively dressed Japanese teens posed as punk rockers and goths and California-girls. They pointed at us through the window and mouthed gaijin as they strolled past. One girl with spiky peroxided hair motioned at us to smile and then took our photo. Trick laughed and blew her a kiss and she giggled and slipped back into the crowd.

"Crazy kids! They'll be wanting my autograph next," Trick smirked, stroking his hair.

"Yeah, it's bizarre isn't it?" I said, dribbling sugar into my tea from a small paper tube. I picked up one of the brown plastic containers of long-life cream. "Can I get some milk? I'm not used to drinking tea with cream."

Trick gave me a strange half smile. "You're going to run into trouble if you can't learn to adapt, Evie-chan. Usually I tell my girls, 'when in Rome' but you're new so let me take care of you. Don't let anyone say I don't take look out for my girls."

I shifted uncomfortably against the hard wood of the stool; I need a gig, I thought, so I'll play.

Trick called the waitress over and spoke to her in rapid Japanese. She looked puzzled but bowed politely and returned with an oversized jug of scalded milk and some bean buns. "Sumimasen," she apologised before placing it on the table. I grimaced and poured some of it into my tea.

Trick stared at me, assessing me. "You know, I can lay my hands on just about anything if you or your amigos ever need a little pick-me-up, Evie-chan."

I shoved some bean bun into my mouth and swallowed quickly without chewing. "Thanks, but I'll be OK. Anyway, I don't know anyone much yet – only Sandra and a couple of guys at Banana House."

Trick frowned. "Let me give you a tip, Evie-chan. Sandra's one freaky chick. She needs to take care of her issues or go live in a tree house somewhere. Anyway, it's totally cool. I just wanted to open up the offer to a new friend. Japan is a trippy place sometimes. It can mess with your energy, baby."

He sighed deeply and gave me a beatific smile worthy of the Bagwhan, then pulled out a silver Zippo lighter and a packet of cigarettes.

"I reckon Sandra's OK," I said, deliberately slurping loudly on my tea. "She can be intense but at least she cares about something. Hey, why did the other girls leave for India?"

Trick looked pained as he picked imaginary speck of dust on

his sleeve and stroked the knot on his tie before looking me up and down and exhaling a low whistle.

"You don't seem to be a stupid girl Evie-chan, so I'll let you in on a little trade secret. Japan conquers most gaijin in the end, especially money-hungry hostesses. I've been in this business for ten years and I've seen it again and again. These chicks finally realize that something's missing and a few million more yen won't buy them peace of mind, or whatever it is they're chasing. So they pack their lives away in a week and disappear to an ashram or a yoga centre or a mountain to try and find soul food. Gone. Just like that." And he splayed his hands in a small circle, like a magician conjuring up a dove.

"Right," I said. "Isn't that annoying for you though?" Actually, pouring a few drinks and lighting some cigarettes didn't seem important enough to trigger a spiritual crisis. And hostessing hardly seemed a serious business.

"It's all part of the cosmic wheel, Evie-chan. Turn, turn, turn. It's all good. Anyway, it's better to have a high turnover. Keeps things interesting for the customers. There's always another girl and my job is to keep finding them."

He offered me a cigarette and his Zippo, then checked out my legs and winked at me. "If you lost a bit of weight you could be a righteous babe, you know. You'll need to keep off the rice and the beer or you'll blow up like a balloon. Fat chicks don't really fly over here – you've seen how tiny the J-girls are. The blonde hair is good, though, the salarymen will like that. You'll do for now. You can start tonight."

The numbness in me shifted and settled. "I betcha say that to all the girls," I said and faked a smile. I pocketed his Zippo, the cigarette and an extra bun for later. Trick paid the bill and we headed out into the crowded street.

"Make sure you dress up nice tonight, Evie-chan. No casual Australians allowed. Hey what were you doing in Australia baby?"

"Studying to be a lawyer. I'm halfway through my degree."

Trick stared at me, puzzled. "Wow! Ali McBeal but not as skinny. Watcha doing looking for work as a hostess in Osaka? You running from something? Maybe looking for something?"

"I'm just taking a break, checking things out," I said, and dived into the gaping swallow of the crowd.

Sandra had been right about Trick getting me a good deal, although I never did find out about his cut. I was on 7000 yen an hour and I got a commission on every bottle I sold. If a customer wanted to take me on dohan and I brought him to the club afterwards, I got a bonus. For smiling and pouring a few drinks, I earned more in a week than English teachers did in a month. Even so, hostesses weren't that well regarded in the gaijin community.

I received a postcard from Mum the day Lucy told me about her Wish List. Mum hadn't mastered email, said she preferred to communicate the old fashioned way. The card had one of those tourist photos of an evening at Cottesloe beach, purple sky ablaze, sun sliding into the horizon. On the back a brief, scrawled message.

Dear Evie,
I visited Hopey today and took gerberas, as instructed! It was very peaceful. You mustn't worry so much. I hope you're enjoying yourself and learning Japanese. Having a second language will be a great string to your bow. People tell me Japan's temples and stone gardens are very peaceful and Kyoto is particularly beautiful. What do you think?
Love Mum.
PS Some sunset for you in case you've forgotten.

I shoved the card in my bag and took it to work to show the photo to Lucy. Perth might not have the British Museum or the

Louvre but we know how to do beaches. Lucy told me it looked like paradise and what was I doing in a concrete jungle like Osaka. Then she pulled out a neatly typed piece of paper from her black silk jacket and told me I should put one together too.

"What is it?"

"A Wish List, sweetie. You write up a list of everything you want from your customers and you make sure you get it. I've been given makeup, jewellery, clothes, holidays. Once I got a ticket to fly home but I just pretended I went and cashed it in. One of the girls who used to work here even got given a car and an apartment in Tokyo."

"What for?"

"Nothing. The customer just liked her and she went on dohan with him. You should do it. Save you feeling like you have to pocket everything that's not nailed down."

I flushed and bit my lip. It's not like I ever took anything very valuable. Just a few bits and pieces here and there.

"I don't think any customer likes me that much," I said. "Not like you and Hiroshi-san. I don't want to get involved in anything like that. I'd feel like I owed them something. Anyway, I can't believe you get a car and an apartment for nothing."

Lucy sighed and rolled her eyes. "You've got a lot to learn about relationships Evie, darling. Particularly here. Hasn't anyone told you about the Two Ten Theory?"

"The what theory?"

"Two Ten," Lucy said patiently. "You know, a guy is a Two but you make him feel like a Ten. That's your job. Hostesses are the fantasy, wives are the reality. Hiroshi-san comes here and I serve him drinks and flirt with him and make him believe he's a Ten. He gives me gifts from my Wish List because I'm a foreign-girl-fantasy. But it's just a fantasy, a business transaction. He knows the rules."

"Even if he's connected with the Yakuza? I didn't think they were big on rules."

Lucy smoothed down her skirt and laughed, all white gappy teeth and glinting eyes.

"I can handle him. It's not real, remember? It's all smoke and mirrors. You're a bit too paranoid Evie. You don't need to be. You could get a lot more out of this job if you relaxed a bit.

"Maybe," I said, unconvinced.

By 10.30pm Amber is pumping. Lucy's still wound up but she's doing a good job of hiding it.

Hiroshi-san has brought in a group of international businessmen for a night on the tiles, Japanese style. He's throwing back the whisky but sweat is forming in cruel droplets above his lip. Maybe he's worried about his English, which is basic and trips clumsily on his tongue. Some of his subordinates have been educated overseas and are fluent, but they pretend they only have the basics and converse mostly in Japanese.

Lucy sits next to Hiroshi-san and pours him shots of whisky and orders his favourite food: tempura, sashimi and sushi. When he's not eating she holds both his hands, which looks affectionate but is a tactic to stop him mauling her.

When I first started, Lucy gave me the lowdown on how to fend off amorous advances tactfully. If you offend the customers or make them lose face Mama will sack you faster than you can breathe.

"Most of these guys will try and touch you at some point, Evie darling," she warned me. "Grab both their hands if you can and hold on tight or else wave your finger at them like a schoolteacher and tell them to stop being naughty. This works most of the time – maybe it reminds them of their mothers.

You can order snacks they need both hands to eat and charge everything to their company accounts. If they still won't leave you alone, pour another round of shots and toast them. The drunker they get the sleazier they are, but you need to keep them drinking because this makes the most profit for Mama and ups our commission. And remember to keep the bottle label-up when you pour, honey. Everyone needs to see that it's an expensive brand."

Most nights I follow all Lucy's instructions but I don't have the knack like she does and every now and then I have to escape to the karaoke stage. I'm no threat to Lucy's 'number one hostess' status but as long as I get paid OK and the customers don't touch me, I don't care.

Lucy's careful attention is making Hiroshi-san relax. He leans back in his chair, legs spread, thigh pressing into hers, and raises his glass in a toast to his guests.

"To new friends. Very special and kind. Welcome to Japan!" he bellows.

"Kampai!" we all shout, downing shots in a communal greedy gulp before moving onto different topics of conversation and a new bottle of whisky.

Sebastian, a tall, thin guy from Ireland, tells me the group's been doing business at the bank all day.

"We're in the money game," he says impatiently when I ask what he does.

Well, we're all in that, I think as I pour him another shot.

I smile politely. "Sebastian doesn't sound a very Irish name."

"It's Greek. My mother chose it. It means majestic."

"That's very flattering. Does anyone call you Seb for short? Australians shorten everything…"

"Never," says Sebastian dismissively and looks curiously around the bar. "Where are all the Japanese girls? I thought we were coming to a geisha house. I can see foreign girls in a bar any night of the week at home."

"If you want the company of geisha you have to pay for them. A lot. This is a hostess bar, it's different."

"Aren't hostesses the modern version of geisha? We're paying for you. Or at least Hiroshi-san is."

I pull out Trick's Zippo and move in slowly to light Sebastian's cigarette, waving the flame a little too close to his hair.

"Sumitomo Bank, not Hiroshi-san, is paying for the privilege of storing a bottle of whisky or sake here with his name on it so he can come and relax with his colleagues after work," I correct him. "Geisha are artists, who study music, dance and the art of conversation. Depending on what you read, some may also be prostitutes. Hostesses pour drinks, order snacks, light cigarettes, sing karaoke. We're the party."

Sebastian leans back and surveys his surroundings. He glances at Lucy, who's listening intently to Hiroshi-san, hands holding his, head cocked to the side, and laughs.

"Are hostesses sometimes prostitutes too, depending on what you read? What about that girl who's gone missing? I read in the paper today that they think there's been foul play. She's an English girl – what's her name again?"

"Katherine Daniels," I say quietly. "Most people say she was just hostessing like the rest of us but I guess it depends on the girl and the money on offer. It happens. Not at Amber though. We're strictly drink pourers here."

I throw back another shot and watch Sebastian through the haze of smoke. I'm not sure if I'm telling the truth or not. There will always be rumours about what the girls do for money.

"It's international business really. Just the same as your banking," I say.

Sebastian's eyes wander up and down my body. "Ah, I see. It's just different kind of whoring. I guess we're all hostitutes here."

I pour him another shot and raise my glass in a salute. It's going to be a long night. "Kampai!" I say cheerfully, biting the inside of my cheek so hard that it bleeds.

We take turns singing karaoke on the small wooden stage at the front of the club. I do the version of The Carpenters song Rainy Days and Mondays that I do most nights because it's too hard to learn the lyrics to anything else.

Sebastian winks at me and requests Roxanne by The Police.

"We're not actually prostitutes," I tell him when he returns to the table.

He winks at me and repeats his joke. "We're all hostitutes here!"

I kick Lucy under the table and she winks and mouthes, "Ganbatte ne," and orders Sebastian a cocktail so lethal that he'll spend tomorrow throwing up his stomach lining.

At 2.00am the group is still lingering and Mama, at 55, elegant and immaculate in a silk kimono, swoops on our table to move them out. They're so soaked in whisky and sake they can hardly stand, and they've ordered platters of expensive snacks throughout the evening. There's no more money to be squeezed from the night.

Hiroshi-san suddenly bangs the table and announces that we, the entire drunken mess of a group, will visit Osaka Dome tomorrow for lunch and then go to the baseball, Hanshin Tigers versus the Yomiuri Giants. The Tigers are his team.

I'm exhausted and about to protest but Lucy glares at me. Smile. I glare back. I don't feel like going just because she wants to tick something else off her Wish List.

"Arigato gozaimasu Hiroshi-san, we'd love to but Sunday is our only day off..." I say.

"Great," says Sebastian, leering at Lucy and me. "It'll be a nice day out for all of us."

Hiroshi-san flings an arm around Lucy. "I will collect you at Lucy's apartment and take you there," he announces.

Lucy catches my eye and I remember the manga drawings and Katherine Daniels.

"Thank you Hiroshi-san but Osaka Dome is quite close to

where we live so we'll meet you at the entrance at midday," I tell him.

Mama smiles and bows gracefully to our table saying that the Dome is a very interesting monument for tourists and we will all enjoy our day there. Her courteous tone and controlled gestures kill the bawdy atmosphere and the men rise obediently and stumble toward the exit. Hiroshi-san is the last to leave and before heading to the small, mirrored elevator located just outside Amber, he bows low to Lucy and I.

"Sayonara Lucy-san, Evie-san," he says formally.

We smile and bow lower. "Arigato gozaimasu. Sayonara Hiroshi-san. Sumimasen."

I flop down on one of the leather couches and light my winding-down cigarette. The table is scattered with half-empty glasses and overflowing ashtrays and the air is a clammy mix of sweat, smoke and the fragments of drunken conversations. It makes me feel tired and dirty and old.

Lucy slides down beside me, wrapping a grubby coat around her bony frame.

"Wanna share a cab, Evie darling?" she asks tiredly, grabbing a couple of cigarettes from my pack.

"Sure," I say, picking up the wooden coasters I've hidden and shoving them into my bag. I'm exhausted and I don't feel like talking so I'd prefer to get a taxi on my own but it's safer with two and at least I'll save a few yen.

"Give me five," says Lucy and goes to pick up the leftover food from the kitchen. I don't know why she does that. It's been sitting there for hours and it's not like she can't afford to buy her own.

In the taxi Lucy leans her head against the window and begins to cry silently. The driver stares at her in the rearview mirror.

"What's wrong, Satellite?"

"Nothing sweetie, I'm just tired."

"Come on. You've been wound up all night so something's the matter. Hiroshi-san was pawing you tonight. Is that getting to you? I know you say he's not a chikan but I reckon he's a bit of a sleazebag."

"No, he's all right, I can handle him. It's just that things are getting weird here. I've been hostessing for three years and I've never felt this unsafe. Those manga pictures are freaking me out and I'm pretty sure it's Trick trying to scare me. I owe him a lot of money and if I don't pay him now he'll make me do something I don't want to do. He's made other girls who owe him money sleep with customers, who pay him back on their behalf."

"Get serious. He can't do that."

Lucy rolls her eyes. "Evie, you're so naïve sometimes. Do you think I'd make something like that up? That's why those girls took off for India."

I digest this information, a hot curve of anger in my chest. The smell from her bag of tempura prawns is filling the cab and making me nauseous. I roll down the window.

"Tell Trick to get lost. He can't make you do anything. You're a modern woman for Chrissake. You're supposed to be empowered."

Lucy shakes her head in frustration. "Evie, you don't get it. You need to accept that it's different for women here. Your ideas about equality don't apply, especially to hostesses. 'When in Rome', remember? What Trick wants, Trick gets. He makes the rules."

"Jesus, Lucy! Trick's a pseudo hippy with a big ego and a wandering eye. I don't know why you're so scared of him. How much money do you owe, anyway?"

"Trust me, darling, he's deceptive and I should know. I owe him 15 thousand US – he makes us pay in dollars."

I pull out my cigarettes and offer her one. "15k! Bloody hell,

Lucy. What for?"

Lucy stares at her knees, her pale skin a smudge against the night. "This and that. A couple of bad business deals. I won't bore you with the details."

I roll my eyes. Goddamn druggies. "That's a bummer. Why don't you sell something from your Wish List? I'm sure you can make some extra cash that way. Advertise a Sayonara Sale and once you've sold your things tell everyone you've changed your mind about leaving."

"I plan to but that'll take a while. I told Trick I'd give him the money a month ago and I think my grace period is up."

"Don't you have any savings? You must've earned bucketloads over the years."

"Not much. You know I'm not much good at saving. Is there any chance you could…" she trails off and picks at a hangnail.

I look out into the black. Never lend money to a junkie. "Sorry Satellite. That's my money for my trip and I need to keep moving. Osaka is driving me crazy."

"Evie, it'd only be for a couple of weeks, darling. Just to get Trick off my back. He said he'd be over tomorrow morning to talk to me about it and I know what that means. Trick only gives you so much rope before he starts having conversations with his fists."

I think of Lucy's fragile frame. She'd be no match for a violent Trick, but who's to say she's telling the truth? You can't really trust anyone here.

"I'd really like to help you out Satellite but I can't lend you $15,000. I can lend you five grand, if that'll keep Trick off your back but you need to pay me back before I leave."

Lucy looks out the window at the dark shapes of houses and apartment blocks whizzing past, jiggling her leg up and down against the seat.

"It's not enough. He wants the lot. What if I give you some of the things from my Wish List as a bond? You can choose whatever you want. I've got a couple of diamond rings, which are pretty valuable but there's heaps of other stuff too. Come on Evie, we're on our own over here. We have to look after each other."

I light up another cigarette and consider Lucy's offer. I remember Katherine Daniels' father, all sweaty shirt and desperation. Maybe I could hold onto the rings and a couple of other things until Lucy organizes the money for me. She showed me the ropes when I first got here and protected me from Mama. Perhaps I owe her for that.

"Please Evie-chan," Lucy pleads.

I groan inwardly. Never lend money to a junkie. Haven't you learnt? "OK, OK! I'll come over tomorrow before the dohan and choose some things and then transfer the money to your account. But you have to pay me back in two weeks, tops."

Lucy sighs, a long, sweet sound. "Thank you, Evie honey. You're a lifesaver. Can you transfer it tonight online though? I want to call Trick and tell him I've got the money so he leaves me alone. I'm scared of what he might do if I let him down again."

I look at her, suspicion curling in the base of my spine. Lucy slips off a ring and hands it to me. "Here take this, sweetie. I know it's not enough but I'm good for the rest. I promise."

"Hostesses' honour?" I ask, holding out my hand and crooking my pinky finger.

Lucy hooks her pinky onto mine. "Hostesses' honour," she says grinning, gap-teeth white against the dark.

Lucy and I head into Banana House and Sandra's slumped across the table with half a bottle of sake and some shooter glasses in front of her. I guess the rest of the party has gone to bed or gone home.

"Hey, it's the hostesses with the mostest. What's up?" she slurs.

"Not much," I say, scanning everyone's shelves for some food to nick. Sandra has a couple of packets of dried miso soup and I pocket one. Matt's food patch is looking pretty bare, which is strange because he's big on nutrition. He still has a couple of cans of tuna though so I take one and add it to my stash. I figure he'll stock up tomorrow so he won't miss it.

"Matt's locking most of his food in his room now," says Sandra looking at me slyly. "Think he got sick of everyone taking his stuff."

"Really. You a thief, then?"

"I'm not the thief around here," Sandra mutters. "Whatever... come and have a drink. Even you, Lucy."

Lucy kicks off her shoes and slips on a pair of slippers from the messy pile by the door.

"Home sweet home," she says. "I remember it well."

"How is it up at the palace?" Sandra asks Lucy, pushing a shooter full of sake across the table.

"OK, gets a bit lonely. I never thought I'd say it but I miss this place sometimes."

"God, this dive," Sandra snorts. "I can't wait to get out."

"Me too," I say downing my shot and shoving some seaweed crackers into my mouth. "If I never have to wipe Matt's shaving hair and the mould off the shower walls again, it will be too soon. Hey Sandra, you got anything else to eat?"

"Jeez you're a scammer. Why don't you ever buy your own food? I guess I've got a Bento you can have. It's two days old but it should be OK."

"What's in it?"

"Teriyaki chicken and rice. Do you want me to nuke it in the microwave?"

There's nothing else to eat and I can't be bothered going to Lawsons to buy snacks so I nod and say thanks.

The microwave rings and I grab the lukewarm chicken, spearing some grayish flesh into my mouth. Tastes pretty old but it will fill the nagging ache in my stomach for now.

"Guess what we have to do tomorrow?" Lucy asks Sandra.

"Go on dohan!" she yells, pumping the air drunkenly with her fist.

"How'd you know?"

"I was a hostess for three months remember? Then I realised the money wasn't worth the assault so I decided to teach Conversational English instead. That's a different kind of hell but at least I don't have to show my legs unless I want to. I don't know how you girls can stand it. And look what's happened to Katherine Daniels," Sandra mutters. "What a waste."

Lucy downs her shot and starts jiggling her leg again. I wish she'd stop doing that. It's starting to bug me. "Nobody knows what's happened to Katherine Daniels. That's part of the problem," she says, voice as high and thin as a bird's wing. "For all we know she's taken off to Vietnam or Morocco for a holiday without telling anyone. Anyway, I'm good at hostessing and it's better money than I could earn back home. I don't even have a highschool diploma."

Sandra snorts. "For fuck's sake, Lucy! You're even crazier than usual if you think Katherine Daniels is holidaying in Morocco. They'll find her in the Dotombori River or at the end of a dark alley somewhere. We all know that. As for school, you could go back and get your diploma. Evie finished... she's halfway through a law degree."

They both look at me as if I've got chicken hanging out of my teeth. Lucy's face is moonstone white, eyes so huge and dark you could swim in them. I spoon some greasy rice into my mouth and kick Sandra under the table.

"Shut up, Sandra. You don't know what's happened to Katherine Daniels any more than the rest of us. Anyway, I'm not sure about Law. I think I might want to be a photographer. You guys know that I'm only doing this for a few months so I can earn enough money to buy a decent camera then I'm off to

Thailand and Alaska to shoot the Northern Lights. I'm just passing through, remember?"

Sandra laughs and stares at me as if she's seen something behind my blank. "That's your story and you're sticking to it, huh? Well, I'm going to bed. Enjoy your dohan and keep it down in the morning will ya? I want to sleep in."

She stumbles into her bedroom and slams the door. I look over at Lucy. "Come on Satellite. Let's go upstairs to my room and I'll transfer the money to your account. I'll be over tomorrow morning to choose whatever I want from your Wish List. Quick, before I change my mind."

My alarm goes off at 9.00am. I groan and switch it to snooze for ten minutes. Then I roll off my futon and walk downstairs to the shower, my mind off and running like train tracks, a sour taste in my mouth.

Now that there's no sake taking the edge off things, I'm not sure about this deal I've done with Lucy. A muscle in my temple throbs. Not much I can do about it now. A promise is a promise.

I make an instant coffee and pull The Japan Times from the letterbox and unfold it. Katherine Daniels stares out from the front page, smiling and happy in another time. Sandra was right. She isn't holidaying in Morocco.

Dead hostess found in barrel!
Police made a grisly find at the back of a warehouse in Umeda yesterday evening. The remains of British tourist, Katherine Daniels, were found in a drum behind two metal skips, filled with rubbish. Ms Daniels has been identified via dental records.

Ms Daniels, who had been working at the popular Sakura Club in Shinsaibashi the night she disappeared, had been missing since July this year.

Police are appealing for information and currently interviewing a number of persons of interest.

I flick on the news. Katherine's father is pushing through a media scrum in London. He's lost weight, looks old and bereft. The journalists are shoving microphones and cameras at him, demanding a comment about his dead child. His hands flail across his face and he stumbles through the pack but they don't let up. They ask how he feels about this terrible development, what he'll do if they find the killer, if he'd like to make a public tribute to his beautiful, much-loved, only girl.

I turn off the TV. I bow my head and whisper a prayer for Katherine, her dad and the long, rolling emptiness ahead. I don't know why. I can't be sure anyone hears or cares; only that this is what I know of sadness, what I understand of grief.

The kitchen is quiet and empty, so I sit at the table for a long time until the white-noise retreats.

Nobody is up yet, so at least I'll get some hot water this morning. I stare at myself in the mirror. I've seen better days. After only a few months on the job I've developed hostess skin: grey and pimply with dark circles under my eyes. I cover up the worst of the damage with some makeup and blow-dry my hair.

Lucy lives just a couple of blocks away in Yuho Mansion, a squat grey building of eight apartments joined by a communal roof garden. Except there's no garden on the roof, just a couple of rusty clotheslines and three broken chairs.

I walk up to Lucy's place on the third floor. Her door is slightly ajar but I knock on it anyway. I stand there for a minute but there's no answer so I knock louder then push it open.

"Satellite, you here?" I call, swapping my flip-flops for house slippers and stepping into the tiny kitchen. I look around me and my temple throbs. The kitchen is bare and the fridge is flapping open.

I stride across to Lucy's bedroom and pull the paper door

across. Her futon is stripped and rolled up neatly, the sheets and blankets folded in a pile on the floor. I push her cupboard door open and the coat hangers jangle. A lone shirt lies in a crumpled heap in the corner.

I sit on the rolled futon and drop my head into my hands. I'm too tired to cry.

Never lend money to a junkie.

I don't know how long I've been sitting there when I hear a soft padding across the floor and I look up and see Trick standing above me, his dreadlocks pulled back in a bright red bandanna.

"Hey Evie baby, what's up? Where's our amigo, Lucy? You helping her move apartments or something?"

I try to focus on Trick's eyes. He clicks his fingers a couple of times in front of my face.

"Evie, are you cool? Have you taken something? You look pretty spaced out baby."

"No," I say. I feel like I'm looking at Trick through a long, tunnel. Everything is translucent, fading away. "Lucy's taken something though. All my money. She's probably on a plane right now."

"Whooo. Evie-chan. Back up sistergirl! What do you mean on a plane? Lucy and I had a little business deal."

"I know all about your business deal you drug-dealing fuck. I lent Lucy the money to pay you back and she's up and left with it. All of it."

Trick takes a couple of steps back and laughs softly. "Has she now. Well, well, well. Maybe it's karma, baby." He rocks gently back and forth on his heels.

"Is that all you've got to say? That it's karma? That was my money for my camera gear and my trip. I was set to leave in about a month. Anyway, if it's my karma it's your karma too and you're out of pocket by 15 grand so I don't know why you're smiling."

Tricks looks puzzled and laughs again. "Easy baby, easy. You seem a little confused. Lucy owes me 500 bucks not 15 grand. I don't let anyone run up big debts, especially skanky hostesses with drug issues. I'll get my cash off Mama from the wages she owes Lucy for this month. I'm sitting pretty, Evie-chan. Don't need to worry about my karma."

The knot in my temple unfolds and a haze comes up between me and everything else. Trick is just a blurred shape but I know he's probably telling the truth. I light up a cigarette, draw the smoke in deep and count to five before I exhale. I do it again and the world starts to fall into focus. Trick's leaning against the kitchen cupboards drumming his fingers against the bench.

"Hey baby, did you hear the news about Katherine Daniels?"

I nod, unable to speak.

"You hostesses better watch your backs. There's some crazy karma going down. Earth-to-Evie-chan! You hearing me, baby? Understand what I'm saying?"

I know what Trick's saying. He's threatening me or giving me a heads up, but all I can think about is my lost cash and if it's somehow connected to Katherine Daniels and the story she's become.

That's all Katherine is now. News. A warning. A cautionary footnote in a traveller's tale.

I tell Sandra what Lucy's done and she says that maybe it's a good thing because I might think twice about working at Amber now. I don't know why she's so worried about me hostessing.

"Maybe you should set up Hostesses Anonymous," I say, "just in case the people who want to get out need some Twelve Step support."

Sandra laughs but her coal eyes flash and she starts running her fingers through her hair, so I say maybe she's right and I'd been thinking about teaching anyway.

"Cool," she smiles. "I'll get you a job at UIES. They'll hire anyone with a pulse who can string a sentence together."

"Thanks for the build up," I say.

She grins and throws me a spliff, tells me she'll make some calls.

UIES offers me six nine-hour shifts and Sunday off, and I pick up some privates who pay 4000 yen an hour to hear me speak. I spend a lot of time discussing the difference between run and running and the merits of shopping as a hobby, and after a while I want to throw myself off the Dotombori Bridge. I don't have to hold anyone's hand to stop them groping me, but teaching McEnglish for sixty hours a week is another kind of beast.

The idea of travelling the world taking photographs lies like a promise under my skin. I tell people I'll head to Thailand first and figure the rest out as I go. That I might even work it so I can finally follow the sun.

I bump into Trick a couple of days before I leave town. I'm at the Saturday Flea Market holding a Sayonara Sale to earn extra cash for my trip. He tells me Lucy's been in touch and she's doing OK. She's backpacking through South America and has picked up some Spanish. She's getting into yoga and steering clear of the drugs.

"I think she's sorry about the money," Trick says picking up a Carol King CD I'm offloading. "Maybe one day she'll pay us both back, Evie baby, or maybe she'll pay us back in another lifetime. Man, I dig this singer. She's not really a babe but she's a pretty cool chick."

I glare at him. "You got your money back from Mama didn't you? So Lucy only needs to pay me back, but I'm not holding my breath. I'd say that money's long gone. Probably up her nose, or into a vein."

"Whoa, Evie-chan. Don't let bitterness cloud your heart, baby. It doesn't suit you and no-one likes an angry chick. Let it go. Let life flow." Trick looks me up and down and gives one of his long, low whistles. "May I say that you're looking very righteous, baby. You've lost some weight. Pity you didn't drop those pounds when you were hostessing. Could have made yourself some serious bucks."

I finger Trick's Zippo, which is shoved deep in my pocket. "You want that Carol King CD?" I ask. "It's 2000 yen."

Trick strokes his dreadlocks and grins. "I can get this new for 2500 yen at Rockin' Records. That's not much of a discount, Evie-chan."

"Take it or leave it. Last chance today."

Trick sighs and pulls two 1000 yen notes out of his pocket. "OK, you're killing me but here's a donation for your travel fund. You drive a hard bargain Evie-chan. You need to soften up and let go of your bitterness, baby."

I pocket the notes and think about asking Trick about the manga cartoons and if he and Lucy were in cahoots. I wonder if he knows if she really owed anyone 15 grand or had taken me for a sucker from day one. I guess it wouldn't matter what he told me, though. Like I said, you can't really trust anyone here. You never know who's lying and who's telling the truth.

I put the CD cover in a paper bag and give it to Trick as I slip the disc under my shirt, where it lies cool and smooth against my skin. When I get back to Banana House I'll return it to Sandra's music collection.

Like she said, Carol King is her hands-down favourite singer.

7
Dear
Josie Henley-Einion

Author

Josie Henley-Einion grew up in the Midlands and attended Bangor University in North Wales, studying Psychology and Linguistics. From 2002 to 2005, Josie studied for Manchester Metropolitan University's online MA in Creative Writing, during which her debut novel *Silence* (Legend Press, 2008) was written. Josie now lives in Cardiff, South Wales, with her civil partner Alys, their son and a host of furry friends. Her short stories have been published in *Seven Days* and *Eight Hours* (Legend Press).

Dear,

I'm writing this letter to you on the train out to a conference. I like trains because I can read or write and don't get as sick. The bus is cheaper but all I do is sleep and still don't feel rested. There is much more to see from a train window. Outside of a bus there are simply miles of motorway embankments and other vehicles, the hypnotising stretch of white lines. In contrast, railway tracks follow fields and rivers, nestling up to private back gardens. From here I can see inside someone else's life, from the rubber gloves on a windowsill to the cat warming itself on a shed roof.

The difference in price doesn't bother me, as I'll be claiming expenses for the fare. I'm supposed to be working so here I am on the train with my laptop being very busy and important.

Of course I'm not working. I've looked over the presentation but I've rehearsed it so much already that I'm bored with it. I hope I can maintain a level of interest so I don't put my audience to sleep! That would be quite ironic given the subject matter. I know that my voice can have a soporific effect because I see the undergrads' eyes glaze over during tutorials. Or that might be too many late nights; too much alcohol and sex.

Do you remember that? They say that if you remember the Sixties then you weren't there. I feel the same about being an undergrad. It feels like a lifetime ago. It actually is a lifetime ago! The students I teach now weren't even born when I was their age. In another reality, they could be my sons and daughters. Doesn't bear thinking about. They have no concept of student grants or life without computers. I'm sure some of them have not been to the stacks, at least not to look anything up. I've heard that people go there for sex because they get more privacy than in halls.

Whenever I think about our time back then, I remember the half pints of milk hanging out of windows in plastic bags, the smoky basement bar where you could walk right past someone without noticing them, that coveted end seat next to the pillar in the main lecture theatre where you could sleep propped up. I remember you in your pulling jeans and me trying to keep track of the endless stream of hopefuls beating down your door. It's a world away from today's micro-managed career students. Or is it? Is it just the surface that is different and deep down it's all the same? Same coffee and cramming, same sweaty socks and sex.

There I go again. That's the third time I've mentioned student sex. I'm appalled with myself, really. I wonder if it's got something to do with turning forty. I'm starting to feel as if I've missed the shiny boat and it's already pulling into harbour for the next cruise and all I'm left is a leaky old rowing boat. Excuse the analogy. Probably something Freudian there.

I do love my analogies. Like this journey which could be seen as a state between states, in comparison to a dream state. I am neither here nor there but somewhere in between, ever in motion yet remaining still. It is the paradox of travelling at high speed. How surprised the Victorians were that their lungs did not explode when their trains exceeded twenty miles per hour! I am rather glad of that, or this journey would take the full day. As it is, two hours is long enough for my comfort.

I'm feeling quite uneasy on this seat. Slightly on edge like a bed of nails. I think that my bones have lost their youthful springiness and become hard and unresponsive, like the body they're encased in. Sometimes if I sit for too long in the same position it feels as if I'd have to break something to straighten it all out. My joints crackle as if they've grown a layer of barnacles. God I'm not that old, surely!

The reason I'm writing this is that I've been mulling over what you said the other day. Well, 'mulling' is probably an understatement. Obsessing could go some way to describing it. You asked me, albeit in a joking way, why it was that I'd never found love. You listed all of your failed relationships, which took some time I have to say and even included people I hadn't known about, and said that you thought I was lucky. I almost choked on my sushi. Do you remember this conversation? We were a tad drunk and it was late. It was never mentioned the next morning so I wonder if you remember. But you'd obviously been thinking about it or you wouldn't have brought it up.

I gave you an evasive answer at the time, I seem to recall. About how it is better to have loved and lost and all that, then changed the subject. Covered my embarrassment by cleaning up the spilled rice. I was shaken to realise that you think I've never found love. I had thought that it was patently bloody obvious who I loved and that you had avoided noticing. I didn't tell you the truth. Could not have looked you in the eye and told you that the truth is I've been in love with the same person for twenty years or so. For one thing you'd have asked me to name the person.

Letters are different. I don't have to worry that you'll interrupt before I can get it all out. And I can re-read and rewrite to be sure I've said what I want to say before posting. I always found writing an easier method of communication than talking.

When you were backpacking in India and I was researching mice in mazes, I loved the letters we sent to each other. I still have yours in my bedroom. I wonder if you still have mine. It might be interesting to read them again. Did I go on an awful lot about the mice and the mazes? You were very eloquent about the hostels you stayed in and the people you met. You never spared me details of your conquests.

We see each other so often these days that it seems daft to write, apart from the occasional email. I wonder how many people do write to each other in that way anymore? I know this isn't really the same because I'm doing this on the computer and can edit, but even so a proper letter is better than a few lines of txtspk, is it not?

I'm going off on a tangent I know. This is what I do isn't it? Avoid answering. The question was about love. It is a sticky subject though. It takes a long time to disentangle feelings and work out whether it is love or lust. And if it is love, what sort of love. Is it the same for you? I mean, I don't mean to be rude but your relationships seem to be the 'dive in anyway' type. From the outside at least. Perhaps you simply process your feelings quicker than I do.

That is the big difference between us, and maybe why I prefer letters to talking. You are the veritable image of the extreme left brain whereas I'm the extreme right brain. I sometimes wonder how we ever managed to be friends. You, so open with your heart on your sleeve, forever giving it to strangers. You say that I'm unemotional, that I'm too analytical and don't allow myself to feel: in essence that I have no feelings.

I realise that I've just been extremely analytical, but I have to tell you that I do feel. I feel so much.

When you talk to me about a new lover and I sit there with a fixed smile, inside I'm dying. Your words are a line of Riverdance, clogs and all, with you as Michael Flatley trampling over my non-existent feelings, beating them into the floor in time to the music of your exuberance.

Sometimes I feel so much that I have to lie down or I might fall off the wall of emotion. The world collapses inwards with no structure – nothing concrete. It is like looking down and feeling the dizziness of vertigo as great waves of passion crash over me from no apparent source. Perhaps this is why I appear unemotional: because I compartmentalise and control it. Otherwise I would be overcome and unable to function. Therefore I exist in a continual state of anxiety as I keep the feelings at bay and concentrate on walking a tightrope over the abyss. This is why I prefer mazes and equations to people. Even mice are tricksters with their random twitchings. So it is not that I am unfeeling, but maybe too feeling?

I can count my friends on one finger. How is it that I am friends with you when this is how I feel? I wonder whether I live a vicarious emotional life through you. You appear to have enough expression of feeling for both of us. Although I have but one friend, my friendship has never waned in all these years.

You come and go like the seasons. Each time a new lover appears, you're off for the weeks, months or years it takes for boredom to set in. Even with both sexes to choose from in your voraciousness, you still manage to endure an occasional fallow period.

I'm the perennial, always sitting and waiting for you to come trawling back with your tale of woe and yet more debts and more children. It never ceases to amaze me how easily you sprout children, like a budding hydra, as if no other person were needed. And they stumble in your wake, wide eyed and worshipping.

I wonder if that's how you see me: as one of your disciples. I have wished for so long that I could be more than this. Every time you're single we get closer and I work myself up to telling you but I'm never quite daring enough. The biggest worry of course is that you'll reject me, laugh or patronisingly turn me down and then we'd drift apart again, and you would always be uncomfortable in my presence. I'd lose you as a friend. That friendship is more important to me than anything I might imagine could pass between us as love.

I may have to delete the above few paragraphs before I send this. I've been a coward for so long, what makes me brave now?

Sitting on a train watching the fields and bizarre station names going past, I'm distanced from you enough to say the things that I can't say to your face. What is it about a journey that makes me so introspective? It might be the rumbling feelings of movement, vibrating through my body and jiggling it all up, unsettling the thoughts that have been contained, like bubbles in a vial of liquid.

It might be the isolation, the lack of eye contact with my fellow passengers who seem afraid that I'm a murderer or rapist or something worse like an evangelist who will collar and regale them with revelations from my particular personal philosophy. It might simply be the absence of anything else to do. Travelling is all about the wait.

I remember that time in the airport when we were checking in two hours early and I complained about how that was longer than the flight time. I joked that in the future when the instant transportation device had been invented, it would not cut down the journey time because one would still have to queue up, go through the equivalent of customs checks and baggage handling, all the related paraphernalia.

I started getting excited by the idea that I'd come up with a brilliant plot for a short story. You told me that it had already been done by Arthur C. Clark. You didn't even look up from your novel to say it. If you had, then you might have seen my expression deflating. You would have your evidence that I do indeed have feelings. Perhaps all this time you've been running a randomised control trial on the question of whether my feelings exist.

I'm getting out at the next stop now so had better flick this off and have my bag ready. I'll write more from the conference centre.

Dear,

I'm now at the conference. It's very interesting so far. It's great to see the people from France. Sleep research is big over there! We've been allocated our rooms and we're going to have an introductions session quite soon so we can get networking. They say that in conferences, the networking is the most beneficial part. I am really looking forward to the keynote speech tonight, though. He is an eminent researcher and has been working on sleep and dreaming for years. He even knew the bloke who studied the sleepwalking cats!

My presentation is scheduled for the first session tomorrow morning. So I won't be drinking tonight. I'm quite hungry. We had coffee available when we arrived but the dinner is scheduled for at least an hour after I usually eat. You will laugh I know but I'm a creature of habit and my stomach is rumbling. I did not think to bring anything to snack on. I'm not used to waiting for someone else to serve the food. My own culinary skills have been sharpening lately, as my new set of sushi knives will contest.

I hope you enjoy your night out tonight. I am thinking of you getting yourself ready to hit the clubs. I hope they have been warned! I have to go and hob-knob now. Probably won't have time to write much this weekend but I will hopefully write more on the train on the way home.

Dear,

It's all going on in the bar. I've done all the networking I can do and it's actually got to the flirting stage now, so I've left them to it. It does nothing for me except make me feel old. I did drink some wine with dinner even though I kept saying that I wasn't going to and now I've got a whisky to help me sleep.

Being a sleep researcher and knowing that alcohol has a detrimental effect on sleep patterns does not stop me from believing in that old adage for myself. I am not nervous about the presentation tomorrow but somehow I feel on edge.

I have to relate to you an incident that took place this evening. It was quite unnerving and one of the reasons that I have come upstairs early. I was talking to one of my fellow researchers. We have been working on the sleep and memory project for some time but have never had a personal conversation. I had thought that she was like me, someone who preferred to keep private life and work life separate.

We were chatting about the project. You remember I told you about the tabletop mazes, adapted from my PhD all those years ago in fact! I built the main board with slots so that the maze pattern could be altered with the walls being interchanged. This was the basis of it originally when it was simply training and reinforcement, for operant conditioning. This year I've been measuring the impact of sleep on the training, in other words whether more sleep makes for better learning. My colleague has been studying the dreaming side of it, although when it comes to mice we cannot say that they are dreaming: only describe the REM sleep pattern. This in essence has been our debate all along, and in the bar she attempted to draw some of the other delegates over to her side.

The discussion was lively but I believe that I held my position well. I am essentially a pragmatist. I do not believe that it is possible to study something that cannot be observed. Dreams are subjective and the experience degrades on the moment of waking, perhaps before. The conscious mind translates whatever nonsense has emerged during sleep and fits it into a narrative format so that the true random form has been disguised.

My colleague's argument is that it is the dreaming itself (or for mice, their REM sleep) that influences learning, measured by performance on retest of a task. I hold that it is sleep only and nothing else can be inferred.

We have had this debate several times, however this is the first time it has occurred in front of an alcohol fuelled audience, where I was forced to shout to make my voice heard. This aspect was not what unnerved me; in fact I was quite exhilarated and poured myself another glass of wine as the conversation drifted towards the German contingency's work.

That was when my heretofore professional colleague turned to me and murmured, "You're knocking it back a bit tonight, aren't you?" I sputtered a little, perhaps, from the shock but did not reply.

She did not take the hint from my silence but continued in a similar over-familiar vein. I wonder if she had had rather too much herself. She began to relate several minor incidents with other staff in the department, to which I only half listened as I cautiously sipped my wine. Somewhere amongst this rambling thread, she mentioned the 'milk thief'. This is an ongoing situation and notices have been placed in the departmental kitchen.

I think that I may have sighed at this point because she stopped short and looked at me. "Well I suppose you're above all that, are you?" she asked, not too politely.

I replied that I did think it rather childish at which point she bristled and I half expected a tirade against my own person. However, a strange thing happened.

She smiled quite deliberately and put her hand on my knee, leaning forward and displaying ample cleavage, which I suppose was intentional or perhaps she was more inebriated than I had thought. I jolted backwards, spilling my drink slightly.

"You need to loosen up," she said and brought her chair closer to mine.

I bit back the ready reply that indeed I did need to loosen my collar slightly and preferably well away from her. Again she missed the hint that my rigid body should have given that this situation was entirely unwelcome. Instead, her hand moved further up my leg and with her face close to mine she whispered some additional thoughts, which I was far too flustered to hear. I believe that she may have been inviting me to her room (which is unfortunately just next to mine).

By this time I had broken into a sweat and stood abruptly. I 'knocked back' my wine and this is the point at which I ordered the whisky. I was in half a mind to take her up on the offer and would need all the courage I could get. I do wonder whether I may rely a little more heavily on alcohol than I should. All to no avail, however, as I think that she had taken my dithering for a rejection. When I turned back I saw that her attention had diverted towards another professor.

Relief and disappointment, unlikely bedfellows that they are, clinked together like the ice in my glass. I stood for a moment quite undecided, but before someone else could accost me, I felt that this would be an appropriate moment to sneak upstairs.

I walked up the back stairwell and along a deserted corridor to this room, in a rather chilly wing of the conference centre, all the while berating myself for a coward and thinking of how you would laugh at my predicament. I wondered what you would have done in that situation. Oh, I'm sure that you could very easily have slipped inside her room and warmed it up for her. I pause for a moment as I imagine the scene, but the image blurs once you are behind the door.

How you would have got from the invitation to the consummation is the mystery to me. When it comes to such matters, I feel as though I am still a fumbling teenager. I wonder if she had expected me to be an experienced lover.

I have heard nothing from the room next door, for which I am quite glad, as I have had enough of being a witness to others' pleasure. Perhaps she has found someone else's room more convivial.

I can't help feeling a slight bitterness and definite frustration that I am yet again facing the night alone. Much as I chastise myself for remaining chaste, I believe that I would loathe myself so much more had I succumbed to her charms. I dare not think how I would feel tomorrow morning, waking up to the realisation that I had betrayed my one true love. The thought disgusts me. I need some more whisky and an abrupt change of subject to shake off this repugnance.

I've been wondering what you're up to. I miss you.

Yes it's stupid, it's not like we live together but we've been seeing a lot of each other lately. I miss you and can't help feeling jealous of whoever you're talking to right now. It's also rather annoying that the phone signal appears to be out of range so if you are trying to text me then it won't get through.

I read through the first part of this letter and I think that it will be heavily edited by the time it reaches you, but I will keep this version for myself. I have my own little private store of letters that I've never sent to you. That's not too stalker-ish, is it?

It is a very strange thing to write something on the computer and never print it, never speak it out loud. The letters on the screen are only dots, each character saved in computer memory as a series of zeros and ones. Does that mean that the words do not exist? They are ethereal, rather like dreams, neither existing nor not existing but stuck somewhere subjectively between the two states.

If the written word is only a symbol of the spoken word, writing without speaking is unreal. But is speaking real? Each utterance of speech is symbolic of the physical world item that it represents, and how many of these items would exist without speech itself? We live in a self-perpetuating myth of representation where the only truly real thing is an action performed without thought. To be human is to be false, where the only honesty is to follow animal instinct.

I am quite philosophical tonight. I can't blame it on the movement of the train anymore but perhaps I can blame the whisky. I am getting quite giggly over the thought of writing all of this to you; that you might one day read it.

It is possible that one day I will simply grab you and kiss you. How I've thought about this! But again, as soon as the thoughts slip in, the action is stalled. And I'm quite convinced by now that this letter will never be sent, at least in its current form.

This letter is a tree falling in the forest with no-one there to hear it. These things that I've been talking about, these feelings, might not be real. My love is the sound of one hand clapping. The cat is not yet out of the bag. Or are you already aware? Perhaps it is a Schrödinger's cat; that I will not know whether it is out or not until I open the bag.

I can tell that I'm drunk now that I've slipped into cliché.

Until it is printed, sent or read out, until it has a recipient, it may as well not have been stated. But I will always know what I have said. I am my own recipient. Therefore it exists because it is viewed which in Descartian terms, or perhaps more rightly Berkeley-ian, means that I am God. The logical conclusion of this is that I am omnipotent within this sphere and able to control everything. I can create a page of rambling text and instantly remove it. I delete therefore I am.

More whisky, imaginary bartender!

I can live in this fantasy world quite comfortably, so long as intruders such as earlier this evening do not interrupt it. I have to work, of course, to teach and write papers, to travel from home to work, keep the flat tidy and feed myself. But all of this may be done in a state of half-awareness while I anticipate my alone time.

Once I am inside my own head, I can be anything and do anything. The hollow reality of our existence does not matter in the non-material, it has no matter and therefore cannot matter. I need no longer be the awkward old buffoon that others take me for. I do wonder if that is how you see me, or do you see the real me?

I have always thought that you do see the reality that is me, behind the façade. Lately, though, I wonder if I have disguised myself so well that you don't see me as you used to, as we used to be always together.

I wonder if the disguise is so encompassing as to deceive even myself. Perhaps I really am a fool. I have certainly been made a fool of enough times.

I wrote a poem on a paper serviette while we waited to be served:

I wanted to kiss you
But I was afraid.
"Are you afraid of me?" You asked.
You smiled. This was funny for you.
"No," I said. "I am afraid of myself."

You will say that this is not a poem because it does not rhyme. Ignoring as you usually do the fundamental question that it raises. Who is the I here, and who is the you? You probably don't even remember the incident to which this refers.

It happened approximately five years ago, at Christmas when mistletoe hung around the bar. Everyone else was kissing and you grabbed me as a joke. So funny it would have been, everyone laughing, but I turned away. I realised that this is how you see me: a joke.

This may be the reason that I fear rejection; that this is a very real fear and not simply my usual level of anxiety. And I am not entirely sure how I would react. I would not be able to cope with the rejection. I would have to kill myself, or you, or both of us.

It reminds me of that slick comment that people make when they're attempting to be seen as important: if I tell you then I'll have to kill you.

Please do not misunderstand me. I do not want to kill you; that is not a part of the fantasy. I would want you to turn to me and say that you feel the same and all this time, these myriad lovers, have been a smokescreen and you also were secretly pining for me.

I simply have not been able to see any evidence that this is the case, and this is what has stopped me from hitherto mentioning my own feelings. If you ever found out, if you laughed it off, that would be the point when it turned. That would be when the kiss became the kill.

It is interesting, is it not, how similar the word 'kiss' is to the word 'kill'? The lines of the l's in kill are straight as blades, where the s's swirl together like spooning lovers. With a penned letter the discrimination can be slight with some handwriters twirling or looping their l's and with others the s's becoming reduced to a single mark. Phonetically, the s and l are both in the alveolar region, it simply changes from a fricative to lateral approximant.

Words words words, to paraphrase Shakespeare. The substitution of one letter for another (twice) makes all the difference to the meaning of the word itself, and to the poem as a whole if it is repeated as you can see:

I wanted to kill you
But I was afraid.
"Are you afraid of me?" You asked.
You smiled. This was funny for you.
"No," I said. "I am afraid of myself."

The truth is that I am afraid. Afraid of what I might do, either way. Once it is out of the bag, how far will my passion go? Would I kils you, or kisl you? That is funny. I've had to break off for a moment to laugh at the absurdity.

No, I can never tell you about all of this kiss/kill business, even if I manage to tell you how I feel. I can scarcely tell myself. I shall probably delete this whole letter and start again tomorrow.

I have envisaged suicide. I do believe that this is how my life will end, eventually. We all have the right to decide when and where we die and I would rather this way than some chronic lingering disease. How close to the act I have found myself at various points in life. As a teen, how enamoured with the sight of my own blood I became. Always controlled, never allowing the cuts to become too deep or infected. Knowing it was wrong made it all the more desirable, secret and delicious. The fantasy of death became almost sexual, replayed in so many different scenarios.

To maintain the charade of modern society with all of its empty purpose, we require a moral code. Without this, those who have already decided they will die have no limitations to their behaviour. We see this in school shootings, and now in universities too, for shame.

What might a person, who knows that death is imminent, has already planned for it, of what might that person be capable? For revenge or to prove a point, or simply out of boredom.

Shooting is such an American Dream; I would not be so crass. Guns appear to be easy on film and TV but in reality I'm sure that I'd fumble with the technology. Better the slice of the knife with which I am already so adept.

The knife is a more accessible instrument, hiding in plain view in everyone's kitchen. A blade is the primeval tool, what differentiated humans from animals so long ago. And the act itself has the synchronicity of metaphor that I relish. Your rejection may feel like a knife to my heart, so what better way to illustrate this than to reciprocate? The cut and the thrust. The blade is capable of a delightful surgical precision; you can see how it would be right up my street so to speak.

But no. It will not happen. As I said, once the thoughts begin the action is stalled. It would require some overriding animalistic rage to take me to the point where I lifted the blade against someone else. But for myself, that is another matter, and one which continues to revisit.

Only I know that I can control myself. So long as I have something to live for, someone who relies on me and some sort of goal each day, I can stave off the inevitable. Mostly these thoughts visit me during long hours awake at night. Perhaps this is why I drink to sleep, to muffle those unwanted feelings.

I've finished the whisky. It was good, a single malt. I think it must have been expensive, but the price barely registered.

I must go to sleep now and try not to dream about the presentation. Or dream about sleeping, that's the worse kind as it gives me no rest.

Dear,

I am enjoying the conference. My presentation is over. I am quite relieved. Now I can take pleasure in the remainder of the seminars and relax before it is time to leave.

I was rather worse for wear this morning at breakfast. I can never sleep properly in a new bed. But thankfully the presentation went down well. I had a very interested response from one PhD student but it might simply be that she's looking for post-doc work.

I'm writing this at the back of the seminar room with half an ear on one of the other presentations, Sleep: The Final Frontier. It may be my front ear, ha ha. To all outside viewers I could be taking copious notes on the nature of non-REM sleep. The professor sitting next to me is dozing with his eyes open. He is obviously a veteran of second-day conference seminars.

I began a letter to you yesterday on the train here, but it became rather bland so I've discarded that and begun afresh. The journey was uneventful and last night was a bore. I think the presentation has been on my mind somewhat. Now it's done

I feel so much better. I didn't think that I was nervous but perhaps I was, just slightly.

A colleague of mine seems to have spent the night in someone else's room. I heard no movement from hers this morning (it is adjacent to my own) and yet she arrived at breakfast at almost the same time as myself. From a different direction. I have been scanning the delegates in an attempt to establish which of the other professors she has attached herself to.

It is not that I am disapproving, only that I hope she will not decide to leave the department to set up home with someone in Europe as this would cause unnecessary delays with our research.

As you are aware, in affairs of the heart I am no expert, but I have noticed that sometimes one falls in love with a wholly inappropriate and inconvenient target.

I've come to some realisations over the past few days. Mainly since our recent conversation when you asked me why I had not found love. Do you remember that? There is something I need to tell you regarding this topic. It is not easy. It is never easy to confess to living a lie. You think I'm not in love with anyone because I've never talked to you about it. I've never exposed myself to that extent. But what can I say?

Words are not enough to encompass the feeling I have. Words just slip around and turn over themselves with their own self-importance when in fact they are nothing, nothing at all compared to the strength of feeling they are so inadequate to convey.

I love you.

It feels so simple to say those three words, yet each is weighted with a heaviness of luggage that it drags around on broken wheels.

There is nothing that I can say that won't become a tired cliché once it is out of my mouth or onto the page. It is difficult to find the right way of saying it that will make you realise that it is not a joke, or some passing fancy. It is very difficult to say it in a sober state, easier to contemplate last night after a glass or two of wine. But I must be sure that you know I'm sober or you might think it's the drink talking.

I had thought that you must know; must have been able to see it burning behind my eyes as it burns me up inside when I look at you. You are a bright, hot sun and I am the cold planet orbiting but never fully turning my face to you for fear of a scorching. You might assume that the cold planet is ice and iron throughout but let me assure you that deep inside is a fiery molten core waiting to erupt at the slightest pressure.

These feelings have been smouldering for twenty years or more. When we first met during freshers' week, when we were both nineteen (so young it now seems and yet so mature we thought we were!) I was immediately attracted to you. Initially I thought you quite irritating, I admit, yet also fascinating.

I was not the only moth drawn to your flame, though, and I soon found that I was vying for your attention with some of the most popular students. I was so happy to snag your friendship with my expertise, but even then I am not sure that I had fallen in love. This came gradually, which is how I knew that it was not merely infatuation but a true and abiding love that would last as it has.

Do you remember that first experiment in our study partnership? The alcohol consumption survey. How we giggled when we discovered that the psychology students scored by far the highest, twice as high even as the medics! Are all psychology students so disturbed and disturbing? It appeared so then, and I doubt that it has changed.

Even then it became obvious that I would remain in the academic echelons when you entered the real world. Yet you did not shun me as some of the others did. They thought me intense and 'strange' (strange even for a psychology student!) but you understood. I always felt that you did anyway.

I can pinpoint the moment when I realised that I was in love with you, but that I would never be able to tell you so. It was the morning I awoke from that nightmare to find you still there, holding my bleeding hand. The others thought that I'd simply had too much to drink (which I probably had) and they laughed at my idiocy: climbing on the bar, breaking glasses against my head and goodness knows what else that I don't even remember. Only you realised that I was having an episode. I don't know how difficult it was for you to coax me down and drag me back to my room. I will always appreciate that you did this, cleaned my wounds and held me, listened to me chattering away all night until I finally drifted off and you stayed with me the whole time. I woke up with a mouth like salted velvet, full of self-loathing, to see the care in your eyes and I knew. You were there for the peaks and always there for the crash.

You are a caring, giving sort of person. You tell me that you need to be needed, and this is your problem. You attract needy people. How can you not see that you have attracted me?

I hate myself for not being able to tell you, and sometimes I hate you for not giving me enough time. Most of all I hate the people you bring into your world so easily, leaving me still on the outside. I hate them so much I could kill. I fantasise the slaughter in a Macbeth fashion, the dagger dripping blood. You'll all be murdered in your beds, ha ha.

Damn it.

Dear,

I'm writing this as I am on the train on my way home from the conference. I have twice now begun a letter to you and been unable to complete it. I don't know how to say what I want to say, but I am determined nonetheless to say it.

This weekend has been a journey of self-discovery. Sometimes it takes moving away from what is familiar to examine our home circumstances afresh. I have come to several realisations

I've loved you for years. At first it seemed like a crush that might wear off, but it's been burning inside me and growing until I can't bear it any longer. I have to tell you. Surely you already know. I have wondered if you would make a move but you never did, though you so easily moved in on others.

I feel certain that you will reciprocate, but if you do not then please don't let it affect our friendship. We are both mature enough to acknowledge our feelings and work around them.

On re-reading these letters I have had my eyes opened to some of the more fearsome aspects of my character. The anger and self-disgust that last night's letter demonstrated has appalled me. I am determined to never drink again. This will be difficult I know, but with you beside me, I am convinced that I will be able to remain positive and abstain. It appears to me that my more destructive side becomes apparent when I have been drinking. I feel sure that were I to remain sober, I could win your love. Will you allow me to attempt that?

I do not wish to sound mawkish. This is supposed to be a love letter. Allow me to begin again.

I love you. I have always loved you. You have been my world and without you I would die. You are like air to breath or sun to bathe in, water for the thirsty and rest for the tired. It sounds like a religion and in a way it is: I worship you.

What more can I say other than that I love you? There are no other words to convey this.

My feelings have gone beyond desire, beyond simple love, have reached manic proportions.

I believe that I may well be on the verge of something terrible. I don't know how to express it. Every time I try to encapsulate the feeling with words, it flits away again and I'm back to angry frustration.

I have ruined several letters with this strength of feeling. I am beating the keyboard, slamming each character in an attempt to capture its essence and control the flow of emotion. Why must I destroy everything? Yet each man kills the thing he loves; the brave man with a sword.

I have to begin again.

Dear,

I'm writing this on the train home. I don't have much time before the stop. I need to tell you something. I love you! I have loved you for so long and tried to tell you but each time I miss the moment. This time I know that I will catch you.

As soon as I get home I'll print this out and hand deliver it so that I am sure you'll have it. I have a good feeling about this and I know that we can talk about it. It may come as a shock to you so I can give you time but I feel very strongly that we should be together for the rest of our lives.

My darling, I wish that I could see your face as you read this; I wish that I could know in advance how you feel. I am excited and quite nervous but I know this is the right thing to do. I am glad that I have at last been able to grasp the valour and to articulate my feelings without spoiling the impression. To reiterate: I love you!

Dear,

I played your message when I got home. I came into the darkening house and saw the flashing red bulb lighting up my hall.

I am so glad that I did play it and not send all of the above in my fit of optimism. I know now that I can never send this letter.

It will never be the right time. I will forever be on the brink of telling you how I feel just as you turn up with a shiny new love. I hate them. Each one individually I hate with a venom that I cannot express. I now know what I need to do and this will begin with destroying these letters.

Dear,

Congratulations! I'm so glad for you. Let's get together and you can tell me all about how you met. Better still, why don't you both come over and I'll prepare a meal. Let's have sushi again. I am sharpening my knives. We can have a few drinks and catch up. Come tomorrow night so I have a chance to clean out the spare room and you can stay over. I'll tell you all about the conference. See you then! Bring wine!

8
Angel Wings
Brendan Telford

Author

Brendan Telford, despite having spent much of his adult life in urban settings, is a country born boy from Queensland, Australia. He has always had an affinity with the written word, when as a child he would make up stories while pretending to read the phone directory. Brendan is a teacher, music journalist, studied Creative Writing and Research as a Masters Degree, and has seen much of the world. His story *Angel Wings* is a road trip, involving love, loss, sex, death, hope… and butterflies. Brendan currently lives in London.

Xavier sat on the bonnet of the shark. He looked around at the MonarchWatch volunteers, all butterfly nets, floppy broad-brimmed hats, hiking boots and ankle protectors. Children, students, middle aged conservationists, senior citizens. All of them hunting the monarch.

He slid off the bonnet and turned to the two cases sitting next to him. He opened the first case and took out segments of the butterfly net. The lacquered dowel felt cool to the touch. He screwed the two segments together, attaching the bamboo hoop to the top section.

The net itself was made of Emma's bridal veil – at least it was getting used.

He placed the rubber grip of the handle in one hand, the leather handle of the second case in the other, and started off into the woods.

Xavier came to the perfect place after ten minutes. In that time he had seen many monarchs, but none of them would make it easy to capture them.

When in flight they were wary creatures. Elusive. No-one seemed to mind this – children's laughter echoed off the trees, bringing a smile to his face. It made the tagging process an adventure. The search for treasure coming to fruition when the butterfly fluttered at the back of a net. But the tagging was only the beginning.

He watched as the butterflies feasted on the nectar of a clump of wood violets growing beside a decaying log. Their wings captured the sun's rays as they broke through the web of the foliage above, moving to and fro to a hypnotic rhythm that only they could hear. Their orange markings glowed.

He moved towards them, his shoulders arched, aching with anticipation. A bead of sweat clung to the tip of his nose. Yet the monarchs did not move. Their undulating wings seemed to encourage the sweep of the net.

He knelt on the pine needles and moss-strewn floor. A quick count showed six butterflies were inside the bridal veil. He flipped open the second case, taking out a sheet of tags and the notebook, its red cover contrasting with the greenness of the surroundings.

24th August, Neenah, Wisconsin (44.19 N, -88.52 W)
– tagged six Danaus plexippus. Found feeding from Viola papilionacea in a wooded clearing. Tags used DOE611 – DOE616.

Xavier turned from the notebook and carefully flattened the net on the ground, ensuring the monarchs' wings were not damaged and instead closing them over their backs. They complied. He eased his hand up under the hoop and into the net, using his thumb and forefinger to grasp the closest thorax, gently bringing it out of its temporary prison.

Xavier held the butterfly in front of his face. The dappled sunlight pierced its wings. A golden hue emanated seemingly from within the wings, possibly the creature itself, cocooning both of them in cascading luminosity.

He let go of its thorax, placing it on his forefinger. Instead of fleeing, it remained there, its wings dancing. He felt the velvet of the auburn wings, interlaced with black, splashes of white dots bordering the tips. Its delicate features belied its true self – a being of splendour, courage, and hope. The sun heightened the colours into a burnt orange, fire, a phoenix.

A rustle from behind brought Xavier around, head spinning from the sudden movement. Before he could stop, the butterfly floated into the air, hovering above his startled expression and outstretched arms.

He saw the child standing there, bewilderment and amazement swimming across her ruddy features. Her red coat enhanced her blue eyes, but they were not focused on him. The monarch in flight transfixed her.

Xavier remained frozen, watching the girl watching the monarch, when her eyes focused on him for the first time. He went to speak, but felt something tickle his outstretched finger. The monarch sat there, lazily moving its wings, inviting him to take it. With careful movements he held the butterfly's thorax with his thumb and forefinger, kneeling as he did so.

The girl smiled, matching the glow of the monarch's golden wings. She made to come forward, then stalled, creases meeting at the corners of her eyes. Her smile faltered, yet a remnant remained.

Xavier gestured with his head to come closer. The girl's fingers twitched, a shadow coming across her face. The smile dimmed further.

"It's OK."

The girl hesitated, then the smile returned in all its beauty. She took measured steps, her gaze never leaving his fingertips. She reached him and squatted down, her eyes sapphires, gleaming in the streaked sunlight. She looked up at him, full of anticipation and wonder.

Xavier took the tagging sheet with his other hand and motioned to the girl.

"Do you want to tag him?"

The girl's fingers answered for her. She peeled the first circular tag from the sheet – DOE611. Sticking it to her fingertip, she looked at Xavier, awaiting further instructions. He moved closer to her, exposing the monarch's hind wing.

"See that baseball mitt shaped part there?"

The girl nodded, her fringe falling into her eyes. She tucked it behind her ear, an absent movement, getting rid of an irritation.

"Just press the tag lightly right there."

Her fingers whispered as she placed the tag on the discal cell. The procedure was completed in reverent silence. Slowly the girl moved away from the butterfly, the tag in place.

Xavier and the girl smiled at each other, both safe in the knowledge that they had participated in a beautiful and life-changing act.

The girl's eyes were so clear, he could see the future in them. Blue skies. Warm suns. And laughter. Lots of laughter.

Xavier's smile hardened like drying paint. He needed to do something before everything was ruined. He moved his hand towards the girl.

"Here. You can release it."

The girl's eyes glistened. She took the butterfly in her hands and held it to her face. She giggled as the wings brushed her face, the first sound she had made. She whispered something into the monarch's wings, and then in one fluid movement she stood and launched it towards the heavens.

The girl laughed in wonderment as the monarch floated above them. Xavier blinked the salt out of his eyes. He turned to the net, where the other monarchs waited, his back to the girl.

"Do you want to help me with the rest?'

Xavier opened the trunk of the shark and placed himself inside.

One car refrigerator. One leather doctor's bag, full of toiletries and personals. One small suitcase, full of short-sleeved shirts and trousers of differing shades of brown. One thin black briefcase – tagging apparatus, glassine envelopes, zip loc bags and all-weather polypropylene tags, individually numbered. One metallic case – butterfly net, self-made. One kerosene lamp. Two floodlight torches. One laptop computer.

He closed the trunk and hopped on top, staring at the stars amidst a haze of smoke, each star telling ancient history to an ignorant audience. Their shimmering form enraptured him, pinpricks of life that kept away the darkness.

Xavier held up the joint and waved it in the air, tracing a course amongst the stars. The burning ember left a trail like a comet. He brought the joint back to his lips and drew a breath. He closed his eyes, suddenly feeling exposed to the elements.

Xavier grabbed the sleeping bag and walked over to the campsite. The fire crackled hungrily. He rolled out the sleeping bag, smoothing out all the creases. He lay on his side, staring into the flames. Blood rushed to his cheeks. The branches fuelling the fire were crimson rods. He felt himself being sucked into the flames, ensconced in its raging heat, yet feeling no pain, only strength.

One of the stars moved. Just above the trees. He rose up onto his elbows and squinted up at the sky. Everything was coloured with a crimson tinge, the flames of the fire burnt onto his retina. He strained his eyes. It was gone.

He lowered himself back on the bag when he saw the star move again. It didn't move like a normal shooting star. It had no tail. It floated along, drifting on the air's currents. It tracked through its myriad cousins, in no hurry to complete its journey, disappearing behind the treetops.

Another star moved. And another. Xavier stood, kicking one of the branches in the fire. A quick flush of heat raced up his leg, the spiraling sparks enveloping him. All of the stars were now moving, slowly at first, then increasing in speed. He ran his fingers through his hair and readjusted his glasses. His face turned up to the sky, he stretched his arms out on either side of him, and palms raised, he began to spin. Each star left an arc of light mapping its movement. The sky filled with curved lines of white light.

Xavier felt the white lines pass by the shark as he traveled down US-151. Wind whipped at his face, his hair flicking at his glasses. A sheet of paper muttered from the backseat, disturbed by the constant turbulence. Earth, sand, sky permeated Xavier's pores. He took a deep breath, feeling some semblance of happiness.

The past two days had been a blur of notating monarch flight coordinates, scouring over meteorological reports and road maps, and watching the MonarchWatch GPS from his laptop, currently situated on the opposite bucket seat.

Xavier barely acknowledged the passing of state lines from Wisconsin to Iowa, except for the automatic marking of notes in his book. Every few miles he would crane his head back, hearing an unsettling crack emanate from his neck. The brown corduroy seat covers prickled his skin through his shirt. He had taken to wearing his leather jacket whilst driving, but before long sweat trickled into his eyes.

The shark wasn't the problem. Its long sleek white body prowled the road, intimidating the few vehicles it came into contact with. It wasn't the constant note taking either – he had done these types of things countless times in the laboratories at the Entomology section of Kansas University. He excelled in reporting and analysis.

It wasn't the roads – the trip had seemed the most exhilarating part for him – the openness of the rolling countryside speaking volumes of the history of the land beneath the shark's wheels.

Since the night of the spinning stars, sleep would not come.

The hitchhiker came out of nowhere. It stood just after the turnoff to Cedar Rapids.

Xavier was barely aware of its presence, let alone its protruding thumb, yet he found himself on the shoulder of the highway, the shark's tyres creating dust devils. He placed his arm on the headrest of the passenger side seat and stared out of the rear window. He strained to focus on the figure that approached. The heat rose off the bitumen, causing the person to become a shimmering enigma. A figment of his imagination.

The hitchhiker rapped on the roof of the shark, making Xavier start, his glasses sliding off his nose. He looked out his window and up into a faceless, sexless specter. The sun shone directly behind the figure, blackening all features.

"Where should I throw my stuff?"

The feminine voice threw him.

"On the backseat will be fine."

"Cool." The figure moved away from the window, causing Xavier to be momentarily blinded by the sudden exposure of the sun. The back door opened, accommodating an oversized duffel bag and a series of smaller backpacks and assorted accoutrements. The door slammed closed, causing the shark to rock gently. Its engine thrummed unabated.

The passenger door creaked open, Xavier snatching up the laptop as the hitchhiker backed into the shark. He cradled the laptop in his arms and watched as she got herself comfortable, moving up and down in the seat, feeling the corduroy, eyeing the cracked leather upholstery, looking around. Weighing it up.

Finally she turned to him as she buckled up. "Ready?"

The shark rolled on.

"Where are you heading?"

"Me? To the Alamo."

"The Alamo?"

"Yeah, you know, that big fort of yours where Davey Crockett got himself killed?"

"Yeah, I know. Why are you heading down there?"

"I'm meeting friends there. You?"

"Huh?"

"Where are you heading?"

"Oh, oh, yeah, I'm heading to the Michaocan highlands. Mexico."

"Oh, OK. What's there?"

"The monarch butterfly."

"Oh. Cool."

Yasmin studied him as the shark moved along the highway. Every ride she ever caught was usually with male occupants, always looking at her sideways, some not even trying to hide their rabid lust. She was cool with that. She knew her body and what it was capable of better than anyone. Yet he seemed determined not to look at her. She leant on the passenger side door, accentuating the curves that lay hidden by her tight black jeans. He didn't appear to notice.

She straightened and stared out the window at the farmland that was sliding by. Iowa was so flat. Its lack of undulating mountain ranges or expansive views of an ocean would have bored many people. She was fascinated by it. The thin layer of heat shimmering above the loamy fields; red shirted farmers coated in dirt, rivulets of sweat carving furrows in their faces, crow's feet encroaching on their glistening eyes. The patchwork of fields stretched to the horizon, a sea of corn swelling on one side, a lake of purple alfalfa rising up on the other. The sense of accomplishment that these people must experience. Content in the knowledge that the fruits of their labour come from the earth, providing for them and for those that depend on them. For those that are still to come.

Yasmin didn't realise he was talking until he asked the question a second time. She looked over at him. His eyes flickered intermittently between the road and the GPS map on his laptop. She nodded even though she knew he couldn't see the motion.

"Yes, I am Australian. Come from Perth, actually. Western Australia."

He nodded without taking his eyes off the road. "I've been there."

"Really?"

"When I was younger. My father studied the behavioural patterns of dolphins. In Bunbury."

"Oh yeah, I've been there! Koombana Bay?" Yasmin nodded

without waiting for a reply. "Yeah, I swam with the dolphins there one time. Not too long ago actually. The way they glide in and out of the tourists, without a care... Amazing."

"Yeah, I guess it would be."

"Guess? Didn't you swim with them?"

"I was too young. My father wouldn't let me." He shrugged. "I'm not a good swimmer."

She nodded. He drove.

Xavier guided the shark off the East 2 highway and moved into Fort Madison. The hitchhiker looked at her watch. 3:41pm. As they moved into the town's wide leafy streets, she turned to him.

"Are we stopping for a while?"

Xavier looked at her, surprise etched on his face.

"Well, yeah. I have to stop here for the night." Realising his error, his expression melted into one of apology. "Oh, sorry, I don't know what I was thinking. I only travel 200 miles a day. Following the route of the butterfly. I should have told you, maybe left you out on the highway – "

She waved his words away.

"That's cool. I can cruise around the town anyway. We're in Lee County after all. The backroads of Middle America." She laughed and looked at her own reflection in the window.

The shark sailed into the parking lot of the Budget Host Mericana Motel, a squat brown brick building stretching back from the street, languishing in the heat. A large sign attached to the front wall said ANTIQUES. The sign seemed an unconvincing attempt at conveying authenticity – a real ranch of a motel that was built at the height of tacky excessiveness during the 1980s. Yasmin's nose twitched.

The shark rolled to a stop. He let his hands fall into his lap, not knowing what to do with them any more.

"Well, it was nice to meet you."

"Thanks for the ride."

Xavier nodded. "No problem."

She smiled, threw the duffel bag over her shoulder and walked towards the centre of Fort Madison.

He lay on the lumpy single bed, staring at the mildew spots on the off-white ceiling. He covered one eye with the palm of his hand, then the other, watching the spots move from side to side. The quicker his hand moved, the quicker the spots danced until he was reminded of the night of the spinning stars.

Xavier closed his eyes and rewound the day. He replayed the time spent with his traveling companion. He could almost hear the crackle and pop of the film stock juxtaposing with the vivid colours of his memory. Yasmin's short blonde hair blinded him. The way she slouched in the seat, so assured, so comfortable in a stranger's car. He saw her reaction to his lack of conversation. Her down turned lips, her eyelids at half-mast. He wondered what colour her eyes were. He imagined ice blue.

Xavier swung his legs over the side of the bed, pushing off the mattress with a grunt. The mattress sunk in the middle. His back ached. He ran his hands over his face. His forehead was damp.

He moved over to the small kitchenette table that served as his desk, and fell onto the plastic chair in front of his laptop. According to the GPS readout the butterflies had stopped 25 miles east of Fort Madison, on the other side of the Mississippi River. He was a little disappointed that he hadn't decided to camp closer to them. But he had already made the booking.

He began going through his notebook, typing his tight handwriting in longhand for the MonarchWatch website. Studying the work as it scrolled onto the screen, he was quite proud of his achievement.

The others wore painted smiles when Dr. Rafferty announced it would be Xavier carrying out the solo migration journey. The expedition provided him with the perfect environment to display his potential as an entomologist and ecologist, whilst presenting a unique opportunity to observe the monarch butterfly in a seemingly one-on-one fashion. Of course anyone could do the trip. MonarchWatch made it a reward for hard work and dedication towards the cause.

He finished typing and perused his work. A small nod, a click of the mouse, and the entries were posted. Everyone interested in the journey would be able to read his admissions tomorrow morning.

He stood up and moved towards the car refrigerator that sat beside the bed. A hiss of cold manufactured air cloaked him as he lifted its lid, reaching in and bringing out the glassine envelope. With slow hands he brought DOE616 out of its cage. She looked lifeless in his hands, cool to the touch. A flicker of a wing denoted the life that beat within.

Xavier held the monarch to his lips, and prayed.

She pulled the bourbon through the straw, the ice chinking in the bottom of the glass, her gaze piercing the smoky air. She felt the looks she was garnering. Her black jeans gripped the curves of her thighs, her red and black striped jumper stressing the message her body was trying to convey – a fish out of water. Each man cut off ties to their friends, deciding which lure to use. Entice her, drag her in. Catch of the day.

Her eyes never left the pool table. Two men battled over the felt, weapons at the ready. The one closest to her bent over the table, lining up the shot, looking to strike the next blow. Concentration etched itself around his eyes, peering out through a curtain of stringy black hair. A cloud of blue chalk erupted from the tip of the cue as it struck the white ball. A ball is sunk. A chink in the armour. The man floats around the table, eyeing up his next kill.

Her tongue flitted over her upper lip, the taste of sweat and sugar biting her taste buds. She drank in the rest of the scenery

– flannelette shirt, ink trailing from both forearms to unknown destinations underneath the shirtsleeves, calluses upon calluses sliding up and down the pool cue. Black stubble crowding his cheekbones. His friend wrapped in black leather, his long hair kept in check by a red cap.

The two men, the entire tavern's clientele, were from another world. She felt drawn by the exoticness, the primitiveness of it all. The smells of sawdust, alcohol and blood mingled to burn her sinuses. Her skin tingled with excitement. She was entering into another society, one that revolved around anger and bravado. She was simply stirring the pot. An exotic intruder.

She placed her empty glass on the bar and slid off her chair. Peanut shells and cigarette butts gave way to the pressure of her heels. Her movements drew all attention. Lips drew back, teeth bared. Shoulders moved forward, anticipating the pounce.

She reached the men and took out a digital recorder and placed it on the pool table. One hand slid into the pocket of one of the men, the other caressed the felt.

"Hello boys. If you let me interview you, I might let you buy me a drink."

The dim light overhead caught the glimmering of teeth.

Xavier steered the shark back onto US-61. The monarchs were in flight, appearing to follow the Mississippi River. He predicted that they would stop somewhere near Summitville to refuel on the nectar of the milkweed plant, one of the few constants on the yearly migration route.

It was only roughly three hours away, but he intended to view them in flight, following their movement by sight rather than the GPS.

He knew that the blonde-haired figure ahead was the hitchhiker from before. His palms began to itch, his heartbeat quickened. He wasn't sure whether he would stop for her or not. The shark made the decision for him.

She shook her head and laughed. Throwing her belongings onto the backseat, she climbed aboard.

"Are you stalking me?" she asked.

He looked over at her, finally taking her in. Her eyes were not blue, but a chocolate brown. There was power within them, fuelling her vibrancy.

He tried to suppress the upturning corners of his lips without success.

"No. But I think you are stalking me."

She leant against the passenger door, looking him up and down.

"Is that so?"

"Uh huh."

She continued to stare at him, pressing her tongue firmly into her cheek. She stuck out her hand, thumb straight up.

"Yasmin."

He looked at her, the smell of daffodils flooding the car. He took her hand in his own.

"Xavier."

"Well, nice to meet you, Xavier." Yasmin laughed and took her hand back, leaving an empty space in its place.

The sun shone off Xavier's glasses, giving him eye sockets of pure light. The needle quivered around 40 miles per hour. He peered out his side window every few minutes before turning his attention back on the road.

Yasmin held the recorder in her lap, pretending to watch last night's proceedings. She took in Xavier's profile. He sat straight in his seat, his concentration on the task all-important. His long fingers embraced the wheel, caressing the gear stick, guiding the shark with a steady hand. At times his glasses would slide down the bridge of his nose, the light disappearing to display eyes of the palest green. They were calm, confident. Then he would push the glasses back up his nose, and the light returned.

"Where are you traveling today?"

Xavier turned to look at her. "Summitville."

"Oh. That's not very far away, is it?"

"About 210 miles, I think."

"OK."

Xavier looked out his window. Yasmin peered out the windscreen up into the empty sky.

"What are you always looking out the window for?"

"I'm hoping to see the monarchs in flight."

"What? Oh, the *butter*flies."

Xavier looked at her, his glasses resting on the edge of his nose. "Yeah, the *butter*flies."

They both laughed. Yasmin watched him watch her, his face smiling, before he broke contact and moved back to watching the road and the sky.

"What's the deal with these butterflies, anyway? What's so important about them that you follow them every day?"

Xavier shrugged.

"Well, it's what I do."

"You do the monarchs?"

Xavier scrunched his face, a prune of disgust.

"No. I work for MonarchWatch, a conservation outreach program out of Kansas University. We monitor the monarch butterfly, its biology, life cycle, natural populations, enemies, migrational habits… We put it all together and post it on our website. It's accessible to all manner of people, but is aimed at schools and schoolchildren."

One hand left the wheel as he spoke, fluttering between them, accentuating his speech.

"So. You're educational? Like a teacher or something?"

"No, I do real research, scientific data, all of that. Our research is the foremost in ecological findings for the monarch. Our pieces are shown in most of the great science periodicals in the Northern Hemisphere.'

Xavier looked at her as he said this, his eyes wide, searching. She could tell that he was nervous, trying to justify his motives. She laughed in spite of herself.

Xavier frowned, his grip on the wheel tighter. "What?"

Yasmin stifled her giggles. "Nothing. You're just so, committed. To the cause and all."

Xavier shrugged in defiance. "And what's wrong with being proud of your work?" Yasmin held up her hands in mock-surrender. "Hey, no offence, I was just saying…"

Xavier looked down at her lap, his mouth agape. Yasmin felt her hands go to her crotch, feeling the cold surface of the recorder. She looked down. The light was red. She looked back up at him.

"You're recording me?"

"I didn't mean it, honestly, I was going to ask you –"

Xavier reached over and snatched the recorder. Yasmin's hands fell lifeless into her lap. He peered at the recorder, a strange relic he hadn't seen other than in picture books. He swung the recorder in her direction, the light still red, reflecting off his glasses.

"So, what is it that *you* do?"

Yasmin made a feeble attempt to get the camera back. He pulled away, the red glare of the recorder focused on her. The road seemed to be forgotten; their world existed within the shark. She began to sweat. She caught the faint whiff of copper. The seat itched.

"Give it back, please."

Xavier shook his head, his words clipped. "No. Look, what is it that you do? That is so worthwhile?"

"I just want my camera back –"

"What do you do?"

"GIVE IT BACK!"

The shout reverberated between them. Xavier became a statue, staring straight through her. Yasmin held his gaze, her fists clenched, struggling to conceal the trembling of her body. He handed her the recorder. She took it, fumbling a few times before she turned the power off. The red light winked once, and then died.

"Look! There they are!"

Yasmin leant forward again. The blue strip at the top of the windshield turned the sky a faint purple.

"I can't see anything," she said, shrugging.

Xavier jabbed the windshield with his finger. "There! Over near those cypress trees!"

Eyes squinting, her forehead touching the glass, Yasmin saw a faint smudge of something hovering in the air.

The shark threw up gravel as it pulled onto the shoulder of the highway. Yasmin's head pushed painfully against the glass before she was whipped back into her seat. Her complaints were met with a slammed door and fading footsteps.

Unfolding herself from the shark, she watched as Xavier waded amongst the yellow grass below the highway. He stumbled a few times over the unfamiliar ground, only once taking his eyes off the monarchs. He looked back at her, his eyes so clear. A tuft of hair had been pushed into the air, standing up as if by static electricity. He began gesturing for her to follow, and then checked himself, a cloud covering his glasses. Shoulders slumping a little, he turned and continued his lurch towards the centre of the field.

Picking her way across the field, taking in the smell of damp earth and straw, she could make out other scents – the cypress pines, the water of the Mississippi, ash from campfires. The wind felt cold and wet upon her cheeks.

Xavier did not react when she came up beside him. The whirr of the recorder produced a cursory glance, but his attention remained in the sky. She watched the monarchs through the eyepiece of her camera. The sky became grainy, the monarchs indistinguishable.

A weight dipped the camera away from her face. She looked up to see Xavier's hand pushing it to her hip. He nodded, and then resumed his observation of the sky. She craned her neck and watched billions of butterflies get caught on the up draught, jostled by strong surly gusts, gliding on slipstreams. A conical shadow sliding across the sky, dancing just for the two of them.

Xavier stared into the fire. Yasmin sat opposite him, the fire lighting her features from beneath, the hollows of her cheeks blackened whilst her skin took on an orange hue.

She ate baked beans; the only sounds the clatter of her spoon on the inside of the tin and the popping of the twigs as they set to combust, keeping them both warm.

Yasmin watched Xavier. She simulated hunger, the spoonfuls of baked beans a mechanical movement. His glasses were impenetrable once more, the fire licking the lens, threatening to engulf his fringe. His skin had softened to porcelain. His fingers twitched as they dangled over his knees.

"What do you film?"

She froze, her spoon halfway to her mouth. A dollop of tomato sauce dropped onto her sleeping bag. She regained composure and brought the spoon to its intended destination. She answered through the beans.

"Nothing. Everything. Anything."

Xavier's eyebrows disappeared under his fringe. "That must make for some great cinema."

Yasmin stared at him until she noticed the glimmer of a grin pass over his lips. She relaxed, allowing a smile to cross her face.

"Sorry. I didn't mean to be rude or anything, I just, didn't think you would want to know."

The light in Xavier's face was eclipsed for a brief moment, he took his glasses off and the furrows in his forehead disappeared.

He began to clean them on his shirt, his head down, expression unknown.

"I really would like to know."

She placed the tin down beside her and picked up the camera, cradling it for inspiration. She took a deep breath.

"I record society, it's what I love. The exoticness, the eccentricities, the earthiness of society. Backwaters, backroads, the boondocks, whatever. I record these things because they are so foreign to me. And that's what makes me love them. Draws me in."

"What types of society though? Like, all over the world?"

"No, just here. There are so many different cultures and societies that exist here. You can go anywhere and be immersed in a totally different experience."

"Where have you been?"

"Everywhere. But I love the South the most. Mississippi, Missouri, Alabama, Georgia. The smells, the sounds… it gives me the shivers just thinking about it."

Xavier studied her for a few moments, nodded and looked back down at his glasses.

"You can look if you want. I have it all in my backpack." She held the camera over the fire towards him.

Shranking away, he placed his glasses upon his nose. "No, it's fine. I was just curious, that's all. Maybe another time."

Yasmin held the camera out for a few moments more before pulling it back into her arms.

"Fair enough."

"So what exactly are you doing? What's the purpose of following butterflies all over the country?"

He shrugged. "Well, they travel from Wisconsin to Mexico to hibernate and survive the winter. I guess I want to know how they can fly all that way, and still make it to the same area every year."

"What, do they have memories of goldfish?"

Xavier laughed. "No, but they have a short lifespan. They can only do the journey once. It's probably their great-grandchildren that do the journey the following year. It's one of the major mysteries of the insect world."

"Oh." Holding his gaze for a few moments, she scraped the rest of the beans out of the tin, shoveling them into her mouth. She looked up at him again.

"Why do you think the butterflies travel all this way to migrate? Aren't there other areas that are closer to their home?"

"Well, technically the Michoacan region is just as much home as Wisconsin is…"

"OK, but still, why go that far?"

Xavier leaned back onto the palms of his hands, looking up at the stars.

"Well, the region does have everything they need. Trees on which to cluster, a temperature that will slow down their metabolism without freezing them, protection from the elements, a body of water…"

"But if there are other places, it's not like it's out of habit, is it? If they die before the next year's journey?"

"No."

"So?" She says, holding up her hands. "Word of mouth?"

He laughed. "Maybe. I don't know. I'd like to know why, and how. There are various theories, all of them sound pretty good. But no-one knows, not yet."

Yasmin shrugged.

"I think you already know the answer."

"What?"

"You said it before. Because it's their home." Yawning, she shimmied into her sleeping bag, "Goodnight."

She watched Xavier pull a blanket around him. He returned the gaze for a moment.

"Goodnight."

Xavier stood at the edge of the clearing, sneaking glances over his shoulder at Yasmin's sleeping form, the fire down to glowing embers. A joint drooped from the corner of his mouth. Invisible clouds drifted across the sky, blocking the stars. A sliver of moonlight came through the foliage, casting minimal light over the clearing. He moved his feet from side to side, a rhythmic action, an uncomfortable dance.

Sleep was ignoring him. Sticks lay at his feet, perfect for restoring the flames to the campfire. He looked down at them and took another puff, the smoke curling out his nostrils and drifting upwards like silver tendrils.

He looked down at DOE616. He had placed her in a zip loc bag after the night in Fort Madison in the hopes of giving her some breathing space. He watched her move her wings and antennae, her proboscis searching the walls of the bag, trying to find herself. He let his fingers trace her body, the thicker vein pigmentation on the wings floating in front of his eyes. Even in captivity, she seemed so strong. So free. He kicked at the sticks and looked over his shoulder again.

Yasmin's mouth was slightly open, her hair veiling her eyes. She looked fragile, vulnerable. He turned away, another drag on the joint. She wasn't fragile or vulnerable, he was sure of that. She seemed so self-assured, so comfortable in her own world, so comfortable with herself.

He didn't realise he had held his breath until the smoke began attacking his lungs in earnest. Air rocketed from his mouth, boosted by racking coughs.

He watched the twigs begin to move as his eyes filled with tears. They stood up and formed a circle. He couldn't see anything inside the circle. The ground had disappeared leaving a black hole in its place.

He watched as he placed his hand into the circle of twigs, entering the hole in the ground. He reached forward, reaching down, yet could feel nothing. He kept reaching until he fell into the hole, dropping lower and lower, reaching down, his hands opening and closing. No matter how hard he strained, he remained suspended in the dark, his hands empty.

Yasmin lay close to the campfire, soaking up the little warmth it gave off, watching Xavier lay down next to a pile of sticks, a joint wedged in the fork of his fingers. He lay still for some time, muttering to himself, before falling silent.

She wriggled free of her sleeping bag and moved towards him. He lay face down, embracing the earth beneath him. Soil stuck to the tear tracks on his cheeks.

She wrapped his sleeping bag around him. Sitting on her haunches, she watches him, patts his hair. Who is this man? Finally she took the joint from between his fingers and placed it between her own. She picked up the pile of sticks and stoked the fire, the flames thankful for the fuel. She sat down, smoking and watched the world light up.

Xavier looked over the smouldering remains of the campfire, he couldn't remember placing the sticks on the fire last night. Their remnants lay in a perfect circle, steeped in the middle, a teepee of fire. He pushed them over with the toe of his shoe. A few sparks were the only protests given.

Yasmin had packed up her gear and was sitting on the bonnet of the shark, looking out over the tree line, recorder held in front of her. He wandered up to her.

"What you looking at?"

She turned to look at him. His hand fluttered towards his hair for a brief moment, then fell to his side. Her eyes returned to the summit.

"Just wondering what the day will bring."

She leant forward to slide off the bonnet. Her blue shorts caught on the matte surface, offering Xavier a glimpse of thigh.

"So you are flesh and bone after all?" Yasmin said, a wry

smile matching her eyes.

Blood flooded his cheeks. He made to look away; she followed his gaze until a grin pressed itself onto his lips.

They climbed into the shark and made their way back onto US-61. He didn't ask her where she wanted to get dropped off. She didn't say.

Xavier finished unfolding his sleeping bag, while Yasmin was finding some wood for the fire. He started rummaging through the refrigerator to find something edible for them both; pulling out what was left with the idea of making a stew.

The sound of a crackle made his hand fly up. He peered inside and saw the zip loc bag. He searched for Yasmin, she was nowhere to be seen. He brought out the bag. DOE616 lay still, frozen. He had not looked at her for the last five days, not since Summitville.

"Hey, what have you got there?"

Yasmin loomed out of the darkness, her hands resting on his. He fought the urge to shrink, to push away. She looked at him as she gently pulled the bag from his fingers, then brought it up above her head, holding it in the moonlight.

"So this is the famous monarch butterfly?"

The wings were etched in silver, the moonlight shining through the wings. Xavier felt compelled to tear the magical creature from her grasp and crush it to his chest. His hands did not leave his side.

"I've seen these before, you know. All the time, actually."

Xavier forced himself to speak. "Most people have. Or seen butterflies that resemble it. It's coloured that way to remind predators that they are inedible."

He grimaced as soon as the words had leapt from his tongue.

She looked into the trunk of the shark and laughed. "You weren't going to feed it to me were you? I'm not that bad a passenger!"

He smiled, a furtive glance at the bag, his fear lessening. "I thought maybe there was a bit of the monarch butterfly in all of us, so why not make it literal?"

Yasmin shrieked, Xavier felt himself begin to relax. Her teeth shone in the moonlight, her cheeks glowing. For a moment he wanted to touch them. He didn't move an inch.

"That's good, Xavier! You can be quite funny when you want to."

He shrugged. "So I've heard."

She opened the bag. His hands finally left his side, clasping on her forearms. She looked at them, not sure what they were.

"What are you doing?"

"Don't open the bag."

"Why? The butterfly is dead, isn't it?"

The monarch spread its wings and floated out of the bag, out of her hands, out of his reach. They watched, Xavier still holding Yasmin as the monarch moved upward, caught in the beams of light, her silhouette imprinted on the moon. She curled overhead.

With one quick movement she was out of the light, and gone.

Yasmin carefully took Xavier's hands off her arms and held them, staring into his eyes. The faint scent of daffodils wafted from her. She was so close to him, the closest he had been to anyone for a long time. He could feel the heat radiating from her.

"It's OK. It was time to let go."

Her hand moved to his cheek, her thumb resting underneath his glasses, coming away wet.

"How about I make dinner tonight?"

She reached into the trunk and took out the food, moving away from him towards the fire.

He remained standing, motionless, caught in the cool night air.

"Why do you smoke?"

Xavier looked at her, the heat making his cheeks red, hiding his embarrassment.

"I've seen you. Every night, when you think I've gone to sleep."

"Oh. Sorry about that. I should have offered…"

"Oh no, that's all right. But that's the thing. I smoke when I'm with people. You know, to chill out. So why do you smoke it?"

He sucked his lower lip as he looked down at the remnants of his stew.

"I don't know. It makes me feel good. It helps me to relax."

She nodded with the reverence of someone imparting sage advice. She cocked her head to one side.

"But why hide it? I think you're intimidated by me."

"I'm not intimidated by I think you are. But still… Hiding it doesn't make much sense."

"Does it matter?" A hint of exasperation in his voice.

She shrugged. "I don't know. Guess not."

She rolled over and closed her eyes, knowing sleep would not come. Silence reigned over the clearing, the flames licking at the shadows beyond.

The shark moved up Alamo Plaza in the shadows of the huge building. The weight of fierce history washed over Xavier in a heavy wave. He took a deep breath. He smelled ash, dirt, gunpowder and blood. Electricity flowed through him.

Yasmin sat still for a few moments, staring out the window at the complex. She stirred as the shark slowed down, approaching Gate 5. She turned to Xavier as he moved to the sidewalk.

"I want to see the butterflies."

Xavier looked at her. She seemed genuine, yet something lurked beneath the surface.

"Are you sure? I mean, you said the Alamo, so…"

"I know, I know. And I really want to see it sometime. Have

you been in there?"

"No."

"Yeah, well, I can come back through this way."

"What about your friends?"

"Friends?" Xavier saw the moment of confusion before Yasmin could continue. "Oh, those guys. They're hanging around for a while." She paused. "Unless you don't want me to come? If not, that's cool."

"No, it's cool."

Xavier sped up again, moving out of the Alamo's shadow.

The Sierra Madre Oriental Mountains stretched before them, the shark weaving its way up the roughly carved switchbacks.

Yasmin looked down over Angangueo. The cobblestoned village was full of tourists proudly wearing their monarch butterfly paraphernalia. All motels and hostels had been booked out for months. Poor families who had been working the land as employees of larger haciendas ran many of the surrounding farms. The monarchs brought in as much profit as a good harvesting season. Large posters of the butterfly were plastered on fences, walls, and billboards. The road ended in a large field, the grass flattened by constant vehicular traffic. Two buses and an abused pick-up were the only signs of human life.

Yasmin jumped out of the shark and ran over to the edge of the field. Tendrils of fog hung over the pine oaks as they sloped down the mountain. The valley curved away to the left, disappearing in on itself.

Xavier opened the trunk. He took a garbage bag out of his doctor's bag, flicking it twice to let the air in. One change of clothes, toothpaste, toothbrush, sleeping bag. He tied a knot in the bag and hefted it over one shoulder, slinging his laptop over the other. He picked up the other case.

Yasmin grabbed her pack from the back seat. "Going for a hike, are we?"

Xavier nodded down at the valley. "About an hour's walk, maybe more."

"How do you know where to go? I thought you hadn't done this before."

"I haven't followed the monarch's migration. I have been to their overwintering site, last year. I only went to El Rosario though."

"What's that?"

"The tourist reserve. There's Rincon de Villalobos also. That's why the buses are here. More will be here soon."

"So where are we going?"

Xavier smiled." It's a secret."

They set off down a goat's track barely distinguishable from the surrounding foliage. Everything was green, except for the black volcanic soil that clung to the soles of their boots. The murmurs of clothing and laboured breathing were the only sounds. The forest spat them out into a great clearing.

Yasmin stopped and watched as Xavier waded through the sea of tropical milkweed that carpeted the ground. The oak trees towered above, reaching limbs over their heads to create an impenetrable roof. Running water could be heard nearby, the sound like ice in a glass tumbler. She shivered and rubbed her arms. Breathing on her hands, she took out her recorder and started filming.

"It's like a refrigerator in here."

"It slows down their metabolism, so that they can live for up to 20 times their normal lifespan."

"Why do they want to do that?"

"They are sexually energetic creatures, some of the most excessive creatures in the animal world. But they are fragile, and burn out and die within two weeks. However, if they can hibernate where everything they need to survive is in one place, they can slow down and survive the winter. The population can continue."

"And their offspring travel to Wisconsin to have all the fun."

Xavier laughed. "Yeah, something like that."

Yasmin knelt down and plucked some milkweed from the damp earth. She ran it through her fingers.

"How long do you need to be here, documenting all this?"

Xavier shrugged. "Three, four weeks. I'll travel around, capturing monarchs, taking down tag numbers, monitoring flight patterns, living conditions, their physical changes... Others from MonarchWatch will be down too."

"All to find out the secrets of a butterfly?"

"Pretty much."

She laughed.

"What?"

"I don't know. It's just, you spend your time watching butterflies and how they work, and I watch people and how they work. I thought that was funny. You know, how far away we are to understanding them."

The night fell down, blanketing the clearing. Xavier and Yasmin huddled together, a kerosene lamp lighting their meal. It was primitive; baked beans and gendarmes she had picked up in Calexico after they had crossed the border. He mopped up the sauce with the last of the bread. She stood up to gather some water.

Xavier had laid out their sleeping bags before Yasmin came back from the stream, two tin cups in her hands. She squatted cross-legged on the end of her bag, handing one cup to him. They drank silently, the cold liquid flowing over their lips and tongues, cooling their stomachs.

He hunched forward, his arms wrapped around his legs. Yasmin rummaged through her pack, then over it, his hand caressing the case. She looked over her shoulder at him.

"What's this?"

He said nothing, rocking forward until he was on his hands and knees, moving over to her. He unclasped the lid and opened it, taking out the segments of the butterfly net. She sidled next to him.

"Modern technology?"

Xavier laughed. "It does the job."

Yasmin reached forward, her fingers tracing the handle. "It looks special."

He nodded. "I made it." He hesitated, then put the net together and handed it to her. She held it in both hands, lending a reverence to the proceedings. The net brushed against her.

"Its so soft."

"It has to be." A pause, then, "It's a bridal veil."

She looked up at him, wide eyed. "Really? Why?"

Xavier rubbed the palms of his hands, looking down. Yasmin waited, then started, a sharp intake of breath.

"Oh, I'm sorry."

Xavier shook his head, still focusing on the ground between them. "She, Emma, she and I were driving to her parents' house. I was tired. There was a deer... " He fell silent. "Its OK though."

She looked at the net, and then held it out to him. He took it without saying a word; taking the segments apart and laying them back in the case.

She picked up a torch. "Well, I had better gather some wood."

"We can't have fire here. This is edijos land."

"Edijos?"

"It belongs to the farmers around here, property handed to them after the Mexican Revolution. It's not exactly reserve land, but..."

"We're not supposed to be here?" Yasmin slapped Xavier lightly on the arm. "Naughty!" A small smile crept across Xavier's lips. She smiled back. Yasmin clicked on the torch and looked around the clearing, the torchlight slicing through the darkness. "It makes sense, though. It feels like a sacred place."

Xavier stood up, pins and needles stabbing his skin. He watched

Yasmin follow the torchlight, staring at the trees. He moved beside her, his presence bringing her attention to him. The smell of daffodils mingled with the pine needles. She stared into his eyes, through them, beyond them. Her chocolate eyes said everything his stammering mouth could not.

The click of a switch echoed over the clearing, and night moved in once more.

Whispering. Xavier stirred. Something brushed lightly across his cheek. He couldn't move his arms. He was entangled. He couldn't break free.

Xavier opened his eyes. The whispering grew louder. He looked around him.

Everything was darkness, except for Yasmin's blonde halo of hair as it rested on his shoulder. He wriggled his arm free from under her body, shaking her softly, whispering in her ear. She flapped at him as if at an irritating mosquito. He tried a second time with the same result. He left her, fumbling for the torches.

His hand grasped the handle of one. The whispering filled the clearing. He pointed the torch in the air and flicked the switch.

Butterflies exploded into view. They moved in and out of the beam of light, a burnt orange double helix spiraling up to the heavens. The beating of their wings saturated Xavier's senses. Saltwater trickled down his face as gossamer brushed his cheeks, his arms, his chest.

They engulfed the pine oaks, the trees filled with flames. He heard the gunshot crack of a branch breaking under the weight of millions of tiny bodies. He closed his eyes, yet the flying and fragile insects of orange and black and white remained imprinted on the back of his eyelids.

The power of their beauty hung palpable in the air, seeping into the pores of his skin, melding with him. He slumped to his knees; his eyes wide open, watching the monarch dance for him.

A sprinkle of sunlight pierced Xavier's eyelids, forcing him to rise. He rubbed the grit from his eyes and looked around the clearing. Tree branches drooped from the weight of butterflies setting up for the long winter ahead. The excitement and majesty of last night flooded him, and he rolled over to Yasmin.

She was gone.

He stood up, spinning around in circles, a dog chasing its tail. Her sleeping bag, backpack, everything had disappeared. He looked at the ground of the clearing. Monarchs surrounded him on all sides feasting on the nectar of the milkweed.

A light sensation tickled his ear. A monarch had landed on his shoulder. As he turned, cupping his hands taking the butterfly in, he recognised the tag before his eyes could focus on the symbols.

DOE616.

Low clouds covered the sun, the clearing becoming a dull imitation of itself.

The parking area was full. Tourist buses, station wagons, Land Rovers, garish headwear, picnic baskets, placards, horses, and bedlam. The enthusiasm pervaded the field. Xavier's shoulders slumped.

Something connected with his foot near the back wheel of the shark. He bent down and picked up a tape. He rushed over to the nearest bus, its driver slouched against the door, crudely rolled cigarette crushed between his lips.

"Hey, you don't happen to have a handheld video recorder do you?"

Xavier jammed the tape in and clicked the door shut. He flipped the play button and watched the little screen light up.

"*... Others from MonarchWatch will be down too.*"

"*All to find out the secrets of a butterfly?*"

Xavier watched until static and white noise filled him. He wiped his hand across his face, rewound the tape, and watched it again.

9
What If You Slept

Anne Devereux

Author

Anne Devereux is a writer of contemporary, romantic and gothic/fantasy short fiction, has written a Young Adult fantasy novel and also writes poetry and song lyrics. Anne was born in England but has called Toronto, Canada home for a long time. She identifies with Pierre Trudeau as a 'citizen of the world'. Her favourite things to do are write, read, sing, fiddle around on the guitar, scrabble about in her garden, sunbathe, and generally avoid work. Her story *What If You Slept* follows the journey of two strangers, both running from their respective daily lives, on a train to nowhere.

There's something surreal about a train station. The vast space seems formless and vague, like a Salvador Dali painting. A blank canvas, ready for a portrait of a thousand disconnected lives. You stand alone in the concourse, surrounded by bodies rushing in all directions, like faceless figures from a tangled dream. Your fellow travellers don't appear to see you; they jostle and bump you without apology or even acknowledgement of your presence. Some even try to walk right through you, as though you had no physical existence at all.

In Suite 620, all was quiet except for the rustling of paper. Nick sat on the edge of the bed in his ecru Italian cotton pyjamas, raking his hands through his hair (chestnut brown with #35 dirty blond highlights, texturized by Bodie of Mikado Salon), reading and re-reading the crumpled page in his lap. He knew this would happen.

'Dear Nick: I can't do this anymore. I've cleared out my stuff from the closet, and I took my CDs. Sorry.'

He screwed up the paper and hurled it at the bin, where it rimmed and then missed, bobbing sadly on the parquet.

"Fuck you," he snarled. What the hell was wrong with women anyway? All this constant whining about self-respect. Men just had to get on with it; nobody threw bake sales for abused men. There were no self-help books for men entitled *How to Balance Career and Family*. The bathroom mirror showed a damp 28 year old with clear blue eyes and a perfectly straight nose. He rubbed his chin and wondered about shaving. But he'd already called in sick, what was the point? She was gone. He traced her name on the steamed-up glass. He was already beginning to forget the colour of her eyes, but evidently, his body remembered more intimate details.

The sound of the shower covered his eventual release, but afterwards he felt empty.

You finger the wooden beads around your wrist. When you're nervous, your hands just refuse to rest. Should you take up knitting? A wry smile crosses your face as you imagine his reaction. He doesn't even approve of you wearing wool.

Irritated, you slide the bracelet off your wrist and unwind it, clicking the beads through finger and thumb like a rosary. You're not even Catholic. The carriage is comfortable, well lit and air-conditioned, with blue velour seating and foldaway tables. There are restrooms and a dining car with white tablecloths and silverware. The eight-hour journey to Cochrane is almost an adventure by train, striking out beyond the city. If you kept going north, you'd hit the Arctic Circle.

You feel secure, comforted by the capsule-like carriage dotted with non threatening strangers, all going somewhere, purposeful, not owing you anything. You feel safe. Beyond anything else, you feel free. The past few months have been suffocating, feeling as though you were slowly being strangled to death in a sterile, spotless, designer vacuum.

The apartment was an eternal clean room where any evidence of human biology was persona non grata. Throughout the ten months, your eclectic mix of almost-antique furniture and yard sale finds had been gradually replaced or eliminated. The space you used to call home was now a cool, brushed-stainless steel reservoir of minimalist chic. It was practically Japanese.

You'd noticed his display of oddly obsessive-compulsive behaviour of late: flicking the light switch off and on, off and on, off and on until you screamed at him.

At night, he tossed in wild nightmares, dripping in cold sweat. More than once you've had to shake him awake, trembling in fear as he violently thrashed around in his sleep.

The carriage door slid open with a crash, snapping the single occupant out of his reverie.

"Fuck!" Nick's bag slid off his shoulder and onto the floor, followed in short order by his BlackBerry. Upon hitting the linoleum it broke apart, the batteries skidding under the opposite seat.

"Fuck, shit, goddammit!"

Nick kicked the disembowelled remains of the BlackBerry, untangled himself from his coat and scarf and tossed them into a corner. He flung himself into the nearest seat.

"Um, you OK?"

Nick looked across the row of seats. He was in no mood for company. "Yeah. Yeah. No. Not really, no." He laughed, to himself rather than to the stranger sitting opposite him. Another spike of rage tore through him and he fumbled frantically for the broken bits of BlackBerry, scrambled them all together in his hand and hurled them at the carriage door, where they shattered into fragments of blue plastic. The Rogers logo skittered cheerfully on the floor. "Fucking piece of shit!" Nick spat, then slumped back into his seat.

"You want a Valium?" The stranger grinned. Nick looked up, a little chastened now that his anger had vented.

"Sorry. I'll be OK in a minute." He ran his hand through his hair.

He could feel those eyes watching him. Oh yes, he'd noticed. Dark espresso-brown, long black lashes, a subtle trace of eyeliner. He shook himself. *Don't.*

"You really don't like that thing, do you?" the voice persisted. Cynical, cavalier, slightly amused.

"I hate it. I hate everything about it. What's it got to do with you, anyway? Mind your own business, I'm in no mood for smart remarks."

"I noticed."

Nick put his head in his hands. He was just looking for a bit of peace. The other cars were full of mums and kids, wailing babies, assholes talking loudly on cell phones, gossiping teenagers, chattering housewives who didn't take a breath in between words.

The train clunked over a switch. Nick looked out of the window and took what felt like his first breath in an hour. He was suddenly aware of the painful throbbing in his head.

"Uh, sorry, this is going to sound rather stupid," Nick said.

"You want to be alone? I can move. Just ask."

Nick shook his head. "No. I mean, yes, but no."

"Yes, you want to be alone, or no, you don't want me to move?"

Nick stared. "Um... "

"You were going to ask me a question, I think."

"Jesus! Yes. Sorry. Where is this train going?"

"You're kidding, right?"

"No."

"You just got on a train, and you have no idea where it's headed?"

Nick stared at the floor. "Yeah. That's about it, yeah." He wanted to cry. *I'm lost.* The brown eyes shone with private amusement.

"Well, you might want to get off at the next stop then, because this is the Ontario Northlander, it goes all the way to Cochrane."

"Where?"

"My point exactly."

"And you're going there, I suppose?"

"Yep."

"Why?"

"Why not?"

Flippant. Infuriating. "What's there?"

"A big statue of a polar bear. Tim Hortons. And my grandma."

Nick suppressed a giggle. "Your grandma?"

"Nothing wrong with visiting your grandma once in a while. It's a very relaxing trip. Although maybe not for *you*," the stranger said, glibly. A smirk, then a frown in Nick's direction, followed by the curious arch of an eyebrow. "Where did you mean to go?"

"What?"

"You got on the wrong train, obviously. Where did you mean to go?"

Kind. Concerned. Patient. Stop it. Don't be so nice to me. "Uh, I don't know. Nowhere. Anywhere. I just ran for a train, any train. I jumped on the nearest one."

"Wow. Did you rob a bank?"

Nick was silent.

"Look, I didn't mean to pry. But if you want to talk about it, it's cool. I'm a good listener. And I have cop friends."

Managing a smile, Nick let out a deep sigh. "My girlfriend left me. I just, I guess I kinda snapped. I didn't go into work this morning. I just ran all the way here, and jumped onto the first train I saw."

"And you broke your little corporate toy."

Nick grimaced. "Corporate leg-iron is more like it."

"What's your name?"

"Huh?"

"Your name. Or did you leave that behind as well?"

"Nick. Pleased to meet you, um?"

"Chris." A smile, a handshake. Polite conversation. "So what do you do that's made you so neurotic?" Chris grinned disarmingly. Nick felt a strange sensation in his knees.

"I'm a lawyer."

"Ah." Chris nodded. "That explains a lot."

"What are those?" Nick pointed to the wooden beads on Chris' wrist.

"Worry beads."

"Are you serious?"

"Yeah. Look, try it. Just slide them between your fingers. Very calming. Helped me quit smoking, in fact." Chris took off the bracelet and uncoiled it, handing the beads to Nick. Their hands brushed together. *Don't touch.*

The train trundled on. Nick gazed out of the window at the endless suburbs, sprawling out of control over what was once prime arable land, now a seamless patchwork of semis and townhouses, and shopping centres. They passed through North York, Vaughan, Richmond Hill, Newmarket. All just the same.

"Subdivision Hell."

"What?"

"You're really quite rude, you know. I was just making an observation."

"Sorry." Nick looked down at his hands. He needed a cigarette. Badly.

"Makes you think of that old Cree proverb, doesn't it."

"What?"

"You're doing it again. No wonder she left."

"What? Who?"

"Forgotten her already, then. That's good. A step forward."

Nick felt nauseous. He shook his head pitifully.

"Some lawyer. Your girlfriend! She left you. Which is why you're on a train to nowhere, with me."

With me. Nick's head began to spin. "What proverb?"

"'Only when we have cut down the last tree, and paved over the last blade of grass, will we realize that money cannot be eaten'."

Nick nodded. "Yeah. Progress sucks."

"Which is why you're a lawyer, presumably."

Ouch.

"So you're getting off at the next stop, then?" Chris asked.

"I don't know. Where's the next stop?"

"Washago."

"Where in the wide world of sports is that?"

It was Chris' turn to stifle a giggle. "Just south of Gravenhurst. Muskoka, you know, cottage country. Your clients probably own half of it."

Nick sighed. He'd had his fill of lawyer jokes.

"You've never been north of Eglinton, have you?"

Those eyes again. Twinkling. Ironic. Stop flirting with me. "Actually, I used to spend summers at Pickle Lake, just outside of Haliburton. So yeah, I have too been north. Well, not as far as your polar bear, but... " Nick felt Chris' eyes on him. He swallowed hard. His mother's voice nagged at the back of his mind. *Don't upset your father. Get yourself a girlfriend. Think of your career. For God's sake, don't upset your father.*

"Come with me," Chris said.

"What?"

"Come with me. To Cochrane."

"How far is it?"

"The end of the line. Eight hours. Well, seven and a half now."

Nick looked at his watch.

"Why not?" Chris urged. "What have you got to lose? You're already running away from everything."

Eight hours with you. The silence fell softly between them and settled like the spring mists coating the faraway pines. Nick rested his chin in the tuck of his palm, and watched as the endless drear of the suburbs flicked past, then melted into the lush rolling pastures of rural Ontario. The early morning world seemed drenched in browns and greens. Chris' eyes traveled to the same spot on the horizon, and they seemed to coast there in an unfocused rendezvous, soaring across the tops of sugar maples, down into misty green valleys, dodging along the banks of rushing streams, flashes of sunlight through pine stands, and up again into the clear sky. Their eyes met at the same moment, brown into blue. "Want a smoke?" Chris suddenly blurted out.

Nick stared. His heart gave a little hiccup. "You said you'd quit."

"I lied."

Nick struggled to his feet and followed Chris, who had bolted down the narrow compartment like a rabbit from a snare. Nick tried not to notice the slim hips in faded Levi's, the impossibly long legs and slender body, the tie-dye T-shirt and long, wild layers of black hair with oddly placed bleached strands. He tried not to notice, like he tried not to smoke.

"This is it." Chris slid open the door to the dining car.

"I didn't know they allowed smoking on these trains?" Nick looked around at the other patrons, and loosened his tie.

Chris made a face. "Only in here. What the hell are you still wearing that for? Dump it, for God's sake. You actually look like a lawyer."

Nick grimaced at the joke, slid his tie off, and paused for a moment, staring at it. He thought about all his other ties, hanging in sad single file in his closet. A tie for court, a tie for client meetings, a tie for dates with girls he didn't like. Something inside him burned. Nick's heart pounded wildly as he crumpled the tie into a ball and tossed it out of the window. "Good riddance."

Nick watched helplessly as it caught on a tree and flapped in the wind like a defiant rebel flag. A mild panic gripped him, and he clutched at the nearest seat back.

"Here." Chris offered a cigarette. They leaned on the window ledge and inhaled deeply.

"Oh, thank God!" exclaimed Nick, exhaling smoke with his eyes closed. Chris smiled knowingly. "Back in a minute," said Nick, as he rested the precious cigarette carefully in the ashtray and headed to the toilet at the end of the compartment.

You inhale the sweet nicotine and the burn hits the back of your throat just before you breathe it down. It's been so long. You're not allowed to smoke in the apartment because he's allergic, and besides, filthy habit, ashtrays stinking up the place and residue staining the paintwork.

You lapsed once. You had to have just one, out on the balcony where you thought he wouldn't notice, but he did. All you remember is the shouting, shouting all the time. Your hands start to tremble and you curse under your breath. *Stop it, stop it, you left him, you're strong.* But you know you're not strong and your hands start to shake so violently, you drop your cigarette on the floor.

You blink back the tears that are pricking your eyelids and swallow hard. *Don't. Don't let him see.* A warm hand covers yours, firmly, stopping the shaking in its tracks. You let out the breath you didn't even know you were holding.

"Hey. Hey, you OK?" Nick covered Chris' hand with his own. "Your hands are shaking."

"It's nothing," he mumbled, turning away. Nick's hand maintained its grip. Chris shivered, although it wasn't cold.

Nick settled himself into the opposite seat, and plunked a cup of double espresso in front of him. Chris took a deep breath, let it out all in a rush, then gave a shrug. "I left my boyfriend. This morning. No big deal. I'm just, my hands start to shake, and I can't... "

Nick took a gulp of his coffee, and wiped his mouth with the back of his hand. "It's OK. It's going to be all right. Hey, look at me." Nick glanced around quickly. The other patrons of the dining car seemed engrossed in their own lives. He took Chris' hands in both of his and held them under the table. Chris stared at him, wide-eyed, lower lip trembling slightly. "Now listen," Nick began in his best lawyer-advising-client voice.

"Sshh!" Chris wrestled free of Nick's grasp.

"What? I'm not trying to... "

"No. I don't mean that."

Nick whipped his head around. "What?" He could hear a muffled bell ringing and a stamping of feet.

"Get your ticket out. The ticket inspector is here," Chris said, matter-of-factly.

"Fuck!" Nick jumped up from his seat.

"What?"

"I don't have one! I don't have a ticket."

"You got on a train without buying a ticket?" Chris muttered.

"I told you, I just jumped onto any train. I was fucked up this morning, I wasn't thinking!"

"Well, they won't buy that excuse." Chris scowled.

"What am I going to do?" Nick hissed under his breath.

"Come on, I have an idea. Here, follow me. Quickly!" Chris got up and dashed to the other side of the dining car. "Here. Get in." Shoving Nick into the restroom, Chris scoped out the other passengers, then slid in sideways and locked the door. "Breathe in!" Nick obediently sucked in his gut, not that he had any, and gave Chris as much room as possible, which wasn't a lot, in the tiny toilet built for about half a normal person.

"But they check the toilets! I've seen them do it on the commuter trains..."

Chris smirked. "Relax, man. I have a plan. You see, I *do* have a ticket."

"But..." Nick squirmed. He'd never cheated on anything in his life. Always paid his bills on time, never accrued any interest on his credit card, never late for appointments. The perfect, impeccable, unimpeachable life. And he'd just thrown his favourite Ralph Lauren tie out of a train window.

A sharp knock on the door announced the ticket inspector. "Excuse me, sir or madam, I need to see your ticket please."

The voice was imperious, no nonsense. Chris motioned to Nick to keep quiet, then called out cheerfully.

"Just a moment!" Opening the door just enough to shimmy out, Chris greeted the inspector with a bright smile and closed the door firmly. "Sorry. Junk food." Chris made a face and the inspector smiled in sympathy. She was a short little barrel of a woman, compressed into her regulation polyester like an overstuffed pork sausage.

"Ticket, please."

"Yes, sorry. Here." Chris fished the ticket out from the depths of the Roots backpack that occupied the window seat. The inspector studied it closely, nodded, and handed it back with a smile.

"That's fine, thank you. Have a good day."

Chris grinned back, pulling down the handle of the restroom door. "If you'll excuse me, I have to go finish what I started."

The inspector, thoroughly disarmed, rolled her eyes and grinned. "Don't fall in, it's a long walk back to Toronto!"

Chris waited until she was tackling the next victim before backing into the restroom. The door closed and locked, the light outside once again flashed 'occupied'.

"Well. Aren't you the dazzling urbanite?" Nick was impressed.

"Nobody can resist my charms," Chris retorted.

"Not even me?" Nick had to give as good as he got. He was a lawyer, after all.

"Especially not you." Warm brown eyes burned into Nick's soul.

When you're shoved up against someone in a confined area, you become acutely aware of the physical world. Normally we are separated from each other by what we like to call 'personal space'. That three-foot-diameter bubble that Da Vinci illustrated to brilliant effect.

We live in a vacuum, each person suspended in a void of their own creation: untouched, untouchable, alone. And we pretend that's just how we like it. The reverse is, of course, true. In our automated, vacuum-packed, homogenized, politically correct, morally desiccated world, we live out our lint-free, ready-to-eat, microwavable, lactose-intolerant lives. We don't reach out and touch someone, unless it's by text message. And we're lonely. We crave that most basic of needs, touch. The closeness of another person; the simple warmth of an embrace. To know that we are still human beings.

Nick softened his stance and allowed his body to mould against Chris. He was warm and Nick allowed himself to feel that warmth, to let it wash over and through him, breaking down the conventions of polite society that had been drilled into him. Don't get close to anyone. Don't let anyone in. Men don't show emotion, it's a sign of weakness. Find a nice girl, get married, settle down. *Don't upset your father.*

To hell with all that. He was tired. Before he even knew what he was doing, his arms were around Chris. Chris folded into him, grateful. A tiny point of moving space, in the vast expanse of time. What did it matter? Nothing mattered, only this moment. Nick closed his eyes and breathed slowly, evenly. Their breathing and heartbeats merged. Their scents blended together; Nick's top-drawer Prada cologne, and Chris, who smelled of wild heather and sunshine. "She's gone," Chris whispered into Nick's shoulder, and the spell was broken. A moment that felt like an hour, was over. Nick let out a breath. Chris opened the door a crack, "All clear. Come on."

Nick looked around apprehensively, but the inspector was nowhere to be seen. Sitting down heavily in the nearest seat, he felt slightly crumpled. Chris sat next to him. Any notion of personal space was a fading memory.

Nick looked out of the window. The train was rocking across an impossibly narrow bridge. The landscape had changed from the gentle meadows and farmland of the south. Now, huge granite boulders jutted out from the railway cuttings and the distant patchwork of forest seemed hemmed with dark evergreens.

Nick, lost in thought, barely noticed the whistle and the muffled announcement.

"This is your stop."

"What?"

"Your stop. Washago. This is where you get off, to go back to Toronto."

Nick's heart began to pound. *Go back*. He looked up. His palms were sweating. The station lumbered into view. Chris stared impassively out of the window. *What do you really want?*

"Grandma, right?" Nick willed Chris to look at him.

"Grandma. Yeah." Chris smiled, still staring out at the tiny station house, standing all by itself at the edge of the river. "You know, she used to say to me, if you don't ever want to be sorry, just do what your heart tells you all the time."

"She sounds wise." But Nick's decision was already made.

When you're seriously attracted to someone, your whole body changes. Your heart beats faster when they're close to you. You feel hot all over and your breath gets all caught up in your throat. Sometimes when you try to speak, nothing comes out. Those few moments when he held you, you could think of nothing else but what it would be like to be with him, and you fought your body's response. You could feel how much he wanted you, but you were afraid. All those words that can never be said.

You twist the beads on your wrist, hoping for an answer. As usual, you have no say in the matter; the choice is his, and his alone.

"All aboard, stand clear of the doors please. Gravenhurst next stop, Gravenhurst."

You stare out at the grey sky. Canada in April is a world toying with the notion of Spring. A day that begins balmy: summer-soft air, suffused with the joyful counterpoint of chickadee, robin, redwing, and spring peeper, turns frigid by afternoon. A line of frantic honking geese flies low past a cold day moon;

snow will follow. The bare bones of trees shiver with silent mirth.

It's ten-thirty and there's snow on the wind, but you don't care because the train is pulling out of the station and he is still sitting beside you. His presence is your lifeline and you cling to it, unashamed.

"Still here then?"

"Yeah."

"Good."

"Would you have missed me?"

"Yeah."

"Smoke?"

"Thought you'd never ask."

They lurched back to the dining car as the train swayed alarmingly. Nick grabbed at the nearest seat back. "Is it supposed to do this?"

"Don't worry. We're crossing the Severn River, it always feels like it's going to fall off the tracks."

"I'll take your word for it." They flopped into a window seat. Chris took out a crumpled pack of Camels and handed one to Nick, which he lit and gave back.

Chris arched an eyebrow. "You don't have to do that."

"Yes, I do. I'm a gentleman, remember?"

Chris snorted. "Don't gentlemen prefer blonds?"

"Not this one. Besides, I'm not sure what colour your hair really is."

"Nobody is. Not even me."

The train wobbled again as it rattled across the bridge. Chris grabbed Nick's arm. "Look, Nick! Look."

Nick followed Chris' pointing finger. Deep in a forested gully on the other side of the river, a family of white-tail deer stood, transfixed at the approach of the train, then bounding away as it passed.

"Wow. They're beautiful."

"You won't see that on Bay Street."

"To hell with Bay Street."

"That's the spirit." Chris grinned at Nick. The train pulled slowly into Gravenhurst station. The pretty station house with its whitewashed wood siding and hanging baskets of geraniums gave Nick the impression of having stepped back in time.

"What?" Chris was regarding him with a knowing smirk.

"Nothing. Well, I was just thinking, how little places like this change. The city just keeps building. More office towers, knocking all the old stuff down, and then you come up here... "

Chris nodded. "Gravenhurst hasn't changed much since Lucy Maud Montgomery vacationed here. She wrote *Anne of Green Gables*."

"How do you know all this stuff?" Nick shook his head in mock surprise.

"I read. A lot." Chris dragged on the Camel.

Nick's cigarette was already almost gone. *You're so bad for me*.

Chris stubbed out the cigarette, and shot a glance at Nick. "I told you, I'm trying to quit. Now let's eat, I'm starving."

"So," said Chris, in between his french fries. "What do you notice about the landscape up here?"

"What? What do you mean?"

"The landscape." Chris licked gravy off one finger. Nick tried not to stare. "What's different about it? Come on, you went to law school, you should be observant by nature."

Nick coughed. Chris took a french fry and dangled it, long artistic fingers twirling just enough to get a quarter-inch of gravy, then expertly nibbling the end off, before biting the fry in half with perfect white teeth. But it was the surreptitious lick of the lips that made Nick dizzy.

"What?"

"Nothing."

"I asked you a question."

"Uh... yeah. Sorry." Nick frowned and stared out of the window. The Muskoka towns of Bracebridge and Huntsville followed in quick succession. Another river, another rickety bridge. "It's um, rocky. And there are a lot of rivers and lakes. And the trees are different."

"Well done, Einstein." Chris gestured out of the window. "We're now on the Canadian Shield. It's a solid sheet of pre-Cambrian rock, mostly granite, left over from the last Ice Age. As soon as you cross the Severn and enter Muskoka, everything changes." Chris leaned across the table. "Here. Eat."

Nick meekly took the offered french fry. It felt like some kind of strange mating ritual. He sat passively as Chris fed him one at a time. He'd never done this before, not even in private. He felt the eyes of other passengers on them, but he didn't care. For the first time in his 28 years, he felt free, like he'd been bound and gagged all this time. It was the tie, it had to be the tie.

Severn, Muskoka, Fairy Lake, Big East River. Chris knew the name of every town, village, lake, river, and highway. Even the trees had names.

"See," said Chris, pointing down into a deep ravine. "The bushy ones are Scots pine, the dark, shaggy-looking ones are balsam fir, and the really tall ones with the wide arms are white pine."

"Branches, you mean," Nick interrupted. "Trees don't have arms." He took a swig of coffee.

Chris shot him a look. "You've never hugged a tree, have you?"

"No." Nick slumped back, defeated. "Doesn't it scare you, being up this high?" Changing the subject, an old lawyer's trick. It usually worked like a charm.

Chris looked out of the window. The sheer rock walls of the ravine plunged down to the dark, forested bottom where a creek meandered, a sparkling reflection of the faraway sun.

"This doesn't scare me. People scare me, sometimes. My grandma always told me, don't be so afraid of dying, that you forget to live."

Chris turned the basket of fries around and around, while Nick pretended not to notice that his elegant, delicate fingers were trembling like the aspen leaves in the valley below.

"Did he hurt you?" Nick was out on a limb, and he knew it. But he had to ask.

"Only emotionally." Chris replied, as though that made it all right.

"I'm sorry, about before."

"What are you talking about?"

"Before. In the toilet, I'm sorry." Nick fidgeted in his seat.

"You're sorry for what? For getting frisky?"

Nick flushed. "I didn't mean to, I just, there was no room, and I..."

"There's no need to apologize. I liked it. In fact, if you wanted to do it again..." Chris shrugged and gazed out of the window.

Nick frowned. "Are you hitting on me?"

"Do you want me to?" Chris arched an eyebrow, and Nick's stomach flipped.

Choose.

"Yes." Nick swallowed hard. His voice sounded hoarse and far away, and all he could hear was the pounding of his own pulse.

"Last one," said Chris, lightly.

"What?" Nick's throat had closed up barely getting the word out.

"Last fry." Chris regarded Nick with amusement. "Wanna share?"

"What do you mean?" Nick already knew, but wanted to hear him say it.

"Oh, come on. Don't tell me you've never done this with spaghetti."

Nick could only manage a nod. Chris held one end of the fry lightly between those white teeth and offered the other end. Nick bit, and swallowed, and bit, until there was nowhere to go but Chris' lips. Nick's heart was pounding in his ears. Chris waited patiently for Nick to take what was being offered.

Does time stop when you hold your breath? Dark brown eyes framed by long black lashes; full lips, waiting. Nick's mind was on hold, so his body took over, surrendering his mouth to the devastating softness of Chris' lips. The first taste was salt, then coffee, tobacco, and finally a warm deliciousness. Nick ran his fingers through Chris' hair.

A voice over the P.A. system announced the next stop, but no-one was listening.

The first time you kiss someone, it's like unwrapping a gift. You've admired the pretty paper, read the clever card, and now it's time to undo the ribbon and see what's inside. A simple touching of lips could never suffice to define what a kiss is. You offer an intimate part of yourself to another person for them to sample. You open the door to your soul, and invite them inside. At first the touch, taste, scent and then beneath all that, the things they try to hide: gentleness, vulnerability, fear, pain. Your body responds to the touch and you pray to the old gods who watch over such matters that you will be allowed to keep them, for just a little while.

Nick closed his eyes. Across the carriage, an elderly lady tutted, but he didn't care. There was no point in hiding anymore. Nick was sinking down, down into a deep ocean from which there was no return. Then, like sunlight on dark water, Chris brought him back. "What did you want to be when you grew up?"

"What?" Nick's head was spinning.

"When you were a little kid. What did you want to be?" Chris spoke softly, as though sharing a secret. Their fingers entwined of their own accord on the tabletop that separated them.

Whispered words between kisses suddenly seemed so normal. Outside the window, the green forested world sped by.

"I don't know." Nick couldn't think, couldn't breathe. Brown eyes smiled into blue.

"Come on, don't tell me you wanted to be a lawyer when you were six."

"No. No, of course not."

"Well?"

"I, um... " Nick closed his eyes as Chris stroked his hair. "I loved horses. My aunt had a farm, and I was fascinated by the farrier, you know, the blacksmith. I used to hang around while he shoed the ponies. Then one time, he taught me how to make a horseshoe. My parents sent me there every summer, so they could take off to Paris without feeling guilty. I learned all about the forge, how to work iron; I loved it. So yeah, I think I wanted to be a blacksmith."

"You think?" Chris traced a finger along Nick's jaw.

Somewhere in the back of Nick's mind, he registered the fact that the train had picked up speed and was rattling along the tracks at a breakneck pace. A wall of green flashed past, punctuated by occasional blue. "Well, yes, I know I did. I was good at it, too. Heck, I made half the metal art in my condo."

"So why didn't you?"

Nick sighed. "My father. He didn't want me working with my hands, said it was blue-collar work. Didn't want any son of his having to use the tradesman's entrance."

Chris made a face. "And a lawyer is better?"

Nick laughed. "You have to understand, it's a dynastic thing. My father is a crown prosecutor, and his father was on the bench. It was expected of me. He was even disappointed that I went into corporate law. Seven years of school just to push paper around an office. Thought it was a cop-out."

"You've spent a lot of time trying to live up to him, haven't you?"

"Yeah."

"And now?"

Nick felt a sudden burn at the back of his eyes, which was ridiculous. He hadn't cried since he was eight years old. He clenched his jaw. "Now? What do you mean, now?" *Why does my voice sound so angry?*

"I didn't mean to push, I'm sorry. Forget it." Chris looked down, fiddling with the wooden beads around the slender wrist that still wouldn't stop shaking.

Nick took Chris' hands in his. "It's not you, it's me. I always end up hurting the people who care about me."

"Is that what your girlfriend said?" Dark eyes, deep and unfathomable, gazed at the wooden beads.

"The only thing she cared about was my bank account."

"Maybe it was because she didn't know who you really were."

Nick ran his hands through his hair. "How could she, when I didn't even know?"

"Do you know now?" Chris ran a finger across Nick's lower lip.

"I think I'm getting closer."

"North Bay, this stop, North Bay." The train, which had been hurtling through space as though it wasn't even in contact with the tracks, suddenly slowed with a whoosh and glided to a stop.

"Rest stop."

"Huh?"

"Rest stop. The train stops here for half an hour. We can get out, stretch our legs, that kind of thing."

Nick looked out of the window. The station was smack in the middle of town, surrounded by bustling streets, restaurants, traffic.

"Of course, if you prefer, we can always go back in the restroom." Chris raised an eyebrow.

"That's not really my style," Nick said, laughing.

"Come on. I *know* a place." Chris stood up, and held out

a hand..

"You know a place?" Nick said, archly.

"Hey, this is my train, man. I've traveled this route so many times." Chris grinned.

Nick sighed in mock exasperation, and took the hand that was offered.

At two o'clock on a weekday afternoon, the station was practically deserted. The few passengers left on the small Northlander train variously wandered around, stretched, visited the gift shop, checked their e-mail. There was one bored ticket clerk behind the glass.

"Here." Chris led Nick around the back of the station house, and stopped at the corner of a passageway.

"The Lost and Found?" Nick frowned. His heart had made its way to his throat.

"Yeah, it's perfect. There's never anybody here." Chris cast a sideways glance at Nick. "Not that I've done this before or anything."

"Of course not." Nick was beyond caring about such details while his body was already betraying him.

Chris tried the door. "It's unlocked." Carefully, they stepped inside. "See? What did I tell... ?"

The words dangled in the air, unfinished as Nick slammed Chris against the wall and effectively removed any lingering doubt. They kissed until they were dizzy. Hands roved over warm skin, fumbling with buttons.

"Nick, Nick... " Chris gasped. Nick just smiled, and kicked the door shut with his foot.

Reaching down, Nick touched him gently, as he groaned and clutched at Nick's shoulders.

"Nick, please, I'm yours, just take me... "

I'm yours. Nick's heart pounded in his ears and his head was spinning. He was breathing hard and fast. Together, they tumbled to the floor, hands roving over each other's bodies, panting breathless open-mouthed kisses.

Chris' breath slowed to a rhythmic huff as he bucked against Nick. A primal grunt from Nick and no more words were needed; he held on until Chris cried out.

"Nick, oh, Nicky, please..."

Nobody had called him Nicky since he was a toddler. But something in Chris' voice made it sound so sensual, so personal, so intimate; almost like a secret that only they could share. Nick didn't need to be told what Chris wanted, what he needed so desperately.

When they were done, they lay on the floor, crumpled and panting. There were no words, just incomprehensible murmurs, the stroking of hair, the fluttering of fingertips, the light touch of lips on earlobe, neck, shoulders, hands. The soft brush of cheek against cheek. Love, made.

Lying in his arms on the floor of the Lost and Found, surrounded by other people's umbrellas, plaid wallets, and shopping bags, you stretch like a cat and relish the delicious sensation of all the cells in your body tingling at once. You remember his warm lips on yours, his tongue in your mouth, his hands on your skin, the longing for more. And when he took you, you cried out his name.

You run long, elegant fingers over his chest. Blue eyes, swimming pool blue. You flicker your fingertips over his stomach and he sighs. You lean over his face, taking in every detail of his features: the straight nose, the perfect skin, the fair hair with chestnut roots, the long black lashes, the soft lips. He smiles, reaches up, and strokes your hair. You must remember his scent, his taste: vanilla and cigarettes, sandalwood and clean, musky male.

You brush his lips with yours and commit the feeling to memory. You kiss like it's the first time. He runs his fingers through your hair and pulls you down, against him, into him, through him. You're a part of him now and you don't want to let go.

Somewhere in the distance, a whistle blows.

"Shit! The train!"

Nick scrambled to his feet, searching for his clothes. Chris picked out jeans, T-shirt, and sneakers from the scattered assortment of unclaimed baggage and forgotten articles that littered the small room. Half-dressed and out of breath, they made the train by the skin of their teeth.

"Fuck!"

"You said it."

Tripping over each other and giggling, they fell into the window seat. Chris leaned against Nick, and Nick instinctively opened his arms. Chris snuggled down against his chest. "You OK, baby?" Nick had never called anyone "baby" in his life. But then there were a lot of things he'd never done before today.

Nick wrapped Chris up in his arms. They kissed in that lazy way that people do, when all the walls between them have been torn down. Nick breathed in Chris' scent and stretched languidly, reaching out to recapture a frisson of remembered pleasure.

"Temagami, next stop, Temagami."

The train sped eastward past the rows of little white cottages along the highway that bordered Trout Lake, narrowly missed Quebec, then veered north towards the old growth forests of the Temiskaming shore. Nick stroked Chris' hair and they nuzzled each other. *This is heaven. I'm in heaven, right now, this moment.* A deep calm suffused Nick's body as he listened to Chris' slow, even breathing, and his head began to nod.

"Nick? Nick Sinclair?" The voice startled Nick awake, and he looked up, blinking.

"It is you! What the devil... " The speaker trailed off. He was staring, somewhat dumbfounded, at Chris.

"Hey, Duncan," Nick said, yawning. "Fancy meeting you here."

"I'll say," said the short, middle-aged man in the grey suit with the rather frantic tie. Duncan Travis was the last person Nick would have counted on meeting today. But with Chris sleeping peacefully against him, he felt invincible. Chris stirred in Nick's arms and looked up at him with a sleepy smile.

"Hey, baby," Nick murmured. "Oh, sorry, Duncan, this is Chris. We're um, on vacation."

"Uh, hi. Pleased to meet you." Duncan shuffled from foot to foot.

"Likewise, I'm sure," Chris purred, without even looking. When it became obvious that neither of them were going to move, Duncan started to back away.

"Yeah, well, I've got a client meeting in New Liskeard, of all places, so I guess I'll see you back at the office then, after the long weekend?" Duncan was studying the pattern on his tie.

"Maybe. Or maybe not," Nick said, shrugging. He was lost in dark brown eyes. Chris smiled, and licked his lips with deliberate slowness. Duncan, flushing to the roots of his sparse ginger hair, stepped backward and sideways at the same time, ducking at the last moment to avoid a collision with the luggage rack.

"I...well. You've got company, so I'll, I'll see you, OK, Nick?"

"Mmm-hmm. Later, man," Nick mumbled, not taking his eyes from Chris. With Duncan safely blundering his way into the next carriage, Nick and Chris clung to each other, giggling.

"We're on vacation?" Chris arched an eyebrow at Nick.

"Just trying to think outside the box," Nick said with a shrug.

"Nick, you only need to know one thing."

"What's that?"

"There is no box."

Nick shook his head in mock exasperation. He stroked the wooden beads around Chris' wrist.

"Here." Chris unwound the beads, and slipped them onto Nick's wrist.

"No, no they're yours."

"Not anymore. You've earned them. Welcome to the human race, Nick." Chris smiled. "Besides, I can always make another one."

"You made this?" Nick fingered the delicately carved and painted beads, strung together on a lace of fine leather.

"Yeah. You're not the only one with talent, you know." Chris stretched lazily, and sat cross-legged, grabbing the backpack from under the seat and rummaging for cigarettes.

"I didn't say I was." Nick looked out of the window for the first time in what seemed like hours, and found himself staring at a flash rainstorm, pelting in angry sheets against the glass. The sky was black. He tapped the cigarette that Chris offered him and stuck it behind his ear. "So. What do you do for a living?" When you've been as intimate as it's possible to be with another person, and then realize that you know practically nothing about them, it can come as a bit of a shock.

"Guess."

"I couldn't possibly."

"Oh, come on. Live dangerously."

"All right. Um, you don't work in an office."

"Duh. You asked what I do, not what I don't do. See, I should have been the lawyer."

"You're a smartass, is what you are. Okay, let me think, you're a designer."

"No."

"A short-order cook."

"Never. I can't even make toast."

"A window-cleaner."

"Close, but no cigar."

"Aha! You work outside."

"Yes. Carry on, Sherlock."

"You work with your hands."

"You noticed."

Nick realized that he had, in fact, noticed the short nails and the slight roughness of Chris' long, artistic fingers. "You're a landscaper."

"How incredibly bourgeois of you." Chris made a face. "I'm a gardener. I pull other people's weeds for a living."

"It's a decent job."

"Bullshit."

"Smoke?"

"About damn time."

The dining car was empty. Nick took the cigarette from behind his ear and fumbled for matches.

"So, where are we headed now?" Nick plunked himself down on the arm of Chris' seat and ran idle fingers through his soft black hair. Chris pushed back against Nick's hand like a contented cat.

"Temagami."

"Ta-ma... what?"

"Temagami. It's Ojibway for 'deep water by the shore'. How long until we get to where we're going?"

"Four hours."

"Plenty of time to get to know each other even better."

"You are so full of shit, Nick."

"I know." The rainstorm had wrung out its last drops as the train pulled into Temagami station, and the world appeared rinsed, with a fresh scent like young pine. There was woodsmoke on the wind. Nick leaned out of the window, watching as a couple with a baby in tow stepped down from the train. no-one got on.

"Cobalt, next stop. Stand clear of the doors, please."

"I think we're alone," Nick said, glancing over his shoulder at Chris, who was gazing at the sky.

The espresso-dark eyes were impassive. "Alone, yeah." The voice that answered him was as unknowable and unreachable as the distant hills that rolled in a blue-green ribbon across the endless horizon. Nick dragged down the last of his cigarette and flicked it out of the window. He turned to look at Chris, but something else caught his eye.

"Shit."

"What?"

"Someone left their laptop."

"Must have been one of the suits who got off at North Bay."

"It's still on."

"Leave it, man."

"Oh, come on. Don't turn all ethical on me."

"Hey, it's your karma, not mine." Chris shrugged.

Nick walked over and sat down, gingerly opening the laptop. He tapped a key and the screen sprang to life, then pressed another key and the Internet browser opened with a jolly flourish of sound.

"What are you doing?" said Chris, curiosity getting the better of judgment.

"Don't tell me you've never Googled yourself?"

"Is that even a word?"

Nick suddenly had the oddest sensation, that he had become Chris and Chris had become Nick. He shook himself, and typed his own name into the search engine.

"You put your name into the Google search. You'd be amazed at what pops up."

"I can't begin to imagine." Chris chewed on already ragged fingernails.

"Nicholas Cameron Sinclair III." Nick read out what he had typed. It used to be something he was proud of, but now it just sounded ridiculous.

"Fancy. Sounds like a Restoration monarch," Chris said, with the faintest trace of sarcasm.

"Three generations, all named after each other," Nick said, looking up at Chris. "But Nick will do just fine."

"So what does it tell you about yourself, that you don't already know?"

"Okay, let's see." Nick read out the first few search results. "Graduate, University of Waterloo, B.A. Honors; Osgoode Hall Law School, Class of 2002; called to the Bar, September 2004; second year associate, Cooper Michaeljohn, Barristers & Solicitors, Toronto."

"Wow," Chris said. "You really are somebody. What the hell are you doing on an empty train with me?"

"Oh, wait a second. I didn't do this just to brag. It's your turn anyway, what's your name?" He looked up at Chris, the brown eyes were sad.

"Chris."

"I know that, your full name."

"No." Chris said abruptly, and snapped the laptop shut.

"Chris, I didn't mean …" Nick jumped up, but Chris was already slamming open the door to the next carriage. It slid shut with a heavy clunk, leaving Nick alone.

"Fuck." Nick slid the laptop onto the next seat and ran after Chris, losing his footing and grabbing at the luggage rack as the train lurched wildly from side to side. Chris was standing at the far end of the last carriage, staring out of the rear window. A sudden shiver of fear sliced at Nick's mind like an ice-cold knife. He ran up behind him and stopped. "I'm sorry. I'm so sorry, please forgive me. I'm a complete and utter jerk, and I have no excuse. No excuse at all."

When he is standing right behind you, so close you can almost taste him, the pain is so intense you can't let him in, and you can't even tell him why; why in your loneliness you reach out to strangers in subways, at bus stops, on trains. You throw out a slender thread, a lifeline, and wait. If only someone would notice and grab hold – pull you back from the edge. You angrily blink back the tears that you didn't even know were streaming down your face. The ever-present blackness opens before you like a deep well and you stare it down. "Please, Chris. I'm sorry. Baby, please." The softest of touches on your shoulder, and the blackness recedes. *You don't get me today. Not today.*

"Nick?" He's still here.

"I'm here, it's OK. It's going to be OK." You fold into his arms and hold on tight.

"I didn't mean to hurt you." They sat together in the last car, watching the late afternoon sun dip behind the tree line. Tom Thomson's white pines had changed to spindly black spruce and tamaracks. The landscape looked parched and sparse. Bull moose ambled unseen through dank muskeg.

"It doesn't matter."

"Yes, it does. It matters to me."

"It's just, it's almost the end of the line," Chris said.

"I'll still be here."

"Will you?"

"Count on it. I'm a lawyer, remember? We're not allowed to lie."

"Cochrane, next stop – Cochrane."

"There's nobody left on the train. Just us."

"How long until we get to Cochrane?"

"Two hours." They kissed, like it was the last time. Making out in the dining car of a deserted train could be construed as a metaphor for something profound, but it was just sex. Chris backed Nick up into the buffet table, sending plastic plates and flatware flying. Once on the floor, it became evident that this time, Chris had the upper hand.

The slender body pinning Nick down was light enough for him to flip with ease, but along with the realization that he really didn't want to, came the unfamiliar sensation of complete surrender.

Nick let Chris kiss him until he was dizzy. There was

something about giving up control to another person that was intensely liberating. To allow another human being to break down the barriers to your secret self; to let him see you at your most vulnerable, is the true meaning of trust. It took the rest of the journey for Chris to teach Nick how to let go, how to accept the gift of pleasure, and how to cut away the bonds of other people's assumptions.

He looks up at you with those insanely blue eyes. You can still taste him. He resisted for as long as he could, but in the end, you taught him to surrender, and you buried your face in his hair as he cried out your name. Now all you have to do is hang on, just hang on and don't let go. Don't let him slip away.

"Cochrane, this is your final stop, Cochrane. This train is now out of service. Will all passengers please leave the train."

"End of the line, man." Chris' eyes searched Nick's face.

"Grandma?" Nick arched an eyebrow.

"Grandma." Chris grinned. They collected their bags and stepped off the train. The platform was deserted except for an elderly man and his dog. Inside the station, a ticket clerk sat behind the Plexiglas, playing solitaire on his computer. He nodded at Nick.

"See, we even have technology up here," Chris remarked.

"I want to see the polar bear," Nick said, feeling a little like a six-year-old on holiday.

"All in good time," said Chris, pulling Nick by the hand. "First, you have to meet grandma."

They crossed the street, walked a couple of blocks, and rounded a corner. Chris led Nick up to the front door of a small cottage with white siding and blue wooden shutters. There was a basket of marigolds hanging from the porch. A gust of wind blew one of the shutters from its hook, and it flapped frantically.

"Go on. Ring the bell and ask for Rose." Chris hung back, arms folded.

"No!" Nick protested. "She's your grandma. She doesn't

know me from Adam."

"Humour me." Chris' expression was intransigent, and Nick knew there was no point in arguing.

"Fine. But you'd better jump in and introduce me." Nick gingerly opened the storm door and rang the bell. The indignant yelping of a small dog, the sound of a chair being scraped back, then the shuffling of feet, and the front door swung open. A short, grey-haired lady in her sixties stood in the doorway, looking Nick up and down. Her dark brown eyes regarded Nick with suspicion.

"Yes? Can I help you?" She looked past Nick, and he turned, more to elicit a little assistance from Chris than to follow her gaze. But there was no-one there.

Nick ran down the path, around the corner, and stared down the deserted road. A street light flickered into life against the gathering dark. It was cold.

"Chris! Chris, what the fuck? Where are you? Quit fooling around!" Nick's heart started to beat a little too fast. He felt a crushing abandonment weigh down on his chest. "Chris!"

Nick ran back to the cottage door, where Chris' grandma was still standing, frowning at him.

"I'm sorry, ma'am, Chris was right here, behind me."

The petite, frail-looking lady shook her head. "That's impossible," she said, flatly.

"What are you talking about? Chris and I, we were on the train together. All the way from Toronto. How else would I know where you lived, who you were? You're his grandmother, right? Your name is Rose?"

"Right. But everyone knows that around here."

"I'm not from around here. I'm from Toronto, I just told you that, weren't you listening to me?" Nick was aware that his voice was becoming strident. His stomach was doing back flips.

The old lady sighed, as though she was worn out. "I think you'd better come in."

Nick followed Rose into her living room, where she sat down heavily in an old leather recliner. Nick perched gingerly on a hard wicker chair opposite her, but almost immediately jumped up again.

"There! That's him, right there!" Nick ran over to the framed photograph on the mantel over the fireplace. Chris grinned at him from the photo. Younger, but the same glossy black hair streaked with bleach, the same dark brown eyes, happy and smiling in the sunshine; and on the slender wrist, a bracelet of painted wooden beads.

"My favourite grandchild," said Rose, wearily.

Nick stared at the photograph. He took it down from the mantel and studied it closely. Suddenly, he remembered. "Here, I'll prove it to you," Nick said, excitedly. "Chris gave me ..." He looked down at his wrist, but there was nothing there. "The bracelet, he gave me the beaded bracelet, it's in the picture..." Nick trailed off. He was at a loss. "I must have dropped it on the road. It must have fallen off, I'll go and look for it right now. I'll ..." Aware that he was babbling like an idiot, He looked back at Rose, only to find that she was crying.

"Why are you doing this?" she sobbed.

"What do you mean? Why am I here? Because Chris told me to come and see you. Because he brought me here. Where is Chris? Why are you crying? What the hell is going on?" Nick heard his own voice as though it belonged to someone else.

"Please leave." Rose snatched the photograph from Nick's hands and clasped it to her heart.

"I'm sorry, I didn't mean ..." Nick stammered. "Duncan! I can phone Duncan, he saw us, just give me a minute ..." Nick fumbled for his BlackBerry, and then remembered that it was gone.

"Get out. You've done more than enough damage as it is." Rose's voice was cold.

"But, I'm not ..." Nick began to protest, but Rose opened the front door.

"Get out. Get out of my house, right now, and don't come back."

"Rose, please!" A note of desperation had crept into Nick's voice.

"Get out!" Nick was unceremoniously shoved out onto the sidewalk. The door slammed shut behind him. Nick stared down the street, a cold swirl of panic rising in his gut. It was after eight o'clock, and night was closing in fast. He started to retrace his steps, looking for the bracelet among the clumps of dirty snow that lined the pavement. *Chris, where are you? Don't leave me here all alone, please, Chris, I need you, please...*

Cochrane in April wears a somewhat bleak aspect. Nick walked on, back towards the train station. He rubbed his wrist where the beads used to be, and tried to ignore the strange hot prickling at the back of his eyes. When the station came into view, tears began to stream down his face. The sensation was so unfamiliar. He reached up to touch his face and found that his cheeks were wet. He hurt all over, with a nameless agony. For the first time since he was eight years old, Nick Sinclair was crying.

Nick wandered aimlessly across the tracks at the station. He had enough on his credit card to buy a ticket back. But why? For what?

"Hey, watch it there, fella." The elderly station attendant's words cut into Nick's thoughts. "Stay off the tracks, the sign says. Youngster came a cropper there, about a year ago now. Some kind of lovers' tiff, you know how it goes. Only 22-years-old – very sad."

Nick stepped up onto the platform. "Chris?" he muttered, his voice sounding hollow.

"Yes, that was the name. Young lad, went to live with some asshole from the city, came home a wreck. Walked in front of the northbound train."

Nick's knees gave way. Bile reached up from his insides, making his head swim. All the breath had left his body and he stared down into the black void that was opening up before him. *Chris...*

"Yeah. Lucky really, if you can call it luck. Hasn't moved or said a word for damn near a year now. The doctors say a coma like that can last for the rest of the patient's life."

"What?" Nick's mind spun back from the edge of the murky dark. "Wait, what?"

"Kid's in a coma. Like I said, very sad."

"Where?" A direct shot of pure adrenaline hit Nick's muscles and he sprang to his feet. "Where is he? Is it far? How can I get there?"

"Hold your horses, lad!" The old man rubbed his chin and looked Nick up and down, as though appraising his market value. "Lady Minto Hospital, ICU. But they won't let you in unless you're family."

"I don't care. Take me there. I'll pay you any amount of money. Name your price, just get me there."

"All right, all right. Give me a minute." The elderly gentleman struggled to his feet and reached for the phone. As he lifted the receiver, he frowned at Nick. "You're not him, are you?"

"What? Who?" Nick said, somewhat at a loss.

"The boyfriend." The man's finger hovered over the dial pad.

"No! No, well not that one, at any rate," Nick replied. "Please. I have to see him."

It seemed to take forever for the cab to arrive, but finally Nick was on his way. Cochrane seemed drab – a grey little town at the end of the line. By the time they got to the hospital, it was pitch dark, and visiting hours were over at the ICU.

"But I've come all the way from Toronto," Nick found himself explaining to the pretty blonde nurse. "The train doesn't get here until 7:45."

"Family only in the ICU, sir, I'm sorry," the nurse said, in a syrupy voice that was supposed to be comforting.

"But I have to see Chris. I have to, you don't understand. I stopped by to pick up Rose, his grandmother, but she was upset, she told me to come by myself anyway," Nick lied. At this point, he'd lie to the Dalai Lama.

The nurse checked a piece of paper under her computer keyboard. "Yes, Rose is listed as next of kin, she hasn't been by for a while." The nurse looked directly at Nick, searching his face. "She's lost hope, I think."

Nick nodded slowly. "Yes. Yes, I think you're right." He held his breath. He could feel the nurse sizing him up, making a mental note of the tear tracks on his face.

"All right, I suppose it can't do any harm. Through these double doors, then the first door on the right."

"Thank you, thank you."

The nurse looked up to say 'You're welcome,' but Nick was gone.

The first door on the right was ajar, and Nick knocked softly, even though he knew that no-one would answer. The room was dimly lit, and beige hospital blinds shut out the night. The regular beep of a monitor punctuated the silence.

"Chris?" Nick whispered. The figure in the bed lay still, propped up with pillows, wired to an I.V. Nick sat down on the visitor's chair. Thinner, for sure, paler, but unmistakably Chris. The same shoulder-length black hair, fine features, long black eyelashes. And around a wrist so thin you could see the bones under the translucent skin, a bracelet made of painted wooden beads.

"Chris, it's Nick. I'm here, I found you. Chris, wake up. Please, I miss you, I need you, please." But there was no answer.

Nick took the pale, slender hand in his own and cried. He cried for his own loss, and for Chris, and for Rose. He cried for a long, long time. When he was done crying, he talked to the unconscious figure in the bed, about his job and how he hated it, about his father's preconceptions and his mother's denial. He talked about how he could never say the words, not to anyone, that was why his girlfriend had left him, it was why everyone always left him, because he couldn't say the words. And then he slept.

Morning came cold and clear, the watery spring sun filtering through the hospital blinds Nick pulled them up, flooding the room with light. He stared out at the sky; a sky so high and blue, it could drown any sorrow. He sighed, and ran his hands through his hair. There was a bustle of noise from the nurses' station. Soon they would be coming in to check the I.V. and turf him out.

"Nick?" It was only a whisper on the wind. "Nick?" The voice was weak and hoarse. But it was there, and it was real. Nick found himself rooted to the spot. His heart was racing, but he couldn't move. "Nicky?" There it was again. With a supreme effort of will, Nick forced his feet to turn. He ran to the bed and knelt down.

"Is it really you? Are you real?" The soft voice could only manage a whisper. Dark brown eyes gazed up at Nick, the long black lashes fluttering.

"Yes, it's me, it's Nick, I'm here, Chris I'm here."

"You came. You found me," Chris murmured.

"You led me here. I was scared, so scared I'd lost you forever." Nick gathered him into his arms.

"I dreamed of you. We were on the train."

"How much do you remember?"

"Everything."

"Is it really you?" Nick echoed Chris' question.

"Don't believe the evidence of your own eyes? Some lawyer."

"It's you."

They kissed, like it was the first time.

"You've been crying. I thought you didn't cry."

"I'm doing a lot of things lately that I haven't done in a long, long time."

"Why were you crying? Was it because of me?"

"You don't really need to ask me that, do you?"

"Yes, I do."

"God! You haven't changed."

"Not a chance."

"Chris, you know how I feel about you."

"Tell me anyway."

As Nick gathered Chris into his arms, closing his eyes and breathing in his warmth, his scent, his life, he realized that he could never go back. Just as Chris had dreamed of him, Nick would dream a future for them. So Nick said the words that he had never said in his life before, and became more than the sum of his parts, more than his father's expectations. In the space of a single day, on a train to nowhere, Nick Sinclair became a human being.

What if you slept
And what if
In your sleep
You dreamed
And what if
In your dream
You went to heaven
And there plucked a strange and beautiful flower
And what if
When you awoke
You had that flower in your hand
Ah, what then?

~ Samuel Taylor Coleridge

10
Curious Case of Jenni Wen

A. J. Kirby

Author

A.J. Kirby has published two novels and a large number of short stories in a variety of media, including print anthologies, magazines and journals, on-line and as pod casts. He was awarded third prize in the Luke Bitmead Writer's Bursary competition 2008 judged by a panel including best-selling authors Deborah Wright and Zoë Jenny, and has also been runner-up in the Huddersfield Literature Festival and short-listed for the Mere Literary Festival prizes. Andy's writing was also featured in Legend Press' 2009 short story collection *8 Rooms*. He lives in Leeds with his girlfriend Heidi and lucky black cat Eric.

Curled into a foetal comma in my wet dress, I whispered prayers that it *was* a comma – simply an intermission – and not the full stop of my life.

Next to me the long, malnourished body of a man became an exclamation mark; it was topped by a bulging head that seemed weirdly separated from his body. Someone had ripped open his checked shirt, exposing his sunken chest and a stomach, which seemed to have gone mouldy; damp patches were everywhere. Under his beige combat shorts I could see knees which knocked together. No musculature. No movement. He was either dead or close to it.

I didn't dare take a similar inventory of my own body. Didn't want to know. I was alive, I knew I was alive and that was all that mattered. I could feel my heart clattering away in my chest; I was scared.

I was scared because I still had some idea at least of who I was and I wanted to protect that tiny piece of myself. And because the three snarling men who stood over us, waving their massive meaty paws around, seemed to be paying little or no attention to the dead man, but were certainly interested in me.

The three men were dressed almost identically: huge clod-hopping boots – shit-kicker boots, my brother Lanh would have called them – and these luminous yellow vests which speared my eyes as though I'd not seen anything bright for a long, long time.

One of the men, the largest of the group, shouted something into my face. I had no idea what he was trying to communicate.

Maybe, I thought, the man just liked shouting. Maybe he was like the mad dog that was parked-up in the yard out back of Romi's Bar in the village. Lanh and I used to laugh at that big, flop-eared dog. We were amused by the way he raged at the very night as though bitterly unhappy about his lot in life. As though he thought he should have been built for something better

But this Dog-Man was no laughing matter, despite his stupid fuzzy moustache, which was now so close that it was tickling my neck.

Dog-Man spat almost continuously. Whether he was clearing his throat before speaking, or mid-sentence, or after he'd finished as though getting rid of a horrible taste in his mouth. He spat so much that it left a snail-trail of saliva across his moustache.

I tried to speak to him. I tried to open my mouth to ask him what was going on – nothing like this had been mentioned in Orientation 101 – but all that came out was a muffled wheeze. Nothing the man would hear. *Come on, it's easy*, I told myself. And in my head I screamed the words WHERE AM I? In my head I demanded to know what was happening to me, how I'd come to be here and what they were intending to do with me. But no words spirited out of my mouth. All I felt was the cracking of my lips, which I now realised were so dry, so parched, that they'd become almost welded closed. Compared to the Dog-Man and his lake of saliva, I was a desert.

And a cold desert at that; I couldn't stop myself from shivering. The second man seemed to find this funny. Or at least he did when he stopped pacing around me. He reminded me of an angry cockerel, the way his head bobbed up and down as he circled. Unable to keep still, he kept reaching down to his belt, twitching for a truncheon with which to batter me. I got the feeling that if the larger, moustachioed man were not here, Cockerel would have quite happily exclamation-marked me (and maybe had already done so to the poor guy by my side).

The third man held my attention for longer. Although he was dressed the same, he didn't have the same violence bubbling just below the surface. Instead, he had a strange calmness about him, which seemed out of place. He was more like a buffalo, I supposed. Or perhaps he was simply drunk. I'd seen the same mindless staring eyes in certain men in our village. Nevertheless, my eyes appealed to his; I begged him to explain what was happening. But it seemed I had stared at his face for rather too long; after a moment, Cockerel gleefully slapped me.

The slap was good. It allowed my head to clear a little. I began to take in a little more of my surroundings.

It was dark and it was bitterly cold. We were outside but the air contained nothing like the humidity I was used to. Neither could I see a single star in the sky. It was as though they'd finally blinked off for good; stopped watching.

But the more I took in, the more I realised was wrong with the scene. Artificial light washed past us every few seconds before leaving us shrouded in darkness again. And every time this light passed it showed that we were in the shadow of a huge articulated lorry; a great dinosaur of a creature, which seemed to creak and moan as if it were alive when the wind hit it. Along one side of the lorry was a jagged tear, as if the three men had attacked it, wounded it. It had spilled its guts onto the floor; crates and crates containing electrical goods which had been hacked open; and me. Evidently I had been spilled out of the lorry's guts too.

I screwed up my eyes. I didn't really understand. Neither, it appeared, did the three men. Underneath all of their whispered, spitting rage at me, they were mystified. They just wanted an explanation.

Even before I re-opened my eyes I felt one of them leaning in closer, his hot breath spraying out all over my face. It had to be Dog-Man. He was repeating the same thing over and over, but I had no idea what it was. As my eyes were fixed on Dog-Man,

Cockerel was able to catch me by surprise. Without warning, he grabbed me under the arms and started to drag me to my feet. His rough hands touched far more of me than they needed to.

Finally, words came out of my mouth, "Let go of me!"

Cockerel simply smirked, he was now marching me round and round the lorry as though we were learning the steps for a dance. Every few moments he would stop and Dog-Man would gesture wildly in my face as though trying to make me understand something. Judging by their frustration, it was a very easy concept they were trying to get through to me, but I just couldn't make out anything resembling a language in their barks, wheezes and grunts.

The only sound I did understand was my bare feet slapping on the concrete floor and echoing back off other concrete things, taller concrete things, which loomed above us, almost invisible. Indeed, the more I looked, the more I saw that everywhere was elephant-grey concrete. Even the three men seemed as though they were made from the stuff. They were like great slabs of dumb no-feeling concrete that hadn't quite set yet. When they moved around the lorry, they moved heavily as though weighed down. Eventually, we stopped marching. A CB radio on Dog-Man's hip had buzzed into life and I could hear a tinny voice seemingly asking questions. Dog-Man moved away from us in order to speak, which I thought was funny, in a sad sort of way. I'd not been able to understand a single word he'd said thus far; what made him think I would understand now? Was it that he simply did not trust me or my kind? I suspected it was. For Cockerel clearly felt the same way. He still gripped me hard, but now his superior had moved away, he took the opportunity to bait me. He sneered and pecked his beak close to my face. I could tell that it took all of his self-restraint to stop from smashing me in the mouth.

Finally Dog-Man finished with his CB radio and came back to us barking orders and spitting even more than he had done earlier. Cockerel nodded compliantly, taking a moment to wipe a little of the excess saliva from his face, and then he took hold of my arm again, tighter this time, extending long fingernail-claws into my flesh. Biting into me; marking me.

They dragged me over to the other side of the lorry where a long, coiled snake of a hosepipe was waiting. Cockerel pinned me to a wall and then Dog-Man turned on a heavy jet of water. It hit me with some force, winding me; almost knocking me over. But the quiet, Buffalo-eyed man held me up. Not with his fingernail-claws as Cockerel had done, but more gently somehow. As though he felt that no human being should have to be subjected to such humiliation.

Being hosed down; in the villages it was what we did to the farm animals or to dogs when they'd rolled about in the dirt. It was a way of cleansing them so they were fit to be touched. I understood the meaning of their water torture completely.

Cockerel was laughing now as it quickly became clear to them that my will was breaking. I tried to free my mind and to simply submit to the humiliation. But suddenly, something struck me as being very strange. Although Dog-Man had been hosing me down for what seemed like hours, I was becoming dryer and dryer by the minute. No longer was my dress sticking to me. No longer was I shivering. When the water was finally turned off, it was as though it had never been there in the first place. Perhaps it was simply my mind playing tricks on me; I was close to the edge as it was. Lanh was always saying it, or used to be. Perhaps finding myself in such a situation, without a single clue as to how I got there, had finally pushed me into insanity.

Strange things continued to happen. Suddenly, Cockerel was pushing me back onto the concrete floor again. For a moment, I feared that he meant to choke the life out of me; such was the grip he had on the top of my dress. But then he moved away from me and made an obvious gesture that transcended language. He scrunched up his face and held his nose as though being near me offended his nostrils. In spite of myself, I took a quick sniff under my armpit and realised that I did indeed smell quite badly. Why did I smell if they had just hosed me down? I sniffed again, getting a good lungful of the me-smell now. And then I looked up and saw the men laughing at me. I realised at once that it was our first meaningful conversation. Our *only* meaningful communication.

And then, all of a sudden, the dead man was by my side once more. I'd almost forgotten him in my terror, in my incomprehension of what was going on. Almost before I even had the time to check whether he was breathing, I felt more hands grabbing at me and lifting me up. I felt those same hands launching me up into the back of the lorry; throwing me as if I were as insignificant as a rag-doll. The body of the dead man came next and his swollen head landed somewhere near my bare foot. I had to choke back a scream as I wriggled away from him.

"You *can't* leave me in here with a dead man!" I cried into the night air.

But leave me they did. It was as though as soon as I was safely in the shadows, crouching petrified in the furthest, darkest corner of the lorry, I was completely forgotten. The three men seemed far too busy re-loading the lorry with all of the broken crates that had been spilled out on the concrete floor outside. They seemed absolutely engrossed with whispering excitedly amongst themselves as though they were on the verge of making some amazing discovery that I'd turned into an irrelevance.

When the final crate was slammed into place and everything was locked down tight, I was trapped. Wedged in. But I found that if I tucked my legs up under my chin and wrinkled up my bare toes, I could at least sit upright. Although it was a tight space they'd left me in, it did seem to fit almost magically around my body (or the other way round). Someone had even thought to leave a blanket for me.

After a last cursory flash of the torch and a couple of half-hearted shouts (and spits) from Dog-Man, I saw Buffalo-eyes and Cockerel climbing up onto the back-lip of the lorry and starting to pull the rolling back door down fully. The last thing I saw of the outside world was the back of Cockerel's high-visibility vest, the word 'IMMIGRATION' written across it.

As the door finally rolled shut, I could hear his cocky, evil laughter echoing through the cogs and wheels and machinery underneath me.

What the hell did that mean? What the hell did any of it mean? I racked my brain to remember if they'd told us any of this would happen at the Orientation 101 classes, but they hadn't. And those classes were the last real thing I could remember. After them, life was just a stinking, cramped black hole.

I must have passed out in the back of the lorry, whether from exhaustion or from sheer unadulterated terror I don't know. All I know is that when I came to we were moving.

Inside the tarpaulin shell, the noise of the lorry's movement was so loud that I was surprised I'd not woken sooner. Straps slapped, roller-shutter doors chattered incessantly, wheels crunched and squeaked, the engine throbbed. It sounded like I was inside the bowels of a ravenous beast. Smelled like it too; the stench of decay was everywhere. The dead man was the obvious source of the stink, but his ripe smell was underscored by other scents, some of which I could tell were coming from me. Prime amongst those was the bestial smell of desperation. Like a caged animal, I'd had some key part of me taken away.

The stink was getting worse. My nostrils quivered as I thought I caught the grace notes of human waste in the overall rotten melody. I couldn't stop myself from retching, but nothing came up. I realised that there was nothing inside me *to* come up.

I tried breathing through my mouth to avoid another retching incident but the air tasted rancid on my tongue. *Mind over matter*, I told myself. Shakily, I tried to climb to my feet but either my limbs wouldn't do what I told them or the crate I was clutching onto wouldn't provide the right purchase. So I sat back down again and stared into the blackness, wondering if I'd ever get used to it. Wondering whether I'd ever see anything again. In my blindness, other senses began to take over. My sense of touch being one of them.

I let my shaking fingers do my seeing for me. I let them stroke the metal wall behind me; the wall that I figured must divide me from the lorry's driver. It was cold to the touch, unwelcoming. But something made me keep running my hands across it. Something told me that there was something there that was worth finding. Finally, after I don't know how long, I found what I was looking for. Deep scratches torn into the metal. I traced my fingers along the tears, trying to work out whether there was a message there for me. Like a flash of light illuminating the whole sorry container, it dawned on me what the scratches actually were. They were the painful, jerky rendering of my name. Or rather, my new name.

Westerners call that walking-over-a-grave feeling *déjà vu*. Literally: seen before. And as my fingers finally picked out the name on the wall that was exactly how I felt. The name was surely written by my own fair hand. Had to be; there was that same looping cat's tail on the 'J'. There was that same attempt at a smiling face over the 'I'. I had dreamed of scratching my name on the lorry's wall and the dream felt as real as the actual sensory perception of the thing. It was almost as though I was in two places at once. The past and present, dream-world and real-world.

The name on the wall was Jenni. A name that took me back to Orientation 101 class and the tight-lipped Madame Dugard. She was the woman who had given us our new names, and mine was Jenni.

"Repeat the names over and over in your head so you can get used to them, so you can't be caught off guard even if they are snarling in your face or threatening you with a truncheon," she said, leaning against the blackboard and showing us once again how to form the alien letters. "Write them too, if you can write. For you'll find that through writing something down, you can memorise almost anything."

The ten of us in the class obediently bent over our notebooks and tried to scrawl out the letters just as she had, but most of us couldn't get our hand-eye coordination in. Madame Dugard picked up one of the books at random, sneered at the poor girl's attempts and then threw the book onto the floor.

"How much are you paying for us to help you?" she barked.

The poor girl turned into a quivering wreck, all blushes and uncertain smiles.

"Two years' wages," I interrupted.

"That's right," said Dugard. "It is costing your family two years' wages to give you this remarkable opportunity to learn. And we are giving you the education, nay orientation skills, which will stand you in much better stead than anyone else who tries to cross borders that aren't supposed to be crossed. And what do you do? Blush and smile. Honestly, girls... Start again from the top."

Madame Dugard returned to her seat at the front of the class and poured herself a large glass of wine. She drank from it fiercely as though as angry at the wine as she was at us. It was our third such lesson and none of the girls (me included) seemed to be getting the message. I felt bad for her. Perhaps the men would, in turn, be angry with her and cut her money.

I knew all about how much these people had kindly invested in us, just to give us a good start once we were in Europe. That's why so many of us were choosing to go the FFF route these days. FFF, like all the other 'people traffickers' took a great deal of money from us in order to arrange our transport, but at least they included these Orientation 101 classes in the price.

After all 'if you sound like a country bumpkin Vietnamese, why, you'll be treated like a country bumpkin Vietnamese,' as Madame Dugard was always telling us. She wanted to teach us how to be proper European ladies. Women with names like Jenni and Laura who couldn't possibly be stuffed into one of those awful camps once they'd reached the tail of the snake. She wanted us to be the kind of women that Westerners would recognise, "remind them of their sisters and their grannies and they'll never turn the hoses on you," she said.

But it was difficult. She didn't understand that it was hard for us suddenly to become other people. Madame's writing the name over and over again technique still hadn't worked for any of us. No matter how many times I drew those cat's tail 'J's or smiley-face dotted 'I's, I still thought of myself by my real, Vietnamese name. If someone were to ask me to write down what I was doing at any particular point, I would have written 'Dung is going to the toilet' or 'Dung is trying to half-run along the alley at the back of Romi's Bar without alerting the mad dog to her presence.' Instead, what worked for me was making it all into a game like the ones that Lanh and I used to play. I made like I was a secret agent. I pretended that my secret new identity was all that was keeping me from great danger...

My fingers traced through the carved name once again and I tried to remember whether I'd actually been here before and not just in a dream. Jenni. I liked the sound of the name; sort of tinkly, *musical*. Not like some of the English names that friends in Orientation 101 were given. Not so long and tongue twisting.

Jenni sounded nice but I didn't know what it meant. Perhaps that was why I had such trouble remembering it. There could be no associations with the name. If ever I forgot Lanh's name (as if) I could think: *what do you call someone who always has a plan, be it to make Mr C fall in his own shit pit (a long story) or to go off and join the Band of Brothers from Romi's Bar? What do you call someone who is street-smart enough to never be caught by the ravenous jaws of the village's mad dog?* Ah! Lanh. That's it.

My own real name was Dung, which in our language meant beautiful (which I hoped that I was, despite the fact that in the long-mirror in mother's bedroom I looked gawky and too young, despite being way-past teenage.) When Madame Dugard first read my name from the register in Orientation 101, she couldn't stop laughing. At first, I took it to mean that she couldn't possibly think me beautiful. Tall for a Vietnamese country bumpkin *sure*, long-legged like Westerners at a push, but *beautiful*? Who was I kidding?

"Mother says I'm an ugly duckling..." I muttered.

But Dugard carried on laughing. Over the course of our week of sessions, we all got used to the almost drunken way she let herself go when she laughed but on that first day, I suppose it scared us. When finally she composed herself she told the whole class that Dung didn't mean beautiful at all in English. Indeed, she began to snort with laughter once more when she tried to explain what Dung *did* mean in that distant language. In Lanh's hand such knowledge would have been an incendiary device, but he was long gone. Street-smart enough to get away. In the hands of the 'Orchids' and 'Placid Ones' in Orientation 101, it was forgotten about almost as soon as Madame had said it.

For a while, I thought nothing. I let myself drift, occasionally feeling a sharp twinge in my legs as the cramps set in, but nothing else. And then I suppose I started to listen to the sounds of the lorry once again. Even over the rattle and hum sound of the engine, I could, if I concentrated hard enough, hear the tinny crackle of what sounded like a radio coming from the driver's cab on the other side of the metal wall. It was playing (or at least I thought it was playing) 'The Scientist' by that droning English band they made us listen to in Orientation 101 class. I couldn't remember the name of that band for a dozen of Lanh's kisses, but I could remember the MTV video; everything happening back-to-front. A little like my life had become, I imagined.

I wondered who was in there. Would it be one of the three from the concrete place? What did he possibly think he was carrying in his truck? I wondered how he could listen to his radio without a care in the world if he knew that there was a dead Vietnamese in the back. But then I remembered the way Cockerel had looked at me. I remembered the barely contained hatred in his eyes and that jerky, scary way he walked around me, head bobbing, readying himself to strike.

The monotony of pain and the mind-numbing battery I'd taken from an almost constant state of confusion were wearing me down. But, as Lanh always said, it was amazing what the human body could get used to, and soon I started to feel a little better again.

I noticed that my eyes were starting to grow somewhat accustomed to the dark. And I clutched onto this small victory as though it was the most important thing in the world. I forced myself to make a mental list of everything I saw when I looked at my immediate surroundings. It was like a life-or-madness game of I-Spy.

"I spy with my little eye something beginning with 'C'," I whispered.

Ah! Too easy. Crate. Try harder, ladeez, chirped the voice in my head. For some reason, it sounded exactly like Madame Dugard. I wondered what she would have made of the fact that she'd suddenly become one of the voices in my half-howling-mad head? She'd probably have simply poured another load of wine into that globe-sized glass, and just leaned back and got on with it.

"I spy with my little eye something beginning with 'P'."

Another easy one. Come on ladeez, what do you think I am? A country bumpkin like you? It's 'P' for plastic bag. As in the two plastic bags that you can see just out of reach behind that third crate there... That's right, near the outstretched hand of your travelling companion. Not much good at this game, eh?

There were indeed two bulging plastic bags close to the dead man. I steeled myself to crawl closer to him in order to check them out, only, as soon as I got any closer, I realised what was in them. I jerked backwards, clipping the side of one of the crates.

You know what's in those bags, don't you Dung? Don't you; dung? That's a good one.

My head was filled with the cackling of Madame Dugard. She was right; dung filled the bags. Dung from Dung, although I couldn't remember doing it.

"Shut up! Shut up!" I screeched, my voice almost as high-pitched as the squeaking of the lorry's brakes. "Get out of my head!"

Not that easy, I'm afraid, Mzzz Country Bumpkin. I'm here for the duration. You didn't think the FFF would just leave you on your own did you?

Lanh used to say that the first sign of madness was talking to yourself, but maybe that was because I did it a lot, and especially when he started hanging out with the men at Romi's Bar. Back then I didn't see the harm in it, but now? Now it felt as though I had altitude sickness. Like I was lost at the top of the peak of my own mind and couldn't find a way out. But at the same time, so pressed in by darkness, by dung and by dead man's hands, I felt cornered. Like I was being crushed in so eventually I'd become so small I could simply be folded away and put in someone's pocket for later.

Now when I tried to speak, it felt as though cockroaches were crawling out of my mouth. When I tried to breathe, leeches latched on to my nostrils. When I tried to listen to the dim radio-sounds from the driver's cabin, all I got was an earful of cotton wool. I was drowning in myself. Dung's body becoming her own tomb before finally becoming what it was pre-destined to be from the moment of slapped-arse naming – dung. Shit. Nothing. So this was what it felt like to be buried alive. This was what my worst nightmare felt like…

Back when we were snot-nosed, raggedy-pants children, Lanh and I used to love scaring each other. While Lanh was squatting over the toilet, I would crawl under the door like a snake and bite him on the ankles. While I was drifting off to sleep at night, he would make his fingers into a spider and crawl them across my face. Together, we were braver, daring each other to confront the huge dog out the back of Romi's Bar in the village. We poked him with sticks until he was spinning-round crazy, throwing up great gobs of saliva all over the place before we ran away giggling into the night. We'd steal up on the drunks out front of the bar while they were comatose, sleeping with their eyes open. We'd stick our mucky paws into their pockets and take a couple of coins from them and then, as our final coup de grace, we'd extricate the glass from their hand and we'd pour the last of the remaining bad-poison onto their crotch so when they woke up, they'd believe they'd wet themselves.

We were very free children. We ran amok in the village, never listening to the adults when they told us to behave. But we pushed it too far when Lanh started in on Mr C. Mr C was a big Yank left over from the big war. Apparently he was something called AWOL, which we didn't really understand. We thought it might have had something to do with that crazed look in his eyes, like his spirit had taken leave of his body and rendered him mad. After a few years, he'd started to look like an old man of the forest. All long red hairs everywhere; wild and matted.

Mr C liked to smoke dope all day long in his tent on the outskirts of the village, where our land bordered on jungle. In fact, that was pretty much all he did. Smoking so much for so long did something terrible to his bowels though, and eventually he built his own pit so he didn't have to keep running off to use the toilets in Romi's Bar. His pit was awful and primitive. Most of the women in the village wouldn't come near him after he dug it, but he didn't seem in the least bit bothered by having this huge grave-thing in what was his garden.

After a while, Lanh and I started creeping up on him while he was at his painful-sounding ablutions. We'd throw small stones at the back of his neck and at his exposed behind so he thought insects were attacking him. We'd make howling-monkey noises so he couldn't concentrate properly. And then, we decided that it would be the funniest thing we'd ever done if we could manage to make Mr C fall in his own shit pit.

We spent ages and ages coming up with a plan that would work, and then finally Lanh saw something on the television in Romi's Bar, (he was always sneaking in there) he decided that we needed to make a trap. We would cover part of the pit with big palm leaves so that in the dark it looked just like it was normal undergrowth. Then we would wait in the bushes and watch as Mr C dived out of his house, ran to the pit and then, as soon as his full weight was on the leaves, he'd go crashing down into it. The plan was foolproof.

That night, our trap laid, we crouched low in the tall grass so as not to be seen. (I think that even if we had been seen Mr C would have ignored us, but that was beside the point; this was our very own military operation.)

After a long time, we heard his shaky wooden door being prised open. We watched him creep across the dark ground, almost bent double such was the sting in his bowels. He was walking with the aid of a stick, we now noted; he was so wasted.

As he reached the edge of the pit, we were sure that he was about to drop through the leaves. I stifled a giggle, Lanh tried to hold back a whoop of joy. He stepped onto the leaves…This was it, the moment of truth…And then, as the big leaves started to give way under his weight, he gave out this terrible wounded sound, like the yelp of a tormented animal. One leg slipped through and down, as if here were on quick-sand. The other started to give way, but right at the last minute he managed to hook his stick onto the trunk of a nearby tree and hoist himself up and out of the hole.

Then he turned to the long grass and started shouting in his own language. He was whipping the stick back and forth. He was a man possessed.

Lanh gave out a terrible groan and then turned on his heels, but I couldn't seem to get my legs to work properly. The ground was wet and it seemed to be eating up my little feet. And now Mr C was gaining on me, batting away long grass with his stick, growling like an animal.

When he found me, he dragged me by the hair back to his pit, screaming questions in my face. I didn't have the strength to fight him off. I could only let myself be dragged. I suppose that was the moment I learned how to submit myself, no matter how painful circumstances may be.

We reached the stinking pit. He lifted me with his string arms and then launched me into its hungry mouth. I landed on soft ground but didn't want to think about why it was soft. I looked up and saw many, many stars glittering around me, watching. I also saw the great shaggy ginger mass of Mr C, peering over the edge looking immensely pleased with himself. I shouted up to him, pleaded with him to help me out. But he simply smiled one of his funny gap-toothed smiles and then started to put each and every one of my blinking friends out of business. He dragged more palm leaves over the top of the pit. Palm leaves and now long struts of wood (which he'd been given free by the village so that he could make his house stand up properly). He was laughing maniacally as he buried me alive…

I woke up in darkness in the back of the truck wondering how I'd managed to fall asleep again and then deciding that it was because my body was so weak. I was lapsing in and out of consciousness, in and out of past and present. Even now, Mr C's pit felt as real and as shitty to me as the hard wood of the crate, which my tender foot was resting on. I could half-see his orange form dancing back and forth as he carried more flotsam and jetsam with which to cover me up. I screwed up my eyes and tried to imagine him away. It had all turned out OK. Why was I so scared by it now?

Maybe it was because the smell was the same. When I'd been down there in his pit, I could smell the human waste, sure. But I'd also smelled something far, far worse. Only when Lanh came back, bringing with him all the men from Romi's Bar did I discover what that smell was. When the men dragged me out, they also dragged out the bodies of at least three dead pigs and a couple of chickens. A dog too, maybe one of the pups from the mad dog at Romi's last litter. Human waste mixed with the stench of dead, rotting flesh. The flesh of various presents that had been given to Mr C over the years by the villagers.

On the long walk back home that night, Lanh was apoplectic. He wouldn't listen to me as I begged him not to tell mother what had happened. He was more concerned about the behaviour of Mr C to even care what I had to say.

"I agree with what the men say. He's gone too far this time. All we wanted was for him to feel a part of the place, even if he didn't grow up here. We told him, if going back to America was too much, then stay here. We tried to make him feel at home with us. Only, he's thrown it back into our faces. Like shit."

I wondered who this 'we' was that Lanh was talking about and felt jealous. I suppose that even then, I could sense that he was drifting away from me. That the shit pit trick would be our final, grand hurrah as a duo. Already he was spending more and more time at the bar. Already he was listening attentively to whatever the Band of Brothers, shaping himself to be one of their gang. It was clear as the Qui River that they liked him because of his 'street smarts'.

As we traipsed down the alley behind the bar, I felt like I was a hindrance to him for the first time. As we passed the kennel, I gestured to a stick (one which would have been perfect for plaguing the mad dog with) but Lanh simply shook his head and looked sad. "Jojo wouldn't like it," he said. Since when had Lanh known the mad dog's name? Since when had he stopped referring to it as Mad Dog? I was starting to lose my grip on us.

"Oh Lanh!" I called.

No response. Of course there was no response. I was all alone in the back of a lorry. Human traffic. And finally the tears I'd been saving up for the whole journey so far started to fall. A raging torrent, eating up whatever reserves of moisture I must have stored up in my body. They came like a river, draining me of everything that was still me. I'd become an animal, a stupid, desperate animal.

"Don't cry," said a voice in the darkness.

"Leave me alone! Get out of my head!" I cried. A cough, a splutter, retching sounds in my head.

"Shut up! Shut up! Can't you see I'm on the edge!"

Silence again. Good. Silent like the grave.

Suddenly I heard another sound from the darkness. It sounded like rustling. Like movement. My imagination ran away with me. I pictured a big animal in there with me. A tiger perhaps. A tiger who was feasting on the dead meat but would soon be hungry for the fresh stuff.

"Who's there?" I called numbly. A tiger wouldn't answer me.

A rasping, croaking sound was delivered by way of response.

"Who's there?" I called again, thinking this is it, my journey is complete. My life's journey is about to come to an end.

A voice in the darkness: "It's me: An."

An. Of course; Mr Peacefulness. An means peace. Mr Death. Ready to come sweeping over me, releasing me from this gawky body. "Take me now!" I whispered.

"Pardon?" asked the voice in the darkness.

"Take me away from this place, this body, this torment,"

And then An gave what I thought was a laugh. "What are you talking about, Dung? Have you finally succumbed to madness? Pass me the water will you? I'm dying of thirst here!"

Dying of thirst, Bumpkin. Think about it. You'll get it in a minute...

I did get it. I didn't *want* to get it.

"What are you wearing, An?" I asked, carefully.

An spluttered a laugh again: "What is this, one of those sex lines? Pass me the water and I'll..."

"Tell me what you are wearing, you ghost!" I demanded.

Still laughing, An responded: "Well, despite the fact that I have such an extensive wardrobe in here, with all the fashions from Tokyo freshly flown in for me, I've decided to plump for the checked shirt and beige combat shorts combo that I know the girls just love."

"Che...Checked shirt," I stammered.

"Come on, it ain't that bad. It's a fake Ben Sherman, for crying out loud!"

"But you're dead," I gasped. "You're the dead man! The dead man from the concrete place..."

"I will be a dead man if you don't give me some water. Come on, Dung. I thought we were both trying to keep each other's spirits up? I thought we were going to keep each other sane so that when we finally reach our destination we won't be gibbering lunatics like that guy from your village. That Yank. Mr C you call him."

Without knowing what I was doing, I reached into one of the two plastic bags. The bag, which I now discovered contained a half-full bottle of mineral water and a few slices of bread. Before I threw it over to my ghostly companion, I unscrewed the cap and let a modest dribble wet my lips. It felt like freedom.

"Ah! Wonderful, life-affirming water," chirped An, as I tossed him the water. And amazingly, for a figment of my imagination (which he surely was) he gulped. Evidently this imaginary friend had a throat and a stomach as well as a mouth. Either the mad visions were getting clearer or something else, something so completely strange even Lanh couldn't have come up with it, was happening.

An woke me with a finger on his lips. I couldn't help but jump backwards and crack my head on the metal wall when I saw him, for his share of the water and a few slices of bread appeared to have done him the world of good. He was still wearing his shorts and checked shirt but his body seemed to have filled out in them. He was no longer so knock-kneed, no longer so sunken-chested. And he was breathing. Despite everything, I couldn't get over the fact that he was breathing.

"What is it?" I whispered.

"Hush! I heard us being loaded onto a boat, that's why I'm waking you. All that clanging and shouting and yet you slept right through it. You could sleep for Vietnam, Dung, honestly!"

I couldn't help feeling my face flush. Over the past few days, we'd shared many intimacies. Hell, we'd crapped right in front of each other into those horrible plastic bags, chucking them out through a small gap in the roller-shutter as soon as we were done. And now he'd filled out, become, well, *less dead*, I had found myself starting to like An. I liked the way he was so funny all the time, like Lanh had been. I liked the way he could make the old tarpaulin cover of the back of the lorry, and the crates within it into some marvellous world that I could almost reach out and touch. He almost made the whole thing bearable.

The only problem was that An quite clearly thought I was mad. And I could completely understand why he'd come to such a conclusion. First, I'd called him a dead man. That's a pretty serious accusation to make about any man without them thinking you're a bit of a, well *mad-dog-barking-at-the-moon type*. Then there was the day when I kept, mistakenly, calling him Lanh (which I got over only after he joked that I had 'a thing' for a dead man that resembled my brother, which was weird in anyone's book) and then there was my constant sleeping. I'd sleep in the middle of conversations; just float off into the past, into the village or into some dream-time which must have been what the Westerners call a 'parallel universe.' And when I wasn't sleeping, I made enough noise to wake the dead (*ha! Very funny, An*).

But the final straw that broke the donkey's back was my proposition that we were not going the way he thought, and all common sense dictated, we would be going. At first, I tried to break it to him gently. "I think we're heading back across France. We'll then be loaded onto a ship and then taken back to where we belong." And he'd said *poppycock* and some other choice words that he'd learned in his own Orientation 101. We'd agreed to disagree, but whenever the subject reared its ugly head, we started to argue. The fact that we were to all intents and purposes being loaded onto a ship was the first time I could actually point to some concrete evidence that we were on some karmic, reverse journey. Deep down, past all the jokes and the petty arguments, we both knew what it meant when we were loaded onto a ship.

We were at sea for long enough for An to admit that he was wrong, and believe me, it takes a *long time* for a man to admit to that. Needless to say, as soon as he admitted that he was wrong, our spirits seemed to lighten. Because we were together, the terrible cramps that we suffered, the back spasms, the muscle-wasting, were all made just that little bit easier to bear.

Alone, as I had been when I first entered the lorry, I had suffered these things and they were ten times the anguish they were now in our strange backwards-together journey. Remarkably, we were starting to become rosy-cheek happy, free from lice, and apparently getting cleaner by the day. It was a sort of, backwards miracle.

Of course, we suffered from bouts of boredom from which we thought we would never emerge. We had our crab-biting moments of fear and we had our pregnant desires for chocolate, for Coca Cola, for television, for the touch of the long grasses, for the sounds of the wind, or simply the sound of silence. We had our moments of sea-sickness too, but I think we both came to realise that the body is a remarkable instrument. Capable of coping with whatever shit pit you subject it to, at least for a while. It was almost as though we were reaping our karmic rewards for our suffering at the same time as we were suffering it. Neither of us really knew what was occurring, and it was probably best that we kept it that way. You don't mess with karma. Not if you know what's good for you.

Certainly, I knew what was good for me. I knew that An was good for me. His real voice was gradually exorcising all of those ghost-voices in my head. Making me whole again. He held me in his ever-stronger arms, squeezing the poison out of me, bringing me back to life.

We made plans, and what further indication do you want that things were getting better than the making of plans? A caged tiger does not make plans. A swatted fly does not make plans. A person buried alive *cannot* make plans. Suddenly, as well as the smudged past and present, there was a new world opening up to us: the future.

"It doesn't matter where we go," I said, rather bashfully. "As long as I'm with you. I feel like I belong with you."

"You think I'm the reincarnation of your darling brother or somesuch weird shit," he said, but not cruelly. "Sometimes I think your Madame Dugard was right about you being a country bumpkin with your country bumpkinish ways."

"Don't bring her into this," I said, tickling at the hair on his stomach, barely even remembering when there had once been patches of damp mould on his dead body there.

He kissed the top of my head, poured some water into my

mouth for me and then whispered into my ear: "Oh Jenni Wen, you are a curious case!"

His straggly whiskers tickled my ears and I couldn't help but laugh. I *was* a curious case. Here I was with all my back-to-front dreams of fighting cockerels and spitting dog men. Here I was telling my stories of how we'd tormented poor Mr C and how we plagued that mad dog out back of Romi's Bar. Here I was with all of my stories of home and the past and nothing, no stories at all about where we were supposed to be going. I didn't care where we were going, I really didn't. I just had one condition: that he didn't succumb to temptation as Lanh had.

Lanh left me because he wanted to be with the men, to *be* a man, and not spend all his time with his stupid sister. At the time, just after my close encounter with the dead animals and his shit pit, the realisation was crushing. Going off to be with the men was what my father did, or so my mother was always telling us, and yet Lanh hadn't taken in a single word that she said. As soon as people in the bar started saying things like 'fighting for freedom' and 'taking back what is rightfully ours', they were the only words he had time for.

He joined the Band of Brothers to fight a guerrilla war against traffickers like the FFF. He'd never have forgiven me for later handing over my money and allowing myself to be treated like a piece of meat by them. But he'd already been gone three years by that time. He'd already said all he meant to say about how much or how little he cared for mother and me. Mother said he was dead to her. I didn't agree, but I still felt betrayed. And when the rumoured attacks by the militia started to become more than rumours, when we actually *knew* some of the victims, we were too alone, too unprotected. The men from the FFF picked the most opportune moment to come a-calling with all their glossy brochures promising a new life with more riches than you could shake Mr. C's wonky walking-stick at; I was ripe for the picking. Ripe to be hewn from that tree, our village. Ripe to be cut off at the roots and left to choke. I was to be chewed up and spat out like a bad seed. I was to become like the countless other victims of the cruel world. And Lanh left me to that fate. He should have been there for me.

An was sleeping peacefully, as he was named. His head rested on my leg. I had been staring at the spider's ornate tapestry in the top corner of the lorry for so long that time seemed to have lost all meaning. I found myself amazed by the intricate patterns of the web; the interlinked road map of strands, which formed not quite concentric circles; the way the moisture in the air glistened off it. Yet again I thanked my mother for this ability to get so lost in idle contemplation. Westerners would have called her lazy; in the good old days, she tended to lie in her hammock in the garden leaving the house to fall into disrepair as she watched a single blade of grass dancing in the wind. Lanh and I knew better. Lanh and I knew that being able to just sit and think, without being bothered by the busy world, was truly An.

I must have been staring at the spider-web for hours and hours. I was staring so hard that it took some time before I realised that the big ship had docked. Finally our journey had reached its end. For a moment, I didn't wake An. I simply sat and reflected on what had come to pass. How a dead man had come back to life, how I'd once been wet but now was dry, how time, as we knew it had ceased to exist.

Before I could wake him, I heard a clattering at the back of the lorry. The roller-shutter doors began to roll up. An opened his eyes, already frantic.

"Remember the script," he whispered. "Remember what we practised."

I nodded, but he didn't seem convinced. Perhaps he still thought me mad. Couldn't blame him.

"Our own Orientation 101," I said. "Or rather our *re-*

Orientation 101."

"That's right," he said, and then, putting on a silly accent, he asked: "Where are your papers?"

"I don't have any papers. I am my own identity. I am me. I am dung. I am shit. I am beautiful," I answered, playing the game.

"What makes you think you should be allowed into our country?" he asked, exaggerating the cruelty of the accent even more.

"Because I have two legs with which I can walk," I said. "Because I am a human being."

The light of a torch flashed through a gap in the crates. I gasped in fright. An continued with his questioning, probably to quell his own terror as much as mine:

"What are you then; an economic migrant, an asylum seeker, human traffic?"

Heavy feet started climbing through the open roller-shutter and then clomping across the lorry floor. It was a man wearing a luminous yellow jacket and heavy workboots. *Shit-kicker* boots.

"We are all human traffic," I answered, in spite of the man whose shadow was now towering above us. He tried to interrupt, but neither of us could understand the man's strange accent. It had been so long since we'd heard the sound of another human voice. And besides, the man seemed to have so much saliva in his mouth that it was as though he was talking through a reservoir. And that moustache? Urgh.

The man grunted again. Made a grab at An, and yet An continued with his questions: "Why are you here?"

A slight smile played on my lips. This was my favourite question of all. "Nobody knows why they are here. That's the point of life. It is a journey; only when you reach the tail of the snake can you truly know the answer to that one."

The man leaned over us. So close that I could smell the fishy breakfast on his breath. He wrinkled his own nose. Seemed to smell nothing. We'd been at sea for so long and yet he smelled nothing. He grunted once again. His voice sounded harsh. Dog-like. I half-suspected that Cockerel would be behind him, just waiting to get his hands on us. Just waiting to dig his womanish claws into my flesh again. But there was no Cockerel. Not here. Somehow, I already knew it.

The man made another grab for An, and this time, An submitted. He allowed himself to be pulled to his feet as though he were

---

The Short Story Reinvented Series
Enjoyed Ten Journeys? Then treat yourself to the other four books in the collection

The Remarkable Everyday
ISBN: 9780955103209
7.99

Seven Days
ISBN: 9780955103230
7.99

Eight Hours
ISBN: 9780955103292
7.99

Eight Rooms
ISBN: 9781906558093
7.99

BATTLE OF BRITAIN

COMBAT ARCHIVE

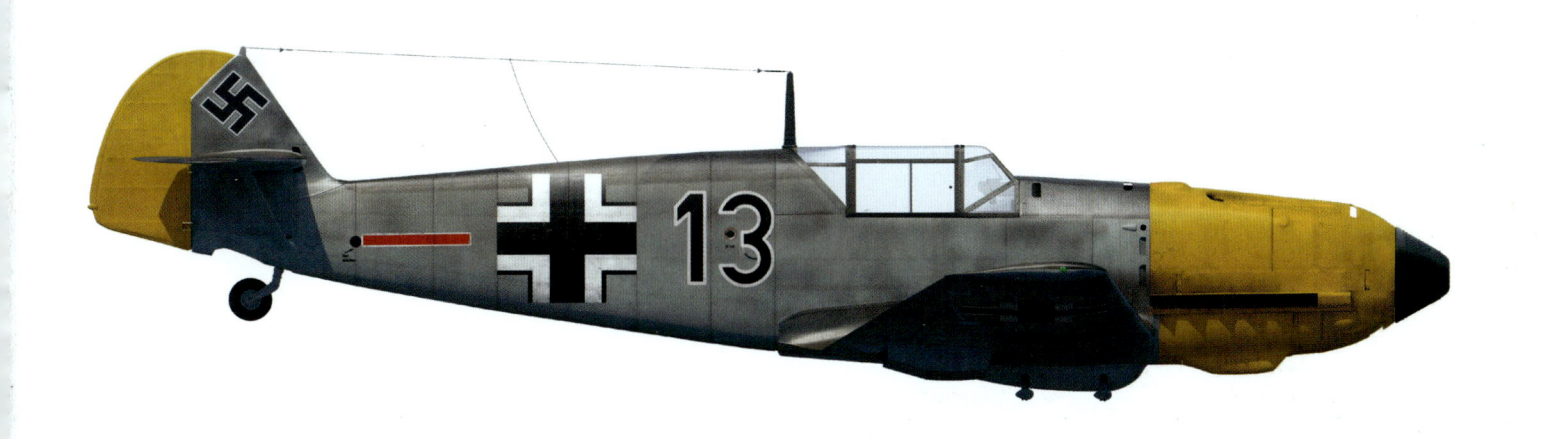

VOLUME NINE

1 – 3 SEPTEMBER 1940

Simon W Parry

THE BATTLE OF BRITAIN COMBAT ARCHIVE SERIES

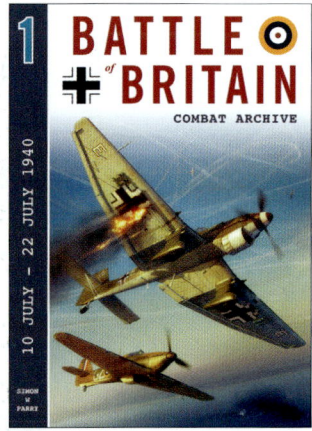

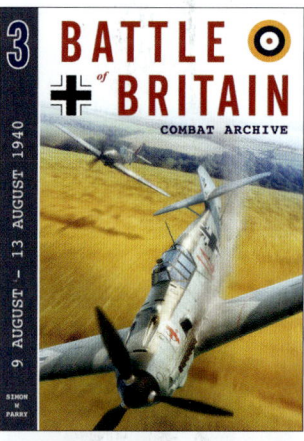

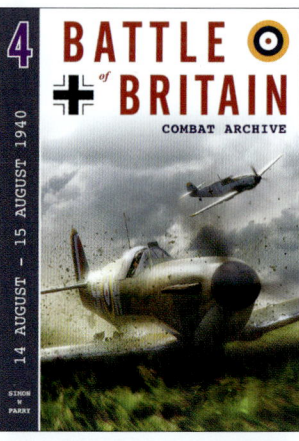

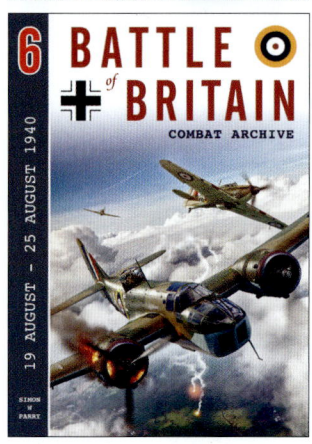

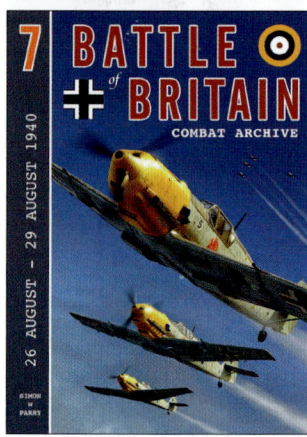

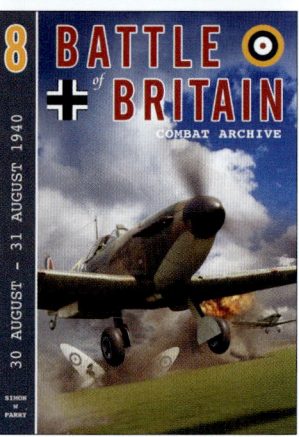

Author: Simon W Parry   simon@wingleader.co.uk

Design/Profiles: Mark Postlethwaite   mark@wingleader.co.uk

Illustrator/Profiles: Piotr Forkasiewicz   info@peterfor.com

Specialist contributors:
Dave Brocklehurst MBE (RAF pilots)
John Foreman (RAF and Luftwaffe Claims)
Nigel Parker and Milan Krajči (Luftwaffe)
John Vasco (Luftwaffe)
Chris Goss (Luftwaffe)
Andy Saunders
Andy Thomas (RAF)
Johnny Wheeler (601 Squadron)
Andy Long (RAF)
Steve Vizard
Peter Tookey
James Barnes
David Smith
Robin Hill

Photo Credits:
Kent Battle of Britain Museum
ww2images.com
BofB Memorial Trust
Geoff Simpson
Andy Thomas
Chris Goss Archive
Johnny Wheeler
Andy Saunders
Dennis Knight
Ian Simpson
Andy Long
Peter Snowden
Philippa Wheeler
Ashley Lamb

First Edition
ISBN 978 1 906592 65 3
First published 2020 by
Red Kite
PO Box 223, Walton-on-Thames,
Surrey, KT12 3YQ.
England
Tel. 0116 340 1085
www.wingleader.co.uk

© Simon W Parry 2020

All Rights Reserved.
No part of this publication may be reproduced, stored in any form of retrieval system, or transmitted in any form or by any means without prior permission in writing from the publishers.

Printed in Poland by Dimograf.

The Battle of Britain Combat Archive Series is a totally unique project that sets out to cover every aerial combat that was fought by RAF Fighter Command during the Battle of Britain. The series will run to approximately 15 volumes and will cover the period from 10 July 1940 - 31 October 1940.
The publishers hope to feature as many of The Few as possible during the course of the series so if any readers have photos or information on any airmen involved in the Battle, please do get in touch with the author.

All volumes available directly from the publishers at www.wingleader.co.uk